Two large male hands settled on either side of her waist…

…pulling her back against a lean, hard body and shoving her heart to an unnatural pace. "Maria." Mariette froze. Soledad had warned her that this man wanted more than just a cleaning lady. Soledad had told her she was in big trouble. For once, Soledad just might be right. Mariette gripped the dishes tighter, trying to keep her hands from shaking. What had she told Soledad? That she could handle this? She would have to, wouldn't she? This time there weren't any big brothers around to punch in the nose of an overly amorous swain.

She really could handle this. Really.

For a steadying moment she shut her eyes. That was a mistake. It only made her more aware of lean hands at her waist, the thumbs making lazy circles at the small of her back, the fingers caressing upward to the base of her breasts, down to her waist. Up. Down. More aware of the heat and sun enhanced scent of him. More aware of his body pressed chest and hip and thigh against hers.

His lips traced the curve of her ear, nipped at her neck, gently sucked at the curve between neck and shoulder, stirring something within her that ran right through her heart and stomach to land in a quivering heap in her loins. She didn't want the sensations to stop, didn't want Alejandro to stop. Mariette was glad none of her brothers were here. Then she wished they were because she suddenly realized that Soledad was right. She was not going to be able to handle this.

Other Books and Stories by Michele Stegman

Fortune's Foe

MICHELE STEGMAN

MYTHICAL PRESS ★ DAYTON, OHIO

Fortune's Foe
ISBN 978-0-9967976-1-0
Copyright © 2011 by Michele Stegman
Cover art © 2011 Jennette Marie Powell Heikes
Photos used under license via romancenovelcovers.com and istockphoto.com

Acknowledgements

My thanks to Ricardo Agrait for his help with Spanish names.

Dedication

To Carole Stegman and Elaine Ropka for their enthusiastic support of my writing, my art, and my family.

Chapter One

St. Augustine, Florida, 1740

MARIETTE GRASPED THE SEAT OF THE SKIFF AND LOOKED across the choppy water of Matanzas Bay as ships sailed into and out of St. Augustine, and the gray stone walls of the Spanish fort, *El Castillo*, loomed over it all.

"Matt is in there," she said, "and he'll die if we don't get him out."

"And we might die trying."

Mariette turned to her younger brother, Nate, in disguise as she was, in old, faded clothing, a droopy brown felt tricorn on his head. He, too, was looking grimly up at the enemy fort, his hands white knuckled on the tiller of the battered little skiff as they sailed by.

Up close, the fort was more forbidding than Mariette had imagined.

There was no way to approach it undetected. Nothing grew near its walls and a moat surrounded the part of it not touched by the waters of the bay.

Guards patrolled the top and the black snouts of cannon protruded from its sides.

"You're the one who sulked for three days because Mama

and Papa wouldn't let you join Oglethorpe's expedition," she said. "Well, Little Brother, you're in this war now." *And so am I,* she thought, folding her hands in her lap and drawing her feet close under her, as if she could make herself invisible to the danger she was about to face.

"Yeah," Nate grumbled, "I get to sail in and out while you go into St. Augustine and face all the danger." He smiled at her, but his eyes held concern and worry.

She could not help but let a fond smile play over her own face. "That's because your sailing is a lot better than your Spanish."

Nate's chin came up. "I can speak Spanish."

Mariette turned to the third passenger in the skiff. "Not well enough to pass for a Mestizo though, does he, Soledad?"

Soledad looked Nate up and down in her somewhat cynical fashion, her smooth red scarf a bright contrast to a face more black and wrinkled than a raisin. "Besides which, dem blue eyes of yours give you away pretty damn quick," the skinny black woman said to Nate, harumphing for emphasis. "Leastways, your sister, she look the part of a half-Spanish, half-Indian with dat black hair and eyes. Long as dat pretty face don't get too much attention, we be all right."

Mariette laid a hand on Soledad's arm, feeling the hard strength in that lean limb. "I want to thank you again for helping us, Soledad."

Soledad harrumphed again and spat over the side, wiping her toothless mouth with the back of a hand that looked too large and work-roughened for the rest of her skinny frame. "Damn fool notion thinkin' we's gonna get them two away from the Spanish dons."

Mariette looked blank and Soledad continued. "You tol' me your fiancé is in there with your twin. I'm guessin' we got to get him out, too."

"Oh. Yes. Of course!" Mariette sat up straighter, determined to show a confidence that had slipped somewhat at the sight of the impregnable fort.

"Somehow we'll manage to rescue them both."

"Damn fool notion if you ask me," Soledad muttered, shaking her head. "Damn fool. Don't even have no plan. Don't know nothin' 'bout that fort."

"That's why I have to talk to some soldiers, find out where the prisoners are being held, what the routine is." Mariette glanced up at the worn sail as Nate smoothly adjusted it, turning them toward the dock.

"Well," Soledad hedged, "most of dem soldiers ain't too bad. Just local folk like me. But dem officers is all from Spain and they's sharp. Don't go talkin' to none of dem."

"I won't, Soledad." She placed her hands demurely in her lap, fingering the well-worn butternut brown skirt she had chosen for her disguise. "Not if I can find out what I need to know from the others."

Soledad sat forward, glaring into Mariette's eyes. "Not for no reason. You get caught, your daddy'll come down here and have my hide. And he knows just where to find me since him and this young'un be the ones who brung me down here."

Mariette gave a noncommittal nod and looked up again at the gray coquina walls of the fort, weather hardened enough that Oglethorpe's cannon balls had just bounced off.

"So you think a woman and a boy gonna do what all of James Oglethorpe's fleet and army couldn't do? You gonna invade dat Spanish stronghold and get them two men out and get all of you home safe?" Soledad sucked her toothless gums and shook her head. "Unh, unh, unh. And here I thought I done something by joining my Cato after he run away to come down here."

Maybe Soledad was right, Mariette thought. Maybe it was a

'damn fool notion'. She had even had a hard time talking adventure-hungry Nate into risking his precious sloop to bring her down here. But then she thought of Matt languishing in there, perhaps being tortured, and her resolve hardened.

"We'll do it, Soledad," Mariette said. "We have to."

Nate turned the skiff toward the dock, mingling with several other skiffs loaded with people going to the market. He let the sail down so that the craft came to a slow stop with its side almost, but not quite, brushing the dock. He threw a line around a stanchion to hold them steady so she and Soledad could climb out.

Mariette hoisted herself onto the dock and stood for a moment looking around. There were several ships riding at anchor and one of them was obviously English. Mariette turned to Nate but he had already spotted it. His brows were drawn into a knot and his mouth was set in a tight line.

"A prize?"

He nodded.

She didn't say anything more. She didn't have to. They both knew that if they weren't careful, Nate's little ship, now hidden in an inlet near Cato and Soledad's hut, could easily be the next prize of war captured by the Spanish and brought in with its English prisoners.

Mariette looked toward the end of the worn, wooden dock. A militiaman paced back and forth there, his uniform old but smartly pressed and creased, a musket slung over one shoulder. He was middle-aged, a Mestizo like she was supposed to be. He glanced in her direction. Then, his attention caught, he headed toward them, the warped boards creaking with his heavy tread.

She almost jumped back into the skiff but forced herself to act calmly. Soledad came to the market every week bringing vegetables and bread and muffins to sell. Surely there was nothing unusual about them to warrant his suspicion.

She bent to take the tray of warm sweet potato muffins from Soledad, helping her onto the dock. Nate handed up her basket of vegetables.

Soledad glanced down the dock at the advancing soldier then quickly bent to give the skiff a little shove to send it off quickly. "You get out of here, young'un. Don't need you talkin' to no soldier. Be back here come noon. We be waitin'."

With a quick glance at the soldier and a curt nod to Matiette, Nate set the sail, the wind caught it, and he headed back up the bay to Soledad's hut.

"Bueños días." The soldier gave them an appraising look, his thick black brows going up questioningly as he glanced from the departing skiff to the two women.

Mariette gave him a tentative smile but before she could speak Soledad was nudging her, herding her past the soldier. When they headed up the narrow, sun-baked street toward the market, Soledad finally slowed down a bit to readjust the basket of vegetables she carried on one bony hip.

"Why didn't you let me question him?" Mariette asked. "He might have known something about the prisoners."

"You ask your questions of some soldier who ain't got his mind on his job. Dat one lookin' out for trouble. You find you a soldier ain't doin' nothin' but lollygaggin' around with nothin' official on his mind."

Mariette nodded.

"And talk Spanish. Nothing but Spanish. Think in Spanish. Don't need nobody hearin' no English."

Mariette glanced around nervously at the shops built of the same gray coquina as the fort, but there was no one close enough to have heard. No English. Not even to Soledad. She must remember.

The market was set up at one end of a large plaza with the fort towering above the shops, the church, and the government buildings, overlooking all. Spanish merchants good-naturedly jostled for space with Mestizos and Indians to set out their wares. Mariette helped Soledad spread out a brightly colored striped cloth and lay out the vegetables on it. The sun was already hot but there were trees and there would soon be shade. The muffins were still warm from Soledad's dutch oven, their enticing smell mingling with the pungent tang of spices from the stall next to them, and with the smell of leather and wool and animals.

Merchants greeted each other over the noise of sheep and pigs and chickens and soon the sound of haggling could be heard in all directions.

Soledad traded vegetables and six muffins to a merchant for some salt and spices and Mariette took the opportunity to ask him about the English prisoners.

"I hope they burn the heretics," he said, slamming the lid to one of his spice boxes. He leaned across a bag of cinnamon and jabbed a blunt finger toward the fort. "They should pay for the destruction they brought to St. Augustine."

"What good would that do?" a woman selling rice asked. "They should be put to work rebuilding what their cannons destroyed."

"I say they should ship them to Spain," a bald oil merchant said. "They are a danger to us here. What if they escape?"

A fat soldier who had wandered over to eye the muffins laughed. "Escape from the Castillo? Impossible."

"If they let them out to work," the oil merchant said glaring at the woman who had suggested it, "they could escape."

"Which is why I say they should be burned at the stake!" the spice merchant reiterated.

Mariette looked hopefully at the soldier. "What will they do with the prisoners?"

The soldier shrugged, smoothing a fat-fingered hand over a uniform that wouldn't stay buttoned, more interested in the muffins than the fate of English prisoners.

Mariette picked up a muffin, cocked her head coquettishly, and asked, "Who would know what will be done with the prisoners?"

The soldier licked his lips and looked hopefully from the muffin to her, then back again. "Perhaps the officers know. But they do not confide in me."

Mariette smiled and handed him the muffin. "For one of the staunch defenders of our town," she said.

Grinning, the soldier took the muffin and went off happily toward the fort.

Mariette knelt on the cloth and leaned close to Soledad. "I have to talk to an officer, Soledad," Mariette whispered.

Soledad wiped her brow and checked the position of the sun. "Almost noon. Dat brother of yours be back soon. We'll come back to the market next week. Maybe you have better luck den." She began gathering up the few vegetables they had left.

"Next week?" She clutched Soledad's arm. "I can't wait a whole week to find out about..." She glanced around and lowered her voice. "A week is too long."

"Can't think of no other reason for us to be hangin' 'round here."

"Then I'll have to find a reason," Mariette said, jamming the packet of spices into Soledad's basket. "And an officer."

Soledad's eyes widened and she reached for Mariette's hand, starting to shake her head but Mariette jerked away. With her jaw set, she looked Soledad square in the eye. "I'll go to the commandant himself, if I have to. Whatever it takes, I'll do."

"Child," Soledad said, "do you think your brother be wantin' you to put yourself in dat much danger? Don't you think he be wantin' you to take care of yourself?"

"Matt's more than a brother, Soledad. He's my twin. Another

part of me. I can't let him die."

"Maybe dat twin of yours is tougher than you think."

"And maybe not." Mariette finished packing the vegetables into the basket. "Soledad, don't you know anyone in town I could stay with?"

Soledad shook her head. "Cato and me, we stay close to home. Don't come here no more than we has to. Some of our friends, dey find jobs here workin' for rich folks. But I don't know nobody who needs help right now."

Mariette's hands knotted into fists. Then she saw the tray of muffins. There were still a half dozen of them left. She snatched up the tray. "I'm going to walk around the market just once, Soledad."

Soledad's mouth opened as if she would protest, but she looked at the determined set of Mariette's jaw and nodded. "Just you be careful, now. And don't be long. Don't want Nate gettin' hisself into no trouble at the dock."

Mariette propped the tray on one hip and turned. That's when she saw the Spanish officer—danger in blue and red headed right for her.

Alejandro de Silva y Morales-Alcover had expected to find an old family friend in the commandant's office in *El Castillo*. Instead, he found himself looking into the face of his mortal enemy.

Ignatio Javier de Silva y Gonzales leaned back in a wooden chair that creaked with his bulk, smuggly folded thick fingers over his belly, and leered up at Alejandro. He had donned the red and blue uniform of the militia, but Ignatio was not a soldier and looked out of place in the ill-fitting outfit. In spite of the ragged Indian slave who stood beside his chair fanning him, his face was oily with sweat, much as Alejandro imagined his own face must look after having been kept waiting over two hours in the sun-drenched compound of the fort. His own clothing, black with silver embroidery, was limp and wilted from the heat.

"You cannot know the pleasure it has given me to hear that you were here in St. Augustine, Alejandro." Ignatio's leering grin widened to bare yellow, tobacco-stained teeth. "And under my command."

Alejandro bowed deeply, giving himself a moment to compose himself, to subdue the snarl of emotions this man always dredged up and to keep them from showing on his face. The man's voice, soft and suggestive as a serpent's, slightly husky, grated on him. Alejandro looked around at the stark stone walls of the office, bare except for a map of the colony. An open cabinet held official papers and an Indian rug covered the floor. Other than that there was no decoration. It was the office of a soldier, not the luxury Ignatio preferred.

"Uncle, it surprises me to find you here. I thought you were in Havana?" Alejandro managed to give his uncle a wary but respectful smile.

"And so I was. But Commandant Montiano came to Havana to meet with the Viceroy and take care of some urgent personal matters, and he needed a temporary replacement." He waved a hand expansively. "I volunteered to help out."

Alejandro cocked one disbelieving brow. "Indeed."

Ignatio shrugged and leaned forward onto the unpainted wooden desk to pick up a small, ornate dagger, fondling it, running his finger lightly over the blade as he looked pointedly at Alejandro. "Of course I had a letter from your…" he paused as if in search of a better word, then shrugged again and continued, "from your father that you were coming. How could I pass up an opportunity to see my nephew?"

Alejandro glanced at the dagger. "Yes, I understand why you

have come."

Ignatio grinned again, twirling the dagger. "Do you, now?" He tossed the dagger onto the desk and sat forward, leaning heavy elbows onto a pile of documents. "I hope you found your accommodations suitable? With the English attack, so many colonials have moved into St. Augustine for protection, there is not much available."

Alejandro inclined his head graciously. "Yes, the house is adequate for my needs. Thank you for making the arrangements."

"And the housekeeper I hired for you?" Ignatio licked leering lips.

A picture of the painted doxie who had awaited him in his bed rose up. Had his uncle really thought he would be enticed by such a creature, even after three months at sea? Learning now that his uncle had arranged to have her there made him gladder still that he had sent her away. Likely she would have infected him with the pox…as well as spied on his every move.

"I thank you for your kindness, Uncle, but I would prefer to find my own housekeeper. I sent her away."

A brief look of annoyance flashed across Ignatio's face before he shrugged. "As you like, Alejandro. But now we must find some duties for you."

Alejandro shifted, tired of standing but unwilling to take a seat without being invited. He was certain his uncle had already found 'duties' for him. And he was prepared for them to be the most unpleasant duties a soldier could be given. Unpleasant and likely dangerous.

"Ah, yes!" Ignatio picked up a sheet of paper as if inspiration had only that moment struck him. "Here is a duty that you will be well suited for, *mi sobrino,* my nephew."

Alejandro's uncle cleared his throat, took a long draught from a wine glass sitting conveniently nearby, grimaced at the taste, took out a handkerchief and wiped his brow, then glared at the Indian to fan harder. He glanced up at Alejandro and shrugged as if in apology at the delay, opened his mouth to speak, then put down the paper to take a moment to straighten his vest, his stock, shift to a more comfortable position in his chair.

Alejandro gritted his teeth at these little purposefully tormenting delays his uncle was so good at performing. He knew from the past that impatience would do him little good. Instead, he forced himself to look about the room as if bored with the wait.

Ignatio cleared his throat noisily and rattled the paper in his hands to draw Alejandro's attention back to him. "Ah yes, Nephew. Now where were we?"

"My duties, Uncle." Alejandro had played this game more than once with his uncle. He knew the rules, and that now was not the time to break them.

"Yes, your du-ties." The words were drawn out as if Ignatio were savoring each of them. He put the paper down on the desk and fastened it there with a meaty finger jabbed into the center of it. "We have need of a guard for some prisoners here in the Castillo."

"Guard duty?" Alejandro's brow shot up again.

Ignatio's pleasure at Alejandro's surprise spread across his oily features. "Do you think guard duty beneath you, Nephew?"

Alejandro may have been surprised that his uncle's choice of duty for him was even lower than he expected, but his pride was not so affronted as Ignatio may have hoped. He bowed in acceptance of the duty, unpleasant as it might prove. "My Uncle, it is you who has always been vigilant of the family's pride."

Ignatio's grin faded, replaced by a glare. "Indeed."

"If giving guard duty to a *capitán* in his majesty's forces—who happens also to be a member of your noble family—does not offend you," Alejandro continued, "how could it possibly offend me?"

"You mistake me, Alejandro, if you think I would assign a member of my family to lowly guard duty." He paused just long enough for Alejandro to wonder if Ignatio was telling him, once again, that he knew who he really was. That even though he would not assign this duty to a member of his family, he would not hesitate to assign it to him. Ignatio smiled smugly. "No, *mi sobrino,* I would not, even indirectly, so offend our family honor."

Ignatio's finger began to toy with the paper before him, running up and down the list written there. "But you see, these are rather special prisoners. Prisoners that are very important to the crown. And you will not just be a guard. You will be the *capitán* in charge of the guards. A much more responsible role, befitting who you are." He paused a moment before grinning triumphantly and saying, "You see, these are the English prisoners of war."

Alejandro reached out to steady himself with a hand to the back of the chair his uncle had not invited him to sit in. It took even him, so used to his uncle's torments and unpleasant surprises, a moment to recover his poise. He bowed once again to his uncle, not only in acceptance of the duty, but in acknowledgment of his uncle's having won this round of their ever ongoing game. With Alejandro's background, one escaped prisoner would be all Ignatio would need to accuse Alejandro of treason. And here, far from Spain, it would be all too easy to make the charges stick, have an execution, and apologize to the crown later. With so much at stake, even the stain of having a traitor in the family would not stop Ignatio.

His uncle once more leaned back in his chair, once more folded his fat fingers across his belly, and smirked in triumph. Prepared now to be a bit more magnanimous, he said, "You may draw a uniform from the Castillo's stores, Alejandro, and have lunch with the soldiers. Then you may have an hour or two to find yourself a housekeeper before you report back to the Castillo for duty this afternoon." Ignatio waved his hand in dismissal and Alejandro bowed once again, taking his leave.

The Spanish officer coming toward Mariette with a scowl on his face was just what Soledad had warned her against. Head held high, he had the proud air of a Spanish noble about him making him doubly dangerous to her. He was handsome in a typical Spanish way with gleaming black hair, black eyes, and olive skin. But nothing else about him was typical. He was taller than most Spaniards she had met and his uniform was almost too tight across powerfully-muscled shoulders. His lips were full and sensuous and she thought that if she had met this man in Charles Town, she would not have let the evening pass without securing his promise to call on her.

But this was not Charles Town, and he stalked directly toward her with an intensity to his long-legged stride that suddenly made her wonder if she had been found out, if he were coming to arrest her. She quickly dismissed that notion. He wouldn't be alone if they knew there was an Englishwoman in St. Augustine intent on freeing the English prisoners. He would have men with him, and they would be armed.

But even alone, Mariette felt that this man was not one to trifle with. It would be a dangerous game indeed to approach this one. Unconsciously she took a step back, for the first time feeling that she may have underestimated the difficulty in rescuing her brother. Maybe Soledad was right. Maybe she should go right back to the skiff, back to Soledad's village, get aboard Nate's sloop and return to Charles Town.

She looked up and saw the fort, massive and ominous. The fort where her twin was held prisoner. Matt couldn't go back to Charles Town unless she helped him. And Matt wouldn't give up this easily, either. If this wasn't her last chance for a week to gain information, she wouldn't be so bold. And if he didn't have that scowl on his face, she thought, and wasn't her enemy, she might have flirted with him.

But that was just what she must do. If she were really the Mestiza she pretended to be, she would certainly flirt with such a handsome officer. For he was handsome, even with those hard angles of his face. Tall and lean and intense. The kind of man who would give unwavering attention to whatever he was doing, war— or seduction. A kiss from him would sear right through a woman and curl her toes.

Mariette swallowed hard and took a deep breath to calm her racing heart. It was not a kiss she needed, but information. Smile, you dolt, she told herself, smile. Gripping the tray tightly, she gave the officer a tentative smile and stepped out to intercept him. This officer was just who she needed to find out about Matt.

"Muffins, *señor?* Freshly made this morning. Only three for a quarter." Mariette stepped right in front of him, lifting the cloth that covered the muffins and thrusting out the hip that balanced the tray.

He was moving so fast that he nearly collided with her, forcing her back an unsteady step. She was about to fall. Instantly, his arm shot out and caught her around the waist. His hand splayed warmly against the small of her back, his mouth a mere breath from hers, his gaze sweeping over her like molten lava.

"Muffins, *señor?*" she repeated weakly. "Three for a quarter."

His nostrils flared as he took in a deep breath and his gaze swept over her again, more slowly this time. More thoroughly. He looked down and Mariette knew that from his angle not even the kerchief she wore tucked into her bodice would completely conceal the upper curves of her breasts from him.

One black brow shot upward but his gaze lingered downward.

"Muffins?" Making certain that she was now steady on her feet, he stepped back from her, his hand slowly skimming around her waist, steadying her, before it dropped away.

His gaze now locked with hers and one corner of his mouth lifted in a mockery of a grin as he picked up a muffin. He bit into it, then nodded appreciatively. He took another bite and a crumb fell onto his coat, like a piece of bright yellow-orange pollen against the blue.

Without thinking Mariette reached up to brush it away, her fingers lingering, feeling the warmth of him, the crisp newness of the uniform, the rough texture of the material…the sudden rise of his chest with his quickly indrawn breath.

He lifted his hand to brush the back of hers with his fingers, sending a thrill up her arm and straight into her heart. Her own breath quickened and she looked up at him. He was smiling now and suddenly she realized how intimate an act brushing away that crumb had been. She jerked her hand away, and handed him a second muffin. "Three for a quarter, *señor*," she said.

He took a second muffin in one hand, fishing for a coin with the other. He bit into the muffin just as he tossed a coin onto the tray. Mariette saw a flash of gold and felt the weight of the coin as it landed with a solid ring. It was a gold quarter *escudo*. More than a laborer would earn in a week. "Señor, this is too much. The cost is one quarter *real*." She picked up the gold piece, feeling the ridges and bumps of a coin newly minted and fresh from Spain. It was still warm from being carried close to his body, alive from the touch of his fingers.

She held it out to him but he ignored it, grinning at her instead. He bit into the second muffin. "What if I have nothing smaller?" Mariette looked to Soledad. The black woman shook her head. She did not have enough to make change.

"I do not have change."

He leaned toward her, grinning mischievously. "Then, I suppose you will have to give me a lot of muffins."

"But I…" She fisted her hand about the coin, holding it close to her breast.

He leaned closer yet, pressing her, close enough that she felt the soft cambric of his shirt against the back of her hand and the heat of his body.

"Or something of equal value."

She could see the individual hairs of his brows, the smooth perfection of his skin beneath a sheen of perspiration inspired by the heat. Her breathing became shallow and quick as if he had suddenly taken all the air and left her struggling for breath.

He moved back just a bit, enough to give her room to breathe, at least. But she reacted to his sudden movement like a spring released from pressure, inadvertently swaying toward him. He responded in kind until he was even closer. Only a breath away. "I need someone to…shall we say, be a live-in housekeeper?" He tapped the hand she still held fisted around the quarter escudo. "I would pay you one quarter *escudo* a week."

Mariette heard a muffled squawk from Soledad but ignored it. A live-in housekeeper? She may have grown up with a house full of servants, but she knew how to clean and sweep and make beds. It was perfect. A place to stay in town, an officer close at hand she could question every day, and plenty of excuses to get inside the fort.

She smiled, again holding the coin up between thumb and forefinger. "My first week's wages?" At his nod, she tucked the quarter into her bodice. She felt it there, branding her. "When do I start?"

"Today?"

Mariette felt a sharp tug on her skirts and looked down to see Soledad wide-eyed, frantically shaking her head no. Mariette gathered the muffins into the cloth and shoved the tray into Soledad's hand, mouthing a quick, "Yes!"

She turned back to the officer with a smile. "Today will be fine."

Soledad gave another tug on Mariette's skirt, so strong as to almost unbalance her. Mariette pushed Soledad's hand away with her foot, but Soledad pinched her. "A moment, *señor*." She knelt down beside Soledad and whispered, "What is the matter, Soledad?"

"What de matter? What de matter?" Soledad hissed back. "You a grown girl and got to ask me dat? Jus' what you be thinkin' dat man want wid a girl like you?"

"You heard. He needs a housekeeper."

"I heard all right. Seems I heard him say a whole lot more than you did."

"I can handle this, Soledad."

"You can't handle nothin'. You's already in the biggest mess anybody ever heard tell of and don't even have sense enough to know it."

"This is just what I need, Soledad. A place to stay in town, a chance to get into the fort."

Soledad took Mariette's arm in a hard grasp and shook her. "What you need is a good whuppin' and a leash. I jus' knowed dis was a damn fool notion. Don't know why I lets myself get talked into it. But you's comin' right home with me and den dat brother of yours is gonna take you straight back to your daddy."

Mariette pried Soledad's fingers off her arm, tightly gripping the older woman's wrist. "No, Soledad. I'm going with this officer. I'm going to do what I came here for. I'll meet you right here next week. With a plan. Tell Nate not to worry."

Soledad reached for her again but Mariette quickly stood up and stepped out of reach. "I'm ready, *señor*," she said and fell into step ahead of the Spanish officer, leaving Soledad behind, muttering thickly.

Chapter Two

ALEJANDRO TOOK GREAT PLEASURE IN WATCHING THE enticing sway of the perfectly rounded hips in front of him. Finally, he thought, something is going right. After a rough three months at sea and the encounter with his uncle, he was ready for a woman. He rubbed his jaw and grinned watching that backside. He didn't think his long abstinence was clouding his judgment in the case of the shapely Mestiza who had just agreed to be his 'housekeeper'. Properly dressed, she could put any woman in the Spanish court to shame. So far, he had not seen her equal in St. Augustine.

And she was his.

At the edge of the market the woman paused, turning back toward him with a hesitant smile, waiting for directions. Alejandro held out one hand toward the Calle del Gobernador and guided her with a light touch at the small of her back.

Her waist, the bones of her back felt so small, so delicate against his palm, he could not bear to remove his hand. He didn't want to remove his hand. He wanted to touch her all over. And it wasn't just being without a woman for so long that was making his pulse race and his loins ache. He suspected that he would be aroused by this woman even after a week in Spain's finest bordello.

She moved away from his touch and he was not sure if it was intentional or if she had just walked on, but he let his hand drop... although it tingled with want and need for her.

Now that they were out of the crowded market and on a broad street, he moved up to walk alongside her. She glanced up at him with a smile and his loins lurched in eager anticipation. Her skin was a warm, even tone, lighter than his and without blemish. When she turned to look at him, her eyes were deep obsidian, black as sin, but wide with innocence. They did contain flecks of brown, probably from her European ancestry, but her hair was even blacker than his, its darkness relieved only by the brush of sunlight playing among the curls.

He licked suddenly dry lips and noticed that hers were lush and full and he thought how soft they would be touching his, parting, perhaps trembling slightly as he took possession of her mouth. He wrenched his gaze away. She was not a whore, but here he was ready to take her without preliminaries, without even knowing her name.

He had to clear his throat and lick his lips again before he could speak. "I am Alejandro de Silva."

Her perfectly arched brows wrinkled a moment and she bit her underlip, then said, "My name is...Maria. You are in charge of many men at the fort?"

She must be ill at ease, he thought. He didn't want her to be uncomfortable and hesitant with him. He smiled. "Not many. Just a few guards."

He saw her catch her breath. "Guards? What do you guard, *señor*? Do you guard the English prisoners?" She was looking up at him, her eyes wide, her mouth slightly parted, as if she were hoping that he did, as if it was important to her that he guarded the Englishmen. Why should it matter to her? he wondered.

"Yes," he answered her. "I am in charge of the English prisoners."

She grasped his arm, nearly dropping her bundle of muffins. "How are they? Are they well? Are they well treated? Are they given enough food and water? Are they given exercise in the open air or kept in a cell?"

He gave a little laugh, puzzled by her intense interest. "I do not know."

Her eyes widened further, "You do not know?" Then she jerked her hand away from him. Her brows came crashing down over eyes turned suddenly fiery and she squared off with him in the middle of the street. "You do not know?"

Alejandro spread wide his hands and shrugged. "*Señorita*, I arrived from Spain only yesterday. I am to begin my new assignment of guarding the prisoners this afternoon. But I wonder why you are so concerned about a group of men who less than a month ago were trying to destroy this colony."

"Concerned? No, I… It is just that…" She turned and began walking again. "I just did not want to work for a soldier who takes his duties lightly."

There was more to her concern than she wanted him to know, he thought. As casually as he could, he asked, "Do you know one of the prisoners?"

She nearly stumbled, grasping the muffins so tightly, he was sure there would be nothing left but crumbs. "No. No, of course not." She looked ahead down the street. "Is your house much farther?"

"No," he answered, allowing her to change the subject.

He found another opportunity to touch her when they reached the street where he lived. Again she turned willingly in the direction he indicated but moved away from his touch like a shy foal. Was she really so untouched or was she merely unwilling to be demonstrative in public? He would soon find out, he thought, as he pushed open the door to the house his uncle had obtained for him and guided her inside with a hand at her waist.

As soon as Alejandro opened the door to his house, Mariette quickly stepped inside. Away from the heat of the day and away from the heat of his hand—which held a heat entirely different from the sun's. And far more dangerous.

Mariette looked about the simple single room that served as both living and dining room and almost burst into tears. Pieces of masculine clothing littered the floor and the sparse furniture just like Matt's room at home. Nate had learned neatness in the cramped quarters of ships and Ty…well…Ty just seemed to have been born neat. But Matt, her twin, now a prisoner in the Castillo, had always left a trail of clothing throughout the house. Maybe because he wore so little of it when he was off with his Indian friends.

She picked up a pair of brown breeches from the floor, a shirt from a worn yellow sofa that was the only piece of furniture in the living room area, and a towel that had been draped over one of the two chairs left askew next to a rough wooden table.

Dirty dishes of crude terra cotta pottery cluttered the table and she began to stack them, scraping the remains of meals into one bowl. Two large male hands settled on either side of her waist pulling her back against a lean, hard body and shoving her heart to an unnatural pace.

"Maria."

Mariette froze. Soledad had warned her that this man wanted more than just a cleaning lady. Soledad had told her she was in big trouble. For once, Soledad just might be right.

Mariette gripped the dishes tighter, trying to keep her hands from shaking. What had she told Soledad? That she could handle this? She would have to, wouldn't she? This time there weren't any big brothers around to punch in the nose of an overly amorous swain. She really could handle this. Really.

For a steadying moment she shut her eyes. That was a mistake. It only made her more aware of the lean hands at her waist, the thumbs making lazy circles at the small of her back, the fingers caressing upward to the base of her breasts, down to her waist. Up. Down. More aware of the heat and sun enhanced scent of him. More aware of his body pressed chest and hip and thigh against hers.

His lips traced the shell of her ear, nipped at her neck, gently sucked at the curve between neck and shoulder, stirring something within her that ran right through her heart and stomach to land in a quivering heap in her loins. She didn't want the sensations to stop, didn't want Alejandro to stop. Mariette was glad none of her brothers were here. Then she wished they were because she suddenly realized that Soledad was right. She was not going to be able to handle this. She didn't want to 'handle' this. She wanted it to go on and on. She wanted to surrender completely to what this man was doing to her.

But she was here to wrest prisoners from the enemy, not to surrender to them. And Alejandro de Silva was the enemy. Not only a Spaniard, but the very guard she must outwit to win her brother's freedom. She had to stop this now while she still had a few of her wits left.

She could have stopped it if he was all she had to fight off. But she had herself to fight, as well. A self that was rapidly throwing away every defense she had ever had. As self that was succumbing so rapidly that soon it would be her who would be dragging him down onto the sofa.

She had to break free of him. She had come to rescue her brother. She had a fiancé—who also needed rescuing. She had to stop this now. Really.

But she didn't want to offend this Spanish officer. She didn't want him to throw her out. She needed to stay here. For the information he could give her about Matt, of course. What better place was there to use as her headquarters for mounting a rescue than the home of the captain of the guard?

Holding thoughts of Matt as a shield against the onslaught to her reason, she slipped sideways from Alejandro's hold, edging around the table. Alejandro let her go, but followed closely, his fingers trailing down her arm.

A door was open to the courtyard and another to a second room. She needed space and air but Alejandro was blocking her way to the courtyard so she went to the second door, pretending not to have been affected by his touch, pretending an interest in seeing the rest of the house.

She paused at the doorway and Alejandro came up behind her, laying a hand gently on her shoulder. She bolted into the next room. It was a bedroom. His bedroom, where his rumpled bed lay in blatant unmade invitation. Hastily she stepped forward, jerking the sheets straight and tucking them in tight and chaste. She added a pair of his drawers to the dirty clothing over her shoulder. She had to get out of here to where there was more space and air, where he was not so close, not hemming her in.

She pointed to a door on the other side of the bedroom. "Is there another room through there or are there only the two rooms?"

He brushed past her to lead her to the doorway set in the opposite wall, and she leaned away from him to keep their bodies from touching in the confining space. "A small storage room only," he said, opening the door, "with another door to the courtyard."

She edged past him, picked her way between his trunks stored in the small room and out into the walled courtyard. Flowers grew along the walls and one huge tamarind tree grew in the center.

"There is a well and an outhouse," he said. "The kitchen is here against the side wall of the house under the overhang. It is a simple house but adequate for my current needs."

She nodded and went back inside. Thanks to the thick coquina walls the interior was much cooler than the street outside. He had left the door to the bedroom and the door to the courtyard open so a breeze wafted through the house cooling it further.

Alejandro watched as she wandered about the small room picking up clothes he had tossed onto the two chairs and the sofa in the sitting room. It didn't seem like she looked at him, but he was sure she was constantly aware of his presence, aware of exactly where he was because she kept the width of the room between them, warily working around him, cautiously keeping her distance.

The house was simple, the furnishings spartan. Until she had come into the house, it had seemed sufficient. He had grown up amidst luxury, but he was also trained as a soldier. As long as the food was adequate and there was a roof over his head, he was content. Now he wished there were carpets and cushions in the little house, curtains and tapestries, more rooms, servants.

He knew she was but a simple Mestiza peasant and probably accustomed only to a wattle-and-daub hut with a thatched roof and dirt floor. But somehow, his heart and his gut were telling him something different. This woman deserved to be dressed in silk, riding the finest of palfreys, attended by servants, eating from fine porcelain and silver.

She cleared away his breakfast breadcrumbs, her fine, slim fingers a stark contrast to the coarse wood of the table as she swept with the fingertips of one hand and held the other cupped beneath the edge of the table to catch the crumbs. She turned briefly to fling the crumbs outside, lightly brushing her hands together to free them of the last of the crumbs. *She should be dancing at a grand ball*, he thought, as he watched the grace with which she moved, *not cleaning my leavings from a coarse wooden table.*

Placing the remaining muffins in a pottery bowl, she leaned across the table to pick up the dishes she had stacked. He snatched them up, holding them out to her—wanting her to notice him, look at him. Really look at him, not just dance away from his presence and keep the table as a barrier between them. He wanted no barrier between them. Not a table, not the length of the room, not even clothes.

When she grasped the dishes, their fingers brushed, and instead of letting go, he held the dishes tighter. She looked up at him then, her eyes widening, her lips parting softly. He could easily imagine her like that lying beneath him with those midnight curls spread across a pillow. He swallowed. Hard. He had never wanted a woman more and he had scarcely touched her. Yet, she seemed totally unaffected. Or was that a slight tremble in her hands?

"*Señor?*"

He let go of the dishes at her question and just as quickly she lowered her gaze. As she turned away with the dishes he heard them rattle within her grasp before she steadied them against her. So it was a trembling he had felt. Perhaps she was not as unaffected by him as he thought. Perhaps she wanted him as much as he wanted her. And perhaps not. Perhaps she was just nervous to be in the home of a Spanish officer. He sighed. He wanted a woman. He wanted this woman. But now was not the time.

She was doing the job he had hired her to do. He should get on with his own job. He had eaten at the fort then left to find a housekeeper. He had found one. He should get back to the fort and check on the welfare of the prisoners that, strangely, she seemed so concerned about.

He sighed, watching her carry the dishes outside to wash them. Perhaps tonight. He went to the door and leaned there watching her place the dishes in a metal pan on the tiled stove top.

"I have already found a boy to bring firewood each day. There is some food in the store room, rice, beans, spices, flour. You will find something to fix for supper."

She stopped in the middle of dipping water from a brimming bucket he had drawn from the well earlier in the day. "You want me to cook?"

"Isn't that part of being a housekeeper?"

She drew in a great breath and pursed her lips before replying. "I…yes."

He tilted his head to look at her through slitted eyes. "You do know how to cook, don't you?"

She gripped the dipper so hard, her knuckles whitened. "I… of course."

It was a reply that sounded a bit too uncertain to him. Especially when he thought of those muffins.

She turned her back to him and poured the water into the pan. Taking up a hard bar of soap she began shaving off bits of it with a knife then dissolving the soap in the water. Her back was ramrod straight and Alejandro could almost feel the tension in her. Was she so fearful of him?

She turned back to him, a question in her eyes. "Is there anything else you wish me to do, *señor*?"

He noticed that she clutched the hard edge of the tile, and although her voice did not waver, she seemed relieved when he shook his head and turned to go.

There was an unusual quality to Maria's voice, he thought. Not quite an accent, although maybe she did have a slight one, as if Spanish was not her native tongue. And perhaps it wasn't. She could have grown up speaking both her native Indian language as well as Spanish. It was something he would have to ask her some-time. Strange, though, that there seemed to be something familiar about it. Even though he certainly had had no chance to become familiar with any native dialect. He shrugged. He had more important things to consider than a Mestiza's bit of accent. Maria promised to be an interesting distraction, as long as he didn't let her become too much of a distraction.

Mariette heard each of Alejandro's footsteps as he walked through the house, heard the latch, heard the door swing open, then shut. Only then did she turn around, bury her face in her hands and give way just a bit to the case of nerves that had been building ever since she had encountered *Señor* de Silva.

"Steady as she goes," she muttered one of Nate's favorite terms and took deep breaths. "I am not in over my head as Soledad warned. I am right where I need to be to rescue Matt. And Douglass. I can handle this. And I can handle *Señor* de Silva." She turned back to the dishes and put them into the pan to soak. "However, I just might be over my head if the *capitán* is expecting a decent meal tonight."

"Here puppy! Now where have you gotten yourself off to, you little sprite?"

Mariette froze. There was someone on the other side of the wall at the back of the yard. And that someone was speaking English. English with a touch of the shamrock.

"Here puppy! Sean Patrick Christopher O'Mally, if you don't show your sweet little self, and soon, I'm going to be givin' this nice bone to some other deservin' animal."

Mariette ran to the gate set in the back wall and peeked into the alley behind the house. Someone was there all right. A thin young woman in a once fine dress, that was now no better than a rag, was bent over searching through the rubble that littered the alley.

Mariette opened the door farther and the woman straightened in alarm, brushing an unruly batch of Irish red curls back from eyes as green as the Irish Sea. Her eyes widened and she whirled to run.

"Wait! Don't go!" Mariette remembered at the last moment to speak in Spanish. A Mestiza might know Spanish, but she certainly wouldn't know English. She wanted to know why this Irish woman was here in Spanish St. Augustine, but she couldn't risk trusting her just yet. The Irish had too much reason to hate the English.

The woman halted, then turned back to face Mariette, quickly hidinga meaty bone she was holding behind her back. "¿Sí, señora?"

"Who are you?" The woman seemed skittish as a young colt so Mariette came into the alley, letting herself be seen, letting the woman know there was nothing to fear from her.

"I'm Irish," the woman replied tossing back her heavy mane of hair with a proud lift of her chin.

Mariette smiled. "So I see from your red hair and from the English you were speaking, but what is your name?"

The woman shook her head in puzzlement. "My Spanish. Not good. I don't understand."

Mariette repeated her question slowly using simple words, wishing she could just speak to this woman in English. But it was not a chance she could take. Not with Matt's life—and hers—hanging in the balance.

"Ah," the woman said in understanding. "I told you. I'm Irish. That's what they call me." Her chin came up another notch as if defying Mariette, or anyone else, to pry any deeper.

"I am Maria." Mariette dipped a quick curtsey, in an effort to identify herself as a servant and on the same plane as Irish. "I am the housekeeper for the *capitán* who lives here."

Mariette spoke slowly and clearly and Irish nodded her head in understanding as she struggled for words to reply. "I belong to the Martíns."

"Belong? You are a slave?"

Irish blushed but the proud defiance in her stance did not alter. "I was on my way to America. The ship I was on was taken by the Spanish. I was sold in the marketplace and the Martíns bought me."

Irish had spoken in a mixture of bad Spanish and English, but knowing both languages, Mariette had little trouble understanding her. She looked at Irish anew. Her status would explain her clothing, the bruises that Mariette now noticed on her arms. She was not being kindly used.

"I see. I am sorry." Mariette stepped forward, hand outstretched in sympathy and comfort, but halted when Irish's back stiffened. Clearly the woman wanted no pity. Mariette changed the subject. "Were you calling someone earlier?"

Irish instantly mellowed, no longer defensive. "Aye. A wee pest of a dog." She held up the bone and shrugged. "I thought he might be wanting this."

At that moment they heard a whimper and a mutt crawled out from under some rubbish and came waggling toward Irish on thin, wobbly legs. He was half-grown and half-starved and completely full of all the qualities that make dogs lovable.

Irish knelt and the puppy jumped to lick her face. She lapsed back into English to lavish praises on the puppy, "Good dog! Sweet little one! Ye needn't lick me to death, now, since I've brought you a good bone still with a bit of meat on it."

She gave him the bone and the puppy seemed torn between food and love, jumping on Irish for one more hug then sniffing the bone then back for another pet. Finally, he settled down at Irish's feet, gnawing at the scraps of meat left on the bone. "There you go, Paddy, ye poor starved thing."

Mariette knelt beside the pair and patted the dog. "What is his name?" she asked as if she had not understood Irish's English.

"It's Sean Patrick Christopher O'Malley."

"Quite a mouthful for such a small dog." Mariette petted the dog's soft floppy ears.

Irish laughed, her smile lighting up her face. "Aye. He put me in mind of the bishop back at home with his pointy nose and curious way. But I call him Paddy for short."

"Paddy's going to need more than an occasional bone to put some weight on. I can count his ribs."

"Aye, I know. But I haven't much to give him. It's likely, I am, to get a caning for taking even this bit of bone for him." Irish scratched Paddy behind the ears and surreptitiously brushed at her eyes.

Mariette thought Irish could use a bit more food as well, judging from her thin arms. She sighed. "There is plenty of food in our pantry and I would be glad to give Paddy our scraps each night, but if I do not come up with a meal for the *capitán* tonight, I will not have any scraps at all…and might just be out of a job, as well."

"And what might be the problem, seein' as how you have plenty of food?"

Mariette winced. "I do not know how to cook."

Irish laughed and Mariette could not help joining her. "And how did a fine lass like yourself get to be of such an age without knowin' how to cook?"

Mariette just shrugged uncomfortably. She couldn't very well tell Irish the truth and she didn't want to lie to her, either. But Irish seemed to understand that there were things a person needed to keep to herself and didn't press her.

"Well, I'm a fine cook when I get the chance. Seein' as how you're willin' to feed Paddy and the Martíns are gone right now, I could get a meal started for you and none would be the wiser."

Mariette invited Irish and Paddy into the patio then watched in awe as Irish took a quick inventory of the food in the *capitán's* storeroom and threw things into a pot. They fed Paddy some scraps and he was soon curled at their feet sleeping deeply, his now rounded belly sticking out beneath his ribs. Irish told Mariette a few things to buy at the market the next day for tomorrow's dinner and then she had to leave before she might be found missing.

"Come along then, Sean Patrick," Irish said, nudging Paddy gently with her toe. The dog rolled over but continued his deep puppy sleep. She bent to pick him up but Mariette stopped her.

"He cannot stay out there in the alley. Something might happen to him."

"Aye, I'm worried every day that he won't be there when I call. But I can't take him to the Martín's."

Mariette bent to stroke Paddy who gave a contented sigh in his sleep.

"Then leave him here. When you want to see him, you will know where he is."

"Oh, Maria!" Irish gave Mariette a quick hug. "How can I ever thank you!"

Mariette shrugged. "I feed your dog. You feed my *capitán.* That is more than thanks enough. You have saved my job."

Mariette watched as Irish gave Paddy one last scratch behind his ear and slipped through the back gate. And suddenly she realized that Irish had not made her task in St. Augustine any easier. She had made it more complex by far because Mariette knew that when she and Nate sailed away from here with Matt and Douglass, Irish would have to be with them. She couldn't leave her behind.

Chapter Three

BACK SO SOON, NEPHEW?" IGNATIO LEANED BACK IN HIS chair, causing it to creak beneath his weight. He propped his elbows on the chair arms, steepled his fingers and leered superciliously over them at Alejandro.

It was even hotter in the commandant's office this afternoon than it had been this morning. The same Indian slave stood beside Ignatio, fanning him, while trickles of sweat ran down his own thin face.

Alejandro clenched one fist in the other behind his back and gave his uncle a quick nod of assent.

"You found a housekeeper in so short a time?" Ignatio mopped his face with a handkerchief and signaled for the slave to fan harder.

"I had no trouble, Uncle." None at all. He'd hired the first woman he had bumped into. Literally.

"You always did have a reputation with women, Alejandro." Ignatio snickered lasciviously, licking thick lips in anticipation. "It will be interesting to 'meet' the woman you chose. Especially considering the very talented woman you refused."

Ignatio also had a reputation with women, Alejandro thought, in spite of the fact that he was married with six children. And that reputation was not a good one.

"I doubt that she would appeal to you, sir."

"Tsk, tsk, tsk." Ignatio pursed his lips and shook his head in mock sympathy. "Don't tell me that you hired some old hag simply on the merits of her housekeeping abilities?"

Alejandro suddenly realized that he did not know a thing about Maria except that she was beautifully alluring. Had he assumed that because she was a woman grown she knew how to keep house and cook? Had her beauty so blinded him to what he really needed?

Ignatio must have misinterpreted Alejandro's look because he gave a shout of laughter, threw himself forward in his chair and slapped his hands down on the desk. "So you did! No wonder you are back so soon and ready for duty. Oh, this is too good!" He laughed until he had to stop to wipe spittle from the corners of his mouth with the back of one hand. "I never thought you would be this amusing, Nephew. Really! I think you are going to make things much too easy for me. I expected more of a challenge from you. But then," Ignatio smirked, "we are not finished yet, are we?"

Ignatio grabbed an apple from a bowl of fruit and some keys from the desktop and lurched to his feet, still snickering. "But come, Alejandro, let me show you the men I have found for you." His uncle led the way down the stairs and out into the central compound of the fort. He snapped his fingers at three soldiers who bumbled their way into a somewhat straight line.

"This is your *capitán*, Alejandro de Silva." Ignatio turned to his nephew. "Here are the men I have assigned to help you guard the English prisoners." Ignatio grinned unpleasantly and polished the apple he was carrying on his sleeve before biting into it.

Alejandro frowned at the three men lined up before him, supposedly at attention. The first one was staring at Ignatio's apple as if he hadn't eaten in a week but his belly protruded so far his coat would not button.

"What is your name?" Alejandro asked.

"Franciso, *Capitán*," the man answered, grinning broadly and giving a limp salute.

"Fasten that button, soldier!" Alejandro commanded.

Francisco looked down, shook his head as if at a naughty child, sucked in as much as he could and managed to get the button through its hole. It popped right back out again and he shrugged apologetically to Alejandro as he tugged at his coat and smoothed a beefy hand over it.

"And your name?" Alejandro asked the second man.

"Paco, sir!" the man shouted in perfect military precision. He snapped to attention, saluted, then nearly dropped his musket. Alejandro caught it and the man mumbled a hasty apology before snapping back to attention.

Alejandro grimaced. "At ease, Paco. You'll have a stroke if you don't."

Paco nodded and took up a sharp at ease position. Alejandro shook his head.

The third man was short and wiry and looked Alejandro up and down insolently, lifting one brow as if he had somehow found his captain lacking.

"Your name?" Alejandro asked.

"Raúl," the man drawled. Then after a pause added, "*Capitán*." He glanced at Ignatio then turned back to Alejandro with a smirk.

This one he would have to watch. The other two seemed merely incompetent. This one, Alejandro was sure, his uncle had set as a spy.

"I can tell, Uncle, that you did not spare any effort in choosing them."

Ignatio shrugged and finished his apple. "What can you expect of colonials? The English attack has made recruitment difficult for the militia."

"Where are the prisoners, Uncle?"

"There, in the corner cell." Ignatio pulled out two large keys and handed them to Alejandro with a nasty grin. "They are now your responsibility."

Alejandro stood tossing the keys up and down in his hand, assessing the men assigned to him. He had observed the colonial militia yesterday on his arrival and this morning at the fort. These men were not typical. It was as he thought. His uncle wanted him to fail. But even with this bumbling lot, how could the prisoners escape? They were inside a fort that even the English cannon had not dented. There were guards all around in addition to these three. Well-trained men on the alert. He would take the prisoners from their cell, exercise them in the compound, see to their welfare. Even if one of them should happen to bolt, he would never make it to the gates, let alone across the drawbridge, across the moat, and across fifteen hundred feet of clear ground without being shot down.

The duty assigned him would perhaps be boring but it would also be uneventful. He wondered what reason his uncle had for assigning it. Ignatio's mind worked deeper than the simple pettishness of giving him a boring duty. There was a trap here somewhere. He just couldn't see it, yet.

Alejandro headed across the compound with his three men trailing behind. The militiaman guarding the cell saluted smartly at his approach.

"What is the routine for the prisoners' feeding and exercise?" Alejandro asked the man.

The soldier shrugged. "We give them whatever we have left over from the soldiers' mess in the evening. A couple of times a week we take them out and run them around the compound."

Alejandro glanced toward the cell door. Even from where he

stood the stink of unwashed bodies and urine was almost over-powering. "And do little else for them, I suppose. Like water for washing?"

The soldier shrugged again. "They are English. And prisoners. They attacked us." He leaned closer to Alejandro as if to impart a confidence. "There are many who say they should burn as the heretics they are in a grand *auto-de-fé*."

It was with difficulty that Alejandro kept from reaching out to strangle the man. "Thank you, soldier," he said through clenched teeth. "You are dismissed."

The soldier saluted and turned to go, then turned back to add, "One of them speaks pretty good Spanish, so don't let them get away with acting like they don't know what you're telling them to do."

Alejandro's lips relaxed into a brief smile at this information and he nodded his thanks to the soldier. With feelings so high against the English because of the recent siege, he had not particularly wanted to reveal to anyone that he spoke the language like a native. They might jump to conclusions that would hit all too close to home. It was bad enough that his uncle knew. If the prisoners knew, they might come to have higher expectations of him than he could fulfill. It was better all around that his dealings with the prisoners be conducted in Spanish.

He handed Paco the key to the cell door. "Let's get them out of there for a look."

The lock grated and grumbled and the hinges squealed as the door was flung open, and the English prisoners began to tumble out of their cell.

Alejandro noticed that Raúl watched each prisoner with ha-tred intent on his face. Francisco stepped back, his face screwed up in disgust at the odor, more concerned with putting some distance between himself and the foul smelling prisoners than in guarding them. Paco watched each prisoner as they emerged, fumbling with his musket and uncertain what to do with the key until Alejandro took it from him.

Alejandro watched the prisoners turn eager faces to the sun and breathe deeply of the fresh air outside their cell. They were all wearing shackles on their wrists and ankles and he gave them a few minutes to walk around as best they could dragging their chains.

One tall, broad-shouldered man in particular seemed, even more than the others, to relish being outside the cell. He stretched like the others and breathed in the clean air like the others, but while they continued to move and talk quietly, this man went to the wall and bent to break off a stem of grass that had found a crack to grow in. He didn't pull up the whole plant. Just that one stem. Alejandro watched as he smelled it, rolled it appreciatively in his hand, then tucked it inside his shirt.

"Paco!"

Paco scampered to Alejandro and saluted so smartly his whole body seemed to quiver from it. "*Sí, mi capitán!*"

"Round up as many buckets as you can and a few bars of soap."

"Soap?"

It took only one small scowl to send Paco off at a run on his errand.

"And a pair of scissors!" he called after him. Then Alejandro turned to the prisoners.

"Which of you speaks Spanish?" he asked.

The prisoner Alejandro had been watching lifted his chin and turned the most amazing blue eyes toward him. Like the rest of the prisoners his clothing was not much more than filthy rags, he was unshaven and his hair hung in greasy locks. But once those eyes were on him, Alejandro ceased to notice.

"I do."

The words were softly spoken but Alejandro noted that all the other prisoners paused in whatever they were doing to listen, to give this man their full attention even though they did not understand what he was saying.

Alejandro motioned for the man to come to him. The man stood,looked him up and down as if taking his full measure, then walked toward him. He had the strangest feeling that the man came only because he wanted to, that if he had chosen not to come, nothing—and no one—could have forced him to.

When the prisoner stood face to face with him, Alejandro could not help but smile. Somehow he sensed that in other circumstances, this man and he could have become fast friends.

"I am Captain Alejandro de Silva. What is your name?"

The man looked at him intently for a moment, those bright blue eyes taking in every detail. Then he quietly said, "Mateo."

Alejandro nodded. The man had given the Spanish equivalent of his name, Mateo. Matthew. He noted that he did not give a last name and Alejandro did not press him for one.

"Mateo, I have been placed in charge of you and the other prisoners."

Alejandro noticed that Mateo cocked one brow and one side of his mouth almost smiled.

"You find something amusing, Mateo?"

Mateo shrugged. "I was just wondering what heinous crime sent a Spanish don to the colonies to stand guard duty over a group of filthy prisoners."

"What makes you think I am a noble?"

"Any number of things," Mateo answered, playing with the links of the chain stretched between his wrists. "Your name, the way you carry yourself, the fact that you are a *capitán*."

Alejandro nodded. Mateo was too perceptive by far. He would have to watch this one closely. "You are right that I am from a noble family, Mateo. But you are wrong about the crime."

Paco came running up at that moment with five buckets, each containing a bar of soap. He set them down and saluted, nearly jabbing his eye out with the pair of scissors he held in his hand.

Alejandro thanked him, took the scissors, and held them out to Mateo.

"You and the other prisoners have two hours to bathe, wash your clothes, and trim beards and hair."

For a moment all traces of a smile were wiped from Mateo's face until the offer Alejandro had made finally sank in. Then his smile came back, full, white, and punctuated by a dimple on each side. Taking the scissors he turned to the other prisoners and told them the news, handing the scissors to one of them.

The prisoners cheered and Alejandro handed Raúl the key to the shackles. As Raúl unlocked their shackles, Paco showed the prisoners where to fill their buckets. Mateo held out his hands to Raúl then rubbed raw wrists while Raúl freed his ankles.

Mateo turned back to Alejandro. "Thank you, *Capitán* for this kindness," he said gravely before he, too, turned to start shedding filthy clothing to wash.

The prisoners were pale from lack of sun and gaunt from lack of food. He would have to see what he could do about increasing their rations. It would not be easy considering how much Ignatio de Silva hated all things English.

"I see you are already pampering your English friends."

Alejandro clenched his fists but crossed his wrists nonchalantly in back to keep from smashing one of those fists into his uncle's nose.

"I hardly call allowing the prisoners a bath after weeks of confinement pampering."

"And what would you call removing their shackles, Nephew? Would you call that wise?" Ignatio casually picked at his teeth with one overlong fingernail.

Alejandro glanced around the fort, noting the men on vigilant guard.

"Within the confines of the fort, as well-guarded as they are, I do not see the harm. How else could they wash and launder their clothes?"

Ignatio also clasped his hands behind his back and rocked back and forth on his heels, a too pleased-with-himself grin on his face for Alejandro's comfort. Alejandro knew that look. He had seen it many times just before his uncle sprang some unpleasant surprise on him. What he could be leading up to now Alejandro could only play along and see.

"And will you leave the shackles off the prisoners when they return to their cell?"

Alejandro considered the question carefully, turning back to watch the prisoners. He knew his uncle was looking for weakness in him, waiting for him to cross the line in favoring English prisoners. But there was no reason to burden these men with shackles while in their cell.

"I see no harm in leaving off the shackles, Uncle," Alejandro said glancing back at Ignatio. "Within the confines of the Castillo, that is."

Ignatio's grin widened, a sure sign of trouble coming. "The prisoners will not be within the confines of the fort much longer."

Alejandro raised his brows and tilted his head.

"The ship that brought you from Spain also brought dispatches. The prisoners are to be sent to Spain when the Eagle returns in two weeks."

Two weeks! He had to guard these prisoners only two weeks and his task was done. Even with three inept guards he could keep twenty prisoners safe within the walls of *El Castillo* for two weeks. He almost breathed a sigh of relief until he chanced to look at his uncle.

Ignatio was smiling much too broadly for this to be all he had to say. And Alejandro was sure he would not like the rest of it.

"I have a feeling, Uncle, that there is more to the story than this."

Ignatio chuckled, ran a finger around his neck to loosen his stock a bit, tugged at his coat to straighten it. "Well, yes," he said. "There is a bit more."

Alejandro would not give his uncle the small pleasure of asking. He merely bided his time and waited for his uncle to speak.

Ignatio took his time about it, drawing out the suspense as only he could do, but finally said, "It is the usual practice that prisoners be used to work."

Ignatio paused and Alejandro could not help giving him a nod to continue.

"Beginning tomorrow, and until the prisoners are onboard ship, you will take them out on work detail. There are considerable repairs to be done to some of our fortifications. Why not make use of the prisoners since we have to feed them anyway?" Ignatio's grin reached its widest. He turned to walk away, saying over his shoulder, "Whether you choose to shackle them or not is entirely up to you."

By the time Alejandro left the fort that evening he was more than a little tired. Although he was worried about taking the prisoners out of the fort the next day, he had at least managed to get a few concessions from his uncle. The prisoners' rations would be increased and once they were locked into their cell at night, they would be the responsibility of the Castillo guard. Alejandro and his three men would only have charge of the prisoners during the day.

That would be bad enough, he thought, walking through the plaza on his way back to his lodgings. Three more inept soldiers he had never seen than the ones his uncle had assigned to him. After they had put the prisoners back into their cell—unshackled—Alejandro had drilled the three guards for the rest of the afternoon. They at least knew which end of their muskets to point at the prisoners now.

The prisoners had been reluctant to go back into that cramped cell, and Alejandro didn't blame them. Mateo had asked him to allow the prisoners to clean it out, so it wasn't as feotid as before. Alejandro noticed that Mateo still had the stem of grass with him, tucked carefully in a button hole. Alejandro didn't blame him. If he were locked within stone walls day and night for weeks, he would want a reminder that life and green still existed, too.

Alejandro hoped that even though they would be working, and working hard, Mateo and the others would enjoy being outside these next two weeks. Once they were put onboard the Eagle and taken to Spain, they would probably be kept in prison there and not see the sun again until the end of this war.

As Alejandro crossed the plaza, now quiet in the hush of early evening, and headed down the *Calle del Gobernador*, his thoughts turned to a bath for himself, food, and the lovely Mestiza he had hired that morning. If she could keep house half as well as she could bake muffins, he would count himself fortunate, indeed, for having met her. He would just have to make sure his Uncle Ignatio never did.

He doubted that, even as skittish as she was, a woman her age was still a virgin. But even if she had had a dozen lovers, she would be no match for his uncle's perverted tastes. He barely knew Maria, but he was willing to wager that she was not a woman who would relish being hurt. Ignatio would want her and he would enjoy hurting her, for no other reason than to thwart his nephew and to take something that belonged to him.

Maybe he should send Maria back to her family. He could

find someone else to keep house for him, cook for him. Some old woman with skin wrinkled and tough as shoe leather, with only three teeth left in her head. Someone Ignatio would not want.

But Alejandro knew that if Ignatio decided to take vengeance on his nephew by hurting his maid, it would not matter to him whether she was an old crone or the lovely young woman she was. He would just have to be careful to protect Maria from his uncle.

In the meantime, it was so much more pleasant to think of returning home each night to a good meal served by the lovely Maria.

Alejandro's pace quickened and by the time he reached his house, he was envisioning being met by a lovely, smiling face and enticing food. He could picture her with slim arms outstretched, skirts swaying and her full breasts rounded above her tightly laced bodice. But when he opened the door, he found instead a small yapping dog, bravely barring his entrance to his own home.

"What the...?" The dog's bark was fierce but its tale was wagging so hard it was nearly knocking it off balance. A puppy. Alejandro ignored it, stepping inside. But unlike most puppies, this one did not back up in the face of a larger adversary. It held its ground, even advancing a step, baring teeth. At that Alejandro stopped. Not that a puppy that young and small could do much damage, but what was it doing here in the first place?

The answer came sweeping through the door from the patio in a flurry of dark brown skirts and flashes of cream colored petticoat. "Good dog! Good dog, Paddy!" Maria scooped up the puppy and, holding it pressed to the very breasts Alejandro had just been thinking of, gave the puppy a vigorous rub from head to proudly wagging tail.

Alejandro glared at the interloping puppy that seemed to be grinning smugly at him. "Good dog? The vicious little beast nearly took my leg off!"

Maria snuggled the puppy closer to those luscious breasts, and bent her head to caress it with her cheek. She looked up at him with wide, innocent eyes, apparently completely ignorant of the chaos she was causing in his loins. "A good guard dog is supposed to growl at intruders."

Alejandro planted fists on hips and this time glared at Maria. "Intruder? This is my home!"

Her chin came up defensively and she held the dog even more protectively close. "Paddy did not know that."

Alejandro's fists came off his hips and his brows rose questioningly. "Paddy?"

Mariette shrugged, turning her attention—and a smile—back to the puppy, running slim fingers over soft floppy ears. "That is his name."

Alejandro watched the play of her fingers in fascination. "And just where did Paddy come from?"

"The alley out back."

Alejandro again placed fists on hips and glared at the dog. He was lapping up Maria's attention like a…well, a dog. "Then he can just go right back into the alley."

"He'll starve!" Maria held Paddy closer and took up a defensive stance, glaring back at him.

Alejandro noted the puppy's rounded, recently stuffed belly that protruded in stark contrast to its plainly showing ribs. He remembered another starving dog that had not been so lucky once Ignatio had realized how much it meant to a small boy to care for it.

He glared at the puppy again and the puppy responded by licking Maria's chin, and then it had the nerve to grin at him. He almost grinned back but he had learned long ago not to let his care of anything show.

Cheeky little devil. Damn dog had her wrapped around its paw and knew it, and now it was working on him. Besides, if he threw it out, Maria would never let Alejandro lick her chin. Or any other part of her for that matter.

"Probably has fleas and who knows what else," he muttered.

Maria cuddled Paddy's head defensively. "He does not have fleas. I gave him a good bath and went over him thoroughly."

Alejandro sighed. He knew when he was beaten. "All right."

Maria's eyes sparkled and it was almost worth the concession to have her look at him like that. "Let him smell your hand."

"What?"

"You have to make friends."

Friends. Another thing he had seldom been allowed to have. Tentatively, he held his hand out for the puppy to sniff.

Paddy gave him an approving lick that sent a melting warmth through him, and he found himself giving the animal a pat on the head before he realized what he was doing. He jerked his hand away.

"I would like my supper now. That is, if you haven't fed everything in the house to this mongrel." The words came out sharper than he intended causing both Maria and Paddy to start, and Alejandro instantly regretted his tone.

But Maria quirked a brow at him and one corner of her mouth flickered in a near grin. The wench was not the least bit intimidated by him after all and that made him wish he had spoken even sharper than he had.

"*Sí, señor.* I have a meal ready for you." She gave Paddy one last squeeze and set him down.

Alejandro gave the dog one more glare—that seemed not to bother him at all—then swiped his tricorn hat from his head and sent it sailing to the sofa. Paddy chased after it but couldn't quite make the leap up onto the sofa where the hat had landed. He whined in frustration for a moment then settled down with his head on his paws to watch Alejandro.

Alejandro loosened his stock, shrugged off his coat and hung it on the back of one of the two chairs. Maria had gone back outside, presumably to bring his dinner, and he looked around. The floor gleamed, even in the corners, and from somewhere Maria had found a cloth for the table. The table was set with the crude dishes that had come with the place, but somehow the addition of the cloth and a bowl of flowers made it seem almost elegant.

Maria bustled in and out putting the food on the table—a steaming bowl of rice and a bean dish, flat bread, sliced tomatoes. She poured a cup of wine and then pulled out a chair for him to sit at the single place set at the table.

He had eaten alone many times, especially in the last months of his mother's illness. He had not felt the slightest bit awkward or uncomfortable sitting alone at the long polished table in his parent's home, being waited on by silent servants. But this was different somehow. Perhaps because for the first time he was truly alone and on his own, thousands of miles from any family or friend who cared for him. He thought he had left his enemies behind in Spain, as well. The presence of Ignatio had proved him wrong. For whatever reason, perhaps the small intimacy of the house, he did not want to sit down alone to eat.

He looked at Maria and wondered how she would react if he asked her to join him. If she became his lover, as he hoped she would, it seemed foolish to begin their relationship so formally. The walls between his class and hers would have to be breached quickly since he did not plan to stay in St. Augustine for long.

"Have you eaten yet?" he asked her.

"No, Don Alejandro."

Her words were meek but there was something about her, the tone of her voice, her stance, that made him feel that their stations were more equal than not. It was almost disturbing. As if she were a lady and he should be holding out the chair for her. But she wasn't a lady, he reminded himself. She was an uneducated Mestiza servant girl and it would be best for both of them if he remembered that. She might provide a dalliance for him if she were willing, but there could never be more than that between them.

"Then set another place and eat with me." The words came out too harshly, too much of a command. He could see her spine stiffen, her chin come up, fire snap in her eyes as if she really were a lady. This was not the way to win her. He gave her a small, stiff bow as if she were, in truth, a grand lady, and, with a smile, added, "Please."

Chapter Four

MARIETTE TRIED NOT TO ACT AS OFF KILTER AS SHE FELT by this bowing Spanish nobleman. She lowered her eyes. "You confuse me, *señor.*"

"Confuse you?" He smiled and took her hand to urge her into the chair. "It is not my intent to confuse you."

At the touch of his hand, she felt a melting within her and her nipples peaked beneath her chemise. It had to be his hand on hers that so affected her. She pulled it away from his. She had to put some distance between them. And keep it there.

"I am your servant. It is not proper for me to sit with you and share a meal."

"If we were in Spain and in my parent's palacio, I might agree." He took her hand again, held it firmly in his, and stepped close enough to brush his lips against her hair. "But we are not in Spain. And this," he dismissed the humble house with a wave of his hand, "is certainly not a palace."

"But still…" Mariette stepped away from him so she could breathe, could think.

He closed on her again. "I am far from Spain, new come to these shores, without a friend. What harm to share a meal with the lovely woman who prepared it?"

Mariette could not squelch a grin at that. If he only knew who had really prepared this meal! She looked up at him and he smiled in response to her smile. A brilliant, white smile that went all the way to his eyes, lighting them, making her feel like the most desired woman in the world.

"Aah, you are giving in to me."

Mariette caught a glimpse of the bedroom behind Alejandro and was afraid she knew just where it could lead to give in to him. But she also knew she would get no information from him playing the part of a humble, ignorant servant. It would not be easy to tease and taunt and yet hold him at bay. Not when her own impulse was to lean into him and...

"Very well, Don Alejandro." She said it before she could change her mind. She had to think of Matt. And Douglass.

She thought he would let her go then, let her get another plate and sit, but he drew her closer instead. She gasped in surprise and made the mistake of looking into his eyes. Eyes blacker than her own. Eyes with unfathomable depths. He leaned closer. His mouth was only a breath away from hers. She thought he was going to kiss her and she forgot how to breathe. But he brought her hand to his lips instead, planting a chaste, gentlemanly kiss on her fingertips. Chaste and gentlemanly, but it warmed her and made her wish he had chosen to kiss her lips instead.

She managed to wrench away from him to turn to the cupboard and fumble for a plate and cup and utensils. She had to be more careful. As Soledad had warned her—she was, indeed, playing with fire. Spanish fire. Enemy fire. It would be wise to remember that. And to douse every flame he ignited. She had to keep her head if she was going to rescue Matt. And Douglass.

But even a Spanish noble would feel compelled to talk about something over a meal. It would be up to her to steer the conversation where she wanted it to go—to information about the English prisoners.

"I would be honored to join you, *señor*." A little flattery wouldn't hurt, either, she thought, trying hard not to bat her eyelashes too coyly. She had to maintain just the right balance between flirtation and humility. She wanted information, not to find herself in his bed.

Quickly she arranged her place setting. When she looked up she was surprised to find him holding her chair for her. Inwardly she shrugged. If he wanted to treat her like a lady, she would respond as a lady. If he thought of her as a lady, perhaps he would court her to win her to his bed instead of pressuring her. Surely she could fend him off for another few days. Just until she had the information she needed to rescue Matt. And Douglass.

Automatically Mariette crossed herself and folded her hands to pray, then gritted her teeth. Would this Spanish *capitán* think her too pious or simple? But he merely smiled at her indulgently, crossed himself and nodded for her to do the honors.

Heart pounding, wondering if her Anglican prayers would be different from Catholic prayers, she hastily mumbled something and picked up the bowl of rice, handing it to him to serve himself first.

Perhaps it was for the best that she had prayed, Mariette thought, as Alejandro finished heaping rice onto his plate and passed her the bowl. Maybe he would be easier to keep at bay if he thought she had strong religious principles. She must think of ways to foster this impression, but for now, she would find out all she could about the prisoners.

"How did you find your new duties at *El Castillo* this afternoon, *Capitán*?" Mariette cast her gaze downward onto her plate, trying desperately to sound as casual as possible.

Alejandro took a loaf of the flat bread Irish had helped her make, tore it in two, and, leaning close, offered her half, touching it to her lips in invitation. "Why spoil our meal with talk of forts and soldiers and prisoners? I am sure I can find a more appropriate topic to discuss with such a lovely *señorita*."

Mariette took the bread from him, the touch of his fingers bringing a flush to her face. She took up the beans, well-seasoned with peppers and tomatoes and onions and passed them to Alejandro, forcing him to sit back from her to take the large bowl.

He helped himself, then held it while she ladled some of the beans over her own rice. He was too close. She needed distance. He was taking up all the air. She couldn't breathe. She found herself wishing she had set her place on the other side of the table instead of next to him. She wished she could crawl into his lap. She handed him the tomatoes instead, leaning as far from him as she could.

"You shy from me like a new foal." His hand found hers and she pulled it away, placing it in her lap. "You have no need to fear me, *señorita*."

"I am not afraid of you, *Capitán*." She lied. She was terrified. But maybe it wasn't the captain she was afraid of after all. It was herself. She didn't want to shy from him. She didn't want to jerk her hand away. But her brothers had spoken plainly with her. She knew where his touches could lead. And her body was begging her to follow gladly.

He suddenly stiffened. "You are not married, are you?"

"Oh, no, *señor!*"

His lopsided grin lit his eyes anew and he leaned close to her again. "Promised to another?"

She shook her head then gritted her teeth. Why hadn't she said yes? Why did she always forget about Douglass? Was it because Douglass was so very forgettable? Or was her memory so faulty because there was a handsome, black-eyed Spanish *capitán* leaning so close she could feel his soft, warm breath on her cheek?

He leaned closer, his lips whispering feather light upon her cheek and in her hair. "Do the men of St. Augustine sing ballads beneath your window every night?"

The thought of men singing for her brought a brief smile to her lips. Again she shook her head.

He pulled back, his brows shooting upward in mock surprise. "Why not? Are they all blind that they have not seen your beauty?" He took a bite of the beans and rice and he nodded his approval. "And your culinary abilities?"

It felt good to be so teased and complimented, even if she hadn't done the cooking, and she gave in to the urge for a bit of flirtation with her handsome *capitán* while they ate. "I do not live in town, señor. I live in a small village and only come to St. Augustine infrequently."

He cocked one dark brow at her and indicated the small room with a wave of one hand. "You live in St. Augustine now, *Querida*."

Mariette's pulse quickened at his use of this Spanish endearment, sounding so right—and so husky—coming from this grandé. She could not help but mouth the word herself, surprised that he would use it with her. "*Querida*?"

He nodded. "*Sí*," he said emphatically. "*Querida mía*."

Mía. Mine. Was he claiming her or simply flirting? Again her gaze went to the bedroom behind him, her pulse quickening still more, and it was with difficulty that she kept her hands from shaking as she forced herself to take another bite.

"I just hope I do not find myself shooing love smitten swains from the door, or chasing away singing suitors from beneath the window every night."

Mariette could not help laughing at this absurd picture. She waved her hand playfully. "I shall encourage them to come only when you are away."

He grasped her hand and brought it to his lips. "Then I shall have to be at home as much as possible and take you with me when I leave."

When he left he would be going to the fort. She jumped at the chance to turn the conversation to the topic uppermost in her thoughts—her brother and how to free him. And Douglass. "Will you take me with you to the fort?"

He gave her a fierce mock scowl. "And have half the militia deserting their posts so they can pay court to you every day?"

Again she laughed lightly, smiling coquettishly at him. "I doubt that they are so poorly disciplined. But the English prisoners might need a woman's touch. They are far from home. Perhaps some of them are ill and need care?"

"The prisoners are doing just fine."

His words were sharp, as if she had ventured too far. He reached for another loaf of the round, flat bread and tore it into pieces as she watched, wondering what had caused his quick change of mood. Did he hate the English prisoners? Or did he simply not want to talk about them with her? But she had to press on. She had to find out about Matt. Was he really 'just fine' as Alejandro said?

She leaned forward, trying to keep her tone light, the anxiety from her voice. "Are they? Are the prisoners doing just fine?"

"They are well enough considering their treatment."

Mariette clutched her spoon to keep her hand from shaking. She was no innocent not to know how badly prisoners could be treated, especially by the Spanish. It was with difficulty that she kept a waver out of her voice. "And how have they been treated?"

Alejandro did not look at her when he answered, continuing to shred the bread instead, glowering at it as if it were some enemy. "Crowded together in a cell too small for them, shackled hand and foot, inadequate food, unwashed." He glanced up at her and stopped suddenly, dropping the bread and taking her hand. "Forgive me! I should not have spoken so to you. You are unused to hearing such things. I have upset you."

She was indeed upset. More so than she could let him know. It was her brother he spoke of. Her twin who was existing in such harsh conditions. Matt, who was used to roaming free, disappearing for weeks into the wilderness and sleeping under the stars with his Indian friends. Matt, who was now chained like an animal. It was with the utmost difficulty that she kept herself from giving way to tears. "Yes, it is upsetting to hear of men, even enemy soldiers treated so badly." She gripped his hand tightly and looked pleadingly into his eyes. "Please tell me that you have helped them."

"I have done what I could, Maria."

Had he? She still wasn't sure how he felt about the prisoners, about the English. Maybe he hated them as badly as the merchant in the market who wanted to see them burn in an *auto-de-fé*.

"And what were you able to do?"

"I had their chains removed, allowed them time outside their cell, and a chance to wash." He shrugged. "It was not so much. But they seemed to appreciate it."

She was sure they did, especially Matt. She laid her hand on Aljandro's arm, happy to know that he had done what he could for the prisoners. For Matt. And that Alejandro was, if not kindly disposed toward the English prisoners, at least humane. She started to say thank you, but that would have sounded too suspicious. Instead, she settled for, "I am glad."

He placed his hand over hers. "You have a kind heart, Maria, to be so concerned for men who, but weeks ago, were trying to destroy this colony."

She shrugged. "They were soldiers, following orders to protect their homes and way of life. Spanish soldiers do the same."

He sat back, picking up his spoon and continuing to eat. "You are very wise for a simple village girl. I am beginning to think you are not so simple after all."

She lowered her lashes and took a couple of bites wondering how she could find out more about the prisoners, what was to be done with them. "I only wonder about the them as do many people here in the colony. There is much talk in the market about what should be done to them."

"And what do people say?"

She shrugged, trying to sound casual, but it was difficult enough to even say the words, "Some think they should die in an *auto-de-fé*." Mariette could not help giving a shudder at the very thought of her brother and the other prisoners being burned at the stake for the simple reason that they were not Catholic.

"The idea distresses you." Alejandro again took her hand, giving it a comforting squeeze.

"How could it not?" She couldn't keep the anger, the horror from her voice. "It is horrible to think of anyone dying in such a fashion."

He looked earnestly into her eyes. "It will not happen, Maria."

She gazed back at him, hopefully, unable to keep from clutching his arm. "How can you be so sure?"

"They are to be taken to Spain in two weeks."

Two weeks! She had been right not to wait and come back to the market next week as Soledad had urged. Shaken, she turned back to her food and pretended an interest in it. She had been on ships enough to know what confinement in the hold for the long voyage to Spain would entail. She picked at her fluffy rice and seasoned beans and red tomatoes, sprinkled with parsley and oregano and drizzled with olive oil. It was not the fare Matt would be eating even now. In the hold of a prison ship she shuddered to think what he would have. And at the end of that voyage…there awaited a dank Spanish prison.

Two weeks! That didn't give her much time for forming a plan.

If she had been driven to free her brother before because he couldn't stand confinement, now she was frantic to find a way. The whole key to freeing Matt sat next to her. She must have more information and she must not lose hope.

"So the prisoners will be taken to Spain. And how long will they be kept there?" She tried to sound casual, to take bites of her food. Food that now seemed tasteless.

Alejandro shrugged. "Until the war is over."

She swallowed hard to get down the lump of food she had spooned into her mouth. "That could be a long time, *Capitán*."

He nodded, brows knotted. "Years. Then more years before the diplomats and politicians hammer out a treaty and the prisoners are set free. It is not a pleasant future they have before them."

Perhaps not a very long future, either, Mariette thought. Unless she could free Matt. And Douglass. But how? And how could she find out specifically about Matt? She couldn't just say, "By the way, did you happen to notice a tall, dark-haired prisoner with brilliant blue eyes? Oh? And how is he?" A sudden thought struck her. Maybe there was a way to find out about her brother. "*Capitán*, how do you communicate with the prisoners? Do any of them speak Spanish?" Matt spoke Spanish. Not as fluently as he spoke French and some Indian languages, but he spoke it well enough.

"As a matter of fact, one of them does speak Spanish," Alejandro answered.

Matt! It had to be! If only she could be sure. Mariette waited for more information but Alejandro kept eating. Something she was finding more and more difficult to do.

"What does this prisoner who speaks Spanish look like?"

Alejandro looked at her suspiciously and she feared she had gone too far, asked too much. She had to keep from arousing his suspicions any further. She shrugged, trying to seem as nonchalant as possible. "It is just that I have heard that the heretic Englishmen have horns and tails like devils."

At this Alejandro laughed outright. He leaned close, squeezing her hand reassuringly. "They are not devils, Maria. They are men. They look much as we do, not as dark-skinned, perhaps, and some have lighter colored hair, brown, blond. I think there were even two or three with red hair."

She almost held her breath as she asked her next question. "And their eyes, Don Alejandro? What color are their eyes?"

He smiled and spooned another portion of the rice and beans onto his plate. "Brown, black, blue." He set the bowl down. "The one who speaks Spanish has the most remarkable blue eyes I have ever seen."

Matt! It was Matt. She gripped the edge of the table to keep from breaking into tears of relief. Matt could never hide in a crowd, not with his height and those eyes. Every woman he met swooned over those eyes. She felt a thrill of hope.

She wanted to ask Don Alejandro if she could see the prisoners, if she could speak to them, help them. But she knew she had shown more interest in them than was wise. For now, she just wanted to be alone and thank God that she had found out as much as she had about Matt. She excused herself and, taking up her plate and utensils, went outside to clean up the dishes and the meal.

Alejandro watched Maria leave the table. It was strange, this interest of hers in the English prisoners. He shrugged. He supposed a lot of people in St. Augustine were curious about them. But to think that they might have horns and tails! He paused with a bite halfway to his lips. He would not have thought she was so superstitious, so ignorant. It didn't seem in character. He shrugged. He did not really know her all that well, yet. Maybe she was as superstition-ridden as any other poor, ignorant, Mestizo. Maybe he just found it hard to believe it of her because he didn't want to think of her as ignorant. But she probably was. What education, what opportunities could she have had? None.

And why should he care whether she was educated or not? He wanted her first of all as a housekeeper. If she also became his lover, well and good. Normally he was not attracted to women who were unlearned and unenlightened, no matter how beautiful they were. But somehow, Maria was different. She had attracted him from the first. And the more time he spent with her, the more attracted he was. There had to be some reason for it.

He glanced at Paddy and the dog came over to sit grinning up at him, tongue hanging out, one hind leg flopped over. Maria had found a starving dog and fed it, loved it, and defended it. Maria had a loving, giving soul and Alejandro could not help but be drawn to her. He would just have to watch himself that he didn't become so attached to her that he missed a chance to leave. He couldn't afford entanglements right now. No matter how close he became to Maria physically, he would have to keep her at an emotional distance.

Paddy whined. He reached down to pat him, then drew his hand back. Not the dog, either. He couldn't let himself get attached to Paddy, either.

Not now.

Alejandro glared at Paddy and Paddy grinned back. "You're just a damn dog," Alejandro growled.

Paddy whimpered at his tone, his ears drooping.

"All right," Alejandro muttered, "you're a damn dog, but you're a damn cute dog."

Paddy's tail wagged so hard his whole body waggled.

"All right, you're a damn cute dog, but I'm not getting attached to you. I'm not going to be here forever and when I go, I'm leaving you—and Maria—behind."

Paddy whined as if he understood and didn't like what he heard.

Mariette finished washing the dishes and putting the food away while Alejandro took a basin and hot water into his bedroom to wash. He emerged just as she finished putting away the last pot and was wiping her hands on a towel she had tied around her waist.

She looked up to see him standing in the doorway watching her. It would have been impossible to keep her pulse from quickening at the sight of him. The clean cambric shirt he had donned was hanging loose, the sleeves rolled up and the front left open. He leaned negligently in the doorway, one hand braced high against the frame. His gaze never left her and there was a world of meaning in it.

Mariette pulled the towel loose and turned away from him, folding it precisely, taking far more time than was necessary. Then, thinking it would be better to hang the towel up to dry, she unfolded it again and hung it on a peg. When she turned, he was still standing there watching her, disconcerting her.

He didn't look dangerous now. Not the way he had when she had first encountered him in the *mercado*, in full uniform with a brace of pistols in his belt and a sword at his hip. Now the danger emanating from him was a different kind altogether, a danger that had nothing to do with an Englishwoman coming in disguise to a Spanish colony in the midst of a war to rescue her brother.

This danger was older than English or Spanish, older than war itself, and she had to keep from being drawn into that age old battle. But how could she when what she wanted to do was fling herself headlong into that danger, into his arms, and surrender?

Matt. She must think of Matt. She wasn't here to have a torrid affair with a Spanish noble. She was here to rescue Matt. And Douglass. Another time, another place, if he had been a visitor at her family's plantation, she would have welcomed the look Don Alejandro gave her. But for now, she must deflect that danger.

"I will make a lamb stew for dinner tomorrow," she said. Irish had told her what she could make the next night and what she would have to buy in the market. "I will go in the morning to buy what I need."

He nodded briefly. "Then you will need coin." He went inside but returned quickly, jangling some coins in his hand, walking toward her.

She backed up, afraid to let him come near her, touch her. Not here in this fragrant garden with the glow of the setting sun turning everything to gold. Not with the sound of someone playing a guitar somewhere in the distance.

She had backed all the way to the counter that ran alongside the stove. And he had followed, pressing close to her.

"I have money, *señor*. I have the gold *escudo* you gave me."

He took her hand, pressed the coins into it, and closed her fist around them, holding it tightly enclosed in his own. "The *escudo* is your wages, Maria. I do not expect you to spend it on food or other household expenses."

She almost asked him just what he expected in exchange for such high wages, but she was afraid of what he might say. She didn't want to think that he had paid for more than just a housekeeper and cook. She was afraid that Soledad had been right, that he had, indeed, hired her mainly for warming his bed.

But he had not said that at the beginning. He had said only that he needed a housekeeper. That was all he was going to get, too. She was not going to be the plaything of this rich, handsome Spaniard. She was, after all, engaged to another man.

But Douglass's face was awfully hard to remember when she

looked up into midnight black eyes that glowed with warm desire, and saw sensuous, softly parted lips lowering to meet her own.

Chapter Five

WITH ALEJANDRO'S LIPS BEGINNING TO BRUSH HERS, Mariette could not remember why she had ever told Douglass she would marry him. Since the night he had awkwardly and hesitatingly asked her, she hadn't let anyone but Douglass kiss her. And Douglass's kisses were...well...chaste and awkward.

How could she kiss another man when she was engaged to Douglass? As Alejandro's lips began to lightly test hers, the thought changed to: How could she not?

She wasn't sure when she closed her eyes. She only knew she was awash in wonderful sensations as his lips tasted one corner of her mouth, then the other. His lips were softer than she would have imagined, pliant, working deftly over hers.

How could she kiss another man when she was engaged to Douglass? But...she wasn't kissing him. He was kissing her. And his kiss was anything but awkward and hesitant. She was in the hands of an expert who knew exactly what he was doing. The difference between Douglass's kiss and Alejandro's was the difference between a child's pencil drawing and a master painter's work of art. You might like a child's drawing, but you didn't keep it forever. You didn't want to own it, be owned by it, surrender to it, live with it for the rest of your life.

As she surrendered more fully to Alejandro's kiss she ceased to wonder how she would live with only a child's drawing after this. She simply surrendered, sucking in as much pleasure as she could, as he sucked on first her upper lip and then her lower. She let herself be drawn in as his lips covered hers and he took full, commanding possession of them, owning them for a time.

How could she be engaged to Douglass when she had just kissed another man? And not just any man. This man. A Spaniard. An enemy. This enemy she hoped would never stop kissing her. Was that what was making this kiss so thrilling? Because of who he was? Or was it just how he was kissing her? Nothing existed for her anymore except that place where his lips met hers. There seemed to be a direct connection from his mouth to her heart and he was instructing it to beat most erratically.

She'd always thought kisses were meant for the lips, but this kiss traveled downward, stirring up every internal organ she possessed, weakening legs and arms and hands.

There was a sudden clatter and jingling and Mariette realized that she had just dropped the coins he had given her. She wasn't sure when his arm had gone around her to pull her closer to him or how her arm had gotten around his neck, but the coins in her hand had been forgotten until the sound of their falling startled her.

What was she doing? Feeling like a plant being jerked roots and all from the soil, she wrenched away from him, away from the warmth and thrill, away from the surrender and possession.

Mariette looked up at him, trying to focus outward. He was grinning at her, his eyes alive and sparkling with one brow cocked high in question. She didn't have to ask him what he expected for the high wages he was giving her. She was giving it to him without a second thought. She pulled away to look down at where the coins had spilled across the flagstones.

One of them was still rolling. Just like her emotions. She had just kissed the man who was keeping her brother a prisoner. The man she would have to deceive and trick to free Matt. She didn't know how many coins Alejandro had given her, silver *reales*, quarter *reales*, but right now it looked like about thirty coins. Thirty pieces of silver.

She stepped back from Alejandro as tears began to fill her eyes. Ducking her head, she fell to her knees and hurriedly began to gather the coins. If she had not dropped them, where would that kiss have led? How far would her betrayal have gone?

"Leave them, Maria. They are not important." Alejandro tried to take her by the shoulders, to lift her up. Mariette jerked away from his touch. She was certain he wanted their kiss to continue, to deepen, though how it could get any deeper she couldn't fathom. She was just sure he wanted more from her. She was sure she wanted more from him, too. But it had to stop. Now.

"No, *señor*." The words were spoken in no more than a whisper, but Alejandro's hands dropped away. She heard him sigh. Then he began picking up coins and handing them to her, careful not to touch her.

When all the coins were again in her hand Alejandro stood. She didn't look up, but she could feel him looking down at her for the longest time before he said simply, "Good night, Maria."

Then he was gone.

Alejandro wanted to reach out and run his hands through Maria's hair as she knelt there on the flagstones clutching the coins he had given her. For just a moment, he stretched out his hand, but then pulled it back, difficult as it was.

She had said no. He had no doubt that he could persuade her to change her mind. It would not be difficult. The depth and passion in her kiss told him that. He wanted her. And over two months abstinence aboard ship had done nothing to make leaving her alone easier.

He could almost feel the passion emanating from her. He could certainly feel what kissing her had done to him. But she had said no, and he would honor that. For tonight at least.

He turned and went into the house intending to go right to bed. But he paused in the doorway to the bedroom, wondering where she would sleep. The linens on the bed had been turned down invitingly and they were fresh and clean. He could imagine her there awaiting him, her hair loosened, her lips soft and inviting. But it was not going to happen this night.

He turned to look back into the one other room. There was the sofa. She could sleep there. A gentleman would give the bed to a lady and sleep on the couch himself. But she was not a lady. She was a servant, hired to clean his house and cook his meals. He pulled a pillow and a light cover from the bed and placed them on the sofa for her. The master of the house did not give up his bed to the maid, no matter how comely she was. So why did he feel a nagging guilt about it?

Gritting his teeth he went into the bedroom, slammed the door shut in spite of the warmth of the night, and went to bed.

The next morning he found her asleep on the sofa. She wore only a chemise and her hair was loosened in a dark torrent of midnight about her. She had put the cover over her legs but one of them was uncovered to the knee, slim and shapely. One arm was flung up above her head. The other was hanging over the side of the sofa just touching Paddy who was curled up on a rag on the floor.

The dog looked up at him, briefly thumped his tail then settled back, reluctant to move from beneath the touch of Maria's hand.

Alejandro nodded. "I wouldn't get up either, Fella, if she were sleeping with me."

Grabbing one of the flat loaves of bread left over from the night before, Alejandro let himself out the door and headed to the fort.

The sun was not quite up as he made his way through the streets but already people were moving about, beginning their day's work. As he entered the plaza, he saw Francisco and Raúl. Francisco was yawning and rubbing his eyes, eating a loaf of round flat bread. Crumbs dotted his uniform and that center button had already popped out of its hole.

He gave Alejandro a limp salute and prodded his companion. When Raúl saw Alejandro, he looked him up and down disdainfully but gave a grudging salute.

Alejandro returned their salutes and the men fell in beside him. Ahead, Alejandro could see Paco already marching briskly across the drawbridge into the fort.

Mentally shaking his head, Alejandro continued on toward the fort. Two weeks. Even with men such as these he could hold out for two weeks. Then the prisoners would be on their way to Spain and Don Manuel would be back from Havana to take command back from Ignatio.

Once his uncle was gone, he should be safe enough under Don Manuel's protection until this war was over. Maybe even before the war was over Don Manuel could help him get to…

He shoved the hope away as he crossed into the fort. For the present, it would be best to concentrate on the job at hand…and surviving Ignatio's machinations.

Paco snapped to attention and executed an eager salute when Alejandro entered the fort. He was waiting beside the cart they had loaded the night before with water and bread for the prisoners, as well as the tools they would need for the day's work.

Francisco glanced toward the prisoners' cell, his brows knotted with concern. "They are not going to like having to work."

"Prisoners never like the idea of working," Raúl sneered, picking up one of the long leather whips Ignatio had insisted they take with them. He ran it through his fingers, almost as if caressing it. "But it will not be difficult to convince them."

"Put that down," snapped Alejandro.

Raúl continued caressing the whip. "You do not think we will need them, *Capitán*?" Raúl's voice was silky, verging on insolence, implying by his tone that Alejandro was being negligent in his duties if he did not order them all to use the whips.

Alejandro frowned. Raúl was pushing him, edging as close to impertinence and downright disobedience as he could without actually crossing the line. "I hope we will not have to use them."

"Ah! So you have some compassion for these English prisoners." Raúl straightened and took a swaggering step forward, softly slapping the whip against one palm.

Alejandro stepped close to Raúl, purposely crowding him, forcing him to press himself back against the cart. "Let us say that it is good that your *capitán* has some compassion or one of his men would be facing several hours of extra duty." He looked steadily into Raúl's eyes for a moment longer then stepped back. "Now put that down and go help Paco bring out the shackles."

One side of Raúl's mouth quirked up in an insolent grin as he slowly let the whip slither from his hand back into the cart. Then he went off with Paco to fetch the shackles that Alejandro fervently wished he could also avoid using.

Alejandro motioned to Francisco and they headed across the compound to the prisoners' cell. The cell door squealed loudly as Alejandro opened it, waking most of the prisoners. Mateo was sitting just inside, and as the door swung wide, he sprang up into a crouch, his eyes wary. When he saw Alejandro, he slowly straightened and gave him a brief nod as if they were equals, which, Alejandro thought, they just might be in other circumstances.

The prisoners came out of the cell eagerly until they saw the shackles Raúl and Paco had laid out. Sullen looks passed between them, and low mutters.

Alejandro noticed that they looked to Mateo for guidance, waiting for his lead. Whether he was an officer or not, he was obviously a leader and the men would follow his example. So far, he seemed to be reserving judgment, waiting to see what would be expected of them.

"I don't think they're going to like what we have in store for them." Raúl cracked his knuckles as if eager to crack some heads.

Raúl picked up a set of shackles and started toward one of the prisoners. The man backed away, looking toward Mateo who stepped in front of him. The rest of the prisoners grouped themselves behind Mateo, glaring at Alejandro and Raúl.

Mateo glanced upward where several militiamen stood guard from the high walls around the compound. He seemed to be assessing the situation, and realizing it was clear that he and the others had no chance of escape.

Glancing briefly over his shoulder as if to reassure the other prisoners, Mateo turned to Alejandro. "Why are you shackling us again? What are you going to do with us?"

Raúl drew back his arm and stepped forward to backhand Mateo, but Alejandro grabbed his arm and motioned for him to move aside.

"Why do you stop me, *Capitán*? These English dogs must be taught to obey without question."

Alejandro ignored Raúl and faced Mateo instead. "You are being taken outside the fort to work. When we return each evening, your shackles will be removed."

In English, Mateo repeated what Alejandro had said to the prisoners. There were a chorus of murmurs and some outright refusals to work for 'the dons'.

Before it could get out of hand Alejandro raised his voice above the complaints and again addressed Mateo. "I understand that there will be some resistance to working for the enemy. But I urge you, Mateo, to convince these men that they have no choice, and that resistance will only result in severe penalties."

Mateo turned back to talk to the men and Alejandro was relieved to hear him sensibly urging them to cooperate if for no other reason than because they had no choice.

"I don't trust them," Raúl snarled, gripping a set of shackles. "And I especially do not trust the big, blue-eyed one. He is probably telling them to attack us."

"I think not, Raúl. I think he is trying to convince them to cooperate." He knew exactly what Mateo was saying to the prisoners. But he did not tell Raúl that. Raúl did not need to know that Alejandro's English was as good as Mateo's.

Raúl spat. "Give me a free hand, *Capitán*. I will convince them to cooperate."

Mateo turned back to Alejandro and nodded. "We will work."

Raúl's lip curled disdainfully. "We will work," he mocked. He turned to Alejandro. "As if they have a choice."

"Oh, they had a choice, Raúl. They could have fought us. They would have lost, but they had a choice. They made the right one. Now start getting those shackles on them."

"Choices! If I were in charge they would do as they were told or else!"

"They are doing what they were told. I suggest you do the same. I gave you an order. See to it."

Glaring, Raúl began fastening the shackles on the prisoners. Some of the prisoners were still muttering and complaining, others giving Raúl sullen looks, but they would accept the shackles for now, and work. Perhaps not happily or whole-heartedly, but they would work. And for the next two weeks that's all Alejandro needed.

When Mariette woke up, the first thing she saw was Paddy squatting down to make a puddle in the middle of the floor. She jumped up and grabbed the surprised puppy, saying, "No, no!" and "Outside". She took him out near the back wall where he finished his job to her praises and pats.

It was only after he was done and started wagging his tail happily and frisking around her feet that she realized where she was and what language she had been speaking—English! In a near panic she ran back into the house, but Alejandro was gone. No one had heard, then. She leaned against the table and ran a shaky hand through her hair. She would have to be more careful. A little slip like that within the *capitán's* hearing could bring more questions than she could rightfully answer and ruin any chance she would have of rescuing Matt.

She frowned. It was still early, but the *capitán* was already gone. She began straightening, folding her cover and making the *capitán's* bed. Bringing order to her surroundings always helped her bring order to her thoughts.

One thing was certain, she wasn't going to rescue anyone by staying i this house cleaning and cooking. She had to see firsthand what she was up against, to start figuring out how she was going to get her brother out of the Castillo, out of St. Augustine, and home. If she was going to rescue Matt, she would have to convince Alejandro to take her with him to the fort.

But how was she going to accomplish that? Did she dare flirt with him? Be coquettish and sultry? She was afraid to try it. Look what had happened the night before when she wasn't even trying. She had been falling into his arms and almost ready to fall into his bed.

The *capitán* had one major fault as far as she could tell, right now. He was too handsome by far. Why couldn't he have been some cheerful, potbellied, grandfatherly type? She could have sat on his knee and batted her lashes and begged him to show her the fort. The thought of sitting on Alejandro's knee didn't make her feel granddaughterly at all. No, she didn't dare flirt with Alejandro. She would have to find another way.

A light tapping sounded at the door. Paddy started yipping and Mariette went to let Irish in. Irish immediately knelt to scoop up the happily squirming puppy who smothered her with quick swipes of his tongue while she smothered him with English endearments.

Paddy finally calmed down a bit and Irish smiled up at Mariette. She had a fresh bruise on one cheek she tried to hide by letting some of her fiery curls surge about her face. Mariette started to say something, but since Irish had tried to hide it, she assumed her friend wouldn't want to talk about it.

With a defiant toss of her head that caused her hair to lift momentarily off her face, Irish looked straight at Mariette, a proud tilt to her chin. Though she looked even more gaunt than before, the twinkle in her eyes was still there and, somehow, Mariette knew it would be until her dying breath. Irish would never surrender to adversity. And she would never accept pity. It would somehow diminish her.

"Are you ready?" Irish asked, putting Paddy back on the floor. Mariette patted the pocket that held her coins. "Yes, except I haven't eaten anything yet."

"Aye, well, I need to go. If I'm not back as shortly as they think I should be, it will be a matching bruise I'll be having on the other cheek. And I'm not such a good Christian that I would willingly turn my other cheek to the flinty-hearted bitch and bastard who lay claim to me." Half of Irish's speech was in English. "Aye, weel," she continued, "I don't suppose you understood the half of what I said, but I'm still having a bit of trouble with the language."

Mariette pulled out the last two loaves of flat bread and held one out to Irish. "I understood enough to know we have to hurry. We can eat these on the way to the market."

Irish hesitated, her pride warring with her hunger. Hunger won out and she took the loaf.

Mariette shooed Paddy out onto the patio and shut the door. Then they went out the front, locking the door behind them.

The market was smaller than the one on Sundays but several stalls seemed to be a permanent part of the square. Mariette recognized some of the merchants she had seen the day before.

Irish headed for the grain merchant and Mariette waited beside her until the woman could tend to them. Irish haggled briefly over the price of the rice she needed but the merchant gave in quickly and began weighing out the rice.

"You were here yesterday, weren't you?" The woman directed her question to Mariette.

Mariette nodded and the woman continued. "We were talking about the prisoners."

"Yes, we were wondering what they would do with them."

"They've put them to work. Just like I said they should." The woman nodded smugly. "About time, too."

"The prisoners are out of the fort?" Mariette tried not to get her hopes up too high, but if Matt was out of the fort on work detail, it might be a lot easier to rescue him.

The woman wrapped the rice in paper and handed it to Irish. "I saw them march out myself. A pathetic looking lot, but at least we'll get some use out of them."

Mariette's heart clutched at the word 'pathetic', but she tried to keep the tremor out of her voice when she spoke. "They have been ill used, do you think?"

The woman snorted. "Serves them right if they have. I hope

they work them until they drop, every last one of them."

Mariette recoiled from such vehemence, but she forced a smile to her face. "Where are they working?"

The woman shrugged, her attention turning to other customers.

Mariette and Irish headed for the meat market to finish their shopping.

"I was here when the English were taken prisoner," Irish said. "The Irish have never had a great love of the English, but the day they marched the prisoners naked through town, taunting and jeering at them, I said a prayer for them."

"Naked?"

Irish nodded and swiped surreptitiously at her eyes. "I wish them all soon safe at home again!"

Mariette touched her arm. "And you, too, Irish."

Irish shook her head and lifted her chin proudly. "I have nothing to go home to in Ireland. But I will admit I have had enough of Spanish hospitality. I would not be adverse to a fresh start on good English soil!"

They soon finished their shopping. Mariette bought some mutton to make a stew for supper, after Irish bargained the man down to half his original price.

"I stand in amazement at your abilities," Mariette told her as they walked back home. "I was beginning to think that meat merchant was going to pay me to take his mutton."

Irish grinned grimly. "I've had to learn to drive a hard bargain. *Señora* Martín counts every coin when I return and if she thinks I've cheated her…well, it's another bruise. Or worse."

"Worse?"

Irish grinned. "Every night I have to kneel and pray with them. If I've done ought that day that they disapprove of, it's extra prayers for me."

"It seems to me, they are the ones who need prayers. How can they claim to be Christian and then treat you so badly?"

Irish laughed good-naturedly. "Now that's the truth. They're always going to mass and confession. And sometimes it does help. Once *Señor* Martín hit me so hard I fell and cracked my head. Apparently he confessed it and the priest made him be kind to me for a fortnight."

She chuckled at the memory. "I could tell he hated it. He kept saying that a proper penance was prayers, not to let a slave get away with so much for so long."

When they reached Alejandro's home, Irish helped her get the stew started and patted Paddy once more before slipping through the alley gate to return home.

Mariette watched her go. "You'll soon be on good English soil, Irish! I'll see to it," she whispered.

She scooped up the puppy and snuggled him under her chin. "But how, Paddy? How can I rescue Matt and Irish?"

She sighed. At least Matt was out in the fresh air and not locked in a dark prison cell. Tonight, somehow, she would find out from Alejandro where the prisoners were working. Tomorrow she would go and see for herself what their conditions were and form some kind of plan for getting them away.

She set Paddy down. She would use everything Irish had taught her about cooking to make the best meal she could. Then, when Alejandro was pleasantly stuffed, she would get the answers she needed. Perhaps even get him to agree to take her along tomorrow.

In spite of Soledad's moaning, accepting the housekeeper's job had been a good idea. She would soon have a plan and Matt would soon be free.

Chapter Six

MARIETTE READJUSTED THE DAMP MATERIAL OF HER SKIRT over the bush. Her blouse was almost dry, but the heavier material of the skirt was still wet.

The stew Irish had told her how to make was simmering nicely on the stove, and since she did not expect Alejandro home until dusk, she had taken advantage of the hot afternoon to wash and dry her clothes. With nothing else to wear, she had appropriated one of his shirts to cover her while her clothes dried. Unfortunately, the garment barely came to her knees so she was especially glad for the Spanish style of high-walled private patios.

"I really need to get back to Soledad's village and bring back an extra outfit or two," she said to Paddy.

Paddy responded with a happy tail thumping.

"I can't stand around half-naked every time my clothes need washing." She smoothed her hand down the front of the fine cambric shirt she had borrowed. "And I doubt that the *capitán* would appreciate seeing me wear his clothes when mine are wet."

"On the contrary, the *capitán* appreciates it quite a lot."

Mariette whirled. Alejandro lounged in the doorway, one shoulder propped against the door frame, his arms crossed, and his dark eyes gleaming as he took in his fill of her. He had discarded his coat and hat and waistcoat in the heat, and his shirt, a twin of the one she wore, was damp with sweat. It clung to every ridge and crest of bone and muscle, outlining each and showing them all to her as clearly as if he were naked.

She had seen nearly naked men before. The Negroes on the plantations often shed their shirts when they worked in the fields in the hot summertime. And she did have three brothers, for goodness sake. But none of them had looked like this to her.

And none of them had seemed to make the day even hotter, the air more difficult to drag into her lungs, or cause her nipples to draw up into a pucker. She tried to move, to speak, but it was as if she were paralyzed in a dream. Paddy scampered over to Alejandro with a yip and jumped up, pawing at his legs, but he was ignored. Mariette could not look enough at Alejandro lounging there so negligently in the doorway. Yet, there was a tension in him, too, and she knew without doubt just what that tension was.

It was the same tension she was feeling as she looked at him, a tension caused by his gaze roving over her. She had been looked at before and by plenty of men. But none of them had ever made her feel this sizzling tension. She could feel his gaze touching her as surely as if it were his hands. And his gaze was touching her everywhere.

Her lips parted as her breathing quickened and she could not help but lean toward him as if drawn by some invisible force.

"As for standing around half-naked every time you wash your clothes, the *capitán* would not mind at all," Alejandro continued. His voice sounded strained, as if it were a task for him to speak at all and his words were spoken in barely a whisper. But she heard every one. The resonance of his voice seemed to work itself inside her, becoming part of her. "In fact," he continued in the same soft, siren tone, "you can stand around half-naked any time you wish whether your clothes are being washed or not."

She blinked and realized just how exposed she was, how vulnerable, half-naked in front of an enemy Spanish soldier who held her brother and her fiancé captive.

"I expected you to be gone until dusk." She snatched up her skirt and swirled it over her head and down to her waist. "I thought I would take advantage of your absence to wash my clothes." The damp material clung soddenly to her as she fastened the waist. The wet skirt was not very comfortable, but in this heat she doubted that she would take a chill. It could dry as she wore it.

She lifted her head, triumphant that she had covered herself from his tingling gaze, but he was looking at her breasts. She glanced down. Her nipples showed as clearly through the fine fabric as his muscles did through the shirt he wore.

With a yelp, she grabbed the rest of her clothes and fled through the door into the storage room. She leaned back against the door and crossed her arms over her breasts as if he could still see her. But she could not conceal herself from the tingling she felt. A tingling she thought she would feel for the rest of her life.

She heard him enter the bedroom next to the room she was in, the scrape of a drawer as he took out clean clothes, the clatter of a tin basin, the splash of water.

She glanced at the door between the storage room and bedroom then quickly finished dressing, folding his shirt and laying it on a storage chest.

She needed to check on the stew and finish their dinner but she hesitated. He would be coming out onto the patio soon. How would she face him? As if nothing at all had happened, that's how, she told herself sternly.

With head held high she went outside. The stew was bubbling in a heavy crockery pot set into the top of the stove directly over the flames. Mariette added some wood to the fire and stirred the pot, casting nervous glances toward the door, waiting for Alejandro to appear.

She did not have long to wait. Alejandro came outside, freshly washed and toweling his hair dry. The sun glistened on his damp hair, hanging in tangled waves to his shoulders. He draped the towel around his neck and ran his fingers through his hair, tipping his face up to the sun and shaking his head.

Holding the ends of the towel, he turned and it did not take long for him to find her. His eyes lit at the sight of her as if she still stood halfnaked before him and she froze, the long-handled wooden spoon dripping stew back into the pot.

She was too proud to turn away, but her breasts tingled from theremembered touch of his gaze. Mesmerized, it took her a long moment before she could tear her eyes away from him, tap the spoon against the pot, and replace the lid.

"I did not think you would be home until after dusk," she repeated, trying to sound casual, as any servant would.

"We took the prisoners out to work today. It was hard on them after being shut away for so long. I decided to cut the day short."

Hard on them? Had they been beaten? What arduous tasks had they been set to? Oh, Matt! She tried to keep her voice steady as she answered. "I heard in the market that the prisoners were being forced to work."

"Yes, it will be good for them."

"Good for them! To be beaten and starved and forced to heavy labor?"

"They have not been beaten. I have improved their rations. Their tasks are no more difficult than that of any laborer. It was hard on them today because they have been sitting in a prison cell for so long, but over the course of the next two weeks, it will help build their strength for their journey to Spain."

She bit her lip thinking of what misery that journey would

entail. Alejandro was right. The work would do the prisoners good as long as they were properly nourished.

Mariette turned away from him, lifted the lid to the stew pot again and began stirring fast and furiously. Anything to keep him from seeing her face. She was sure it would reflect the horror she felt. Spain! She had heard about the prisons there, dark and damp, hot in summer, freezing in winter. The Inquisition greedily awaiting its next victims. All of that awaited the prisoners if they even survived the trip there, locked away as they would be in the foetid hold of some ship of war.

Two weeks. She must contrive a way to see Matt, see how they were guarded, see for herself what condition he and Douglass were in, plan some kind of escape for them.

The stew was done. She would stir it into mush if she didn't leave it alone. She forced herself to put down her spoon and replace the lid. Reaching beneath the pot with a poker, she pulled the fire away so that it would just keep the pot warm until they were ready to eat.

"I would like to see these English monsters before they are shipped away, *capitán*."

"Maria, they are not monsters or devils. They are human, just as you and I are."

Mariette tried hard not to let her relief show. Alejandro may be an enemy soldier, but at least he seemed to be a little more compassionate than she had expected of a soldier of Spain.

"I would still like to see them for myself, *Capitán*."

"I cannot understand your fascination with these men, Maria. Likely you, and all the rest of St. Augustine, will see them when they are marched through the streets and onto the ship that will carry them to Spain. Until then, it is best that you forget about them and stay as far away from Ft. Mose as you can."

Mariette's eyes lit up with that piece of news. The prisoners must be working out at Ft. Mose! That was close to Soledad and Cato's village. She had planned to walk out there tomorrow to get some clothes anyway. She could see Matt!

Triumphant, she turned away to begin setting the table she had dragged out to the patio. Tomorrow! Tomorrow she would see Matt. And Douglass.

"We are eating out here?" Alejandro asked.

"I thought it would be cooler."

He nodded and went into the house. He came back carrying the two chairs which he placed at the table then sat on the one facing her. He leaned back, watching her every move, disconcerting her.

She tried to ignore him, tried to ignore the long length of him sprawled there, one arm hooked over the back of the chair, hand dangling. The other hand played absently with the napkin she had folded by his plate. But his eyes never wavered from watching her.

She placed rude cutlery beside each plate—knives and spoons. She poured red wine into each of their rough pottery cups and set the bottle on the table. The sun was beginning to set so she lit a thick candle and set it in the middle of the table. It cast a golden glow on his face, lighting the table in its little bower as if in invitation to intimacy.

She had not realized how romantic, how appealing, the setting would be. She had only thought of the coolness on the patio rather than the stuffiness of the house. But his eyes glowed as if a flame burned within him as well as on the table.

She straightened and glared at him, lifting her chin. Let him think what he would. She could afford to let him flirt with her a bit now. Now that she knew she would see Matt tomorrow and would soon form a plan to free him. And Douglass. Now that she knew she would soon be gone from this place forever, he could look at her all he wanted, as if he were going to devour her rather than the mutton stew she had made. He would find his prey gone, his bed empty. She would not be here.

She set the heavy pot of stew on the table, the rice, and a basket of flat bread. Mariette ladled rice and stew onto Alejandro's plate, filled her own, then passed him the bread.

He took a flat loaf and tore it in two, smelling it appreciatively before biting into it. "Did you make this?"

She had bought it at a stall in the marketplace, but he didn't have to know that. She shrugged noncommittally.

"When will you make some more of those sweet potato muffins?"

She looked up, startled, with a spoonful of stew halfway to her mouth. "Muffins?"

"Those muffins are the reason I hired you. I thought I would have had some more of them by now."

Mariette swallowed hard and set down her spoon. "Muffins?"

He leaned forward, taking up her hand and rubbing the back of it with his thumb. "Muffins. The sweet potato muffins you were selling when I met you." He sat back and began spooning up stew. "Maybe you could make some tomorrow."

No one could make those muffins like Soledad. Mariette gripped her spoon, forcing herself to take a bite of stew. Tomorrow? He wanted some of those muffins tomorrow? She would be at Soledad's village. She would see Soledad. Maybe she could convince her to make some for her to bring back.

"Yes, I'll make some tomorrow."

For a few minutes they ate in silence, the only sound the scrape of wooden spoons against rough pottery plates.

Paddy was eating, too, and it was easier to gaze at him than Alejandro. Paddy's tail wagged happily as he chased the last bit of his lamb around in his bowl, licked it clean, then sat looking up at the two of them. His round little belly bulged so much he could barely sit up.

Mariette's attention was drawn back to Alejandro when she heard him push his chair back from the table. He slapped his belly which, unlike Paddy's, was flat and firm. "You have stuffed us both, Maria. The meal was delicious. Paddy and I agree."

On hearing his name, Paddy stood up on wobbly legs and wagged his tail.

"Thank you, *señor*." She began clearing the table and Alejandro disappeared into the house, returning moments later carrying a lute.

He sat on one of the chairs, propped one ankle on the opposite knee and began to tune the lute. It took him a long time, working with each string, plucking it over and over before going on to the next, returning to the first ones to readjust them. After a few minutes, he began to play.

The soft sounds of the lute seemed to float in the warm night air and Mariette hummed as she finished washing the dishes and putting everything away.

The song he played was an old English ballad and she almost started to sing before she remembered that she only knew the words to the song in English.

She finished the dishes and pulled the other chair around to sit and listen. He was perhaps not the most gifted player she had heard, but he was good, and it was pleasant to listen to the sounds of a lute. Not many people played them anymore.

She closed her eyes as he began to sing softly. It was a song of love. She knew this one and in Spanish, but she was content to merely listen, letting the soft sounds of the lute and his rich baritone mingle on the warm summer air, wafting around her.

Abruptly he stopped, not singing the last verse. She opened her eyes and looked at him in surprise. "Why did you stop?" she asked.

He set the lute aside and reached across the table to take her hand. "The last verse is a sad one. The lovers part. I never sing that last verse."

Mariette looked down at his hand touching hers. She pulled her hand away and stood up. "Sometimes, that is the only choice lovers have. Sometimes, there are too many obstacles in the way for them."

He, too, stood and stepped close to her, lightly touching her cheek, drawing a finger along the line of her jaw. "Then they are not very determined lovers. True love will overcome any obstacle. True love would find a way."

He bent to kiss her and she forgot to breathe, letting her eyes drift closed as his lips found hers, lightly, lightly touching.

It was only the second kiss Alejandro had given her, but it was the same as the first one, touching her everywhere. It wasn't just lips touching lips, it was soul touching soul. She felt profoundly stirred, deeply within, as if he were touching places no one else could even find. He seemed to pour into her like rich wine, filling all the empty spaces that had gone wanting within her for so long. It was more than just a kiss. It was a melding, a union, a joining, a blending of their essential essences. There would always be part of him left behind in her, just as she knew that there would always be something of herself left behind with this enemy Spaniard when she returned to Charles Town. She would never be as complete again as she was right now, standing here in an enemy stronghold with the arms of her foe embracing her.

He lifted his head for a moment and she felt bereft. She opened her eyes and looked up into his, shining black. Black Spanish eyes full of fire. A fire that could easily consume her if she weren't careful. A fire she could not let herself fall into, no matter how much she wanted to. And she did want to. She knew in that moment that she had never wanted anyone as much as she wanted Alejandro.

She may never want anyone this much again the rest of her life. Suddenly the rest of her life seemed to stretch ahead of her—empty, bereft of love. For no matter how much she wanted Alejandro, he was the one man she could never have.

Alejandro merely looked at her and she knew her life was forever changed. He was the one she wanted, the one she could never have, and he had ruined her for anyone else. Douglass would be her husband. It was he who would father her children and sleep beside her each night. And all she could think of was the insipid, tepid relationship they would have. There would never be any fire with Douglass. He would be good to her, but there would never be any fire. But neither would she be consumed.

With a sob she pushed Alejandro away and fled, out the patio gate and down the alley. She ran until the heat of the night forced her to stop and she leaned against a wall, sobbing. Douglass had never kissed her like that. Neither of the Rolfes twins had ever moved her when they took turns kissing her the night of their sister's engagement ball. She had thought that there was something wrong with her that she could not respond to any of their kisses. She had thought that there was nothing more to kisses than a physical touching of lips. Now she knew better. Now she knew what a kiss should be. And it was from someone she was going to have to deceive and lie to and leave forever. A foe she would never see again once she had rescued her brother and returned to Charles Town. A foe who had forever spoiled her for anyone else. A foe she would never forget.

Chapter Seven

It was late when Maria returned to the house, slipping inside, shushing Paddy. The door to the patio and Alejandro's bedroom door were ajar to allow the cool evening breeze in and she heard him stir. Perhaps he was awake. Perhaps he heard her talking quietly to Paddy. But he didn't say anything and she was glad.

She undressed down to her chemise and lay on the couch, letting her arm hang over the side to pat Paddy as he curled up on his pile of rags. She listened to the sounds of the night and thought she could hear Alejandro breathing softly. She thought of the song he had sung but left unfinished. He thought there were no obstacles true love could not overcome. How wrong he was. But perhaps theirs was not true love. Not at this point, anyway. For now, it was simply lust. And it would never have a chance to grow into anything else.

So their obstacles would have to remain unconquered, their lust let die, their love stillborn. There was no future for them. They would each have to find their own path, and those paths would not cross again. Mariette lay there a long time, playing with Paddy's ears and thinking of the song of unrequited love.

After a nearly sleepless night waking each time Alejandro

stirred, each time he turned, listening with a smile the one time he snored softly for a few moments, finally, Mariette heard him get up. She could picture him stretching, long sinewy arms lifted, fingers brushing the beamed ceiling, one hand lowered to scrub across a stubbled jaw, a muscled chest, lean belly. She opened her eyes. Wide. She had no business letting her imagination run in that direction.

She heard the scrape of shoes being pulled from beneath his bed and jumped up, jerking on her blouse and skirt. After the kiss that had sent her fleeing into the streets last night, she did not need to have Alejandro find her sprawled half awake and nearly nude across a plush sofa as if in invitation.

She rousted Paddy and scooted him outside then made a fire in the stove and set a pot of water heating for Alejandro's shave. With Paddy chasing her skirts she went to the well and pulled up the pitcher of milk she had stored in its cool depths. She poured a little into Paddy's dish then set the rest on the stove to warm for Alejandro's morning chocolate.

She was just breaking bits of chocolate into the milk to melt when his arms came around her and his lips brushed against her ear. She stopped, outwardly frozen, his touch setting a spark to the barely banked fire within her.

"There will never be a reason for you to run from me, Maria. I would never hurt you or force you." He lightly kissed her ear, ran his hands up her arms to her shoulders and squeezed them reassuringly. Then, before the fire he had set to blazing with that simple, chaste kiss could thaw her limbs, before she could turn and throw herself into his arms, he stepped away from her and poured some of the hot water she had heated into a basin to wash and shave.

Alejandro had tacked a mirror onto one of the posts that supported the roof over the kitchen. He set the basin on a small stand there and washed his face and hands then soaped his face.

What was there about watching a man shave that spoke of domesticity, home, and comfort? Mariette had had those same feelings when she had seen her brothers shave. Well, perhaps not exactly the same feelings. She had never wanted to run her hands over her brothers' backs or feel the muscles in their arms or cup the round firmness of their buttocks.

She looked at the mirror. Alejandro was looking back at her. Their gazes held for long moments, his hand paused with the razor held in shaking fingers by his left jaw.

She turned away and began stirring the chocolate, taking deep breaths to calm her racing pulse while he bent his head to savagely rinse the razor in the basin.

Alejandro quickly finished shaving, nicking himself a few times in the process. When he turned she was waiting with a cup of chocolate for him. With gazes locked he took the cup and drank the steaming chocolate while something of a different kind simmered between them. Handing her the empty cup, he went back inside and she could hear him gathering his things to leave. She stood by the door with the cup in her hand as he came out of his bedroom buckling on his sword. He gave her a swift kiss which could easily have turned into a much longer one had she leaned toward him instead of away.

"I'll see you tonight, Maria," he said. Then he was gone, clapping his tricorn on his head as he strode down the street.

With one brow arched, she watched him go, thinking how very domestic their little scene had been, how wifely of her. But she was not his wife, nor would she ever be. He was the enemy and he would see her much sooner than tonight. She was going to Ft. Mose today to see her brother for herself.

Mariette hurriedly tidied up and got ready to go. She put out a loaf of the flat bread from the previous night's supper and poured the rest of the chocolate into a cup. She couldn't stand the bitter drink herself, but she saved what was left for Irish who was soon there to check on Paddy before heading to the market.

Mariette walked as far as the market with Irish, then, with a wave, headed out past *El Castillo* toward Ft. Mose and Soledad's village. It was a long walk and the day was already getting hot. Mariette stopped to remove a stone from her shoe and wipe sweat from her face and arms. On the way home she would not only have a bundle of her clothes to carry, but hopefully, some of Soledad's muffins. And the day would be hotter then. She groaned. Maybe Nate would bring her back in Cato's skiff.

She sighed. Matt wouldn't be able to take the skiff back to town. He would have to walk and after working all day in this heat. She felt a surge of gratitude that Alejandro had shortened the work day for the prisoners yesterday. Maybe he would let them off early again today.

Soledad was right about Matt, though. He was tough. He could work all day in this heat and still walk back. He was used to long treks in the woods with his Indian friends. It was the imprisonment itself that would be hard on him, being locked away in a cell.

Mariette wondered about Douglass as she put her shoe back on. How was he doing? The work was probably harder on him. As a rich planter's son turned lawyer, he was not used to hard physical labor and he already had just a bit of a paunch. And with his coloring, pale red-gold hair and fair skin, the sun would not be very kind to him. He was probably more in need of a rescue than Matt.

They're probably already out there working, she thought. Alejandro had told her to stay away but she wasn't going to. Not when she had this chance to see Matt and plan some kind of escape. But she would need some excuse for showing up at Ft. Mose.

She started walking again and began to feel a bit hungry. She had been too nervous to eat even a piece of bread this morning. She hoped Soledad had some of those muffins already made. She could use one right now.

"Lunch!" Mariette chuckled out loud. She would take Alejandro some lunch, along with some of Soledad's muffins. He certainly wouldn't refuse to let her come near if she had some luscious lunch packed for him.

She quickened her pace and soon came in sight of Soledad's village. Except for Soledad and Cato, the village was deserted, most of the huts damaged or destroyed from the English invasion a month ago. The inhabitants had fled to St. Augustine and were now afraid to return home.

Soledad was bent over an open fire in front of her wattle-and-daub hut stirring a pot hung over the flames. Mariette could see Cato and Nate working in the vegetable garden and she smiled. Like Matt, Nate liked to be busy doing something.

A couple of dogs spotted Mariette and began to bark. Soledad looked up, straightened, and propped one hand on a bony hip. "So you's still in one piece." A smile played momentarily about her mouth, but she wiped it away with the back of her hand. "You 'bout ready to get in dat boat you come here on and go back where you belong?"

Mariette let the dogs sniff her hands and, satisfied, they trotted away. "One way or another you'll be rid of me soon enough, Soledad."

"Rid of you! Humph! Just worried somethin'll happen to you and if'n it does your daddy gonna come down here and strip this black hide off'n these bones. And since him and this young'un here are the ones who brung me down here to my Cato, he'll know 'xactly where to find me."

Mariette hugged the older woman. "I love you, too, Soledad."

"Humph!" Soledad turned back to her pot, wiping her eyes

with the back of her hand. She replaced the lid and straightened. "So what you need, chile? You 'bout to give up on dis notion to rescue that no 'count brother of yours?"

Mariette shook her head. "We have to get them out sooner than we thought. The prisoners are being shipped to Spain in less than two weeks."

Soledad sat down on a low stool. "Don't leave much time for makin' a plan and getting dem two out of here."

Mariette sat on the ground next to Soledad. "No, but there's a good chance we can do it. The prisoners are working at Ft. Mose."

Soledad nodded. "I seen 'em yesterday."

Mariette grabbed Soledad's hand. "You saw them? You saw Matt? How does he look? Is he all right?"

"Couldn't get close enough to tell nothin' much 'bout him. Dem guards won't let nobody get close." She turned to Mariette, taking her by the shoulders. "They's three guards with pistols and muskets plus that captain of yours. They's spread out and watching all the time. Dem prisoners is shackled and got manacles on. No way one little girl's gonna get two of dem away from there."

The image of Matt, manacled and shackled, rose in Mariette's mind. How could he, who was used to roaming free in the forests, tolerate being chained and held captive?

"But it won't be just me, Soledad. I have Nate to help," she said smiling as her younger brother came trotting up.

"Help with what?" Grinning, Nate sat down on the other side of Soledad and leaned eagerly toward Mariette. "Do we have a plan to free Matt, yet?"

Soledad smacked him on the back of the head. "No, nobody's got no plan 'ceptin' to take this sister of yours straight back home to Charles Town."

Nate's shoulders slumped, his grin wiped away by disappointment. "Is that true, Mariette? Are we giving up?"

"No," Mariette said, giving Soledad a determined glare, "we are not giving up. I just need to see Matt and the other prisoners and come up with a plan. Once I've talked to Matt–"

"Didn't you hear me, girl?" Soledad rolled her eyes. "How you think you's gonna get close enough to Matt to talk to him?"

Mariette's eyes glinted and a grin played around her mouth.

"Oh no! I know dat look." Soledad folded her arms across her sagging breasts. "I knowed you since you's a little girl and dat look always means trouble."

"Now, Soledad," Mariette said batting her lashes prettily, "all I need from you is–"

"No, no, no!" Soledad jumped up, arms flapping, head shaking so hard Mariette thought her bright red scarf might fly off. "I ain't gonna do nothin'. It's enough that I let dis rapscallion brother of yours stay here while you go puttin' yourself in danger cozying up to dat Spanish captain of yours. But I ain't doing nothin' else. Nothin'!" For emphasis the black woman stood ramrod straight, crossed her arms, and nodded her head one firm time.

Mariette stood up next to Soledad and ran her fingers back and forth across her crossed arms. "But Soledad, all I need are some of your muffins."

"My muffins?" Soledad propped her fists on her hips and glared at Mariette. "What you gonna do with my muffins? Throw 'em at dem guards?"

"I just want to take a little lunch to Captain Alejandro. Once he has some of your muffins, and maybe a bit of that stew you're cooking, surely he'll let me get close enough to the prisoners that I'll be able to talk to Matt."

"No. I ain't gonna do it. It's just too dangerous."

Mariette looked pleadingly at Soledad, her mouth in a pout. "But Alejandro is expecting me to make him some muffins today. If I don't, he'll be even more suspicious."

Soledad looked through narrowed eyes at Mariette. "Even if you get close to Matt, he's gonna be suprised to see you. How are you gonna keep him from giving you away?"

"Matt won't give me away. He's too smart, and he's been in enough situations with his Indian friends to know how to maintain control."

Soledad tilted her head, still disbelieving. "And what about dat fiancé, of yours? Is he smart, too?"

Mariette shrugged. "Matt will take care of Douglass."

Soledad sighed heavily, her shoulders slumping in defeat. "All right. I'll make you some muffins. Maybe once you see the situation for yourself you might get smart enough to give up and go home."

Mariette threw her arms around Soledad. "Thank you!"

"Humph! Cain't see no good come from dis at all. No good at all!

Cato!" Soledad turned to call to her husband. "I need me some sweet potatoes!" But Cato was already there, sweet potatoes in hand, grinning from ear to ear and giving Mariette a wink.

Soledad harumphed again. "Best thing can happen is for you two to get yoreselves back to Charles Town 'fore yore daddy come down here and strip the hide off'n me for not sendin' you back soon as you showed up."

Mariette grinned at Soledad's grumbling. "He won't. He and mother don't know where we are."

"He knows where to find us, Mariette." Nate's chin jutted up at a defiant angle and he looked steadily into her eyes. "I left a letter."

Mariette's mouth dropped open and her fists went to her hips. She turned to Soledad. "Lucky for this traitor that Mom and Dad took our big brother to Boston for a visit before he leaves for England. They won't see that letter for two weeks."

Soledad chuckled. "I wondered how y'all got loose. Dat big brother of yours, Tyrus, always kept a tighter rein on you than your daddy."

Mariette's brows lifted mischievously. "Well, he's out of our hair for the next two years. He'll be studying in England."

"So you right away set off to bring these Spanish dons down and end dis war all by your own self."

Mariette glared at her brother. "Well, maybe not the whole war. Just a little piece of it."

Mariette heard the sound of men working even before she reached the edge of the ruined village surrounding Fort Mose. She paused to move the strap of the canvas bag she carried from one shoulder to another. It was heavy with a clay pot of Soledad's stew, several thick slices of bread, a jug of wine, and, of course, those muffins.

The huts of the village surrounding the fort were in ruins, thatched roofs burned, walls missing or leaning crazily, shattered pottery littering the ground, a doll with its head missing crushed into the dirt. Mariette shuddered, imagining the violence that had occurred here less than a month before.

"Move along, now! Put your backs into it!"

She cringed at the shouted order and jumped when she heard it punctuated by the crack of a whip. Shaking, she walked along the deserted street until she could see the walls of the fort—and the prisoners. Anxiously she searched for Matt. He was a lieutenant, but after their siege of St. Augustine and the fighting and nearly a month in prison, it was hard to tell one prisoner from another by the rags they wore.

But Matt was tall. He should stand out in any group of men. As she got closer, she could tell he was not with the group clearing rubble from the gaping hole at the entrance to the fort. There was no sign of the gates at all.

Another group of prisoners were atop the fort's earthen embankment struggling to remove broken stakes from one of the two gaping breaches in the walls. They were bent to their task with a guard standing over them, whip in hand. One of the prisoners straightened, a length of broken stake on his shoulders. Matt!

He was alive. Tears sprang to her eyes. Soledad had told her she had seen Matt, that he seemed well. But it was not the same as seeing him herself, knowing without a doubt that her twin was alive and well.

Another prisoner held the other end of the thick stake on his shoulder. Douglass. It was hard to tell at this distance, but he seemed more stooped than before, as if beaten down. As Mariette walked closer, she could see that his clothes hung loosely on him and his fair skin was burnt.

Her throat felt tight with tears she did not dare let fall now, not now that she was within sight of the guards. It was just as Soledad had said. The prisoners toiled at the fort, a fort surrounded by a dry moat planted with prickly palmetto royal and cactus. There was a large cleared area surrounding the fort and the three guards kept close vigilance.

She heard the crack of the whip once again and jumped. But no one cried out. The lash had not landed on anyone's back. The soldier guarding Matt had snapped the whip seemingly for the mere pleasure of seeing the effect it would have on the prisoners in his power. He began coiling it once more, running it through his hands with a smirk on his face.

Mariette's gaze sought Alejandro. He was not in the second breach in the walls where another group of prisoners worked. Then she caught sight of him, striding purposefully out the front gate of the fort, uniform coat removed, shirt sleeves rolled to the elbow, two pistols tucked into his belt, and a sword swinging at his hip.

He stopped dead when he saw her, chin going up in surprise, then lowering again as his eyes narrowed and he came toward her, fists clenched.

Heart pounding, Mariette stood her ground in the face of his angry charge, smiling as prettily as she knew how, hands gripping the canvas bag tightly.

He halted mere inches from her, jaw clenched, harsh winter in his eyes—every inch the arrogant, Spanish aristocrat. Mariette swallowed hard then straightened. Alejandro's expression was no worse than her brother Ty's, but she still had to take a deep calming breath before she could speak. "I brought you some lunch."

The anger on his face seemed to melt away. His gaze swept her and his lips twitched as if suppressing merriment. He leaned into her, lifting a hand to caress her jaw with one finger. "And to see whether the English prisoners have horns and tails?"

His touch sent shivers through her in spite of the heat of the day. He was too close. There seemed to be no air left to breathe, but she could not move away. Did not want to move away. His body touched hers at toes and thighs and chest. Her breasts tingled with that contact, but still she did not move away. "That might be part of the reason I came," she admitted, coyly lowering her lashes before looking up at him again.

His fingers moved to caress her along the curve of her neck. His voice was low when he spoke. "And the rest of the reason?"

Mariette found it difficult to find enough breath to respond, "I have brought you a lunch."

Alejandro laughed and stepped away, taking the heavy bag from her. She felt bereft. "So you have delivered the lunch and seen the prisoners. Now you must go."

Mariette thought quickly. She couldn't let him send her away already. She had to get closer to the prisoners, to Matt. "But you have not eaten it yet and…and I thought we could share it."

His arm came around her pulling her up against him again. She gasped and her lips parted. His lips hovered only a breath away. "And what else will we share, Maria?"

Would he kiss her here? And now? She was sure some of the prisoners were watching, maybe even Matt. If Matt recognized her, what would he do if he saw a Spanish *capitán*, the very Spanish *capitán* who kept him prisoner, kissing his sister? Matt had never been as strict a guardian as her older brother Ty, but then, Matt had never seen her kiss his enemy, either.

She put her hand on Alejandro's chest, trying not to notice how hard and firm it was, how the heat of her palm blended with his heat and sweat. She pushed away. "Why, I also have a jug of wine." She batted her lashes as she smiled. "And some of those muffins you are so fond of."

"Then how can I resist?" Alejandro's hand slid further down her back to quickly caress her buttocks before he let her go. "Over there," he said, jerking his chin toward the closest ruined hut, "in the shade of that house. Set out the lunch and I will join you shortly." He handed the canvas bag back to her and headed toward the fort. "Paco, Francisco! Bring the prisoners down to the wagons and get lunch for them."

The prisoners didn't wait to be told to drop their tools and head for the wagons. Their guards walked behind, herding them along.

Mariette kept her back to the men as she set out the lunch she had brought. Now that the time was actually here, she was suddenly fearful of just how Matt would react if he recognized her. She looked over her shoulder at the prisoners as they shuffled past the food wagon and slumped against the side of the ruined building. Most of them were giving her curious looks, some grinning lasciviously at her backside, but they were all staring. Uncomfortable with all the attention, Mariette knelt down on the edge of the cloth she had spread but she continued to watch for Matt.

Like the other prisoners Matt stared at her, too, as he went by, but he suddenly stopped, his eyes narrowing as he looked at her. He shook his head just as a guard prodded him to move along.

Douglass was right behind Matt but he gave her only a cursory glance before jerking his eyes downward and moving on to join the other men in the shade. Dear, straightlaced Douglass. It was just like him to refuse to even look at another woman because he was an engaged man. Guilt stabbed Mariette. What would Douglass think of her to know that she had done a lot more than just look at another man? That she was finding it very difficult not to give herself completely to Alejandro de Silva because she knew she would find something in his arms that she was never going to find with Douglass?

She set out the basket with the sweet potato muffins and opened the cloth that covered them. Still warm from Soledad's dutch oven, their aroma was enticing, but she resisted, waiting for Alejandro to join her.

Mariette watched Alejandro position the guards, setting them in such a way that even if one of the prisoners decided to break and run, one of the guards would have a clear shot at him. Her hopes sank at his efficiency. She could not see a way to rescue Matt while he was working inside the fort, but she had hoped that there would be a chance when the prisoners took their lunch break, or perhaps on their way back to the Castillo. Now that she had seen the situation for herself, she knew that the chance for rescue was slim, indeed, but she was not ready to admit that Soledad was right and that there was no chance at all. Surely, she would figure something out. She had to.

When all the prisoners had been given their noon rations, Alejandro dropped down beside Mariette and leaned against the wall of the hut facing the men, his musket within handy reach.

Mariette glanced over her shoulder at the prisoners as she spooned some of Soledad's rabbit stew into a bowl for Alejandro. Douglass kept his eyes stoically on his food while Matt seemed to be studying her through narrowed eyes. The rest of the men watched her hungrily, biting into their bread and cheese as if it were her they were devouring. She shuddered uncomfortably.

When she held out the stew to Alejandro, he gave her a reassuring touch on her hand before he took the bowl. "It has been a long time since they have seen a woman."

She lowered her eyes and busied herself with filling her own bowl and placing round flat loaves of bread within reach.

"Did you carry this all the way from town?" Alejandro asked.

She shook her head. "My village is nearby. I…" she started to say she had made the food there but couldn't quite bring herself to add further lies to her deceptions. "My friend and I made it there."

"And what of your family? Do they live there?"

Mariette could not help glancing at Matt. "Some of my family is close by," she said.

Alejandro ate quietly for a few minutes, cleaning out the last of the stew with a piece of bread and relaxing back against the wall with a satisfied sigh.

"More?" she asked.

He shook his head. "It's hard to eat a lot in this heat. But I do think I could manage one of those muffins."

She handed him a muffin and he bit into it with a moan of pleasure and a nod of approval to her.

"So, have you seen enough of the English prisoners? Can you tell that they do not have horns and tails?"

"From the looks they are giving me, I would assume that they are much like other men."

Alejandro laughed. "As I said, it has been a long time since they have seen a woman. And an even longer time since they have seen one as lovely as you, Maria."

The heat of the day was as nothing compared to the look he was giving her now. The stares of the prisoners seemed crude and lascivious. They made her want to cover herself and turn away. Alejandro's look made her want to throw off every stitch of clothing she had on and fling herself into his arms.

Yet, Alejandro was the one person in all St. Augustine she had to keep her distance from. It was the prisoners she had to find a way to get closer to. Somehow, she had to find a chance to talk to Matt, to let him know an attempt to rescue him was being made, to tell him to be alert.

"I would like to see the prisoners closer, Alejandro. Perhaps talk to them." She tried to appear like a child in awesome wonder, wide-eyed and curious.

Alejandro caressed her along her jaw with the knuckles of one hand. "They do not speak Spanish, Maria."

"Oh." She lowered her eyes. "Of course not." She looked back up at him. "You said there was one who did. One of the prisoners who knew a little Spanish…" She broke off trying to sound hopeful. In reality, her heart was pounding, her palms sweating.

Alejandro nodded. "Yes. Mateo. You may have noticed him. He's the tall one with black hair sitting there on the end." He pointed, but there was no need. She knew which one was Matt. Mateo. Hair black as sin and the devil in the twinkle in his eyes. That was how their mother always described him.

Mariette pretended to scan the row of men. The prisoners had finished their meal and, since looking at her could gain them nothing, most of them had taken advantage of their time and dropped off to sleep. Only Matt was still looking at her, eyes narrowed. She could tell he suspected she was his sister, but at this distance he couldn't be sure. Hopefully he knew her well enough to know she would try to rescue him and wouldn't be totally surprised when he saw her up close. She had told Soledad that Matt was smart enough not to give her away. Right now, she was going to stake both their lives on it.

"Ah, yes. I see the one you mean. Can I talk to him?" She tried to sound curious and anxious, but not as anxious as she felt. It seemed an age before Alejandro shrugged and gave her an indulgent grin.

"Raúl! Bring Mateo over here."

Chapter Eight

MATT GLARED AT HIS SISTER WHILE HE GNAWED AT THE hard bread and cheese each of the prisoners had been given. Every one of them was ogling her and making comments to each other that, in other circumstances, he would not have countenanced from the patrons of a brothel. Even the guards were snickering about *Capitán* de Silva's woman. And there wasn't a damn thing he could do about what they were saying. Whatever she was up to, he didn't dare give her away.

Even if he was her twin brother, he had to admit his sister was shapely enough to deserve the attention she was getting. But he wondered how she was using those assets of hers with de Silva. He just hoped de Silva wasn't giving her more attention than she could handle.

How the hell had she managed to get herself to St. Augustine? Matt washed down a particularly hard piece of bread with some water. Probably talked that half-wit brother of theirs into bringing her. When he got home again, he'd give them both the hiding of their lives. Did they really think they could rescue him? There wasn't any other reason he could think of for her being here.

She always thought she had to mother him. Yes, it was hard being a prisoner, but God—how did she think he would feel if she got herself or Nate into trouble trying to help him? Big brother Ty must be losing his touch to have let these two idiots get loose like this. Or… Good lord! What terrible evil had they perpetrated on Ty to keep him occupied long enough to slip the leash? Had they hogtied him in one of the upriver storage sheds like the time they'd slipped away to Williamsburg for a few days? God, he hoped not. This time of year there were no furs due and no crops to store. It might be days before anyone found him. And what about Mother and Father? He shuddered to think.

And just how had Mariette managed to get acquainted with de Silva? Matt bit down hard on his bread, glaring in their direction. More than just acquainted from the looks of things. The *capitán* was looking at her a bit too lustfully to suit Matt. He really would hate to have to murder the man. He was quite decent for a Spaniard.

His fist clenched around his hard chunk of bread. He had to think of a way to speak to her, to tell her to go home. He glanced at Douglass sitting beside him placidly gnawing at his bread and devoutly keeping his eyes downcast. Good old staid and proper Douglass, never deigning to look at another woman since he'd become engaged to Mariette. He probably didn't understand half of what the men were saying—if he were even listening. Matt doubted that Douglass had ever seen the inside of a brothel. The man was too good for his own good. He was probably still a virgin. He would make a good, if not exactly exciting, husband for Mariette… if he didn't call it off once he realized that his fiancée was cozying up to their captor in an ill-intentioned attempt at rescue.

Matt sighed. No, Douglass would still marry her. He might be wounded to the core of his being once he realized what Mariette was doing, but he would honor his commitment. Especially when he realized what a social outcast Mariette might be if her escapades became generally known. Douglass would marry her and give her the protection and honor of his name, and defend her to the death. The only problem with Douglass was that he might bore Mariette to death.

The problem right now was not only to speak to Mariette, but to keep Douglass from realizing she was here. Good-hearted as he was, there was no telling what his reaction might be. He could deliver her into the hands of the Spanish as a spy without meaning to. Matt gritted his teeth. If he could just think of some pretext to speak to de Silva, he might find a way to let his sister know he didn't want her here.

Raúl was watching the prisoners while the other two guards ate. That mean little toad would never let an English prisoner talk to the *capitán*. Matt glanced at Mariette. She was practically hand feeding de Silva. At this distance it was hard to tell, but he would bet she was even batting her lashes at him and giving him that simpering smile that made her seem like a total idiot, the smile she usually reserved for her most detested suitors. Suddenly he leaned back and chuckled. Mariette would want to talk to him just as much as he wanted to talk to her. He knew his sister. He was sure that somehow she would weasel an interview with the English prisoner out of de Silva.

Matt relaxed and finished his lunch. Mariette wanted to be the heroine here. Let her figure out how to talk to him. She'd do it, too. Most men didn't stand a chance against her. Chuckling to himself, he leaned his head back against the wall and closed his eyes. He almost felt sorry for Captain de Silva.

It was only a short time later that Raúl nudged him with his toe and gestured for him to walk over to where Alejandro and Mariette sat. Matt wasn't the least bit surprised. With a hard grin on his face he stalked across the compound just ahead of the pompous little guard.

Raúl may have thought he was herding Matt over to the hut

where Mariette and the captain sat, but even encumbered with leg shackles and wrist manacles, Raúl and seventeen wild horses could not have stopped Matt from crossing that compound to confront his twin.

When Matt saw Mariette cringe, he knew she could see the danger in his eyes. He grinned, but it was not a grin designed to reassure his sibling. He could tell it was all she could do not to bolt and run.

Matt knew who she was. Watching the way he glared at her as he crossed the compound, Mariette could tell. And he was angry. She took a shuddering breath. Matt was usually mild and easy going, slow to anger, but once he was mad, his retribution usually consisted of some rather nasty tricks his Indian friends had taught him. Not that he would ever actually hurt her. Matt would die himself first. But she had known some decidedly uncomfortable and rather embarrassing moments when they were children.

Well, he was angry now. But even in his anger Matt had always had good sense, had always waited until the right moment to exact his revenge. She would take whatever he cared to dish out to her once they were safely home. She just hoped he wasn't so angry that he wasn't willing to wait. When he finally stood before her, she gave him a tentative grin and a look of wide-eyed, innocent curiosity. Matt answered with a narrow-eyed look that told her she would be sorry later.

If he could have spoken freely she knew exactly what he would be saying to her. "Are you unhinged? How the blazes did you get yourself down here? Did you talk that lunatic brother of ours into bringing you? How did you get loose from Ty and our parents? You get back to Charles Town right now! Isn't it bad enough that one of us is in this mess?"

She blinked back tears thinking of the familiar things he would say to her if he could speak freely, if there weren't shackles and chains and a Spanish *capitán* keeping him silent. She wanted to throw her arms around him, and she bit her lip to keep from wavering. For just a moment she saw his eyes soften as he looked at her, but the glare snapped back and she knew that this time her twin was really angry.

She gulped and cringed against Alejandro, finding herself in the strange position of seeking protection from the very enemy who was the whole problem in the first place. Matt looked from her to Alejandro and back to her, and his eyes narrowed even more in suspicion.

Alejandro slid a protective arm around her, patting her comfortingly. Matt's eyes narrowed still more. Mariette wondered how he could even see, but she knew he was angry for sure. And now, Alejandro was included in that anger. Even though Matt was a chained prisoner, he would find a way to avenge each liberty Alejandro took with her. Poor Alejandro had no idea what he was up against. For his sake, Mariette tried to move out of the protective circle of his arm, but he only tightened his grip.

"You are frightening Maria with your scowl, Mateo," Alejandro said.

Matt cocked one brow, shifted his weight to one leg and, with a rattle of the chain that bound him, folded his arms across his chest, looking as stern and domineering as their older brother, Ty.

"Maria?" Matt tried out the Spanish version of her name she had given Alejandro.

Alejandro smiled fondly at Mariette. "My housekeeper. She wanted to see the English prisoners."

"And now that she has seen us, she can go home." Matt glared hard at Mariette, emphasizing his point. Then he looked at Alejandro, communing man-to-man that this was no place for a woman.

She looked from one to the other and felt like kicking both of them. Even as enemies—even as prisoner and guard—men could form a bond that locked women out. If it was Ty and their father who were here in disguise to rescue him, Matt would have been anxious to help form a plan to escape. He didn't have to glare at her like that. She knew he did not want her here, in danger. But she was not some fragile flower to be protected. She was here to rescue him and she was going to do it whether he liked it or not. Just how many times did she have to prove to her brothers that she was just as clever and strong as they were? Men only had to pass that test once. Women had to face it in every new situation that came along.

Mariette's chin jutted out and she gave Matt a glare that she had given him enough times in the past. A glare that he would have no doubt meant she intended to stay. She could see Matt's jaw clench in response and she allowed one side of her mouth to twitch in a quick grin of triumph.

"Have you seen enough of the English 'devils', Maria?" Alejandro asked, giving her a teasing squeeze.

"Enough to know that men the world over are much alike," she said, again glancing from man to man.

Alejandro laughed, gave her one last squeeze then stood and stretched. "Then it is time to take the Englishman's advice and go home, Maria." This time it was the corner of Matt's mouth that twitched into a brief grin of triumph.

Mariette lifted her brows and smiled sweetly. "Not yet, *Capitán*. I have some things to do with my friend Soledad in her village. My brother will take me back to town in his skiff later this afternoon." There! She had managed to let Matt know that Nate was here with her and staying with Soledad. Surely he would be on the alert for whatever plan she came up with.

"Very well, Maria. I will see you this evening." He started to turn away then looked back at the basket of muffins. "How many of those do you have left?"

Mariette counted quickly. "Eleven."

He handed the basket to Matt. "Divide them with the other prisoners." Then Alejandro turned to Raúl with instructions to get the men back to work.

Matt gave each of the twenty men half a muffin, with extra going to a couple of prisoners who looked thin and sick. The prisoners glanced her way, nodding their appreciation as they ate and shuffled back to the fort. This time there was nothing lewd in the way they looked at her. Just simple appreciation.

Mariette took her time putting the lunch away and packing it back into the bag. She watched everything the guards and prisoners did. Raúl seemed to take delight in tormenting the prisoners in little ways, but he was vigilant. One of the guards was fat and slow and seemed more interested in his own comfort than guarding the prisoners. He was the same soldier she had met in the marketplace when she was there with Soledad. The third guard, like Raúl, was vigilant, but seemed inept. Perhaps there was a chance that she could rescue her brother after all. But somehow, in spite of the unspoken pact between Matt and Alejandro, she would have to find an excuse to come back here—and on a regular basis.

"He's fine, Nate," Mariette assured her brother when she got back to Soledad's village. "I saw him myself. I even talked to him."

"You were able to talk to him?" Nate's eyes were round with admiration.

"I didn't get to say much since Captain Alejandro was there, but I did manage to let him know you were here with Soledad."

Nate beamed.

Mariette turned to Soledad with pleading eyes. "I'll need another batchof muffins. Captain Alejandro gave the extra ones to the prisoners."

Soledad harumphed. "Don't know what you need more muffins for. You seen dat twin of yours. You know he's fine. You and dis here scamp can get on home now."

Mariette put her hand on Soledad's arm. "I didn't come all the way down here just to see Matt. I came to rescue him."

"Matt knows dat ain't possible even if you don't," Soledad retorted. "Best for you two to just get on home. You don't seem to know what danger you is in. You ain't just some English girl here to rescue her brother, not with dat daddy of yours raiding the Spanish like he is. Dem dons find out who you is, who Matthew is…"

Mariette managed to squeeze out a tear. It wasn't too hard to do. "Matt is wearing chains, Soledad. Chains. On Matt. On his wrists and ankles. He's not even used to staying under a roof all that much. How much longer do you think he can stand that?"

Soledad jabbed a bony finger at Mariette. "I'm thinkin' dat twin of yours is a lot tougher than you give him credit for."

"We need your help, Soledad. I'll give you whatever you want, but I need your help." Tears were coursing freely down Mariette's cheeks now.

Soledad swallowed hard, put her fists on her hips and looked upward as if seeking help from a higher source. "Chile, I ain't lookin' for payment. Your daddy already helped me enough when he brought me down here to join my Cato. And dat money you brought to me gonna take care of us for a long time. I just want you safe at home."

"So do I, Soledad. But with Matt there, too." Mariette looked from Nate to Soledad to Cato who, as usual, sat on a stool whittling and saying very little. "I can't go home now. Matt's seen me. He'll be expecting a rescue. If he doesn't see me again, he might think I've been caught. Now that he knows we're here we have to do something."

Soledad sighed and threw up her hands. "All right, Chile. I'll do whatever I can. Just you promise me dat you'll be careful."

Mariette nodded vigorously.

"And if you don't get to rescue Matt, you'll leave as soon as dem prisoners is on their way to Spain."

It took her a moment, but Mariette nodded in agreement.

Soledad turned to find Cato, but he was already heading for the garden. "I know," he said. "You need some sweet potatoes."

Late that afternoon, Soledad and Cato helped Mariette into the skiff for the trip back to town. Nate was already onboard, checking the sail, straightening the ropes and oars, a gleam in his eyes, anxious to set sail.

Cato handed Mariette a pot of rabbit stew Soledad had helped her make for Alejandro's supper that evening and she stowed it carefully under a seat. Soledad handed her the batch of muffins, wrapped in cloth and still warm from the Dutch oven, but when Mariette started to take them Soledad held on, causing Mariette to look up at her questioningly.

"You take care now," Soledad said gravely.

"I will, Soledad."

Soledad nodded toward Nate who was coiling the last line into place ready to go. "You take care of dat boy, too. Don't you even think of letting him run loose in St. Augustine."

"I won't, Soledad."

"Not even for a minute. Don't even let him set his foot on dem docks. Don't want to have two Fortune brothers to rescue." She let go of the muffins and Mariette sat down, cradling them on her lap.

Nate shoved off with an oar and began setting the sail.

"And you, Boy," Soledad called after them, "get that gleam outten your eyes. You ain't doin' nothin' but droppin' your sister off and headin' straight back here. Don't go gettin' any ideas in dat scatterbrain of yours."

Nate gave her a lopsided grin and a jaunty salute. "Don't worry, Soledad. I promise not to stay in St. Augustine more than a day or two!"

Soledad's mouth dropped open, her fists came up to sit atop her bony hips and she actually started forward as if she might try to catch the skiff and bodily haul Nate back to shore.

But the skiff was well out into the river and the sails had caught the breeze. Nate let out a chuckle.

Mariette found it hard to stifle a chuckle herself. "You really shouldn't tease Soledad like that, Nate. Not after all she's doing to help us."

Nate sat down at the tiller. "Who said I was teasing?"

Mariette whipped around to look at her little brother. The gleam was still in his eyes and he was grinning, but she wasn't sure if it was because he really was teasing or if he actually planned to go into town.

"Don't even think about it, Nathanial Winthrop Fortune," she said as sternly as she could.

His chin came up. "Why not? You've been in and out of St. Augustine for days and nothing's happened to you."

She glared at him. "I don't have fair skin, blue eyes, and a strong English accent, either."

"I could keep my head down, not speak to anyone." Nate's shoulders had slumped and his argument was half-hearted at best. Mariette knew her brother had seen reason, but she didn't want him to feel so glum.

"Nate, you know we have to keep you safe. We're counting on

you to get us home. No one else can sail the *Fortune* like you can. If we have any chance at all of rescuing Matt, we'll be depending on you."

He nodded gravely, seemingly mollified. What she said was true and he knew it. He busied himself with turning the skiff out of the river and into the broad estuary that would take them past the fort, *El Castillo*, and to the docks.

Nate looked up at the fortress looming ahead. "So how are we going to rescue Matt? Did you see enough today to come up with a plan?"

Mariette shook her head. "I think there's a chance we can do it, but I'm going to have to be out there. Every day. The guards and the prisoners are going to have to be used to seeing me around, begin to take my presence for granted. Then I'll have a better chance to talk to Matt. When the time comes for the rescue, I'll have to be able to let him know what to do."

Nate trimmed the sail, turning them more to head for the docks. "Then take your captain lunch again."

"That worked once. It might work twice, but then I'm sure Alejandro would tell me not to come again. Besides, I need a reason to be there several hours every day, not just an hour at lunch time."

"You need to be there for a reason," Nate said. "You need to be part of what is going on, serving in some capacity."

Mariette moved the muffins off her lap. Their warmth was too much combined with the heat of the day. "Hmm," she mused. "Serving.

Alejandro gave the muffins I brought today to the prisoners. Maybe I could bring something to the prisoners every day, something he would let me serve them myself."

Nate looked up, grinning. "Water."

Mariette's eyes started to spark. "Water! Yes!" She began plotting out loud, "But how would I convince Alejandro to let me serve the prisoners water? He doesn't want me close to them."

"It would save time. The prisoners wouldn't have to take as many breaks," Nate said.

Mariette shook her head. The Spanish were just using the prisoners to work. They didn't seem to be in any particular hurry to get anything done.

"The guards wouldn't have to do it. They could remain on guard?" Nate suggested.

Mariette thought a moment then discarded that argument too. They remained silent, thinking, as the walls of *El Castillo* slid ominously by.

"I would have to have a reason for being there. Something Alejandro could not argue with. Something beyond even him."

"God?" Nate said with a laugh.

Mariette looked up wide-eyed. "That's it!"

"You're going to tell him God sent you?"

Mariette chuckled. "Exactly!"

"Are you sure the sun hasn't gotten to you, Sis?"

"I'm going to confession!"

"What?" Nate was truly incredulous now. "We're not even Catholic."

Mariette gave him a sly grin. "No, but Alejandro doesn't know that. What if I went to confession—or rather told him I did—and confessed how I thought the English were devils and the priest gave me a penance to do."

She quickly told him about Irish and how her master had to treat her better after going to confession. "I must serve those I had maligned! I must take water to those imprisoned!"

As Nate shook his head doubtfully, Mariette continued. "It has to work! The Church is the one authority no Spaniard dares question. They don't want to get into trouble with the Inquisition.

Captain Alejandro may not like it, but what choice would he have?"

"You can make it work, Mariette," Nate said.

"Yes, I'll make it work," Mariette said with determination. "I won't be able to come out there too early tomorrow. I'm still supposed to be a housekeeper, after all. So I'll have to do some cleaning and laundry in the morning. And go to confession." She grinned at Nate. "But if you could meet me at the docks just before noon, I'll be ready. By the time I get there, the prisoners will be ready for their lunch. Then afterward, the day will be at its hottest, and they'll be needing water."

Shortly, Nate had guided the little boat to the docks and Mariette scrambled out after lifting the pot of stew onto the dock.

"Are you sure you don't need me to help carry that pot?" Nate asked, a hopeful look on his face.

"No, I don't." Mariette gave Nate a stern look and the skiff a shove.

Resigned, Nate sighed and set the tiller and sail to carry him back to the village.

It was Paddy who alerted Mariette to Alejandro's presence. She had the rabbit stew Soledad had made simmering on the stove and the muffins were being kept warm in the oven. She was just giving the stew a stir when Paddy yipped.

She looked up to see Alejandro leaning in the doorway, arms crossed over his chest, watching her with an amused grin on his face.

Mariette breathed a sigh of relief as she replaced the lid on the pot. She had been worried that Alejandro would be angry, that he might even dismiss her for going to Ft. Mose today.

"Your supper is almost ready, *señor*."

He pushed himself away from the door and sauntered over to her. "Will it be as entertaining as my lunch was?"

"Entertaining?" She looked up at him, widening her eyes and blinking innocently.

"Yes. It was very entertaining to see you looking for horns and tails on the English prisoners." He reached out to fondle an errant curl beside her cheek.

Mariette lowered her head as if embarrassed to have been so naive.

"Are you convinced that I told you the truth, that they are merely men?"

"*Sí, señor*. It was stupid to think otherwise. I will go to confession in the morning."

"Confession? I hardly think it was a sin for you to be curious."

"Oh, it is not for curiosity that I must go to confess. It is for thinking ill of others. For thinking they were devils." She decided to lay it on as thick as possible. "And for feeling hatred toward them. I even felt resentful that you gave the muffins to them. Does the Holy Book not tell us to love our enemies?"

"Hatred? You? When we first met were you not concerned about the treatment of the English prisoners?"

Mariette swallowed hard at being caught in an inconsistency. She wasn't used to being so deceptive. She would have to be more careful. "Yes, I suppose I was concerned about them. I do not want them mistreated," she said, trying to explain her way out of the mess she had created. "But it is not easy to love an enemy that has invaded your home."

He chuckled. "No, it isn't. But they were merely soldiers, doing their duty for their country. We should feel a little more compassion for them. I'm sure there are Spaniards who have also been taken prisoner in this war. These men have so little and I have not been very successful at getting them better provisions."

"That is true, *señor*. I will talk to the priest about it. I'm sure he will give me the proper penance to do."

Alejandro laughed outright. "Do you still think you need to go to confession?"

"Oh yes, *señor*." Oh yes, she thought, I still need to go to confession, or at least make you think I went. I still need that reason to be around the prisoners.

Chapter Nine

ARIETTE COULD TELL THAT ALEJANDRO WAS STILL chuckling over Maria's need to go to confession when they sat down to dinner. He didn't seem to think less of her. He just seemed to be amused at her seeming naiveté. But Mariette began to worry that perhaps this was one Spaniard who would not be afraid to go against the injunctions of his church. What if he refused to let her bring water to the prisoners tomorrow?

It was dark by the time they began to eat and she placed a candle in the center of the table. Its glow reflected in Alejandro's eyes, giving them a warmth and luster that began to spark an answering glow within her. She knew what was on his mind because the same thing was on hers. It was true that the Bible said to love your enemy, but she was pretty sure that this was not what Jesus meant.

Alejandro never put pressure on her to share his bed. He had never threatened or cajoled. But she felt that pressure all the same. And the worst part was that most of that pressure was coming from within her own self. She wanted him. She wanted to be with him. She wanted him to touch her. All over. She wanted him to kiss her again. And it did no good at all to remind herself that she was engaged to Douglass. Douglass had never made her feel this way. She knew she had agreed to marry Douglass because it seemed the logical thing to do. But when she was with Alejandro, none of those logical reasons seemed to matter.

Mariette quickly finished eating and hastily began clearing the table. She set the muffins in front of Alejandro and began washing the dishes and giving Paddy his share of the rabbit stew.

Paddy's tail wagged so furiously as he ate that his wobbly puppy legs could barely keep him in place. She gave him a pat on the head and he stopped eating long enough to quickly lick her hand.

Alejandro brought out his lute and sat tuning it while Mariette finished cleaning up. Paddy, the traitor, curled up at Alejandro's feet and between tuning strings the *capitán* would reach down to pet him.

Mariette sat down with some mending to listen to Alejandro play. It was Alejandro's shirt she held in her hands. She had noticed the ripped seam while getting the laundry ready to do the next morning. The music stopped and she looked up.

Alejandro was tickling Paddy's stomach, the puppy's hind leg scratching at air. The scene was so wrenchingly domestic her fingers shook as she placed the next stitch. This was the way her life would be when she returned to Charles Town. But it would be Douglass, not Alejandro, who would be sitting with her in the evenings. She had a wild thought. What if she didn't go home? What if she just stayed here? She made a knot at the end of the seam and bit off the thread. As what? Alejandro's housekeeper? His mistress? What would she do when he tired of her? A noble like Alejandro would never marry a lowly Mestiza housekeeper. And she certainly could never tell him who she really was. What kind of life would that be? And what about Matt? Could she leave him to languish in some Spanish prison so she could be the mistress of their mutual foe? No, she needed to keep her mind on her purpose for being here and squash any foolish dreams of domestic bliss with *Capitán* Alejandro de Silva.

She stuffed the shirt back into the laundry basket and put her needle away. They stood up at the same time, she with the basket under her arm and he with his lute. They stood looking at each other for a long moment. Then Alejandro stepped toward her, one hand outstretched. Quickly she turned away but he stopped her with a hand on her shoulder.

"Maria."

It was only her name. And not really her name at all. But the sound of his voice seemed to penetrate like a spear into her heart. How she wanted to turn into his embrace, lean her head on his shoulder, feel his arms about her. But it would not end there and she knew it.

She shrugged off his hand. "I must be abed now, *señor*. And since I am going to confession in the morning, I need to pray."

Mariette set the basket inside the door and knelt by the sofa where she slept. She kept her head bent but watched as Alejandro closed the doors and went into his room. She didn't know whether to sigh with relief or cry with disappointment, but she figured that since she was on her knees, it might be a good idea to pray after all. She was going to need every ounce of strength she could find to avoid a very strong and virile temptation.

Matt leaned his head against the wall, closed his eyes, and tried to imagine that he was in a Hitachi sweat lodge. He wiped sweat off his face with a shirttail. But even a sweat lodge was not this hot. Nor this foul smelling.

With twenty men crowded into one tiny, airless cell, with scarcely room for them all to lie down at once, the heat was nearly unbearable. Some of the men grumbled about having to work for the Spaniards. But even wearing shackles and manacles, Matt thought that being out in the open air every day was preferable to being confined in this stink-hole. The work itself did not bother him. Unlike Douglass who lay snoring beside him, he was used to physical labor. Matt looked down at Mariette's fiancé. The work had not been easy on him. He was a scholar, not a laborer. His law office in Charles Town did a good business and Douglass was well-respected. Being a prisoner was not easy on him. His soft hands were blistered and his fair skin burned.

Matt hated to wake the man, but he had to talk to him. And he didn't want to be overheard by the other prisoners. He had waited until most of them were sleeping. There was still some shuffling, coughing, and not a few groans, but that went on all night. There wouldn't be any better time than now.

Gently Matt shook Douglass's shoulder. The man moaned and burrowed deeper into the shirt he had wadded beneath his head as a pillow.

"Douglass, wake up."

Matt shook him again. This time Douglass's head came up and he looked around in confusion. There was not much light coming in through the small barred window in the door and precious little air. Matt couldn't see the expression on Douglass's face but he was sure he wasn't smiling at being awakened in the middle of the night. But Douglass was too good-natured to complain. He just rubbed his face and sat up, leaning against the wall next to Matt.

"I need to talk to you about Mariette," Matt said.

Matt could see Douglass scrub his hand back and forth across the top of his head as he was wont to do when he was puzzled. He shook his head and took a deep breath and Matt knew he was fully awake now.

"As much as I love and care about your sister, Matthew, as much as I enjoy talking to her or about her, right now I think I'd rather be sleeping. Can't we talk tomorrow?"

"She's here, Douglass."

"She's…"

Matt was prepared for an outburst and clapped a hand over Douglass's mouth before he could wake anyone. He leaned close to Douglass's ear. "She's here. In St. Augustine." He could feel Douglass struggling to speak but Matt kept his hand firmly in place. "You have to be quiet. We can't endanger her by letting anyone else know."

Matt waited until Douglass nodded his head in agreement then slowly took his hand away, ready to clap it back in place if he had to. But Douglass was no idiot. Boring, maybe, but no idiot.

"Mariette's here? How…? Why…? How do you know?"

"I saw her."

"Dear Lord," Douglass said, and in his case it was a prayer. He would never take God's name in vain.

"My thought exactly," Matt said.

"My poor Mariette. Captured by these filthy idolaters." Douglass's head fell into his hands.

Matt rolled his eyes. His poor Mariette, indeed! Only Douglass would jump to the conclusion that Mariette had been captured. He had a lot to learn about his future wife. Matt almost felt sorry for the man. Mariette would lead him a merry chase.

"She hasn't been captured, Douglass. She's here to rescue us."

Douglass scratched the top of his head again. "But how did she get here?"

"That pea-brained brother of ours brought her."

"Tyrus?" Douglass shook his head. "He's much too levelheaded to do something like that. Surely he would not so endanger a fragile woman."

Fragile? Mariette? Matt wondered for a moment if they were talking about the same woman.

"Not Ty. Nate. Nate brought her down here."

Douglass shook his head again and turned to face Matt more

squarely. "How do you know all this?"

"I talked to her."

Douglass started sliding down the wall, his head aimed for his shirtpillow, his back already turning toward Matt. "You're dreaming, Matthew. Go back to sleep."

Matt gripped his shoulder. "The woman with Captain de Silva at the fort today. It was Mariette."

Douglass stopped his slide into slumber. He turned to look at Matt, then sat up again, leaning close to speak to him. "That was my Mariette?" he asked as if there might be another one Matt had been talking about.

Matt nodded.

"She's in danger! We have to—"

Matt clapped his hand over Douglass's mouth again. "She'll be in danger for sure if you don't keep quiet."

Even in the near darkness Matt thought he could see Douglass's fair skin turn a shade whiter.

Douglass nodded and pulled Matt's hand away. "What are we going to do?"

Matt shrugged. "Do? We're not going to do anything. There's nothing we can do."

"But we just can't…" Douglass's thought trailed off.

"Exactly. She's out there and we're in here. I told her to go home, but she won't. So there isn't anything we can do. But you needed to know so you won't give her away if she comes around to the fort again."

"Do you think she'll come to the fort again?"

Matt's mouth twisted although Douglass could not see it in the darkness. "I can almost guarantee it."

"But how can she do that? How can she just walk in there like she did today?"

"De Silva says she's his housekeeper. Somehow, Mariette managed to get that job and is using it to try to rescue us."

"His housekeeper? He wasn't treating her like a housekeeper. His hands were all over her. I'll–"

Matt's hand found Douglass's mouth once again. "She's playing a role, Douglass. It doesn't mean anything."

Douglass nodded. "My poor, sweet Mariette! To put herself in such danger! To hire herself out as a lowly housekeeper! To put up with the likes of de Silva all for our sakes!"

Matt had been thinking about the same thing. Just how much was his twin putting up with from de Silva? Thinking about it almost made him laugh out loud. Knowing Mariette, she was "putting up with" only as much as she wanted to. He never knew a woman better able to put any man in his place and still keep him smiling. "Just remember, Douglass, when you see her, she isn't Mariette. She's de Silva's housekeeper and that's all she is to you. If anyone sees you speaking to her, or if you give her away, then she will be a captive of the Spanish and we'll be left here to rot along with her."

"I'll be careful, Matthew. I'll be careful for her."

If there was anything that could keep Douglass in line, it would be his fear for Mariette. He had never known a man so besotted. "I know you will, Douglass. We just have to be alert for whatever she does. I don't know what her plan is or even if she has a plan yet, but when she makes her move, we have to be ready." Matt patted the man's shoulder. "Now we'd both better get some sleep."

They lay down and Matt was just about to go to sleep when he thought of something else. "Douglass?"

"Hmmm?"

"She's calling herself Maria."

Douglass's head came up. "Maria? But that's not–"

Matt shoved Douglass's head back down and turned over.

Alejandro mopped sweat from his brow as he peered up at the positionof the sun. It was close enough to noon to call a halt in the work. The prisoners were exhausted already from working in this heat and he could see no reason to keep them at it through the midday hours.

He had tried to keep them in the shade as much as possible, but the really fair-skinned ones were already badly burned. He had insisted that his Uncle Ignatio allow for the purchase of hats for them and he had stood his ground even when his uncle had claimed he was coddling them because they were English. He had won the hats for the prisoners, even though he knew he was giving his uncle a bit more ammunition to use against him.

He watched them now, clustered around the well as Francisco gave them water. In this heat they needed to be watered more often, but his uncle was pressing him to finish the repairs on Ft. Mose. As their northernmost fort and first line of defense against the English, Ft. Mose had taken the brunt of Oglethorpe's assault. The black runaways from the English colonies to the north who'd manned the fort had acquitted themselves well in the battle. It was they who had taken the English prisoners, the twenty men he was in charge of, during the siege of St. Augustine.

Alejandro leaned against the side of a ruined hut in the shade, where Maria had served him lunch the day before. Today, as usual, he would share the rations of the guards, which were not much different from the prisoners'. He glanced down at the ground where he had sat with Maria and smiled. She had seen the prisoners and satisfied her curiosity. She would not be returning today. But he almost wished she would. Being with her had been a pleasant interlude in the day.

Their thirst satisfied at last, the prisoners lined up for their portions of cheese and bread and then sat in their customary spot along the shady side of a wall. Many of them dropped off to sleep with their food still in their hands.

Alejandro nodded in satisfaction at the performance of the three guards. They had taken the precautions he had taught them and kept a vigilant eye while giving water and food to the prisoners. Perhaps he could get through these next few days without incident after all.

A movement at the corner of the ruined hut caught his eye and he turned. "Maria."

She smiled hesitantly and came forward to set down her load. He could smell freshly baked bread and, in spite of the heat and general lack of appetite because of it, his mouth watered.

She shouldn't have come. This was no place for her. Not here with enemy prisoners. He would have to tell her not to come again. He should send her on her way now. But she was so beautiful. A shining gem in a day of ceaseless drudgery—forcing men to work on a defensive fort for their enemies. What could it hurt to enjoy another lunch with her before he sent her on her way?

He started to smile, but decided that he should be stern, let her know that she should not come here again even though he wished she could come every day. But when he started toward her and her smile broadened, sparking an unexpected joy in him, he found it impossible not to return the gesture.

"You should not have come again." His words did not carry the stiff, forbidding tone he had intended. She leaned slightly toward him and he caught her scent, a subtle mix of soap and woman and he wanted to take her by the shoulders and pull her up against him and kiss her. He craved the taste of her mouth far more than the bread he could smell.

She did not move or turn away but stood transfixed as if expecting, hoping for that kiss. Then her eyes sliced to where the guards stood watch over the prisoners and her tongue tip moistened lips he knew he could not touch with his own in this too public place.

"I thought you enjoyed the lunch I brought yesterday," she said.

Oh, I did, I did, he thought. But he didn't want to say it to her here. She must not make a habit of this no matter how much he enjoyed it. "This is no proper place for you. Haven't you seen enough of the English prisoners?"

She didn't answer. She pulled out a cloth and spread it on the ground and began pulling items from her basket. "I brought new baked bread. It is still warm from the oven. And here are beans and rice and a honey cake for each of us." She stopped her chatter and her busy preparations and looked up at him. Her eyes seemed ready to brim over with tears.

Relenting, he knelt down and took her face in his hands, using his thumbs to swipe at the tears that had started to overflow. "I enjoyed the food very much, Maria. Even more than the food, I enjoyed having you with me, but…" He sighed. He would eat the food she had brought, then he would send her on her way. He would tell her tonight not to come again and if she looked at him like that tonight, he would pull her into his arms and… He shook his head. It was best not to think of things like that. Not when he had the responsibility of twenty prisoners hanging over him.

Alejandro looked at the guards. They were properly stationed and watchful. The prisoners were either sleeping or eating. Some of them were eyeing Maria, but that was to be expected of men who had been without women for over a month. One prisoner seemed to be taking an especially acute notice of her, though. The fair-haired one that seemed to be Mateo's friend. But Mateo pulled him down and the man looked away, settling down to his food again.

Alejandro sat down and took the plate of food Maria handed him. The beans were savory and the bread crusty on the outside but soft and white inside. Luck had indeed been with him the day he had hired her to be his housekeeper. She would make some man a wonderful wife someday. At that thought he moved closer to her, wanting to touch her even in the heat. *It is just the way the prisoners are looking at her,* he told himself. *They need to know that she is not for the likes of them.*

He looked at the woman beside him. She was modestly dressed, but it seemed that every lovely curve of her was outlined in soft material, doing more to inspire the imagination than if she had been sitting there stark naked.

"Will the prisoners continue working on repairs here until they are sent to Spain, *capitán*?"

With his mouth full of beans and rice, and his thoughts full of what she might look like with fewer clothes on, Alejandro could only nod.

"It looks like there isn't much more to do. The breaches in the walls have been repaired."

Alejandro took a drink. "The breaches, yes. But we must still replace the gates and finish clearing out the rubble inside."

"So the prisoners will work every day inside the walls of the fort?"

He waved a hand toward the overgrown field surrounding the fort. "In a few days they will be set to clearing around the fort. A lot of ground cover has taken root in the last month. Ft. Mose should have as much cleared ground around it as *El Castillo* so an approaching enemy will have no place to hide."

Maria looked around. "Will they clear everything all the way to those woods over there?"

Alejandro nodded.

She studied the scene for a few moments. "There is much to do. Will you get all this cleared before they are shipped to Spain next week?"

"I don't know. I just know that I have been instructed to get as much of it done as I can."

"It will be hot work out there in the sun. It cannot be easy for them."

Alejandro scooped up the last of his meal and took a drink. He sat with his arms resting on his upright knees, hands dangling. His mouth tightened into a grim line as he looked out at the weed and brush choked field burning in the hot August sun. "True, but it matters not to my uncle. He would just as soon all the English died from the work."

"Your uncle?"

"My uncle, Ignatio de Silva. He is in command of the fort."

A look of puzzlement crossed her face. "I thought Montiano was in charge."

"He is. My uncle is simply a temporary replacement while Montiano confers with others in Cuba."

The puzzled look deepened on Maria's face. "Guard duty seems a rather low assignment to give to the nephew of even a temporary commandant. Especially when that nephew is a *capitán*."

"I was never his favorite nephew, Maria," Alejandro said wryly.

"Still…"

"There has never been any love between my uncle and me. To be honest, I think he is actually hoping some of the prisoners escape so he can use the excuse to dishonor me." Or stand me up in front of a firing squad, he thought, but he didn't want to say as much as that to her.

"I see," she said, and he noticed that her hands clenched tightly in her lap. She was obviously worried about him, but he doubted that she understood completely. How could she? How could she understand the hatred that Ignatio felt for him simply because his birth had disinherited Ignatio's own children from the title and lands? It was hard enough for Alejandro to understand it himself even though he had been the brunt of it since his birth. And now his father hated him, too. Well, not his father. The man he had thought all his life was his father. That was also fuel for Ignatio's hatred. At least when he was small, his uncle had managed to be kind to him at times. But as he grew and looked less and less like his father... He sighed and stood up. "I will see you tonight, Maria. I am going to give the prisoners an hour or so for a siesta while the sun is so hot, and I think I will relieve the guards one at a time so they can get a little rest, as well."

Alejandro walked to where Francisco sat with his musket across his knees. The heavy man lumbered to his feet and gave his *capitán* a rather sluggish salute.

"I will take over for a while, Francisco. You go get some rest."

A huge grin plumped Francisco's cheeks so much it almost made his eyes disappear. "*Si, mi capitán! Gracias!*"

Alejandro watched the guard settle his huge bulk under a tree. It took only seconds before snores grand enough to match his body reverberated across the small plaza.

Most of the prisoners were taking advantage of their time to sleep. Mateo and his fair-skinned friend were talking intently, with the friend glancing over at Maria from time to time. But at last they, too, subsided and slept.

Maria seemed to be in no hurry to pack up the lunch and leave. Watching her graceful, unhurried movements, he could easily imagine her on a dance floor. All eyes would be on her. How could they not? Properly dressed, she would enhance even the most elegant court ball with her beauty and grace. He wished he could take her to such a ball. He would love to see her reaction to the silk and brocade gowns, and the glittering jewels, and the rich food. He would love to see the reaction of the grand nobles who would see her. The young bloods would all rush to dance with her.

But he doubted that he would ever have a chance to show her off at a ball. Maria would live her life here in this colony. Live and die here. What chance would she ever have of seeing Spain? For that matter, what chance would he ever have of seeing Spain again? He had fled and he could not go back.

Alejandro was surprised to glance over and see Maria lying down. Why wasn't she leaving? He shifted, moving the musket into a more comfortable position across his lap. The heat was making everyone sleepy. Perhaps she had decided to take a siesta now and wait until the worst of the heat had passed before returning to town.

He must tell her tonight not to come back again. It was too hard for her to walk all this way every day just to bring him a lunch. It was usually too hot to eat much anyway. He smiled at her curled up there on her side with her back to him, the deep inward curve of her waist, the rise of her buttocks so innocent yet so provocative. He found himself having to move again for comfort's sake. But this time it was not the musket, but a stiffened part of his anatomy that needed to be shifted. Yes, tonight he would tell her not to come here again. He needed to keep his mind on the prisoners, not Maria's shapely backside.

Alejandro woke Francisco after a while and let the other guards take a siesta one at a time. He would like to have joined them, but dared not. But he could let them all rest. What did it matter to him if the repairs on the fort were not completed before the prisoners were shipped to Spain?

But he did not dare risk letting any of them escape. His uncle would see to it that he paid too dearly for that. But if the repairs were done slower than Ignatio wanted, there was nothing he could do. He might sneer and accuse Alejandro of coddling the Englishmen, but he could prove nothing against him.

When it was well into the afternoon, Alejandro stirred up the men to get them back to work. There were more than a few groans and curses, but the guards managed to prod the prisoners back into the fort. On their way, the prisoners took the opportunity to ogle Maria. She sat with her knees drawn up watching as the men were herded along, their chains rattling as they marched past her, craning their necks and nearly stumbling to get a better look. She gave them a small smile.

"Hey, *señorita*!" one called. "You come to me tonight and I'll give you a good time!"

"Pretty lady, don't pay no attention to him. I'm the one who'll make all your dreams come true!"

One after the other they called to her, some making remarks so crude he was glad she did not know English. Alejandro felt like smashing in a few heads, but he was not supposed to know English, either. It was Mateo who finally put a stop to the worst of it. Mateo's friend looked like he was about to lash out at one of the men but Mateo gripped his arm, turned to the men and quietly said, "That woman is a lady and even if she does not understand English, she does not deserve to be spoken to like that."

The catcalls stopped but the men continued to look at her, grinning and nodding to her. Alejandro could not blame them for looking. He couldn't help looking at her himself. She was too beautiful for her own good and certainly did not need to be here, a tempting morsel that could do nothing but tease these sex-starved men. And he was one of them, he thought. He was just as sex-starved as they were and Maria was one lovely distraction none of them needed here.

He wondered why she had not gone home, yet. Was she really so fascinated by these Englishmen? He watched as the last of them tromped into the fort. He would get the men back to their work then he would tell her to leave.

"Mateo!" Alejandro called. "I need three men to haul this rubble out to the plaza to be burned."

As soon as Mateo translated the order, Alejandro was surprised when several men stepped forward to volunteer for the work. Then he grinned as he realized their motivation. Maria was out there. Inside the fort they couldn't see her. Maybe it wouldn't be so bad having her here after all, he thought. He picked three of them and set Paco to supervising the work.

From where he stood he could look out through the gates and see her. He noticed that the prisoners kept finding reasons to pass by the gates for a look, too. It was time for her to leave. He started out the gate but a shout brought his attention back to the work. A timber had fallen, just missing two of the prisoners. By the time it had been reset, with Alejandro loaning a shoulder to help, several of the prisoners were standing by the gate staring across the plaza. He put them to work tearing down a ruined shed.

An hour later he was about to call a water break when he noticed that the men had all stopped their work and were staring toward the gates.

Maria was standing there wearing a tremulous smile. This was too much. It was bad enough that she was here at all distracting everyone with her very presence. She had to leave. Now. He stalked toward her, determined not to be swayed by those big black eyes or the smile on those luscious lips or...

Chapter Ten

As Alejandro headed Maria he saw her chin come up. She could just put that determined little chin right back down. She might think she was going to stay, but she wasn't. There wasn't any reason for her to be here, no excuse she could give, no argument that would persuade him to let her stay. She was too much of a distraction, and not just to the other men. It was hard enough looking at her every night and being denied her bed without having her shapely little derriere swaying in front of him all day, as well.

He halted in front of her, hands on hips, glaring down at her, but she did not seem the least bit intimidated. What was wrong with her? He had turned officers under him to jelly with that look.

But Maria just gave him that soft, sweet smile of hers. "I brought water for the prisoners."

"Water?" He stepped back in confusion. He had just been ready to call a halt to the work so the men could have some water. Now here she was like a dark-eyed angel, carrying a water jug and a cup, offering to bring drink to the thirsty. He looked down into her sweet face, glowing with perspiration. He could just imagine her glowing like this after a passionate mating. He wanted to touch her face, let his fingers trace down her throat to... He swallowed hard and forced himself to remember that he was determined to send her home.

"*Sí, mi capitán*. It is so hot and I do not think the prisoners are used to working so hard in this sun."

Her compassion unmanned him. After thinking that the English were devils, here she was trying to make amends by bringing them water. He took her gently by the shoulders, wanting to draw her to him, kiss her. But not here. Not now. Now he must tell her to go. Gently, but firmly. "You are kind, Maria, and bringing water to them is something they need. But this is no place for you. You see how they look at you. It is time for you to go home."

She glanced around. The prisoners were continuing their work but every one of them had their eyes on her. "They will soon get used to having me around, *Capitán*."

He gripped her shoulders tighter, looking at her with lowered brows and tight lips. Was she that innocent? What made her think the men might get used to having her around? He wasn't used to having her around. He felt like a randy stallion with a sleek mare penned in the next paddock.

"No, they won't, Maria, because you are going home now and you are not to come back."

She looked down briefly, her fingers twisting anxiously in the strap that held the water jug. "But *Capitán*, I must bring them water. I have no choice."

He knew women could be stubborn, but his lovely housekeeper was a master. He could be stubborn, too, however. Firmly, he turned her around toward the gate. "That's right, Maria, you have no choice. You are leaving now."

"But you don't understand, *mi capitán*!" She turned back to him, tears beginning to glisten in her eyes. "When I went to confession this morning, the priest told me to bring water to the prisoners as my penance. I cannot go against Holy Mother Church.

What about my immortal soul? What if I would be brought before the Inquisition?"

Alejandro stiffened, sucking in air. Then he relaxed. Maria seemed so intelligent, so sophisticated at times that he found it difficult to remember that she was really an uneducated peasant girl and probably highly superstitious. Of course she would be terrified to go against whatever the priest told her.

He smiled down at her. "The priest will understand if you are not permitted to do this. He will give you another penance."

She shook her head vehemently. "No, *Capitán*, I begged for another penance. He insisted that this is what I must do."

Alejandro began urging her toward the gate. "Go home, Maria, and do not worry. I, myself, will talk with this priest."

Her eyes widened so in fear he thought she might faint and she clutched at his arms like a drowning victim. "No! You must not do that!"

Her eyes turned moist and pleading. "Please, *mi capitán*, let me do this. It will help me and it will bring relief to these men."

Alejandro sighed and slumped. What could he do? She feared the Inquisition for failure to do her penance. That was nonsense, of course. But if Ignatio heard that his nephew had prevented one of the faithful from performing her set penance, how would he twist it to his own ends? It was not Maria who might be in danger of being hauled before the Inquisition, it was him. And he was sure Ignatio would make sure they knew about his many trips to England, his 'favoring' of the English 'heretics'. Perhaps his summers in England with the De Vere family had also tainted Alejandro with heresy, as well. It was not something he could risk.

"All right, Maria." His hands dropped from her shoulders. "Take water to the prisoners."

Her eyes widened in surprise and began to glisten again with tears. But this time she was smiling with joy. He thought she was going to throw herself at him and kiss him. She even leaned toward him. His arms began to come up to embrace her. But she stopped, her glance taking in the prisoners surrounding them. Were her eyes giving him a promise of something more tonight? His hands trembled at the thought.

She swallowed hard. "Thank you, *mi capitán*."

As she turned toward the nearest prisoner Alejandro growled a surly, "You're welcome," and vowed that if any of those men so much as touched her he would forget his kindly thoughts and have him flogged.

Mariette could scarcely contain her joy at being given access to the prisoners. She had let a little of it seep out as if only glad that Alejandro was permitting her to fulfill her penance. The rest of her triumph she had firmly tamped down. It was hard to resist going directly to Matt but she was determined that Alejandro not suspect any connection or favoritism on her part toward that particular English prisoner.

The first man she approached, a short wiry fellow with straight brown hair, eyed her with a combination of lust and suspicion. But when she held out the rough pottery cup brimming with clear cold water, the suspicion in his eyes turned to surprise and then gratitude as he took the cup from her and drank.

He handed the cup back to her with a leer, his fingers straying over hers, holding on longer than necessary. "I got another thirst that needs quenching anytime yer ready."

Mariette jerked the cup away. She felt like cleaning her hand where he had touched her. But she tried to keep her expression neutral. She wasn't supposed to understand the crude remarks he had made in English. She did give him a frosty glare as she turned away. His only response was a leering grin.

Mariette glanced over her shoulder. If Alejandro thought the men might take advantage of her he might refuse to let her continue. She could not let that happen. Alejandro was watching all right, but since her back was to him he had not seen what had happened. It was just as well. She could take care of the situation herself. Skipping the little bastard the next two or three times she made her rounds might put him in a more amenable frame of mind.

The next man was young, perhaps even younger than Nate's seventeen years, and he was as polite as any well brought up young man. With a nod toward her jug he asked for a second cup and downed it. "Thank you, ma'am," he said, smiling shyly.

She gave him her sweetest smile before moving on down the line of thirsty prisoners, who reacted with varying degrees of courtesy or crudeness. Mariette kept Matt in sight as she worked her way toward him, glancing occasionally at Alejandro. Both men were keeping a sharp eye on her. It might not be possible to say much to Matt today, not with Alejandro watching so closely. But surely over the next few days, when she continued her rounds without incident, Alejandro's vigilance would lapse. There would be opportunities to speak briefly, to forge plans. So intent was she on Alejandro and Matt that Mariette was taken by surprise when the next prisoner addressed her by name.

"Mariette, you must return home. I cannot bear to see you in danger."

Mariette turned to the man and for a moment did not recognize Douglass. Gone was her pale, well-groomed, blond fiancé who always dressed in precise, immaculate clothes. In his place was a sweating, redfaced man with lank, poorly cut hair, and a three day's growth of beard, wearing the grimy, ripped remnants of his uniform.

She could not keep tears from welling up in her eyes. He had looked so…well…not grand, but good, in that uniform the day he had set sail from Charles Town. He had been smiling then and bold enough to kiss her on the lips right on the docks in front of everyone. Hastily she pressed the cup toward him.

He took it but did not drink. "You must return home, Mariette."

She looked around. Alejandro was temporarily occupied with helping two prisoners move a heavy beam. Nearly every other eye was upon her.

"Drink!" she hissed.

Douglass drank and handed back the cup.

Under cover of pouring him another cupful, she whispered. "I have come to rescue you and Matt, but you cannot talk to me, Douglass. I am not supposed to know English."

He ignored her plea and leaned toward her instead. "Go home. It is too dangerous here. I could not live knowing you had been captured for my sake!"

She swallowed guiltily. It wasn't exactly for Douglass's sake she had come. It was Matt's capture that had kept her awake and in tears until she had resolved to rescue him herself, since no one else seemed inclined to do it. It was Matt she could not bear to think of chained in a filthy Spanish dungeon. If it had only been Douglass who had been captured she doubted that she would have dared so much. Did that mean she did not love Douglass? She shook her head. This was no time for pondering such questions.

She thrust the second cup into his hand. While he drank she whispered, "I want to rescue Matt, too, Douglass. Now don't talk to me any more. Just be alert to follow my lead when I have a plan worked out."

He looked at her with pleading in his eyes, then, glancing at the other men who were still watching her every move, he did not say anything else. He drained the cup and handed it back to her and she moved on to the next man who was already reaching eagerly for the water.

The next prisoner, a man with watery blue eyes and a cough, drank three cups in quick succession. While he drank, she glanced at Matt. He was next and he was already glaring at her in that way he always had when he was determined to either get his way or make her sorry for not giving in to him. Her own throat began to feel dry, but thirst had nothing to do with it.

As much as she had been looking forward to this moment when she could at last speak privately with Matt, she suddenly found she needed a moment to compose herself. Knowing what he might say and how he would react to her being here to rescue him, she needed another moment to strengthen her resolve. She was not going to let him talk her out of this. Not by threats or appeals. She took her time rinsing the cup and wiping the rim before walking over to Matt.

Head held high and with just as much steely determination in her eyes as her twin had, Mariette handed him a brimming cup of water. She knew they were opposed in their feelings about her being here, but they also loved each other much more than normal brother and sister. They were twins. No matter how much they had fought as children, or still did on occasion, they had always stood up for each other and supported each other in whatever trouble they got into. And right now she wanted nothing more than to throw herself into his arms for a fierce brotherly hug. But a hug was impossible. Not until she could effect his escape. Right now, she had to convince him that she was going to try to rescue him no matter how opposed he was, and that he had just better accept it.

She almost dropped the cup she held out to him when he simply asked, "Do you have a plan worked out yet?"

"N-not yet," she said, stumbling over her words in her surprise. "I thought you'd try to talk me out of this."

He shrugged as he handed the cup back for a refill. "Is that possible?"

"No." She filled the cup again.

"That's what I figured. So why waste what few moments we have arguing about it?" He took his time with the second cup, stalling as much as possible.

"Nate's here with me. We came down on the *Fortune*. I don't have a plan all worked out yet, but I have an idea. We have to pull this off soon. They're shipping you to Spain in less than two weeks."

Matt stopped drinking and looked down at her with real apprehension in his eyes. "Then I hope you can come up with a plan soon." He tossed the rest of the water on the ground, handed the cup to her and turned back to his work.

Mariette clutched the cup in her hand so tightly that the rough texture cut into her palm. Matt would never say it out loud, even to her, but his free spirit would never survive a long and dangerous sea voyage in the stinking hold of a Spanish ship with no light or air, and with only a dark, dank dungeon at the end of it. And now that he knew what was in store for him and the other prisoners, he would do whatever he could to ensure the success of any plan she came up with.

She made her rounds with her jug of water three more times, refilling the jug with fresh clear water from the village well each time. Only on the last round did she give in to the begging of the skinny, brown-haired man who had insulted her and give him water. He drank it quickly, holding out the cup in a plea for more. She gave him a second, then a third cup. When he had slaked his thirst he gave the cup back, this time offering no insult beyond an angry glare. That did not bother her. She simply gave him a polite smile in return and walked on to the next man.

Matt did not say anything more to her that day, merely accepting the water from her and turning back to his work. There was nothing to be said until she had a plan. Douglass pleaded with her to return home each time she came to him, but she merely shook her head and continued her rounds.

Late in the afternoon, Mariette paused to take a drink herself, leaning against the gatepost in the shade. The sun was getting lower and she looked for a place to stow her jug until tomorrow. She wanted to get back to Soledad's village. She needed time to talk to Soledad and Nate before he took her back to town in the skiff. She had a barely formed rescue plan but she needed their help before she decided whether or not to try it.

Alejandro was looking her way, watching her as he had all afternoon. She set the jug and cup beside the gate and walked to him. "I must leave now, *mi capitán*."

He glanced at the position of the sun and nodded.

Alejandro watched her go, her hips swaying enticingly as she walked across the plaza and gathered the basket that had held their lunch. He swallowed hard when she bent to heft the basket and he caught a glimpse of ankle. She was all the way across the plaza, but she might as well have been in his bedroom and naked for the effect that glimpse had on him.

Yes, he had definitely been too long without a woman. He watched as she disappeared down the path into the woods. He would see her tonight and his loins tightened with the thought. She was a passionate woman. He knew that from the kisses they had shared, especially that one particular kiss that had sent her fleeing from him and left fire skimming through his veins. But he doubted that she would share his bed. He sighed. He wanted a woman. But not just any woman. He wanted Maria.

As soon as Nate saw Mariette set her basket down beside Soledad's door he came running to meet her.

"Did you get to talk to Matt? What did he say? Is he all right?"

"Yes, I was able to talk to Matt. And to Douglass, too. They're both fine, although Douglass is badly sunburned."

Soledad and Cato had come out of their garden in time to hear her report. Soledad nodded.

"Do you have a plan yet?" Nate asked, his blue eyes lighting with anticipation.

"Not yet, but you'll be happy to know I have a job for you."

Nate rubbed his hands together in gleeful anticipation. "What do you want me to do?"

"You ain't givin' dis chile nothin' to do dat's gonna get him in more trouble than he's in already." Soledad emphasized her words with a fist to one bony hip as she shook a long finger at Mariette.

"I'm not a child, Soledad," Nate complained, straightening to his full height.

Soledad turned her glare on Nate. "Don't you go puffin' dat chest out at me, Nathanial Fortune. You's a chile as long as I say you's a chile. And 'pears to me you got a ways to go yet 'fore I call you a man. I reckon I can still turn you over my knee and give you a whuppin'."

Nate grinned abashedly but he gave Mariette a conspiratorial wink.

"It's nothing dangerous, Soledad, especially if Cato will help."

"You know I'll do anything I can to help you and your family, Miss Mariette," Cato said.

Mariette touched his arm in gratitude and looked from Cato to Soledad. "I appreciate all you're doing for us. Both of you."

"So what do you have for me to do, Sis?"

Mariette squatted down, found a stick, smoothed the dirt, and began to draw. "This is the fort where the prisoners are working. The river runs by it here. To this side are trees. What I need to know is if there is another river or creek beyond those trees big enough for the *Fortune*. And I need to know how far it would be through those trees to the river."

Cato nodded. "There is a river there. There's creeks and waterways all over in here. Don't know just how far it is through them trees, though. And I don't know how deep it is."

"Can you find out?"

Cato nodded. "We can take the skiff, make some soundings. But I got to tell you, them woods ain't like the woods back in Carolina."

"Would there be a problem?" Mariette asked.

"Might be. Woods here are thicker. And there's lots of Spanish bayonet. That's a big plant with hard sharp leaves. It can cut you to pieces."

"What you got in mind?" Soledad asked Mariette.

"Alejandro said the prisoners were going to be clearing brush outside the fort in a few days, right up to that tree line."

"If Matt and Douglass can slip away," Nate jumped in excitedly, "the *Fortune* can be waiting in the river, take them on, and be gone before the alarm is sounded!"

"Exactly!" Mariette beamed.

"What about all them other men?" Cato asked.

Mariette bit her lip. "I've thought about that. I feel bad for them, but there's no way we can take them all. I wish we could, but we can't. If they all run, there's bound to be shooting and someone, maybe several people, are going to get hurt or even killed. And with all of them running, there will be an instant alarm. There's no way we could get them aboard and get away before we were sighted. At least," she sighed, "when they are imprisoned in Spain, they will be closer to their home. Except for Matt and Douglass, they are all

Scots."

Cato nodded. "Soon as Nate gets back from taking you to town, we'll go look at that creek and those woods."

Mariette was putting the finishing touches to the table while the meal of rice and lamb stayed hot on the stove. She had once again placed the table out on the patio to catch the last of the cooling evening breeze. Even if the garden setting did evoke a romantic mode, it was just too hot in the house, especially since it had been shut up all day.

Paddy followed her from cupboard to table with a constantly wagging tail, hoping for a falling crumb or two—or better yet, a pat on the head. Tongue lolling, he finally sat to watch Mariette check once more on the dinner.

The time for Alejandro's return was near as the day passed into twilight. She was just leaning over the table to light the candle when she heard an angry shriek from next door.

"Thief! Insolent tart!"

Several loud whacks followed the sharp words. There were more accusations and whacks followed by a gasp of pain.

Mariette moved next to the fence separating her patio from Irish's. It had to be Irish who was being beaten. She laid a hand to the gate that led to the alley thinking to run to her friend's aid. But what could she do? It was the right of her mistress to punish a slave. There would be no lessening of the strokes if she interfered. Indeed, there could well be more.

The accusations were finally stopped as Irish's mistress ran out of breath. The beating also slowed, then stopped. All Mariette could hear was the sharp gasp of the woman's breathing as if she were tired out. Mariette heard a sound like a stout stick being tossed aside then the woman spoke again. "That will teach you, you brazen hussy! And you can sleep out here tonight with no supper!"

As soon as she heard a door slam, Mariette was through the gate and down the alley to the next house. The gate was unlatched and Mariette wasted no thought to the propriety of entering another's yard without invitation. She gasped when she saw Irish crumpled on the patio struggling to rise, a hand groping blindly for a nearby chair.

"Irish! Are you all right?" Keeping her words at a whisper to avoid drawing attention, Mariette knelt to help her friend into the chair. Irish bit her lips to squelch a groan when Mariette took her arm to lift her, but did not otherwise cry out.

Mariette got her into the chair but Irish slumped forward. Her bright red hair had come loose and fallen across her face. When Mariette brushed it back her hand came away sticky with a red that had naught to do with the color of her friend's hair.

"Irish, is there a candle I can light? You're bleeding and it's getting too dark to see."

Irish grabbed her arm. "No! Don't light a candle. *Señora* Martín will come out and…"

Mariette nodded and gave her friend's arm a reassuring squeeze of understanding. "Can you stand? I'll take you next door and tend your wounds there."

Irish gave a nod and Mariette put an arm around her waist to help her stand. After two wobbly steps, Mariette shifted Irish so that she supported more of her weight. A few steps at a time she got her friend back to Alejandro's patio where several candles and a lantern were lit. She settled her in a chair by the table and brought the lantern closer.

Paddy trotted after them then sat at Irish's feet, giving a worried whimper. Irish managed to smile at him even though it made her wince in pain.

Mariette pushed Irish's hair out of the way and gave a low,

"Oh!" when she saw the gash above her eye. Irish reached up to feel, but Mariette caught her hand. "It's a bad cut. Better not touch it."

Irish looked her directly in the eyes. "I'm not a thief, Maria. The money she found was mine. Even the lowliest slave is allowed to earn money if they have free time. I have been doing laundry for some of the neighbors. I hope to someday buy my freedom."

Mariette smiled at her. "And there was the money I insisted you take from me for your help in the market and with the cooking. I did not doubt you, Irish."

Irish let out a breath of relief and nodded.

Mariette brought the lantern closer and began running her hands over Irish's arms and legs checking for further injuries. "Nothing seems to be broken, but you have another bad cut on your back, just on your shoulder blade. I think both cuts need stitches."

"Stitches?"

Both women looked up to see Alejandro standing in the doorway, his coat slung over one shoulder and a questioning look on his face.

Irish's eyes widened with apprehension and she started to get up. "I'd better go."

Mariette stopped her with a hand to her shoulder. "Not until those injuries are taken care of."

Irish glanced at Alejandro. "I don't want to get you into trouble," she whispered.

Mariette leaned close and smiled, giving Irish a reassuring squeeze on her hand, one of the few places she could touch her friend without hurting her. "*Capitán* Alejandro is not *Señora* Martín." She said that with confidence and realized that she believed what she said. She was very sure that Alejandro would not be angry at his servant for helping another servant who had been abused.

Alejandro came to the table, dropped his coat onto a chair back, then reached out to Irish, lifting her chin with a gentle touch. "What happened?" He was studying Irish's injuries, but his question was directed to Mariette. "And," he smiled at Irish, "who is *La Roja*?" Mariette went to the stove, filled a basin with warm water and brought it to the table with a cloth. "*La Roja*, the red-haired one, is my friend, Irish. Her owner beat her."

"Damn."

Irish flinched at Alejandro's explicative, but Mariette knew it was not directed at her friend.

Alejandro glanced down at the basin Mariette had placed on the table.

"I'll send for a doctor."

Irish grabbed his hand before he could move away. "No, *señor*, please. No doctor."

"Those wounds need to be tended," Alejandro said. "You need stitches."

Irish's gaze flicked from Alejandro to Mariette and back again. "I…I will be all right. This has happened before."

Looking at the wound above Irish's eye, Mariette bit her lip. She knew why her friend refused the services of a doctor. She had no coin to pay him and too much pride to either admit it or allow another to pay for her.

"Irish." Mariette knelt before her and took her hand. "You know those gashes need stitches. If you will not have a doctor, will you trust me to do it?"

Irish started to speak but Mariette forestalled her by squeezing her hand again and hurrying ahead with what she had to say. "I have some skill at healing. My grandmother was a doctor. She taught me. And with three brothers always getting into one scrape after another, I had plenty of chances to practice."

Mariette could feel Alejandro staring at her in surprise but she was focused on Irish and waiting for her answer. Finally, Irish gave a terse nod of assent.

When Mariette stood up and turned toward the basin, Alejandro stopped her with a hand to her arm. She looked up at him. The line of his mouth was hard, his gaze piercing.

"Are you sure you can do this?"

She nodded. It was not just her brothers she had stitched up and dosed a time or two, it was the people on her family's plantation, as well. Her grandmother had taught her well, insisting that she read all the latest medical books. She had even been called upon a few times by neighbors. But she could not tell Alejandro any of that. She could only nod and say, "I'm sure."

He looked at her, seeming to appraise her anew. He dropped his hand from her arm. "What can I do?"

"The sewing kit," she answered, "and some wine."

He moved away to do her bidding and she wet the cloth in the water. Tilting Irish's head back, and with the cloth poised above her cut, Mariette paused to give warning. "This is going to sting because I dissolved salt in the water."

Irish's eyes widened and she pulled back. "Salt?"

"My grandmother found that cleaning wounds with salt water helps keep them from getting infected."

Irish bit her lip but then leaned forward and closed her eyes so that Mariette could continue. Irish winced and clenched her teeth as Mariette dribbled the salt water into the wound then cleaned the area around it. By the time she had finished, Alejandro was back with the wine and sewing kit.

She threaded a needle and poured wine into a shallow pottery bowl then dropped the needle and thread into the bowl of wine. She dipped the scissors in the wine, as well.

"Ready?" she asked Irish.

The woman took a deep breath and gripped the sides of her

chair.

Mariette worked as quickly as she could, pulling the edges of the cut together and placing five stitches, cutting the thread after each one and knotting it. Only one quick whimper escaped Irish's lips and it was answered by Paddy who pranced anxiously just out of the way.

"All done. Now lean on the table and I'll stitch the cut on your back."

Loosening the ties on Irish's tattered gown to expose the wound, Mariette finished her work as quickly as she could. Irish's back was already beginning to bruise from the beating and Mariette knew with a certainty that somehow, Irish had to be part of her rescue plan. She could not— would not—leave her friend here in slavery.

Chapter Eleven

SUPPER THAT NIGHT WAS SUBDUED. IRISH HAD INSISTED that she return home before she was missed and earned herself another beating. She would scarcely wait long enough for Mariette to wrap her some bread and cheese to take with her. Alejandro had wanted to call her mistress to account but Irish feared that it would only make her situation worse, so he gave in to her and simply took her home.

When he returned, Mariette was setting the supper of rice and lamb that Soledad had made on the table. "Thank you for your help, *Capitán*."

He stood across the table from her, his fingers resting lightly on the boards, his eyes studying her as if it were the first time he had seen her. "Isn't it about time that you called me Alejandro?"

She paused with the bowl of rice in her hand and looked at him, from his fine, long fingers up sinewy arms to a lean, chiseled face now shadowed by candlelight and stubble. "I am only a servant, *Capitán*."

He shook his head. "I think you are far more than what you seem, Maria."

Mariette gripped the bowl in alarm but she tried to remain calm. What could he know? What had she let slip? Frantically, she went over what she had said to Irish. Had she inadvertently lapsed into English with her friend who still struggled so much with Spanish? No, she was sure she had not. What had she done? "*Capitán?*" she asked trying hard to keep the waver out of her voice.

"I have been on many battlefields, Maria. I have not seen finer work by any formally trained surgeon. Your grandmother taught you well."

Mariette's grip on the bowl relaxed but her hands shook a bit, so she set the bowl down before she spilled its contents. "I will convey your compliments to her the next time I see her."

"I will convey your compliments," Alejandro repeated softly. "You speak Castilian like a courtesan or a noble. You carry yourself like a countess. You perform surgery, simple surgery, but surgery, nonetheless, with the cool skill of a military field doctor. Yet you claim to be no more than a simple Mestiza servant girl. You intrigue me, Maria."

Mariette lowered her eyes. Her hands moved over the table pointlessly rearranging the cups and plates and spoons. Soledad had told her it would not be easy for her to play the role of a simple servant. Mariette never realized how much there was to the role, how many ways she could—had— given herself away in only a few days. How many more ways would she give herself away in the next few days? She might intrigue *Capitán* Alejandro de Silva but would he still turn her in if he knew she was an English spy come to help two of his English prisoners escape? She could not take a chance that he would.

The silence stretched. He had asked no question but she knew he was waiting for an explanation. He was waiting for her to tell him how a halfcaste colonial who supposedly had never seen the courts of Spain, never learned to read, never lived anywhere but a wattle-and-daub hut, could speak and move and act as she did. Her mind was numb. She could think of no answer to give him.

She lifted her eyes to look into his, cooly, as she did when faced by a too ardent suitor who needed to be set in his place, as her father and grandfather had told her one should act in the face of enemy fire. She lifted her chin. "I am only being myself, *Capitán*."

"Alejandro," he corrected, his voice husky, rasping upon something within her like a bow on a violin string.

"Alejandro," she said, barely able to get the name out in a whisper.

"And just who are you, Maria?"

The table setting before her was being rearranged again. And again. Until he reached across and took the cup from her fingers, set it in its place and took her fingers in his. "Who are you?"

She pulled her hand away. "I am just Maria, *mi capitán*, the woman you hired to clean your house and cook your meals. And if you don't sit down to this meal right now, all the food will be cold."

He stood for a moment, his hand left adrift between them when she had taken hers away. He let it fall and, with a sigh, shrugged his acquiescence. He pulled out a chair and held it for her as if she were, indeed, some Spanish *condesa*. She sat in it as gracefully as any noble lady well-trained in the gracious arts. He bowed gallantly before sitting down himself and offering to pour her wine. She nodded benevolently. And so they ate their meal.

Mariette handed a cup of water to Francisco with a smile. During the last three days while she had been taking water to the prisoners she had been quietly getting to know the guards. She thought it would be wise to know their strengths and weaknesses, to know who to watch out for when they made their escape. Francisco seemed a good sort. Simple, but pleasant, with a wife and four children, he had told her, and one on the way.

Her fourth afternoon as water girl for the prisoners was going well. She had been able to speak to Matt a few minutes, giving him some news from home, and the skinny bastard who had given her trouble her first day seemed to have learned his lesson. The only thing he gave her when she brought him water was a glare. Glares didn't bother her.

Francisco wiped sweat from his heavy face with his sleeve and handed the cup back to her. "*Gracias, señorita*. You are an angel to bring water to us."

"Perhaps, Francisco," she leaned conspiratorially close, "for you, next time I'll bring wine."

"Oh no, *señorita*. We cannot drink while on duty!" the guard protested.

But Mariette noticed that his eyes lit up with delight at the prospect and she thought that it might not be so difficult to persuade him to take just a bit. At least enough to slow his ponderous bulk even more. Enough to give escaping prisoners a bit more of an edge.

Francisco was the soldier she had met in the market her first day in St. Augustine, and like Alejandro, he had a fondness for Soledad's muffins. She would have to remember to bring him some the day of the escape. Maybe a full belly would further slow him down.

The other two guards would be more difficult to deal with. Especially that pig, Raúl. Mariette glanced to where that guard stood watch, whip in hand, casually slapping his thigh with it. Only Alejandro's command had kept him from using it on the prisoners when one of them faltered under a load or because of the heat.

The third guard, Paco, seemed totally incompetent, but his enthusiasm for doing his duty might make him dangerous.

Mariette gave Francisco a second cup of water and was about to move on when he suddenly straightened to attention, looking out through the gates. Three men on horses were approaching. Two were guards, but the third, the one in the lead, was obviously someone of importance, to judge from the braid and gilt on his uniform.

"It is the commandant!" Francisco said in an awed whisper. Then, remembering his duty, he shouted to Alejandro, "The commandant is coming, *Capitán!*"

The other two guards came to life, springing to attention and straightening uniforms. Mariette was torn between taking Soledad's advice to avoid officers, and curiosity to meet Alejandro's uncle, the man who temporarily commanded the Castillo. Alejandro headed toward the gate and Mariette saw his face take on a grimness, his mouth set and tight.

The commandant rode a sleek chestnut stallion and he handled the beast well, even when the horse fought the bit and pranced as the man brought it to a halt just inside the gates of the fort. In spite of his round bulk he dismounted with alacrity, tossing the reins to one of the guards who had accompanied him. He looked around at the work being done, and immediately spotted Mariette.

His eyes glittered and he looked at her with an intensity that set every nerve in her body to full alert. His thick lips turned up in a smile that was slightly reminiscent of a cat about to pounce and she felt very much like the mouse. She wanted to run but felt spellbound by the gaze that raked over her. This was exactly the kind of Spanish soldier Soledad had warned her about—one who would never be fooled by her guise as a simple Mestiza, one who would ferret out her every secret.

The commandant stepped close to her and took her shaking fingers into his hands. His were thick and hot as they lifted her hand to his lips. He kissed the back of her hand as if she were some grand lady instead of a Mestiza servant hauling water for English prisoners. Then he smiled again, a smile that might have been charming if she had really been who she was pretending to be.

"*Señorita*, may I introduce myself?" he asked, then went on without waiting for her answer. "I am Ignatio de Silva y Gonzales, commandant of Castillo el Moro and your humble servant. Never have I seen such beauty. What are you doing here in this broken fortress when you should be living in a palace?"

Mariette was not sure just how to answer him. She should have listened to her own advice and hidden someplace before this man had seen her. She took a deep breath. It may seem like he was trying to charm her, but he probably treated every woman he came across this same way. Some men were like that. He would have said the same thing to her if she had been a wizened crone. There was no reason to worry. He would forget her existence the moment he went back to St. Augustine. She was nothing to him. He was a grandee of Spain. She was only a simple peasant girl. So why were her hands still shaking?

Suddenly, Alejandro was there, gripping her arm and pulling her behind him. The protective wall of his body made her feel safe. She placed her hand on his back, leaning close to him, not caring what anyone might think, not caring if they all assumed she really was his woman in every sense of the word. She could feel the tension in the muscles of his back and wondered why that was, what enmity had come between him and his uncle.

"Uncle," Alejandro said, nodding to the commandant.

The commandant looked back and forth between Alejandro and Mariette then his brows rose, and he looked at his nephew as if assessing him anew.

"Your 'housekeeper'?"

"Yes, Uncle. My housekeeper and under my protection."

"I must congratulate you, Nephew, on your choice. I never realized the dirt of this primitive colony could nurture such a rare flower. I cannot believe I did not unearth her myself."

"I am sure you did not come all this way to discuss my choice of housekeeper, Uncle. May I show you what we have accomplished?"

The commandant shrugged. "I can see well enough from here." He looked around at the fort and the prisoners. "I must admit you have done more than I expected, especially considering what you have to work with."

"They are good men, especially now that they are no longer treated like animals."

"You have treated them well, Alejandro." He eyed the water jar she still carried. "Perhaps too well. It could make some people wonder about your loyalty to Spain."

"I do not see disloyalty in keeping them fit enough to work hard for the glory of Spain."

The commandant gave a brief shrug. "You always could twist words, Nephew."

"If there is nothing else, Uncle Ignatio…" Alejandro motioned for the guard to bring his uncle's horse.

The commandant took the reins and the horse nudged him fondly. He looked at Mariette, giving her a smile and running his tongue over his lips as he gave the animal a piece of carrot from his pocket then caressed its nose. It was as if he were blatantly telling her that he wanted to caress her in the same way, feed her from his hand. Then his gaze snapped back to Alejandro.

"We are giving a small party Sunday night at the mansion. Your aunt has insisted that I invite you, Alejandro." He bowed in Mariette's direction. "And I insist that you bring your lovely… companion."

Alejandro's grip on her arm increased. "I doubt that you would want a servant there as a guest, Uncle."

The commandant mounted his horse. "Such a lovely woman should not be a servant. Bring her." With that he whirled the animal and set off at a gallop that his guards were hard pressed to keep up with.

"I cannot go to your uncle's with you," Mariette said as she set dinner before Alejandro that evening.

He looked up at her, his mouth set in a hard line. "No, you cannot."

She turned to bring another dish to the table, surprised that he had so readily agreed with her. She had thought about the invitation all afternoon, knowing that it would be dangerous beyond reason to attend, to have the commandant's scrutiny on her for an entire evening. She had been prepared to argue with Alejandro that she had nothing to wear, that surely his aunt would not want to entertain a servant as an equal, that she would embarrass him with her ignorance. Not that she wasn't accustomed to grand homes and balls, dancing with the governor in Charles Town on more than one occasion, but here she was supposed to be a simple peasant, awkward and humble in the presence of greatness.

As she spooned rice into a bowl she felt tears well up. And then she felt anger. Just why didn't Alejandro want her to go? Was he so ashamed of her? Wasn't she good enough for him? She gritted her teeth. Well, of course not! He was a grandee of Spain. She was a Mestiza servant. There was enmity between Alejandro and his uncle. The commandant probably just wanted to embarrass his nephew with her and Alejandro was not going to let it happen. So why should she feel so hurt? Surely she didn't think that Alejandro—in spite of insisting that she eat at the same table with him each evening—was beginning to feel anything for her besides lust? She set the bowl of rice onto the table, perhaps a bit more forcefully than normal.

Alejandro's brows shot up questioningly as he looked from the bowl to her.

"I am glad you agree, *señor*. An ignorant peasant has no business at the table of the commandant of St. Augustine." Then as if to belie her words she floated gracefully into her chair and pointedly poured wine into his glass as if pouring tea for the queen.

Alejandro's lips quirked up at the corners. "And you probably have nothing to wear."

She looked down at her gown, now soiled with the day's wear and no better than the only other one she had with her. A simple gown. A peasant's gown. For the peasant she was pretending to be. Perhaps it was her he was trying to spare, not himself. She thought of the gowns she had at home, brocade, soft Indian muslins, silk, trimmed with lace from Belgium and seed pearls from the orient. But even if she had them here, she still could not dare go to the party.

"No," she agreed. "I have nothing to wear."

"I will go tonight to see my aunt. She will understand that you cannot come."

"Alejandro!" The woman who held out her arms to him was short and round with hair that was beginning to gray. Alejandro scooped her up and twirled her around, making the older woman giggle like a school girl. If his uncle had done his best to make his life hell, his aunt had made up for most of it by being infinitely sweet and loving, hugging a boy too proud to cry and slipping him food when he was sent unjustly to bed without his supper.

"Aunt Inés! How good to see you." Alejandro held her at arms length and looked at her. "You are younger than the last time I saw you."

She pretended to scowl at him. "Naughty boy! That is not true and you know it. But I love you all the more for saying it." She took his arm and led him to a sofa, and sat beside him. "I was so sorry to hear of your mother's death, Alejandro. I have six children and I love them well, but I think your mother loved her only child more than I loved all six of mine."

He squeezed her hand. "Thank you, Aunt Inés. She looked on you as the sister she never had."

Inés nodded as she patted his hand. "Your father, is he well?"

Alejandro stiffened and pulled his hands away. His father. Or rather, the man he had always thought was his father. When had he begun to suspect that he was not? During those summers in England as a boy when he had felt more at home with Lord Randall's family than his own? Or when his father began to push him away, treating him with scorn? "He was well when I left Spain," he answered. Well, and full of hatred for the only son his wife had given him. A son who was not his own, after all.

"But tell me of your family, Aunt. How are my cousins?"

They chatted amicably for an hour, catching up on news, laughing over the antics of the younger children. When Alejandro stood up to take his leave, she clung to his arm, walking him to the door.

"I will see you tomorrow night, then, Alejandro, with your... your friend?"

Alejandro smiled down at his aunt. He knew she had been ordered to invite, and accept, a woman she must believe was no better than a whore. And he knew she dared not defy her husband.

"She will not be coming, Aunt."

He saw panic rise in her eyes. "But you must bring her. Ignatio implicitly specified that she be here."

"She is a simple peasant woman," Alejandro said, thinking that nothing could be further from the truth. There was nothing simple about Maria. And he had never known a peasant to carry herself with such grace and poise. "She would not feel comfortable."

"Oh, there would be no problem, Alejandro! I would make sure of it."

Alejandro could hear the fear in his aunt's voice and his anger toward his uncle grew, knowing it was he who had put it there. "Besides, she has nothing suitable to wear. She told me so herself."

"No, I suppose not," his aunt said slowly, "but Ignatio will insist that she attend. You know he will. Even if she has to wear rags." She tapped her chin with one finger, thinking. Then, eyes brightening, she said, "Wait right here!" and hurried off.

When she returned a few moments later she laid a heavily wrapped package into Alejandro's arms. "Your friend is slim?"

Alejandro nodded.

"Tall?"

Again Alejandro nodded.

"Then this gown will fit her well enough. I bought it for Aña, but your cousin has more than enough gowns. Give it to your friend."

Alejandro's heart swelled at this outpouring of goodness from his aunt. She could not want to entertain a woman she must think of as a peasant and a whore, yet she could still be generous enough to provide a gown so Maria would not feel so out of place.

Alejandro bent to kiss his aunt. "Maria will be grateful, Aunt Inés. And so am I. And let me assure you, Maria is not…" He faltered to a stop, feeling his face grow red. How could he tell his aunt that Maria was not a whore? "Maria is… that is, we have not…" He cleared his throat, trying to find a polite way to say it.

Inés squeezed his arm, smiling with relief. "I understand, Nephew. And it would not matter in any case. I am sure that any woman who has caught your eye must be very special."

When Alejandro returned home, Maria was sitting on the sofa

mending one of his shirts, bending to catch the last rays of light coming in through the front window. It gave her skin a warm glow. Her hair, still damp from a washing, glinted with depths he wanted to plunge into. She glanced up and her eyes were soft and inviting, more brown than black in the light. Her lips were slightly parted as if awaiting a kiss, a kiss he longed to bestow. He stepped toward her and nearly tripped over Paddy who had scampered from somewhere to sniff at his shoes and wag his tail in happy welcome.

Maria laughed softly and he could not be annoyed at the puppy if it could draw laughter like that out of her. "You see," she said, "he does not snarl at you now. He knows you belong."

Do I? Alejandro thought. Do I really belong anywhere?

She set her mending aside and straightened her skirt.

Oh yes, he thought, I belong. I belong wrapped about you, naked in my bed. I belong inside you, with you arching your neck for my kisses, clawing my back to urge me closer. Alejandro swallowed. Hard. He needed a woman. Not just any woman. This woman. The woman he had just assured his aunt was a good woman and not his whore. Did he really want to make a whore of her? Then what would she do when he left? For he would leave. And she would stay here.

He wrenched his eyes away from her, away from the softly curving mounds of her breasts, the arms folded across her belly as she leaned forward to smile at Paddy.

Paddy rolled over on his back and Alejandro bent to tickle his belly instead of Maria's. One hind leg kicked while Paddy's tongue lolled happily. "Perhaps he will make a good watchdog after all," he conceded.

She would need someone to watch over her when he was gone. He gritted his teeth thinking of another man having what he refused to take. Did she already have a *novio*? A boyfriend? No, she had said she did not.

"He already does make a good watchdog." She leaned forward to caress Paddy's ears and their hands touched.

It was a brief touch. Barely a brushing of one finger against the back of his hand, but he felt it all the way up his arm and down into his loins. He jumped as if scalded, dropping the package as he got to his feet. She sat back, looking up at him questioningly.

Forcing a smile to his lips, he picked up the package and laid it in her lap. "My Aunt Inés sent this to you."

"Why would your aunt send me a gift? I do not even know her." She looked up at him with round wondering eyes and he could not wait to see her expression when she opened the wrapping and saw what was inside.

He could not wait to see her in it, wearing a dress that would befit her far better than the simple clothes she normally wore. He squatted beside her, as careful to avoid touching her as he would a flame, for she could cause him to burn far worse. "Open it and you will see why."

"What is it?" she asked, but she was already plucking eagerly at the strings that held the cheap muslin wrapping, pulling them free.

She paused a moment then folded back the covering cloth. "Oh!" she said as she pulled out the gown. She stood, lifting the gown to her shoulders.

Coral embroidered roses cascaded down a cream colored underskirt. The gown itself was coral with wide creamy lace ruffling the sleeves. Dainty silk slippers, embroidered to match the underskirt, tumbled to the floor and Alejandro scooped them up just before Paddy was able to pounce on them. Panniers and other underthings were also in the package.

"I told my aunt you could not come because you had nothing to wear. So she sent you this." He looked at her holding the gown before her, fingering the embroidery, smoothing her hand over the coral silk, and he thought how much better she would look in it than his cousin. How much better Maria would make the dress look than Aña ever could.

"Oh, Alejandro, I cannot accept such a rich gift as this!"

He stood and looked down at her, and at that moment her beauty overwhelmed him. "You are right, Maria. It is not nearly fine enough for you."

She tilted her head and then grinned, obviously thinking he teased her. "You know very well what I mean. Fine feathers indeed, for such as I. It is a beautiful dress but it will not make me into something I am not. It will not make me fit in." She touched the roses once more then began folding the dress back into its wrapping. She seemed almost anxious to put it away and out of sight, and he noticed that her fingers shook.

"You must return it to your aunt with my thanks. I cannot attend her party. I would not dishonor her, or you, by attending."

It might not be proper for Aunt Inés to invite someone of Maria's social station to her party, but Alejandro knew that his uncle would count on his wife to convince Alejandro to bring Maria. And it would be Aunt Inés who would bear the brunt of Ignatio's anger if Alejandro didn't bring her. His uncle had seen her now. There would be no hiding her from him, not even if he sent her back to her village. He could only hope to protect her. And he must protect his aunt, as well. He had to convince Maria to go.

"She is counting on you, Maria."

She whirled to face him. "Why? Why would a Spanish noble-woman want a Mestiza servant as a guest in her home?"

He shrugged, trying to make it seem nonchalant. "The rules of society are more lax here in the colonies."

She looked up from her folding to eye him wryly. "Not that lax, *Capitán*."

"There will be dancing."

Her fingers paused in their work and he knew he had found her weakness. He stepped close behind her and she straightened. "The night will be filled with fine wine and laughter. We will sit at the table together and I will feed you sweets from my fingers." He whispered the words into her ear, the curve of her neck inviting his kiss as he took in the clean scent of her. "The other men will wonder who you are, where I found you. They will think you are a princess newly arrived to the colony and we will not deny it." They stood for a long time like that, their bodies drawn to each other but not quite touching, not quite igniting the flame that was banked within them both. But he could sense her softening in the warmth of that heat.

He leaned closer, his breath touching her where he dared not. "After the dinner there will be music and dancing. We can dance together, just you and I. It will be as if no one else is in the room." He heard a soft moan coming from somewhere deep within her and he longed to catch it with his mouth on hers but he dared not.

"Maria." He said her name and it was like breathing. He must continue or he would die. He could no longer hold himself in check. He lifted his arms to embrace her but she ducked beneath his arms and whirled away, a look on her face that was less frightened than it was agonized with denied wanting.

"Say you will go, Maria."

She backed all the way to the wall. Her chest rose and fell quickly with shallow breaths and she looked at him as if she were starving. She turned her head away and her face was cast into shadow. When she spoke, the words were so soft he could barely hear them. "I will go."

Chapter Twelve

THE NEXT MORNING, MARIETTE PRETENDED TO BE ASLEEP when Alejandro got up. She could hear the slap of his razor on the strop as he sharpened it, heard him talking to Paddy, heard the sound of cloth on cloth as he put on his uniform jacket. Paddy followed Alejandro to the door, whining when he left. Mariette sat up feeling like whining, too. She was such a coward not to want to face him this morning.

She had tossed and turned for hours before she slept last night, thinking of the party tomorrow, thinking of dancing with Alejandro, moving sensually to the beat of passionate Spanish music. To move in his arms without fearing that she would pull him down onto the floor and allow him—beg him—to have his way with her. For if she let him embrace her here, within the privacy of these walls, kiss her as she knew he could, as she knew he wanted to, she knew she would not be able to stop. But in his uncle's house, surrounded by a crowd of Spaniards, she would be safe.

Safe? How pathetic was she that she was willing to face not only the censure of Spanish St. Augustine society, but possible exposure just to safely dance in Alejandro's arms? It was a good thing that she would be leaving soon, perhaps in just a matter of a few days. Certainly less than a week.

She wanted him. She wanted his arms around her. She wanted his hands touching her. Everywhere. She wanted his mouth upon hers again. She had never known such wanting. She had never known such wanting could exist.

She had certainly never found such passion in any of the men she had danced with, flirted with, or sneaked kisses with in the garden of her home in Charles Town. She had not found it with Douglass, either. She had decided that passion was something her friends had rated too highly. So what difference did it make who she married? Douglass was a good man. He would provide well for her. They were good friends. What else did she need? Her family had been happy for her when she told them she and Douglass were going to be married.

But now she knew. She knew what wanting was, what it felt like to tremble with desire merely to hear the sound of a man's voice vibrating through her body. She knew what it was like to begin melting from the inside out from a look, a glance, a brushing of fingers on an arm. She knew what it was like to feel as though time crawled slowly from one hour to the next until she could see him again.

But if she let him touch her, she feared there would be no end to the wanting, the touching. Not until she gave herself to him completely. That was why she was willing to risk so much to go to that party. There she could dance with him, let him hold her in his arms, caress her cheek, and what could happen surrounded by a throng of people? The thought of those arms around her sent her jumping from her bed.

She fed Paddy and put him outside, then got out the dress Alejandro's aunt had sent. It was beautiful. As fine as anything she owned. When she left, she would take it with her. It would remind her of him. She shook her head. As if she needed reminders. She would never be the same again. How could she forget the man who had changed her?

She put the dress on. It would need just a tuck in the waist to fit well enough to wear. The length was just a bit too short, but it would do. She took it off, tucked and pinned the waist. As soon as she finished she would have to go. She needed to find out if Cato and Nate had made any progress in finding a creek near enough to Ft. Mose to rescue Matt. And Douglass.

She was just beginning to sew when Irish peeked into the open door.

"How is Paddy this morning?" Grinning, Irish held up a bone with a bit of meat still on it. "And how do you think my darling will be liking this?"

There was no need for Mariette to answer because the puppy came waddling in from the patio as soon as he heard Irish's voice, tail wagging, tongue lolling. Paddy's tail wagged almost as wildly over the bone as it did when Irish petted him.

"How are you this morning?" Mariette asked. She set aside her sewing and stood up. "Turn into the light and let me see how those cuts are healing."

Irish turned toward the light from the door and lifted her hair. There was some redness and a bit of swelling, but nothing to be concerned about.

"I...those stitches will have to come out in a few more days." She had started to say she would remove them, but she would not be here. When the Spanish warship, the Eagle, left for Spain, whether her brother was onboard with the other prisoners or not, she would be leaving for Charles Town. Hopefully, Matt and Douglass, as well as Irish and Paddy, would be aboard the *Fortune* with her. The question was, would Irish want to come with them when they made their escape? She still did not dare to trust the information to anyone that she was English and in St. Augustine to rescue two English prisoners of war. Not even to an Irish woman enslaved by the Spanish. But she would have to find out how Irish felt.

Irish smiled. "I know a good doctor when it's time."

Mariette sat back down and fussed with her sewing for a moment.

Irish knelt beside Mariette's chair and fingered the fine fabric of the dress she was altering. "What a beautiful gown! Whose is it?"

Mariette held the gown up to her chest, spreading the skirt out. "It's mine."

Irish's eyes grew round with wonder. "Yours?"

Mariette laughed. "The *capitán*'s uncle, the commandant of the fort, has insisted that Alejandro bring me to a party at his home. Since I had nothing to wear, his wife sent me this gown."

Irish ran her hand lovingly over the fine embroidery of the stomacher. "I have never seen a gown so beautiful."

"Haven't you?" Mariette touched the now ragged sleeve of Irish's own gown. Irish had never said anything about her life in Ireland, but judging from her once fine clothes she must have come from a grand family. She had the bearing of the nobility and when she spoke to Paddy in English, her accent was of the upper classes.

Irish brushed futilely at some stains on her skirt. "Aye, well, it's not so fine now, is it?"

"Do you ever hope to get back to Ireland?"

Irish looked up and Mariette thought it was almost with an expression of alarm before her mouth hardened and she looked away. "No. I will never go back to Ireland." When she turned back to Mariette, there was determination in her face. "But someday I will be free."

"How will you gain your freedom? Do you plan to run away?"

Irish sat back on her heels. "I have thought about it. I have even talked to some of the black slaves who have made their way south from the Carolinas to freedom here with the Spanish. Their stories are all full of the dangers, the hostile Indians, poisonous snakes, hunger, losing their way. I have the courage to try it. I'm not sure I have the strength." She sighed and shook her head. "I thought I might have a better chance to buy my freedom by earning the money. But how can I when my mistress takes my hard earned coin and claims I stole it from her? But one thing I know, I will do anything it takes to gain my freedom."

"So if you had the chance, you would gladly make your way to an English colony?" Mariette probed.

Irish nodded. "I may not be a whole lot better off than I am here, but at least I would have my freedom and a chance to better myself. And I would be among people who speak the same language."

Mariette leaned forward to place her hand on Irish's arm, to tell her who she really was, but Irish jumped up, as if embarrassed to have revealed so much.

"I must be going. *Señora* Martín will thrash me again if she thinks I have dallied too long at the market." She leaned down to give Paddy one last pat and he stopped chewing on his bone long enough to give her hand a lick, then she was gone.

Mariette sat with the gown in her lap, watching the Irish woman hurry away down the street toward the market. Perhaps it was best that she hadn't exposed herself to Irish for now. She thought she could trust her, but Irish had said she would do anything for freedom. Would that include betraying an Englishwoman who was bent on rescuing two of the English prisoners of war in exchange for her own freedom? For her own sake, she would trust Irish. But she had Matt and Nate and Douglass to think of, too. Perhaps it was best, until the last possible moment, to keep silent.

By noon, when Mariette went to the docks, she found Nate

already waiting, his eyes shining and a barely suppressed grin on his face. She climbed down into the skiff and Nate set the sail.

"I take it you and Cato found a creek suitable for the escape."

Nate grimaced. "How could you tell? I wanted to surprise you."

Mariette laughed. "Your face is like an open book, Nate. You couldn't hide anything from anybody. Which is another reason you can't come into St. Augustine. You could never pretend to be something you aren't."

"True," her brother admitted. "You and Matt never let me into any of your schemes."

"One look at your face and Mama, or worse, big brother Ty, would know we were up to something. We couldn't let you know our plans."

Nate looked up at her from under a lock of black hair that had fallen across his forehead and grinned. "I'm glad you didn't have any choice about letting me in on this adventure."

She leaned forward and placed a hand on his arm. "It wasn't just a lack of choice, Nate. You were the best man for the job. No one knows the coastal waterways better than you. And no one, except for Papa, is a better sailor."

Nate blushed and turned away to make some unnecessary adjustment to the sail. But she could see a pleased grin on his face, as well.

"So tell me what you and Cato have found."

"I thought I'd show you instead."

She nodded and leaned back as Nate headed into the creek that flowed past Soledad's little homestead. Shortly Nate trimmed the sail and they headed into what looked like a solid bank but instead of land there was a narrow channel with two twists that put them into an even narrower, sluggish stream.

"Isn't this where we hid the *Fortune*?" Mariette scanned the edges of the stream but could find no trace of Nate's little ship.

He grinned. "It's there," he said, pointing.

The ship was in a little cove well-camouflaged with brush. Nate had even fastened branches onto the mast and slathered mud on the hull, which for Nate would have been hard to do. He was proud of his neat, trim little vessel and usually kept her spotless.

The skiff glided past the *Fortune* and after several more twists and turns, Nate let down the sail. He sat back and grinned at her. Then he pointed into a seemingly impenetrable jungle. "Straight through those woods is Ft. Mose."

"Can you bring the *Fortune* this far?"

Nate shook his head. "No, but the skiff can make it. Once Matt and Douglass get this far we can ferry them to the ship. There may be a search in this area so I've found another hiding place for the *Fortune*. We can stay there until the tide turns and then sail home."

Taking out the oars, Nate nudged the skiff into the bank and helped Mariette out. He led the way, but they had gone only a few feet when they were forced to a halt by the undergrowth.

"I see what Cato meant about the woods here being different from those at home." Mariette pulled her skirt loose from some thorny bushes. "How far is it through this to the clearing around the fort?"

Nate stood looking into the tangle of brush with his hands on his hips, a frown of concentration on his face. "We figured about a quarter of a mile."

"That far?" Mariette's heart sank in despair. "How can we ever get two men in shackles through a quarter mile of that before the guards catch up with us?"

Nate turned with a shrug. "Our driveway at home is longer than that."

"Our driveway at home is not clogged with undergrowth."

"Cato and I figure we can clear it by Monday afternoon."

"Two days?" Mariette shook her head. "The two of you can't do it."

Nate turned with a grin. "We've already started. He led her a few feet farther and pointed. She could see a narrow path that was still overgrown but cleared of the worst of the brambles and Spanish bayonet. "We don't have to cut everything," Nate explained. "Just the worst of it. Just enough that the path is still not obvious to anyone not looking for it, but clear enough that Matt and Douglass can get through. Once the path is done we just have to wait until the prisoners start clearing around the fort. When Matt and Douglass get near the path…"

A slow smile spread over Mariette's face. "We can do it. We are going to rescue Matt and Douglass."

Nate's chin came up at a jaunty angle. "Was there ever any doubt?"

When Mariette arrived at Ft. Mose with Alejandro's lunch, the prisoners were not in the fort. They were out in the field clearing around the fort.

Mariette set the lunch down in the shade of the ruined house. She had not expected them to be doing the clearing so soon. For a few moments she watched their steady progress. It would not take them long to reach the woods. Probably not today, but surely by Monday when the path was cleared and all in readiness. With the little diversion she had planned, Matt and Douglass would be able to make their escape and get to the skiff.

This was Saturday. By Monday evening they could well be on their way home. And she would never see Alejandro again. Her gaze went to where he sat astride a horse, his jacket discarded in the heat, his shirt open at the throat and the sleeves rolled up. A slight breeze molded the fine cambric to his sweat-soaked body, outlining every muscle. One hand rested casually on his thigh. The other held the reins loosely.

An almost imperceptible command set the horse into a canter to where Raúl sat much less expertly on his horse brandishing a whip, cracking it uncomfortably close to a prisoner who kept flinching. Alejandro spoke to the guard and Raúl coiled the whip and took out a musket instead.

It was the first time Mariette had seen Alejandro mounted, but from the way he sat the horse, seemingly a part of it, and guided the animal along the line of prisoners, she could tell that he was an even better rider than his uncle.

She feasted on the sight of him. There would be no work tomorrow for the prisoners. There would be the party tomorrow night at Alejandro's uncle's, and then she would be going home. Less than two days. She wanted to memorize every move he made, to take at least the memory of him with her.

She saw Matt toiling along in the sun. Beside him, Douglass worked, and his shirt also clung to him from sweat, but the sight left her as unmoved as looking at Matt. She loved them both, but now she realized that her love for them was the same. Douglass was like a brother to her.

Until Alejandro had come into her life she had not known what love and desire were. But now she knew that what she felt for Douglass was not desire. She would never melt for him, pant for him, want to press herself close to him. She could never marry Douglass now. Not knowing what it could really be like between a man and a woman. She was spoiled. She could never settle for just friendship in a marriage. She had to have passion. And love.

Mariette looked again at Alejandro. Just looking at him made feelings she had never known before well up inside her. She clenched her teeth to keep tears from flowing and made a decision. She would never marry. Not if she couldn't have Alejandro. And she couldn't. He would stay here or return to Spain, and she would return to Charles Town. They would never see each other again.

Would he miss her as she would miss him? Would he ever think of her? Would he marry, raise children? He had never really held her in his arms, but he would probably hold another. The thought of it made her throat tighten so much she could scarcely breathe. She tried to relax, to take a deep shuddering breath. She would do what she had to do. She would rescue Matt and Douglass like she had set out to do. Then she would break her engagement with Douglass and live miserably alone for the rest of her life.

Straightening her shoulders, she took up her water jug. The prisoners would be thirsty, and there were two of them who would be very happy to hear that their rescue was near at hand.

Mariette strode briskly toward the line of toiling men, trying hard not to look at Alejandro as hungrily as she felt. She waved at him when he spotted her but turned toward the men to begin giving them water. When she reached Matt and Douglass they were indeed happy to hear that the escape was set for Monday. But Douglass also had other things on his mind.

"Has he tried to touch you, Mariette?" Douglass took the cup of water from her and drank slowly, giving her time to answer.

Dear, sweet, Douglass. Only he would phrase it that way, asking if Alejandro had tried to touch her. To Douglass there was no question in his mind that she would not allow herself to be 'touched', that she was completely virtuous, trustworthy.

"He is a gentleman, Douglass," she said, taking back the cup to refill it.

Douglass shook his head. "Even a gentleman sometimes–"

"Not Captain de Silva." She handed him a second cup of water.

He held the water thoughtfully for a moment. "It's just that I've seen the way he looks at you." He drank the water quickly and handed back the cup.

She started to move on to the next man but Douglass took hold of her hand. "I've also seen the way you look at him." She let him hold onto her for a brief moment before pulling away. She had felt nothing in his touch. No fire, no thrill.

He did not try to hold on to her. "It's over between us, isn't it, Mariette?"

She looked at her fiancé. He was the same good man she had known all her life. The man she once thought she could spend the rest of her life with. She always knew he was very intelligent. She had not known how very perceptive he was. But standing there red-faced and sweating, chained hand and foot, a prisoner of the Spanish, she could not find it in her to burden him further right now with her decision not to marry him.

"We'll be going home in two days, Douglass. We'll talk about it then. Things will be different once we are back home," she said.

As she turned away to give water to the next man she heard him say, "I think things are already different," but she didn't answer.

Alejandro sat down at a rough wooden table and tossed down several *reales*, calling for wine. A tired, heavyset woman scooped up the coins, set down a cup of wine and shoved it toward him. The blouse gathered loosely over too generous breasts was surprisingly clean as was the establishment. Perhaps he had come to the right place after all. He had always been particular about the women he bedded.

Maria would be expecting him home, would have his dinner waiting. He ruthlessly squashed a twinge of guilt. There was no reason he should feel guilty for what he was about. He was the master in that house and he could do what he pleased. Maria was a servant, not a wife. A wife would let him in her bed and he wouldn't need to be here.

He wanted a woman, and though he had told himself this afternoon that any woman would do, he knew that was not quite true. He wanted one who, well...he wanted Maria.

He sighed and took a drink of the thin, sour wine. He couldn't have Maria. He had watched her all afternoon taking water to the prisoners, talking to them as if they understood her Spanish. They seemed to appreciate her being there and thankfully, there had been no incidents. For the last week, the prisoners had all behaved themselves around her. Better than he had.

He had seen them looking at her, heard their remarks to each other. He had wanted to bash their skulls in. He had wanted to shout at them that she was his and to keep their eyes and their lust to themselves. But she wasn't his. And wouldn't be his. She had made that clear to him night after night when she primly and cautiously walked around him, never touching him, never letting down her guard, never giving him one bit of encouragement or hope that she would ever share his bed.

She wanted to. He knew that from that first kiss they had shared. But she was a good woman and would not settle for anything less than marriage. That was the one thing he could not give her. And not because he was a Spanish don and she a Mestiza servant. He wouldn't have cared if she were pure Indio. Maria was special. She would make any man proud to claim her.

But he could not marry Maria. He was leaving St. Augustine as soon as he could. As soon as Commander Montiano returned from Cuba. And he couldn't take her with him. Not where he was going.

He looked around at the barmaids. He had been without a woman for far too long. He'd thought when he had hired his 'housekeeper' that he had solved his problem. But since Maria was intent on driving him crazy with her beauty, her smile, her skills, her sweetness, yet not let him touch her, he had to find another outlet.

He should have found some scrawny old hag to keep house for him. Then he could at least have brought a willing woman home with him occasionally. But he couldn't bring another woman into the house with Maria there. So he was here, looking over the barmaids and wondering which of them would be willing to slake his lust for a few coins. He shook his head. Had he really descended to this? Disgusted with himself he finished his wine and banged the cup on the table for more.

The same heavy, middle-aged barmaid again filled his cup, leaning low to give him a view of what she had to offer besides wine. He shook his head. He was not that desperate. She gave him a tired, knowing smile and gestured to a young, slender woman working behind the bar.

"You prefer Conchita?"

Alejandro looked at Conchita who smiled prettily at him. She was shorter than Maria and rounder. Voluptuous, with full red lips. Her hair was long and black and straight. Not like Maria's curls that seemed to trap his gaze in every curve. Not like Maria at all.

Suddenly Alejandro stood up, shoving back his chair so hard it fell over. "Hell." He threw down several coins and left. He couldn't have Maria but he didn't want any other woman, either. Yet, just being with her, talking to her, watching her, playing the lute for her, was better than anything these, or any other woman, had to offer him.

He would go home and somehow get through the evening without kissing Maria, without taking her to his bed, without touching her. Hell is what he had said and hell is what she was putting him through, but if hell was filled with Maria, it just might be worth going through.

Mariette jumped when the door slammed open, crashing

against the wall. Paddy ran growling then came to a skidding halt at Alejandro's feet. He gave a tentative wag of his tail, then sat down with a whimper when he did not get his customary pat.

Mariette set down the plates she had been carrying outside to the table and looked up at Alejandro. He was not coming in, was not giving her his easy smile. He just stood there in the doorway, one hand braced against the door he had just violently flung open. Just stood there staring at her.

She cocked her head, wondering why he was acting so strangely. "Are you all right, *Capitán?*" She reached out to him.

For a long moment he continued to stare at her, jaws clenched, the muscle there jumping, his nostrils flaring. "Alejandro." His voice was low and husky.

"What?"

"Alejandro. My name is Alejandro. I want you to call me Alejandro."

She nodded warily. "Very well."

He straightened, his chin coming up. The hand holding the door open dropped to his side. He seemed casual, but there was a strange intensity to him. "Say it. Say my name."

"Alejandro."

"Again."

"*Capitán?*"

With a growl he kicked the door shut behind him so hard she flinched and took a step back. He came right after her, taking her by the arms and pulling her close.

"Alejandro. I'm Alejandro. And you," he took a deep shuddering breath, "are the most beguiling, beautiful, desirable woman I have ever met."

Before she knew what he was about, before she could pull away or even turn her head, his mouth came crashing down onto hers and her breath was no longer her own.

Chapter Thirteen

As soon as his lips touched Maria's, Alejandro knew he had made a mistake. She did not fight him or try to wrench away. He could feel her body melting into his, soft breasts pressed against him, hips warm and sweet, slim thighs slightly parted, even her toes pressed his through the leather of his boots.

He had thought he would steal just one more kiss. Just one more kiss to remember her by when he left St. Augustine. He would take the kiss to treasure and it would be enough.

Just once he wanted to breach the walls she had built around herself, walls stronger than those of *El Castillo*. He wanted to breach those walls, see her one time without her defenses, to hear the syllables of his name fall from those lush lips, to taste just once his name on her lips.

But he had never expected this response from her. Never expected that she wanted him quite as much as he wanted her. Never expected that she would offer no resistance, that her flesh would become one with his the moment the kiss began, that to part from her now would be like tearing flesh from flesh.

How could he stop now what he had started? He wanted her, more now than ever. And she wanted him. Why had they resisted each other for so long?

Her fortress walls were breached, the drawbridge was down. One sweet salvo and she was won, as if she had been waiting for, anticipating—hoping for—his attack.

He deepened the kiss and she followed his lead, softening her lips, parting them, allowing him access. He had told himself that he would not touch her beyond this one kiss. That it wasn't fair to her that he would be leaving soon, that he could not marry her, and she could not go with him. But they were doomed now. She would be his.

He splayed one hand on her back, feeling the indentation of her spine, the narrowness of her waist, the gentle curve of her hips, feeling at last the curve of that sweet little backside he had been watching with such fascination all week. It was firm and solid but with a feminine give that was better than anything his mind had been able to imagine.

His other hand slid down her arm then to the side of her breast. She did not protest or pull away, but her arms slid upward until they were about his neck pulling him even closer. He could feel the softness of her breast against the heel of his hand but she was pressed too close to him for him to cup its fullness. He contented himself with easing his thumb between them to caress over her nipple. He felt it harden instantly and heard her moan softly.

There were too many clothes between them but he didn't want to stop the kiss to fumble with fastenings. But he wanted—needed—to touch her skin. He traced his fingers along her neck down to the barrier of her blouse. He pushed it off her shoulders, enjoying the smoothness of her skin, the ridge of her shoulder blade. He had to have more, to bare more. He trailed a kiss across her cheek, down her neck, over her collarbone, to the rise of her breast and beyond, baring body as he went. The nipple he had felt only briefly with his thumb was a mere inch away from tongue and lips and he hungered for it as he had never hungered for food.

At last it was his and he drew it deeply into his mouth. She gasped and arched her back, going up onto her tiptoes to aid his eager quest. He felt her hands clutching at his neck, holding him in place, urging him onward, as if she feared he might stop what he was doing. Unfounded fear! He reveled in the taste of her, the little gasps and moans he was eliciting from her, the passion that seemed to flow out of her.

Her hands and his moved from neck to back to waist to buttocks in a fevered dance, trying in these brief moments to capture every part, as if to memorize and treasure each one. He reached for her skirt, grasping a handful of it, lifting it and grabbing for more, trying to get to the bottom of it, to touch her thighs. The damned skirt seemed endless. It defied him, falling back down if he let it go, tangling around his hand. But he was adamant. He was determined. And at last he reached his first goal, the silkiness of her thigh.

"Maria! Where are you? Did you know your rice was about to burn?"

Alejandro heard the voice of the Irish slave from next door, and then a loud gasp. He and Maria sprang apart. It was too late to pretend that what Irish had seen was anything other than what it was.

"Oh!" Irish's eyes were wide. "I'm sorry, I…"

Silently cursing the interruption he stepped in front of Maria to give her time to straighten her clothes.

Nodding to the Irish woman as if she were a welcome guest was not easy but politeness was inbred in him. He managed to give her a smile instead of a snarl.

Maria stepped around him, took Irish's arm and led her back to the patio. "Thank you for saving our dinner," he heard her say. Alejandro wanted to punch a wall. Marching into his bedroom he slammed the door closed as hard as he had slammed the front door open a few minutes earlier. He poured cool water into a basin and splashed it over his face and head. What he needed was to roll in a Pyrenees snowfall.

He took a deep breath, drying his face on a linen towel. What he needed was to be shot. Had he no more control than that? Had he not promised himself not to touch Maria? That it was best not to get involved with her since he would be leaving soon? He shook his head. Apparently, when it came to Maria, he had very little control. If she had given him the slightest encouragement, she would have been in his bed days ago. But she was always walking around him cautiously, never coming too close, never giving him the slightest encouragement. And all this time, she had wanted him as much as he wanted her.

But he was the one who had acted on their desires. She was the wise one, the one in control. She had wisely withheld herself from him, knowing how impossible a relationship with a Spanish nobleman would be for a Mestiza servant. She withheld herself, staying pure and chaste until he had kissed her, unleashing all that passion.

She had once run from him when he had kissed her. He should have had more consideration for her. She was not a whore, not a woman he could dally with for a few days or weeks or however long he was here, then desert. She might think it was because of the difference in their stations. With a woman like Maria, the difference in their social stations meant nothing to him. It was because he was leaving that there could be nothing between them but lust.

Well, he chuckled to himself, lust with Maria just might be pretty good. But, he thought, sobering, it would not be fair to a woman like her. He could not take her chastity and then leave her, perhaps even with a child. No, there could be no more dalliance with his 'housekeeper'. No more kisses, no more touching, no more hoping.

He had been so right when he left the tavern. Hell. Between Maria and his Uncle Ignatio, life was going to be hell until he left St. Augustine.

Irish give a last glare at *Capitán* de Silva before allowing Maria to lead her away. Outside she leaned close and asked, "Was he forcing himself on you?" Her eyes were blazing, her hands clenched into fists. Maria could feel the tension in her friend as if she was ready to lash out in her defense. They heard the door to Alejandro's room slam and they both jumped.

"No, Irish, he was not forcing me. But perhaps it is well that you interrupted when you did." She looked away. She could not admit, even to Irish, how much she had hated, yet needed, that interruption.

She felt Irish relax, then, and Mariette let go of her arm. Irish nodded.

"I did not think your *capitán* would do something like that, but if this is something you do not want…"

Mariette laughed to keep from weeping. "Don't worry, Irish. I know how foolish it would be for me to think there could be anything between a Mestiza servant and a Spanish noble." Or between an Englishwoman and a Spaniard when our two countries are at war, she finished to herself.

"If you ever need me…"

Mariette's heart swelled at this offer from someone so vulnerable herself. But she had no doubt that Irish would face down Alejandro and anyone else who would harm her. If only she could protect herself, as well.

Mariette sighed. In just two more days, if all went as planned, she would be gone—and Irish would be with her. She would take

Irish and leave her heart.

She took a deep breath and shook her head. She would do what she needed to do. And right now, supper needed to be taken care of. She went to the counter where Irish had set the rice and lifted the lid. It was dry and just beginning to stick. "Thank you again for saving our dinner, Irish."

Irish shrugged and stirred the lamb stew. Satisfied that it was fine, she pulled some coins from her pocket. "I was wondering if I could keep this here. I did a neighbor's laundry and I don't want to lose my coins again to that old witch who thinks she owns me."

Mariette chuckled at Irish's terrible mixture of Spanish and English. If she didn't know English, she doubted that she would understand half of what her friend said. "Of course you can. Find someplace in the storage room to hide them. I'll tell *Capitán* de Silva not to bother them."

Irish went into the storage room for a moment and when she returned, she patted Paddy then gave Mariette a quick hug before hurrying off to finish making dinner for her mistress.

It was not easy that evening to eat with Alejandro, to sit across from him at the tiny table, knees almost touching, their intimacy heightened by the light of the three candles between them. His hair, damp from a washing, gleamed in the candlelight and she wished she dared to touch it. Instead she held up the bottle of wine beside her. "More wine, *Capitán*?"

He held out his rough pottery cup and she poured the ruby liquid. When he drank, his eyes never left hers. They smouldered. And her body responded. It was as if the *capitán* had shouted, "¡*Atención*!" and her whole body had come to alert attention. Nipples tightened and lifted, her chin came up, eyes widened, breath quickened, and a warmth suffused her.

She forced herself to look down at her plate but she could only move food around, pretending to eat. He set his cup down and she was acutely aware of his movement, the soft clunk of the crude cup on the thick wood of the table, the scrape of his spoon on his plate as he scooped up another mouthful of the lamb and rice. He shifted again. His booted toe touched her bare foot and they both jerked their feet away.

This might be their last dinner together, she thought. Tomorrow was the party so they would eat there. Then Monday, if all went as planned, she would be gone, the escape to take place in the afternoon. She hoped it would not bring down too heavy a penalty on Alejandro. But she could not think of that. She must think of Matt.

This was their last intimate meal together and she could not bring herself to look at him. She did not dare. He would see the longing in her eyes, he would reach across the table and touch her hand, she would lean forward, lips parted in invitation, he would stand, bend toward her and...

Stop it! she told herself. Thinking like that will land you right where he wants you! She dared a quick glance at him. And right where she wanted to be, too. Almost viciously she shoved a spoonful of food into her mouth, trying hopelessly to concentrate on the taste, the texture. But all she could think about was Alejandro, and that in less than two days she would never see him again.

At last she gave up even pretending to eat. She got up with her plate and cup in hand, took them to the counter and put them into the pan to wash them. She heard Alejandro also get up and she held her breath, hoping he would not come near, would not touch her, would not continue what Irish had interrupted.

She didn't look around, but she heard him leave the house, slamming the door as hard when he left as when he had entered. Mariette braced her hands on the counter, hung her head and cried, glad he had left her alone, wishing he had not.

Alejandro stopped short at the end of the street. Just where the hell did he think he was going? Hadn't he been through this once today? He turned and, with fists on hips, glared down the street at his door. He was a man grown and that was his home. If he could not control his desires around one Mestiza serving woman, then he was not much of a man. Admittedly she was one very special Mestiza serving woman. And very lovely. But she did not deserve to be seduced into a relationship she would very likely regret later.

He took a deep breath. He could do this. For Maria's sake if not for his own. It would not be easy, but she would remain untouched while he was in St. Augustine. Just one brisk walk around the plaza to give himself a few minutes to calm down, to steel himself against her provocative charms, to give her time to rebuild her defenses. Then he would return to live in the hell he had created for himself until he could escape.

Mariette allowed herself only a few tears before she swiped them away and straightened. Why should she cry because Alejandro had not pursued her further? Although their reasons might be different, they both knew there could be nothing between them. She should be glad he was an honorable man who would not take advantage of a servant. But she still felt like pounding something, kicking something. Instead she grabbed her dishcloth and attacked the dishes, finishing them in record time. Then she filled a bucket with water and set to mopping a floor that was in no need of cleaning. Paddy yipped and skittered outside, away from the water she was flinging.

She had just about worked out her frustration on the floor

and was wringing out the mop when Paddy came back into the house growling. At the same time a heavy knock sounded on the door. Mariette shoved mop and bucket onto the patio and, shushing Paddy, stared at the door wondering who it could be. Alejandro would not knock. Irish would call out or tap lightly. And Paddy wouldn't be growling at either of them. Who else in St. Augustine would come pounding on her door?

The knock came again, impatient and authoritative, and Mariette's heart began to pound just as hard. Had she been found out? Were there soldiers on the other side of that thick wooden panel waiting to carry her in chains to a cell in *El Castillo*? Had Matt or Douglass inadvertently said something to give her away? Had they found the *Fortune* and Nate? Should she scoop up Paddy and flee while she still had a chance? Or could she simply pretend not to be home? But what excuse could she give to Alejandro if the visitor was looking for him and she had not answered the door?

She straightened, pushed back her hair, and forced herself to calm down. If they were soldiers, there would be musket butts, not a fist, doing the pounding, and they would not have waited this long before breaking in.

Taking a deep breath, she flung open the door. Alejandro's uncle, Ignatio, stood there. His fist was poised to strike the panels again and there was a scowl on his face. But when he saw her the scowl turned to a wolf-like grin. His gaze raked over her and he licked his lips as if he were, indeed, a wolf, ready to devour her. With a flick of his hand he gestured to the two guards with him to remain outside and, without invitation, he moved inside, kicking the door shut behind him.

Mariette had to step backward to keep him at bay but Paddy charged at him, growling. In alarm, she scooped up the puppy and held him close, trying to give him a reassurance she did not really feel herself. She knew she should welcome the commandant in, offer him something to drink, but she could hardly find breath and her heart seemed to be pounding. She swallowed hard to steady herself. It was only a reaction to her previous fear, she told herself. This was Alejandro's uncle, not the feral wolf he seemed at the door. Well, not at the door anymore. He was well inside looking around, loosening his cravat.

Uncertain why she should be feeling so ill at ease, she at last found her manners. Perhaps he would excuse her since he thought her no more than a servant who would naturally be awed and fearful in the presence of her 'betters'.

"Welcome, Commandant. *Capitán* Alejandro is not at home but you are welcome to wait for him. Would you like to come sit outside where it is cooler?"

Paddy continued to growl and wriggle to get free so he could chase this intruder away. Nothing she did was soothing him so she thrust him inside Alejandro's bedroom and shut the door. She could hear him continuing his growling, scratching to get out to bite the commandant's leg.

When she turned around she was surprised to find that the commandant had followed her. She backed against the door and he leaned a hand against it, beside her head.

"I'm sure Alejandro will not be long. Could I offer you some wine?" She tried to slide away from him but he leaned into her, pinning her where she stood.

"He will not be long, hmmm? Then we haven't any time to lose." With his free hand he fingered her hair, then caressed her jaw.

Mariette turned away from his touch, and Paddy's yipping and scratching turned as frantic as the pounding of her heart. Her breathing was quick and shallow through her parted lips. She had told the commandant that Alejandro would be home soon, but would he? She had no idea.

Ignatio chuckled and his hand slid around her throat, holding her prisoner with that hand while the other began a slide down her arm, across her chest, and down to cup one breast.

"I'll wager you do not turn away from Alejandro's touch, do you?"

She gasped when he pinched the tip of her breast, holding it painfully. She tried to wiggle out of his grasp but he pressed harder against her throat.

What could she do? This man was the most powerful in the colony, commander of the fort, uncle to Alejandro. She was supposed to be a mere servant.

He shoved a knee between her thighs and she knew that, no matter who he was, she was not going to peacefully submit to being raped. One of his knees was between hers, but one of hers was also between his. As hard as she could she lifted that knee, aiming for the most vulnerable place on a man, that part her brothers had taught her to aim for if ever cornered.

The commandant must have felt her shift her weight because he stepped back and away from harm just in time. "I take it you do not like our little game."

There was a quick rap on the door and the commandant stepped completely away from her. "That is my guard," he explained. "Alejandro must be returning." He raked her again with his wolf-like gaze and straightened his clothing, tightening his cravat.

"Perhaps we can continue this at another time," he said, giving her a smile that she would have thought charming in another situation. She simply glared at him.

The door crashed open and Alejandro stood poised in the doorway, balancing lightly on the balls of his feet, ready to spring whichever way he needed to…a warrior on full alert.

Ignatio turned toward the intrusion, spreading his hands innocently wide. "Alejandro! Maria said you would return at any moment. I was just assuring myself that she would indeed be attending our little gathering tomorrow night. Inés would be devastated if you didn't bring her."

Alejandro glanced quickly at Mariette and she nodded assuringly to him in response to his unspoken question whether she was all right. He apparently knew what his uncle was like but she did not want to be the cause of any further enmity between the two of them.

"I have already promised Aunt Inés that we will be there, Uncle," Alejandro said inclining his head in frosty politeness. Then he stood aside, his arm out in an invitation for the man to leave. "If there is nothing else?"

"No, there is nothing else." Ignatio gave Mariette a lustful look, licking lips and raising brows. "Not at this time." He gave a brief bow to each of them. "Until later."

When Alejandro shut the door behind his uncle, Mariette slumped in relief. Should she tell him what his uncle had tried to do? She looked at the tight set of his mouth, the tension in his shoulders. Whatever was between the two of them, she wanted no part in it. They could work out their problems without her adding to them. After all, she would be gone from here in two days. Then Ignatio de Silva would simply be a bad memory.

Alejandro took a step toward her, uncertainly holding out his hand. "Are you all right?"

She managed to stand up straight and paste a smile on her face. "I'm fine."

"My uncle didn't...?" He let the question hang.

She shook her head, unable to answer more than that.

Alejandro seemed ready to take her into his arms to comfort her. His hand faltered mere inches from her hair. But they both knew where that would lead and he let his hand drop.

He gave her a falsely bright smile. "Then if you are sure you are fine, would you please release Paddy before he gnaws a hole through my door trying to protect you?"

"Oh!" She turned to the bedroom door and pushed it open. A still growling Paddy charged into the room. He sniffed around the perimeter, satisfying himself that the intruder was gone. Then he plunked himself down between them and seemed to grin proudly, expecting to be thanked for dispelling the threat.

Mariette and Alejandro laughed and both bent to pet him, flinching each time their fingers happened to touch.

Chapter Fourteen

MARIETTE LOOKED DOWN AT THE BASKET OF SWEET POTATO muffins sitting on the rough table on the little patio. As soon as Alejandro had left to check on the prisoners she had gone to the market to meet Soledad, and Soledad had pressed them into her hand.

"For the captain," she had said. "Keep him in a good mood so he don't suspect nuthin'."

What a lie. Her whole relationship with Alejandro was based on lies. She wasn't really a Mestiza, she wasn't a servant, she didn't even belong in the colony. And she sure couldn't make sweet potato muffins like these.

There was only one part of their relationship that was true. She wanted Alejandro more fiercely than she had ever wanted anything in her life. She closed her eyes. She wanted to put her arms around him and have him kiss her and touch her. All over. She wanted no barriers between them. No lies. No clothes. And it was the one thing she couldn't have.

Her eyes popped open. And why not? She was no longer committed to Douglass. Even he knew that. There was no one else in her bleak future. After Alejandro, how could there be? Unless she lay in Alejandro's arms, she would never know what is was like to love a man. Unless Alejandro took her to his bed, she would never know what it was like to be possessed by a man. Unless she gave herself to Alejandro, she would never know the joy of giving herself to any man.

But how could she give herself to him when she would be gone tomorrow? She looked around at the little patio where she and Alejandro had shared the meals Irish or Soledad had helped her prepare. She was no cook. That part was a lie. But it would be no lie to give herself to Alejandro.

And what if she got pregnant? She put her hand on her abdomen, smiling softly. A baby? Something to always remind her of him. Something that would be part of them both.

She had only one night left. She could not stay in St. Augustine, but she could have one night to treasure, to remember when she went home. She could think of no one else she wanted to 'save' herself for. She wanted Alejandro. And tonight, she decided, she would have him. One night out of her whole life that she would do what she wanted to do and the dictates of society be damned.

She broke apart a muffin and sank her teeth into it. Tonight. After the party. She would be his.

Alejandro hurried through the market on his way home from the fort. Already vendors were packing up their wares and there were few shoppers wandering about. It had taken him longer than he expected to check on the prisoners, to see to giving them an opportunity to bathe and some time outside their cramped cell, and he was worried about Maria. He had not wanted to leave her so long unprotected.

He loosened his stock and unbuttoned a couple of buttons of his vest. It was more than the heat of the day that was causing him to sweat. He knew his uncle was not finished with Maria. He didn't expect Ignatio to return so soon but if he did, Paddy would not be much help to her.

Just what he needed. Someone else to worry about. As if keeping his own neck out of his uncle's greedy clutches was not enough. He had protested when Maria started coming out to Ft. Mose to bring his lunch and take water to the prisoners. Now he was glad. She would be under his watchful eye. But she was home in the mornings, easy prey for his uncle. How could he protect her then?

Should he insist that she come with him in the morning as well? He shook his head. He had hired her to clean his home and cook his meals. She couldn't do her job if she was never there. But he had gotten her into this mess by hiring her in the first place. He had to protect her. He thought of her backed up against the door, terrified from his uncle's visit but trying so bravely not to show it. He had wanted to scoop her up in his arms and comfort her then in the age-old way of a man and a woman. He could not do that to her. He would be leaving here as soon as he could and he would not leave Maria alone and possibly with a child of his to care for. No, it was not just his uncle he would have to protect her from. It was his own horny desires—and hers as well, if he had read her response to his kiss aright.

He should have hired some dried up old crone.

He sighed as he headed out of the market and into the *Calle del Gobinero*, the Street of the Governor. His uncle would have found Maria sooner or later on his own. He was an expert at finding and defiling the innocent. At least this way, Maria had some protection. But now he was trapped. Even if an opportunity presented itself, he could not leave St. Augustine until after Ignatio returned to Cuba. He would die a little bit every time he looked at her and had to turn away. And he had to turn away from Maria. He had to leave her as untouched as he had found her. If his uncle only knew the hell he was going through, it would greatly satisfy his sadistic pleasure.

How out of place she felt, Mariette thought. It had to be the dress. She smoothed the embroidered stomacher and fingered the soft coral silk of her skirt. She looked around Alejandro's little two-room house as she waited for him to finish getting ready for his uncle's party. She had never felt odd or out of place here in spite of the fact that she was used to something much grander, that here she was servant instead of mistress, that she was English in the stronghold of the Spanish enemy.

It was the dress. This was the kind of clothing she was used to, the kind of clothing she wore at home just as often as she wore the simple garb she had donned for her disguise as a Mestiza servant. Perhaps she felt so out of place simply because the dress made her feel so English. The design was pure English with its flowers and light colors, not a stiff, reserved Spanish design, and she wondered if it had come from one of the English ships taken as a prize of war she and Nate had seen in the harbor.

Other than Alejandro's tiny shaving mirror there was no way for her to see how the dress looked on her, but Irish, helping with her hair out on the patio, had gone on and on in her Irish-tinted English about how fine she looked. They had just been finishing when Alejandro came home and went straight to his room. Now she waited for him impatiently. She could only hope he would like what he saw because as soon as he came out that door she was going to begin her campaign to get herself into his bed tonight.

She grinned and rocked up onto her toes, clasping her hands behind her. She did not think it was going to be much of a campaign. Indeed, she would have to be careful or she just might end up in his bed instead of dancing at his uncle's party. She knew what all those smoldering looks were that he had been giving her ever since he had literally run into her in the market.

When the door to Alejandro's room opened, Mariette turned, tilting her head to give him the most provocative smile she knew how to give. It worked because he came to a complete halt in his doorway, one hand holding his tricorn hat and the other still on the door latch. His eyes widened and his gaze travelled over her. She saw his hand tighten on his hat, saw him swallow.

He was not the only one affected. It was the first time she had seen him in anything other than his uniform or the casual shirt and breeches he wore in the evenings. Tonight he looked every inch the fine nobleman and as out of place in this simple home as she did.

His cream silk coat, matched by his waistcoat, was embroidered in colored flowers similar to those on her stomacher. She wanted to run her hands over his waistcoat, touch the fine cambric of his shirt, lift her face to his for a kiss... She found herself swallowing hard, not sure when she had taken her last breath. The first salvo had been fired in her campaign and she had no idea which of them had taken the worse hit.

Lifting her chin, she stepped close to him, lightly touching the embroidery on his waistcoat. "It seems we are a pair."

His eyes gleamed as he looked at her. She warmed beneath his gaze as his eyes seemed to warm. "It was not by chance, Maria."

She cocked her head. "No?"

"No. I would have everyone know that you are mine."

He leaned over her, his mouth softening, his lips parting and she thought then that he would kiss her. She lifted her face to his and her eyes were beginning to close in anticipation when his head snapped up, he straightened and he stepped backward, away from her, his eyes cooling.

She followed, pressing closer. She could feel her skirt swirl about his feet and legs, touching him enticingly. Again fingering his waistcoat, she slipped her fingers between two buttons, the back of her hand touching the fine cambric shirt beneath. She felt the warmth of him, felt the rise and fall of his chest quicken.

"Am I yours, Alejandro?" she whispered.

He ignored her question. Instead, he took her wrist in a gentle, but unbreakable grip and pulled her fingers free of him. His mouth was no longer soft. It was hard, his lips thin. "If you are ready, we should be going."

If it had not been for the slight trembling she felt in the hand that held her wrist, she would have thought him completely unaffected by her. Not a word about how lovely she looked, not the smile and twinkling eyes she had come to expect from him every time he looked at her. If not for that tremble, she would have thought he preferred the servant to the lady. But she knew he wanted her.

Perhaps it was simply that he had promised his aunt and uncle they would come to their party that held him back for now. Very well, she could wait until after the party. But she would make him pay for this little setback. If there was one thing she knew how to do and do well, it was flirt. Giving him a smile—that her brothers would have known instantly meant danger—she stepped away from him, turned in a way that set her skirts twirling, scooped up her small matching bag and light shawl, and swayed toward the door. He could not see the victorious grin that came to her face when she heard his growl of frustration.

She almost felt sorry for him...and the evening had just begun.

Alejandro looked at his 'housekeeper' through narrowed eyes as they made their way the short distance through St. Augustine's streets to his uncle's house. There was something different about Maria tonight—and it wasn't just the gown she wore.

Her hair was styled and curled and pinned in a way that

confounded his male senses. He knew it was a typical high-piled fashion. He had seen similar styles at court in Spain, but Maria's night-black hair seemed to make the style completely new. And though he knew the elaborate coils and curls were held together by an army of pins, it looked like it would all come tumbling softly down into his hands if only he could find the one key pin that locked it all together. It was a puzzle. Like Maria.

He knew she was a simple colonial servant, but she wore the hairstyle and elegant gown as if they were completely familiar to her, as if she wore them every day. And then there was her strange behavior this evening. He glanced sideways at her. That smile, for example. It was more like a smirk. Like she knew something he didn't, some secret she wasn't about to share. It made him want to drag her right back to his bed, shove her down on it, find that key pin to loosen her hair, and kiss the secret from her. He forced that image from his mind. That was just piling wood on the hell fires he had already created for himself.

Alejandro heard the music from his uncle's house when they were still two doors away. He put his hand on the small of Maria's back, thinking to comfort and assure her. He smiled down at her, expecting to see his Mestiza servant apprehensive and unsure of herself. What he saw made his brows arch in surprise and puzzlement. There was a happy glow on her face, a look of anticipation, and although she really was walking, it seemed more like she was dancing in time with the music. It just added to the puzzle.

A servant ushered them inside Uncle Ignatio's house, taking her bag and shawl and his hat. Alejandro spotted his Aunt Inés and she waved and headed toward them, her hands outstretched in greeting. Ignatio also saw them enter, and excusing himself from the man he was talking to, headed their way.

"Alejandro! It is so good to see you again. I am so glad I have family here in the colony." Aunt Inés took his hands in hers and stood on tiptoe to receive his kiss on her cheek.

"Aunt Inés, may I present Maria…" Alejandro faltered. It suddenly dawned on him that he didn't even know Maria's last name.

His aunt's cheeks pinked, but, ever gracious, she pretended not to notice and simply turned to Maria, took her hand and welcomed her with a kiss to her cheek.

"Alejandro tells me I have you to thank for the gift of this lovely gown," Maria said.

Still holding Maria's hands, Aunt Inés leaned back to survey her. She glanced up at Alejandro. "The gown looks lovely on you. It is just right for your coloring, my dear."

"It was generous of you to give it to me."

"I see now that it was a completely wrong choice for my daughter. She probably never would have worn it anyway," Aunt Inés said. "I am glad to see it put to proper use."

"Ahh, Inés," Ignatio's voice grated like sandpaper, intruding. "I see you have met Alejandro's lovely…housekeeper."

Alejandro noticed that his uncle paused before the word 'housekeeper' just long enough to give it a questionable meaning, causing not only his wife, but Maria to blush. Maria's head came up proudly, however, and Aunt Inés, bless her, squeezed Maria's hand even more warmly.

"Commandant." Maria inclined her head as graciously as a duchess. But she warily kept her distance.

Good girl, Alejandro thought.

His Aunt Inés cast a quick glance from Maria to Ignatio, and Alejandro thought, she knows. He had often wondered just how much his aunt knew about Ignatio's escapades, how he terrorized the serving girls, the mistresses he kept and how he mistreated them. But even if she knew, what could she do about it? Nothing, if she valued her own safety.

"There is another reason Aña would not wear that dress,

Alejandro." Inés's eyes were shining and her cheeks pinked again. She fanned herself and Alejandro could tell she was fairly bursting for him to ask for the reason. He would not disappoint her.

"And why is that, *Tia* Inés?"

Inés leaned closer and spoke modestly behind her fan, but proudly and loudly enough for all to hear. "She will need something larger. She is going to have a baby. Our first grandchild! We had a letter today!"

Alejandro and Maria both chimed their congratulations. Alejandro could tell that his uncle was also pleased, but would never admit it.

"Bah! Women and babies! They think of babies when I am near to ruin."

Alejandro looked at his uncle with a lifted questioning brow.

"I've also had a letter today and the news was not good. That pirate, Sean Fortune, has taken another ship and with it a good portion of the sugar from my plantation in Cuba."

It was Mariette's turn to fan herself. She knew exactly which ship Ignatio was talking about. It was sitting in Charles Town harbor at this very moment being refitted to add to her father's fleet. He had brought it in just three days before he and Mama left to take Ty to Boston. As a very successful privateer in this war, her father had taken many Spanish prizes.

"If I could have that bastard in hand for one day…" Ignatio's hand came up, fingers curling into grasping claws that slowly closed as if upon his enemy, tightening, trapping, crushing.

Mariette swallowed hard and fanned herself faster. If he knew who stood here beside him… If he knew who he held prisoner in the Castillo… And, oh, God! Nate! If he found out he had three of Sean Fortune's children within reach, he could indeed exact his revenge. She felt weak but she knew that now was not the time to show that weakness. She had come this far. Hopefully, she and

Matt and Douglass and Nate, and Irish, too, would be on their way home by this time tomorrow.

Mariette clutched at the one word Ignatio had used that would stiffen her spine with enough anger to get her through this evening—pirate. He had called her father a pirate. He was not a pirate. Maybe Grandpapa had once been a pirate, but her father was a privateer with legal letters of marque to raid the Spanish during this war.

"Is this the same privateer who has troubled you before, Uncle?" Alejandro asked.

Mariette gave Alejandro a brief smile of thanks. Not that he would ever know what she was thanking him for, but she was glad, nonetheless, that he had used the term privateer and not pirate.

Ignatio waved a hand in disgust. "Not just me, but half the Spanish Main. But we'll catch him someday and he will pay for his crimes."

"In the meantime," Inés boldly cut in, "let us think on more pleasant things for this evening. We will have dancing after dinner."

Alejandro smiled down at his aunt who was trying to keep the tone of her party a happy one.

"I already told them," Ignatio said, as if correcting a recalcitrant child.

Inés colored again, casting down her eyes and fumbling with her fan, and for this small slight alone, of a woman who lived only to love and care for others, Alejandro could have hated his uncle. But over the years he had seen so many more. "Of course, Ignatio," she said.

"Well!" Ignatio rubbed his palms together briskly. Then he turned avaricious eyes toward Maria, looking her up and down as if evaluating a slave in the market. He stepped closer to her and took her by the upper arm, his thick fingers wrapping tightly about her delicate skin. "Come, my dear, I'll show you around."

He clearly meant to shut out anyone else, but Alejandro was not about to let his uncle take Maria off to some secluded spot and do God knew what with her. He took his place on Maria's other side, and placed his hand at the small of her back. "Thank you, Uncle. I did not have time for Aunt Inés to show me your home the last time I was here."

Ignatio threw him a black look but smiled at him in a way that said Alejandro might have won that round, but he would win in the end.

Alejandro was sure Ignatio's tour was cut short by his presence, but they made the rounds of the public rooms, stopping to chat and be introduced to the other guests.

"You may have seen some of these people before, my dear," Ignatio said to Maria, "but I doubt that you have ever been formally introduced."

Alejandro almost laughed out loud at Ignatio's pretentious words. As if this small colony contained an abundance of nobility! His uncle was only trying to humiliate Maria by implying that one of her status could not possibly know anyone of any importance in the colony.

Ignatio stopped beside one of his guests. "*Señor* Lopez, may I present Maria?"

An older man turned and when he saw Maria he smiled broadly and reached to take both of her hands. "Maria! How are you tonight? You have made the evening shine!" He winked at Ignatio. "Maria and I are already acquainted, Commandant. She comes to my shop and bargains so sharply that I sometimes think I pay her to take my good meat."

Maria laughed. "I pay you outrageously for those tiny strips of lamb, but you are such an old man I take pity on you and try to keep you in business by agreeing to your inflated prices."

Señor Lopez's eyes twinkled. "Each time you come into my shop I am so overcome by your beauty that I give you twice what you pay for. You will soon make me a ruined man."

Ignatio impatiently waved away their teasing. "I'm sure the business I have given you for tonight's party alone will save you from ruin, *Señor* Lopez," Ignatio said. The grin that had been on his face moments ago had now faded.

The merchant gave Ignatio a small bow. "I am certainly grateful for your business, Commandant. I hope I may continue to serve the needs of your household."

Señor *Lopez* turned back to Maria. "I hope you will save at least one dance for an old man."

Maria chuckled. "If you really think you can keep up with me!"

Oh, God! The dancing! Alejandro thought. How could he have been so stupid. Where could Maria have learned to dance? At best she knew some simple village dances. She would be lost trying to dance the complicated steps of the formal dances tonight. Another embarrassment to protect her from.

Ignatio introduced them to several more people before leading her toward the dining room. "Alejandro, since I am taking Maria in to dinner, would you be so kind as to bring your aunt? I would hate for her to have to find her way alone."

Alejandro doubted that Aunt Inés would have trouble finding her own dining room or that his uncle was really concerned about his wife not having a partner for dinner, but it would be rude to leave the hostess with no one to see her in to her own table. Maria was safe for the moment. There were enough people milling about, beginning to head in to dinner.

Alejandro inclined his head toward his uncle in acquiescence and went to find his aunt.

"You were right about Maria, Alejandro," his aunt said as he was seating her. "She is very much a lady. And a lovely girl. I'm glad I got the chance to meet her."

Alejandro squeezed her hand gently. "Thank you for making her welcome in your home."

There were about fifty people at the party, seated at two tables. Ignatio had managed to separate Alejandro from Maria for the meal since Alejandro had to stay with his aunt, and she played hostess at one table while Ignatio headed up the other one.

But by turning his head slightly Alejandro was able to see Maria. She seemed to be enjoying herself even though she was seated next to Ignatio. She spent most of her time talking to *Señor* Lopez and an older woman. But one time he caught her eye. She was just picking up her wine glass and was looking his way when he turned to check on her. She stopped with the glass halfway to her lips and stared at him over its rim, and he felt as if everything else faded away except for the two of them.

Her wine was red and he could almost imagine it breaking into a boil from the heat he felt between them. And then she laughed. And winked at him! Winked! He could have throttled her! What was she doing to him? But she seemed totally unaffected, turning back to her friend to chat. Probably talking about the price of lamb chops while he squirmed uncomfortably imagining them back at home with her in his bed, her hair in unpinned abandonment.

He turned back to his own dinner partner, a waspish wife of one of the officers at the fort. He needed to get his mind off thoughts of Maria in bed. It shouldn't be long before Governor Montiano returned. Then Ignatio would be gone, Maria would be out of danger, and he could at last be on his way out of this blasted colony...and away from his own danger and possible death.

He would also be away from Maria, away from temptation, away from the most tantalizing woman he had ever met. He was born and bred a noble and when it came to Maria, he would have to be just that—noble. He would not dishonor her. He would not take her to his bed and then abandon her.

He would not.

When the dinner was over, servants began clearing away the tables, making room for the dancing to come. A different set of musicians was taking its place in one corner, tuning instruments, sorting through sheets of music. Maria chatted in happy conversation with his aunt and another woman, and Ignatio was giving instructions to the musicians, one hand punctuating his orders with a sternly pointing finger.

As the strains of the first song filled the air, Ignatio headed directly for Maria. Alejandro set down his wineglass and hurried to intercept, hoping that his uncle merely meant to ask his own wife to dance. But no, it was Maria Ignatio had his sights set on. As Alejandro approached the group, Ignatio was already bowing over her hand.

"Will you do me the honor of opening the dance with me?" Ignatio asked Maria.

Maria flicked her fan open and shut and glanced at her hostess, at the woman who should have been asked to open the dance. "I wouldn't want to…"

Ignatio's face began to darken, but before she could be submitted to further insult, Inés reached out to pat Maria's hand. "You run along, my dear. I need to freshen up." Giving Maria's hand a squeeze, and a cautionary glance to Alejandro, Inés hurried from the room.

"Perhaps Maria does not want to dance," Alejandro said trying to save her the embarrassment of admitting that, as a serving girl, she had never learned the intricate steps of the Allemande the musicians were playing.

"Of course she wants to dance. Every woman wants to dance. Unless she does not know how?" Ignatio laughed, but it was not a light dismissing laugh. It was a challenge, as if he were hoping to humiliate her. It was a tactic Alejandro had seen his uncle use more than once. Ignatio had singled Maria out as his next prey and was on the hunt. Alternately charming and vicious to confuse, humiliate, then dominate and control.

It was the same tactic he was trying to use on his nephew, giving him lowly guard duty, the worst of conditions, waiting for the worst to happen so he could take control of his very life.

Maria dropped her fan to let it dangle by its cord from her wrist and, chin held high, she laid her hand on Ignatio's arm, inclined her head in regal acceptance of his challenge and allowed herself to be swept to the head of the room. Alejandro could only watch and hope she could follow the steps well enough to get through the dance.

Once Ignatio and his partner were on the floor, other couples joined to form the squares of the dance and Alejandro watched in amazement as Maria executed the steps as flawlessly as a trained courtesan. But he couldn't help gritting his teeth each time the pattern called for Ignatio to hold Maria's hand while they turned or when he put his arms about Maria in the embraces of the dance.

He hated having to allow his uncle to touch her at all. But he could hardly accuse his uncle of molesting a serving girl during a dance. Even when Ignatio stepped closer and held Maria tighter than the dance required, the man stayed within the bounds of propriety—barely.

Ignatio was smiling and Alejandro could see that he was making small talk with Maria when they came close in the dance. His ploy to humiliate had failed. He would try charming to throw her off balance. Alejandro could only hope he would be there when his uncle decided to swoop in for the conquest. And that time could not be far away. Surely Ignatio's days in St. Augustine were dwindling. Governor Montiano would return soon.

When the Allemande ended Alejandro was waiting to take Maria as his own partner. Ignatio continued to hold Maria's hand as if he planned to partner her in every dance of the evening.

"May I have this dance?" Alejandro asked her.

"She already has a partner, Nephew." Ignatio held Maria's hand tighter, a victorious expression on his face.

Alejandro opened his mouth to retort but Maria forestalled him, deftly pulling her hand free and placing it in Alejandro's. "You flatter me too much," she said to Ignatio. "Your other guests will be devastated if I were to keep you all to myself. Alejandro will have to put up with me for a dance or two." Smiling, she turned away from Ignatio and gazed up at Alejandro.

If she could have seen the look his uncle gave her, she would have been quaking in fear. He did not like being bested, especially not by those he considered his inferiors...and most especially not by a mere woman. But there was naught he could do but give her a stiff bow and stomp away to stalk some other female guest.

The musicians began a contredanse, a simple enough set, but only if you knew the steps. Alejandro led Maria to line up with other couples to form a set.

"You continue to surprise me, Maria."

She merely cocked her brow at him as she moved to the line of women and out of earshot.

When they came together for a turn, he continued. "Where did a Mestiza serving girl learn to dance?"

She shrugged and gave him a smug little grin. "At home." Then she was gone again in the lacy pattern of the dance.

There were not many chances to talk while doing the footwork required in the line of dancing, sliding sideways, clapping hands, making the star formation with others. He would have to wait until they were home again before he could question her about this latest mystery. And from that superior little grin she was giving him—and from his past experience with her—he doubted that he would get much information from her at all.

Chapter Fifteen

THE NEXT DANCE OF THE WAS A FOLIES D'ESPAGNE, AND, once again, Alejandro was her partner. It was a complicated dance but with many chances for her to brush close to him. She knew she was playing with fire by baiting him, but tonight she wanted to burn, to be branded with his imprint, to take home with her a memory of passion to keep close to her for the rest of her life.

She enjoyed dancing and had learned every dance her teacher would show her, including some that were seldom performed in the polite society of Charles Town. The Folies d'Espagne was complicated, but she had learned it well. She could move through the steps almost without thinking. Alejandro was having far more trouble than she was. But he was a good dancer, smoother than his uncle, and certainly more enjoyable to dance with.

She laughed out loud as she used her fan in one of the movements of the dance, fanning herself then hiding her face behind it, peeping coquettishly up at Alejandro. He scowled at her as he moved uncertainly into the next step of the dance. His fumble made her smile even more smugly. He knew the steps. She was causing his uncertainty, not the dance. He was mystified by her actions and she planned to keep him off balance until he fell into his bed tonight—with her.

She would give him no time to continue his questions about her. Let him wonder all he liked about where she learned to dance. Let him guess all he wanted about her upbringing. She would soon be gone and he would never know that she was a member of a rather wealthy English family with plantations and a shipping empire that stretched from Charles Town to the Caribbean to Europe. And if Alejandro tried to pursue the matter, she had the perfect distraction planned.

Tonight, her perfect gentleman who had studiously been avoiding touching her because she had said 'no' was in for a surprise. His housekeeper' was finally going to say 'yes'. In fact, she was planning to make a few rather indecent demands.

She brushed her fan across Alejandro's cheek in one of the movements of the Folies d'Espagne, drawing it along his jawline slower and more lingeringly than the dance called for, pulling him toward her. He leaned close, his gaze intent, his breathing quicker than the exertions of the dance should have caused. His lips parted and she could feel his warm breath on her cheek, sending fire coursing through her. Hastily she moved back a step. She was playing with fire but she hadn't planned to get singed quite so early in the evening.

With the next movement, she made good use of her fan to cool her burning cheeks. She wanted to inflame Alejandro, but she needed to keep her own head cool. She needed to remember that the danger she was in here in Spanish St. Augustine was far from over.

When Ignatio claimed the next dance she felt like her hand was being held by a toad. One of those poisonous ones from the Central American jungles she had heard about.

Fortunately, the dance ended quickly, the musicians decided to take a break, and Alejandro was waiting to claim her once again, and lead her outside into the slightly cooler air of the garden. Inés was sitting on a bench and they joined her. Servants brought light refreshments to the guests, most of whom were also taking advantage of the cooler garden.

"Alejandro, would you play the lute during our break?" Inés asked.

He nodded and a servant soon placed an instrument in his hands, and he began the laborious process of tuning it. Mariette smiled as she watched him, knowing that it usually took him several minutes to tune. The break just might be over before he finished.

Suddenly the instrument was jerked from his hands. Ignatio stood over him with the lute, motioning a servant to bring a chair. "Bah! You never could tune a lute properly, Nephew." Seating himself Ignatio bent to the task and in moments had the fourteen strings vibrating in perfect harmony as he played a few testing chords. Then he returned the instrument to Alejandro.

Mariette fanned herself languidly and listened as Alejandro began to play. His uncle was right. Alejandro's playing sounded far better tonight with a properly tuned instrument. She thought of the evenings when he had struggled so long to get it tuned and wondered if it had been Ignatio who had taught him to play.

She still felt uneasy in Ignatio's presence after his attack on her, but she also knew that many men in positions of power seemed to feel it was their right to treat the females serving them in any fashion they pleased. She had heard some horrid tales of some of the slave owners back in Charles Town. Men who would defend the honor of their own wives and daughters to the death but who had no such feelings when it came to forcing their attentions on their hapless slaves. She was glad her own family had never owned slaves.

Perhaps Ignatio would not be so bad, respectful even, if she and Alejandro were married. Her hand tightened on her fan. That would never happen and she would be gone from St. Augustine long before she became any closer acquainted with Alejandro's relatives. For now, she would relax and enjoy the evening…and anticipate the night ahead. Her last here before she left St. Augustine—and Alejandro—forever.

Alejandro played several songs she did not recognize but which had a Spanish flavor. Then he played one by Vivaldi that she did know. With a wistful, faraway look in his eyes, he began playing another song she knew well, an English composition. Almost immediately the lute was jerked once again from his hands.

"You may enjoy English music, Nephew, as you seem to naturally enjoy all things English, but I'll not have it in my house."

Mariette looked at Alejandro curiously. He enjoyed all things English? Why naturally? Was this the source of the enmity, that rubbed painfully like a stone in a shoe, between uncle and nephew? No, the enmity was too deep. There had to be more to the story. A story she would like to know but there would be no time tonight to ask, and tomorrow, she would be gone.

Ignatio sat down and cradled the lute in his arms, readjusting the tuning. Then he began to play, and groups of guests scattered about the garden who had been talking quietly while Alejandro played, now hushed and began drifting closer.

Mariette couldn't blame them. While Alejandro played well and was enjoyable to listen to, his Uncle Ignatio was a master, commanding silence and attention. Every guest was soon gathered around them in hushed appreciation. When he finished the song, applause and cries of, "Bravo!" came from the guests with quick appeals for more.

Shrugging, Ignatio carelessly strummed across the strings while he thought. Then, he looked directly at Mariette, one brow raised provocatively and a slow smile grew. Without taking his eyes from her he began to play, another piece by Vivaldi, a slow and sensuous piece that she had never before heard played to such perfection. It was a piece that, for her, could nearly bring her to tears. Now, hearing it played so masterfully, she felt a swelling in her chest and tears began to form but she was too entranced by the music to bother brushing them away. Ignatio's fingers slowed on the last chords of the song, drawing them out, and his grin widened triumphantly. Mariette felt like she could not quite catch her breath, could not disengage her gaze from his. Then wild applause broke out and she felt that she had been released from a spell. A beautiful spell cast by a devious enchanter.

She wrenched her gaze away then, and found Alejandro. He was standing, applauding his uncle along with the rest of the guests.

"Wonderful, Uncle," Alejandro said. "I don't think I will ever be able to play half so well."

"I don't think so, either, Alejandro, though I did my best to teach you."

In spite of entreaties to continue, Ignatio stood up and handed the instrument back to a servant. "I see that the musicians have returned to their places. Shall we continue the dance?" Then he was gone, taking the hand of a merchant's wife to begin the dancing.

Ignatio danced with several of his guests while Alejandro alternated between partnering Mariette and his Aunt Inés. Neither of them lacked for partners when he was not dancing with them, but Alejandro seemed wary of his uncle, making sure that Mariette had himself or some stolid merchant or soldier for a partner for each dance.

Most of the guests had left by the time the musicians announced the last dance of the evening. It was to be a sarabande. Mariette caught Alejandro's eye from across the dance floor and her heart pounded. A sarabande was seldom done any more. It was considered far too sensual for polite company. But she had seen

Ignatio speaking to the musicians and was sure he had ordered the dance because he was bearing down on her with a glitter in his eyes.

He had almost reached her when Alejandro took her hand. "I think it only proper for a man to partner the woman he escorted for the last dance, Uncle." Inclining his head he swept Mariette away, but not before she saw the look on Ignatio's face—pure, unadulterated hatred.

She might have other things on her mind for tonight, but sometime before she left tomorrow, she was now determined to ask Alejandro why his uncle seemed to hate him. For the present, she was going to enjoy this last dance with Alejandro.

This dance of slow cadence and close embraces was perfectly suited for her to begin her night's seduction. Of the few guests left to enjoy the last dance, fewer still took places to participate. It was not one many knew since it was generally considered too scandalous to be performed. More often, a sarabande was only played to be listened to. But tonight Ignatio had ordered it played for the dancers.

Mariette was just glad that Alejandro had so gallantly stepped in to save her from a mauling by his uncle. Little did he know that he was going to receive that mauling himself.

She couldn't help but smile as Alejandro held her for the first steps of the dance, a smile that she turned into the most seductive she could manage. And when it came to smiles, she had been told by many, that she could manage quite well. Alejandro certainly seemed to be taken aback by the look she was giving him. She couldn't help but chuckle deep in her throat when she saw his surprise, and that caused his eyes to widen even further. She saw him swallow hard.

"If you'd rather not dance the sarabande," he said, "we can excuse ourselves and go home now."

Mariette moved closer to him, knowing that it was not for her sake that he offered to forego the dance. "Oh, no, Alejandro! I love the sarabande. What a shame it is that one so seldom has a chance to dance to it."

"You have danced it before?" Was that a tinge of jealousy she saw in his suddenly wrinkled brow?

"A time or two," she answered, brushing his body with her own as she moved around him. She could swear she heard him swallow audibly. And was that sweat beading on his forehead? She completed a turn and came back to him, purposely bumping into him and pretending it was accidental. He tried to take a step back from her, but she followed, determined not to allow her quarry to escape now.

"Who did you dance the sarabande with before?" he asked.

Mariette smiled smugly and gave a little shrug. "A man," she answered cryptically before again moving away in the steps of the dance. Yes, a man, she thought, her brother, under the watchful eyes of her dancing instructor.

When the steps of the dance brought her back to Alejandro, he clutched her hand and this time it was he who pulled her close, and held her there. When he spoke, his voice was a growl. "What man?"

He was jealous! She did not answer him except with a merry laugh, then she sank into a deep curtsey as the dance ended.

Musicians began putting away their instruments and the final guests began leaving. A servant brought her shawl and bag and Alejandro's tricorn, and they went to the door to say their farewells and thank you's.

Mariette kissed Inés's cheek and thanked her once again for the gown. When she turned to Ignatio he took both her hands in his before she could avoid it. His thick fingers slid down to her wrists and, with a smile that would have been pleasant if there had not been such a hard, reptilian glitter in his eyes, he brought her forearms against his chest, forcing her to step far closer to him than she would have voluntarily.

"It was so nice to have you here this evening, my dear," he said pleasantly.

He was hurting her wrists but she did not want to cause a scene now, just as they were leaving anyway. She glanced at Alejandro but he was deep in conversation with his aunt. She hoped he did not notice what Ignatio was doing to her. There was no reason to add to the hatred she sensed between uncle and nephew. For she was sure Alejandro would come to her rescue if she cried out, possibly coming to blows with his uncle. She did not want to be the cause of that. After all, after tonight, she would never see this horrid man again.

"I enjoyed meeting your lovely wife," she answered, gritting her teeth against the pain in her wrists.

He leaned closer to her, his gaze flicking downward where her breasts were pushed upward by the way he was holding her. "I will enjoy having you in another way very soon."

She tried to wrench away from him, but without success. He was too strong and held her in a way that it was difficult to struggle. She glared at him. "Never!"

"Don't be so sure, my dear." He kissed her lightly on one cheek. "Don't be so sure." Then he let her go, turning to shake Alejandro's hand goodbye.

As they started down the street Mariette was not sure what she was feeling. Angry, soiled, violated. She wanted to scream, to cry. She couldn't help but seek the solace of Alejandro. She had taken his proffered arm as they went down the steps of his aunt and uncle's home. Now she moved closer, leaning her head against his arm for comfort. For protection. Strange how safe she had always felt with Alejandro. A Spaniard. An enemy. The very man whose job it was to prevent her from doing what she had come to St. Augustine to do—rescue Matt. What would he do, she wondered, if he found out just who she was, that she had a ship hidden in a swampy stream ready to sail away with two of his prisoners? He would have to turn her in or be branded a traitor himself. But could he really turn her in to his Uncle Ignatio? He must have some idea of what his uncle was like.

She snuggled closer into Alejandro's embrace and he put his arm around her as they walked. She would just have to make certain she was not caught. As for Alejandro, surely the loss of two of his prisoners would not be too devastating to his career as a soldier in his Spanish majesty's army. After all, he was a noble.

At this late hour St. Augustine's streets were quiet, and the sound of their footsteps echoed off the walls. A cooling breeze freshened the air and a lonely dog barked in the distance. Mariette put her arm around Alejandro beneath his coat, letting her fingers strum along his spine. A spine that stiffened with the contact. She smiled. He tried to pull away. Her gentleman Spaniard, trying so hard not to let himself be enticed beyond his ability to resist. She did not let him go but added her other hand to the front of his waistcoat to heighten his discomfort. In the most casual manner she played with one button then the next, then traced along the intricate lines of the waistcoat's embroidery.

Alejandro was so stiff he was practically marching like the good soldier he was. But it was another little soldier she wanted marching stiff and hard. She had never appreciated more than now the fact that she had three brothers, who had had no qualms about informing their sister of the details of masculine thinking, anatomy, and predatory skills. Of course they had told her in an effort to protect her from the machinations of dastardly men. She was sure they would be aghast if they knew how she was using that knowledge now.

Taking her hand, Alejandro tried to dislodge her from his side. "It's very warm this evening," he said.

"Hmm," she answered, pushing even closer, "I thought it was pleasantly cool. Perhaps it was the dancing that warmed you."

They had reached Alejandro's home and he opened the door, and pushed her in ahead of him. But she did not go far. Certainly not far enough for him to get around her and make his escape to the bedroom. She turned to face him, standing very close.

He looked down at her and she could see him swallow convulsively. "Yes," he answered, "the dancing."

"Of course," she continued, "that last dance was not very strenuous."

"The sarabande," he said. He cleared his throat but his voice still sounded strained. "No, it was not strenuous at all."

"Perhaps you are taking a fever." She unbuttoned one button on his waistcoat and slipped her hand inside. "You do not feel overly warm. But then, if you were feverish, you would be having chills."

He pulled her hand out of his waistcoat. "I assure you," he said, his voice a mere croak, "I am quite well."

Yes, she thought, grinning inwardly. Quite well. And reacting very much like a typical male. "Of course, that is not the way my mother always checked for a fever."

"No?"

She leaned closer to him. "Shall I show you?"

He took her by the upper arms and tried to move her aside. "Perhaps another time."

She captured his face with her hands and brought it down closer to hers. "I insist." Going up on tiptoe she kissed his forehead, lingering long. Then she kissed one cheek. "No, I detect no fever, though you are a bit warm."

"The dancing."

"Yes, the dancing," she agreed, testing the other cheek. "Although that last dance…" She let that thought slide, letting him remember the close rhythmic feel of her beside him in the slow cadence of that slightly scandalous dance.

"Was not very strenuous," he finished for her in barely a whisper.

"Still, it might be wise for you to take off some of these clothes." She let her fingers slide down his neck and wiggle under his coat, slipping it down his arms.

"Yes, you're right. I'll…um…undress myself and get into bed." He stepped back away from her, coming up against the door.

She followed, not allowing him to escape. She began working at his cravat, undoing the casual knot. He grabbed her two hands with his, pulling them down. "I really am quite well, Maria, and quite capable of undressing myself." With that, he slid past her and into his room.

She let him go, and indulged herself in a wicked grin. Tapping her fan against her palm, she hummed the strands of the sarabande, taking a few of the dance steps about the room. She chuckled to herself. She had him right where she wanted him and he had no idea. He was in his bedroom taking off his clothes. Just like the dance she would let him retreat, then follow, retreat then follow, until they were at last entwined.

She gave him a few moments longer then went to the door of his bedroom and, without knocking, let herself in.

Chapter Sixteen

ALEJANDRO WAS SITTING ON HIS BED WHEN SHE CAME IN, one shoe kicked underneath, the other dangling from his fingers. He had already removed his shirt and she caught her breath at the sight of him in the candlelight. For the past week and a half she had watched the English prisoners work without their shirts. The sight had left her unmoved. Even the sight of Douglas had not excited more than her pity for his sunburned skin.

Alejandro, however, was all that she had imagined him to be those times she had seen him in his sweat-dampened shirt. The soft light of the single candle bronzed his skin, casting shadows of dark umber in the hollows of his cheeks, and beside each clearly delineated muscle of his chest and abdomen. The black hair on his chest trailed downward to the waistband of his breeches. But Alejandro had loosened the top two buttons and that dark trail led onward into a deeper darkness.

The sound of the second shoe dropping from Alejandro's fingers brought her gaze back to his face. He blinked as if he could not quite believe her presence in his room. He straightened and hastily refastened the buttons on his breeches before he stood up.

Before he could question her or ask her to leave, Mariette came fully into the room and kicked the door shut behind her. She lowered her head as if suddenly shy and looked up at him coyly. "You may have no need of assistance getting undressed," she said softly, "but I do. Irish helped me into this gown, but I find I need some help getting out of it."

The sound he made then was of a man drowning, and he wiped his palms on his thighs as if they had suddenly become quite sweaty. "I…" He cleared his throat. "Turn around."

She presented her back to him, but left her hair for him to lift, to finger. She had heard her brothers speak often enough of some woman's hair and how they would like to touch it. Let Alejandro touch. See if he could stop touching.

She waited. She looked over her shoulder at him, her brows lifted in question.

"Your hair," he managed to croak out. "If you'll just lift it out of the way."

She turned away from him, rolling her eyes and lifting her hair. He had certainly seemed intent on getting her into his bed when he first hired her. When had their roles changed? She would just have to be more clever, more seductive, than he was honorable.

As soon as she felt his fingers at the top of her gown, she let some of her hair slip loose. She felt his fingers still and she smiled. "Sorry," she said, reaching back with her other hand to catch up the fallen strands. She turned her head just slightly, arching her back and taking a deep breath.

She had been careful to stand so that the light of the single candle fell on the front of her. From his vantage point just behind her shoulder, she was sure he could not help but see the tops of her breasts, enticing him further.

She felt a warm huff of breath on her neck as if the wind had been knocked right out of him. Oh yes, he was looking right where she wanted him to look. She took another very deep breath. She felt both his hands clasp her shoulders as if he were a drowning man and she his only means of salvation. She felt his hands tremble slightly.

"Perhaps if you turned your back to the light I could see what I am doing," he suggested.

Yes, but then you couldn't see what I am doing, she thought. But she complied and he again began his work on her gown.

"There!" he said. "You can go now."

Her loosened bodice sagged forward and she began slipping it off.

"You have no further need of me," he said stepping around her to reach for the door, inviting her to leave.

"Oh, but the skirt also fastens in the back." She smiled prettily and turned so that the candlelight fell on her back. She could almost hear his teeth grind.

"Of course." He bent to work on the skirt and it was soon loosened.

She began to shimmy out of the skirt and this time he actually managed to get the door open, saying, "I think you can handle it from here."

She managed to look slightly embarrassed. "I don't think so. There are the panniers and…and other things. Thank goodness Irish knew what to do with all these things your aunt sent."

He groaned. "No, I don't suppose you've worn such formal clothing before."

Little did he know, she thought. "Oh, thank you," she said, again presenting her back to him.

He unfastened her petticoats and she turned to hold on to him as she slid them down and stepped out of them, again affording him an excellent view of her décolletage. The panniers were also fastened in the back and she again turned to give him access.

That her slow state of undress was beginning to affect him she had no doubt, especially when he began to snarl softly at the panniers' ties. But he finally got them undone and she set them aside, again turning her back to him.

"More?" His voice was almost a squeak.

She shrugged and looked as helplessly as she could over her shoulder.

He began to work on the black silk cord that tightened the corset but she could tell his hands were not as steady as they usually were.

"There!" he said when the corset was loose. Again he stepped aside so she could avail herself of the door and leave. Instead, she began to wiggle out of the corset, slowly sliding it down over her hips and thighs.

His control was remarkable. Here she was down to her chemise and under petticoat and he still hadn't thrown her onto his bed. But she could see the cracks in that control. The fingers gripping the door were taut, their knuckles white, and he was trying desperately to look anywhere but at her.

"There is just this one more petticoat," she said, trying to make her voice sound small and helpless.

He bit his lip, but nodded, and she again turned her back to him.

It was only a moment's work for him to release the ties and she let the garment fall to her feet.

"If there is nothing further," he said, and again invited her to leave with a wave of his hand toward the door.

"Oh, yes," she answered. "If you could just rub my back a little."

His brows nearly disappeared into his hair. "Rub your back?"

"That corset was so uncomfortable. I just feel like I need to be rubbed good all over." She turned to him then, lifting her chin and letting one strap of her chemise fall off her shoulder. The loose chemise hung precariously on the tip of one breast, threatening at any moment to join the petticoat at her feet.

He stood looking at her a long moment like a starving man who must deny himself a feast. She had hoped his resistance would have failed by now, but he was far stronger than she had supposed. When he spoke, his voice was quiet. "Maria, what do you think you are doing?"

She stepped over the petticoat to stand close to him, bare chest to nearly naked breast. "Do you really need to ask?" she asked softly, lifting her face to him, inviting a kiss with a touch of her tongue to softly parted lips.

"Maria." The word was a surrender, his hands came up to take her in his arms and his head began to lower, but then he stopped. His hands dropped. He straightened. "You don't know what you are asking." His voice was strained, but she could hear the care in it. Still the honorable gentleman in spite of her blatant invitation.

"I know."

"You are an innocent, Maria. I will not dishonor you."

"I may be an innocent, *mi capitán*, but I do know what I want."

"I cannot marry you, Maria." When she opened her mouth to protest, he placed a finger across her lips, then gently caressing, running that finger along her top lip, then the bottom, he continued. "Not because I am a noble and you are a servant. I am not so proud as that. But I will be leaving St. Augustine soon and I cannot take you with me."

Mariette could not show him the relief she felt that he would be leaving St. Augustine. If all went well tomorrow with the escape, she would simply disappear from his life. If he left as well, he would not be searching for her, would not think that she was disappointed or that she never wanted to see him again. She leaned into him, putting her arms around his waist and smiled up at him. "Then we should not waste any more time."

He groaned and took her into his arms, leaning his head down to rub his cheek in her hair. "Do you not understand? I would not dishonor you then leave you alone, possibly carrying my child."

She kneaded his back, reveling in the feel of his muscles, willing them to relax, to unbend and take her to him. "I have thought of that, *mi capitán*. If it happens, then I will always have a part of you with me."

"And your family?"

"Will love me and care for me and the child. I have no fears about that."

"How incredibly fortunate you are, Maria, to have such a family." He held her just a little tighter then, as if wanting such a family for himself.

She thought of her parents and brothers. They would not be happy with her if she came home pregnant. But they would not throw her out, either. They would care for her and the child and never, ever throw recriminations at her feet. She knew it down to her very bones. "Yes, I am."

"I wish I could marry you, Maria. And I wish I could be a part of that wonderful, accepting family of yours."

She shrugged. "If it is not to be, then we must take what we can and be grateful for what we have."

He pulled back from her and looked into her eyes. "Are you sure? Are you sure this is what you want?"

She reached up to run her fingers through the shoulder length strands of his hair. "I never thought I would ever feel this way about any man, want a man as I want you. Yes, I am sure."

He held her tighter and looked intently at her a moment longer before a smile began to play about his lips. "Then if you are certain, Maria, there is one thing I must insist on."

She looked at him questioningly.

"I think it is time for you to stop calling me *capitán* and call me Alejandro."

Mariette laughed and tried, but his kiss stopped all speech, all thought, all time. All she knew was the touch of his mouth on hers, freely and without reserve at last. She sank into him, glorying in the hard length of him against her. Her mouth opened to him and his to her. She felt like they were taking each other in, exchanging breath, and life, and a part of their very souls.

His hands slid down her back and over her buttocks and he chuckled against her lips. Pulling back just enough to speak he squeezed her and said, "I have wanted to touch you here ever since I first saw you. Do you know what a beautiful, enticing shape you carry around with you back there?"

She grazed her hands over his bottom. "I've had my eye on yours, as well. I must say they feel as good as they look."

He laughed then, and she realized that it was the first time she had heard him really laugh, really let go of the stern *capitán*. It was an exhilarating sound. But it did not last long.

He looked into her eyes for a long, silent moment, then again bent to kiss her, his arms coming around her to hold her tightly as if he would never let her go. How she wished that could be true. But they both knew that this was just a temporary thing. He might think it was only for a few days or weeks. She knew it was but for a single night. If he thought their time together was precious, he did not know just how little and how precious it was.

He scooped her up and carried her to the bed, placing her propped up against his pillows, then sat at her feet, facing her. He took one of her feet into his lap and reached for her garter. One pull on the bow and it was gone, tossed onto the floor beside her discarded petticoats. Slowly and sensuously he slid his hands down her calf, taking her stocking with them. He smiled at the sight of every newly uncovered inch of her.

He tugged at the second garter but this time, he was watching her face. "Did you know," he said, "that in England a king once took a woman's garter, tied it around his arm, and made it a symbol of the highest order of knighthood?"

Mariette knew that story, and was surprised that a Spaniard would. But a Spanish colonial servant girl would certainly not know it so she shook her head no.

"I wonder if that woman's legs were as lovely as yours?" He slipped the garter off and tied it around his arm then he took off her stocking and kissed each of her feet, first on the top, then on the instep. He slid his hands up her legs, pushing her chemise up over her bare thighs, pushing further until he stood up to draw it off over her head, lifting her arms and letting them back down to lie above her head. He stood beside the bed looking down at her stretched out naked before him, her arms upraised, vulnerable to his gaze, his touch.

"I have wanted you from the moment I saw you in the market."

"I have wanted you as well, *capit*..." His finger across her lips silenced her.

"Alejandro," he corrected, taking his hand away.

"Alejandro." She turned to him, taking a deep relaxing breath, breathing out his name slowly, "Alejandro."

He removed his own socks and breeches and lay down naked beside her, and buried his face in the curve of her neck. "You do not know how long I have wanted to hear my name from your lips. Not *capitán*, or *señor*, but my name. I want you to know me, who I really am, not what I am."

Mariette bit her lip and swallowed hard, wishing for the same thing for herself. She wished she could hear him call her Mariette, know her for who she was. She wished she could use English endearments to him, call him my darling instead of *mi amor*, but she could not. She had to lie. Even in this most intimate of moments, when there should be nothing between two lovers except truth, she could not reveal even the most superficial thing about her real self.

He ran his hand over her from the line of her jaw, down her throat, along her side, to her hip. She started to touch him but he caught her wrists and lifted her arms back over her head and held them there. "No," he said. "Not yet. Let me."

Propped on one elbow, he held her wrists gently imprisoned with one hand while the other played lightly over her body, strumming along her ribs, drawing music from her nerves as he would from a lute. She felt exposed, vulnerable, open to his every desire, yet she was not embarrassed beneath his gaze.

"Why tonight, Maria?"

"Why tonight...?"

"Yes. If we have both wanted each other, why have we wasted days and days. Why didn't you come to me before? Why tonight?" He stroked down her throat and down to the crest of one breast. She gasped and her whole body shuddered. She felt like he was tormenting her, asking her these questions, then demanding a response from her body, a response she could not help but give.

"Oh!" was all she was able to say.

He repeated the question and the gesture. She felt that touch all the way through her body. It brought parts of her to life that she had never been aware of before. She could feel her most intimate part begin to soften like beeswax in the sun. She would have told him anything, answered any question, to have him touch her again...if she could find her voice.

He looked into her eyes and bent over her. She thought he was going to kiss her, and he did, but not where she had expected it. He kissed her where his hand had been moments before. Then he took her nipple into his mouth. His previous torment had been nothing compared to this. Nothing in her limited experience could compare to this. When he stopped, she could not help but arch upward, lifting herself nearer, hoping with her whole body for him to continue.

"Why tonight, Maria?"

Was he so unaffected that he could still talk?

"Was it the dancing?"

He took her into his mouth again and hummed a bit of that last sarabande while his tongue played a different tune upon her. She could feel the vibration of the music all the way through her. He lifted his head again. Wretch! Why did he stop?

"Was it the gown you wore?" He ran his hand along an imaginary décolletage, a low décolletage that barely covered her nipples. He touched her there. Twice. Once on each breast. She groaned and he chuckled wickedly. He must be related to Torquemada, she thought, of Inquisition infamy.

"Or the panniers?" His hand slid over her hip.

"Perhaps it was that lovely stomacher?" He traced one finger down the center of her body to the point where the stomacher would have ended. Just inches from where she now ached to be touched.

His finger inched downward and he bent to taste her breast again. His fingers splayed into the nest of hair between her thighs then cupped that part of her that was melting. She willingly opened her legs to give him access. She could feel her whole body opening for him, opening, wanting. His fingers stroked her, searching, then touched a part of her that made her cry out. She felt as taut as a lute string, strung between his mouth on her breast and his hand, and he was playing her expertly. Her hands opened and closed, wanting, needing to touch him in return and at last he released her wrists.

Finally freed, starving for touch, her hands fed on his body, every part she could reach, straining for parts she couldn't. He lifted himself above her and she saw him fully erect, dripping with the same wanting that was melting her. He took a moment to position himself and then slid partially into her, pausing at that feminine barrier and looking into her eyes before he thrust into her. He took the cry caused by that sharp pain from her mouth into his own, soothing her with a thrust of his tongue while he waited for her to adjust to him.

Her fingers dug into the muscles of his back and then relaxed, and he began to move within her. Again he hummed that sarabande, thrusting into her with the same rhythm, reminding her of the seductive touches they had shared in that dance that had promised fulfillment later.

Now that time had come and now came the fulfillment, in a shattering throbbing shared crescendo.

Chapter Seventeen

MARIETTE GRADUALLY RETURNED FROM WHEREVER THAT thundering, pounding crescendo had sent her. She took a deep breath and felt Alejandro, still stretched atop her, do the same. He leaned a bit more of his weight on her, turning his head to rest it upon her shoulder. That weight on her felt wonderful, the tight fullness within her felt wonderful, his hard chest muscles against her felt wonderful. She felt wonderful. And beneath her lightly caressing fingers, his back felt wonderful.

"Mmm," he said, shifting his back a bit.

Mariette took her cue and caressed him more, all the way down to his nicely rounded buttocks, all the way up to the nape of his neck and into his hair. He relaxed more, putting more of his weight on her. A little too much weight.

She squirmed and he jerked himself up onto his elbows. She took a deep breath and laughed up at him. "Someone likes to have his back tickled."

"Mmm," he replied, again snuggling down against her but keeping his weight off her this time.

She drummed her fingers against his back. "I wonder who it could be?"

"Mmm," he said again and jostled his shoulders where her

hands rested.

"Could it be some proud Spanish noble?" He shifted again.

"Or perhaps some stern *capitán* of the guard?" He bit her shoulder playfully and she squealed.

Alejandro lifted his head to look at her. "I know two or three ways to torment a saucy, uncooperative wench."

She lifted her brows. "Oh?"

He gave her a little thrust. "One," he said. He bent to briefly flick one breast with his tongue. "Two." He licked the other breast, lingering there much longer. "Three." He kissed her on the mouth, then was barely able to say, "Four."

She felt him swelling again within her. She smiled smugly up at him.

"I doubt that you will make it to ten."

Neither of them did.

When Mariette awoke the next morning it was to a steady drumming rain. She was nestled with her back against Alejandro, his arm around her, his breath against her shoulder. She took a deep breath. For someone who was in disguise in enemy territory with the strong arm of the captain of the guard around her, she was feeling awfully relaxed. In fact, she had not slept so well since coming to St. Augustine.

Alejandro's bed might be just a bit more comfortable than her place on the sofa, but not overly so. She had certainly had a raucous bit of exercise last night with the dancing and the…the activity in bed. But it was no more strenuous than carrying water to the prisoners every day. She ran her hand along the length of the arm that held her. Alejandro pulled her tighter against him. A safe, encompassing tightness. Protecting. Now she knew why she had slept so well. She had felt safe. Safe in the arms of her enemy.

She let herself revel in the feeling, in his closeness, for a while longer, but then began to scoot toward the edge of the bed. It was hard to leave that snug haven, especially knowing that she would never experience it again, but today was when Matt would at last be free. By the end of the day, they would be on their way back to Charles Town.

Alejandro woke just as she slid from beneath his arm and he reached for her, snagging her around the waist and pulling him back to him. "Where do you think you are going?" he mumbled, his head still deep in his pillow, his eyes still closed.

She turned to kiss him. "To make your morning chocolate, start your lunch and supper, to get dressed."

He pulled her closer and began to caress one breast. "There's no need to hurry. We are not going anyplace today."

She froze. If they stayed here, how could she help Matt and Douglass escape? Would her whole plan fail because she had slept with Alejandro last night and now he was going to keep her here making love all day? Not that that thought didn't have a lot of appeal, but there was not much time before the Eagle left for Spain and took the prisoners.

She tried to keep the tremor out of her voice as she turned in his arms and smiled at him. "But what of your prisoners, *capitán*? Do you not have to take them to work today?"

He rolled to capture her beneath him. His eyes glittered as he looked down at her. "Not today, *querida*. I have another prisoner right here and I have a lot of plans for her."

She shut her eyes as he bent to kiss each one, but she could not enjoy it. How could she enjoy being with him if it meant that giving in to her lust for him last night had cost her brother his freedom?

"But Alejandro, it would be a shame to deprive them of a day outside when they will be leaving for Spain so shortly."

He chuckled. "Such concern for men that only a few days ago you thought were devils."

"It is just that they must be expecting you at the fort," she argued lamely.

"*Querida*, do you not hear the rain? I cannot take the prisoners out in this. And even if it stops, the ground will be too wet out by the fort. The land there is low and swampy to begin with."

The rain. It was not because of her. She could have wept with relief except that, for whatever the reason, there would be no escape today. Tomorrow. There was nothing she could do to help Matt today. The rain had ruined their chances of escape. But it had also given her one more day in Alejandro's arms. One last day to savor and treasure, to store up and save, to be taken out and remembered time after time for the rest of her life. But tomorrow… She turned then to Alejandro to begin storing as many memories as she could. He was wonderfully cooperative and helpful.

Later, they sat under the overhang on the patio and drank chocolate. Alejandro played tug-of-war with Paddy with an old rag she had knotted while she put together some leftovers for a late lunch. By early afternoon, the rain had stopped and only quickly drying puddles gave evidence of the downpour. They ate, feeding each other tidbits and sharing wine. He told her of places he had visited in Spain, about the Roman aqueduct still being used in Segovia, the new palace in Madrid, the mosque converted into a church in Cordoba, a city fragrant with orange blossoms.

They went to bed early and Alejandro loved her long and slow, drawing out their pleasure until she begged him for release. Sated, they lay in each other's arms, touching palms, measuring the length of his fingers to hers, comparing the length of their noses, the width of their mouths, the darkness of their hair.

But as night fell, Mariette's thoughts once again turned to her escape plan. If they did not escape tomorrow, it would be too late.

The day after tomorrow, the prisoners would be taken aboard the *Eagle* to go to Spain.

"Surely, it will be dry enough by tomorrow to take the prisoners out, will it not?" she probed.

He shrugged, more interested in tasting her breast than talking about rain and prisoners.

"It will be their last chance to be outside before they are taken to Spain," she said as offhandedly as she could. "It would be a shame if they had to stay cooped up in the fort."

He began to nuzzle her ear. "It would be a shame, but I would be glad not to have to take them out again."

"Would you be glad to see them leave for Spain without one last chance for fresh air and sunshine?"

"I will take them out if I can, but I will also be glad to see them on their way. It has not been easy wondering if there will be an escape."

She managed a little laugh. "And where would a chained, half-naked, English prisoner go even if he did manage to slip away?"

He laughed, but it was mirthless. "You do not know my uncle very well."

"Your uncle?" She pulled back to look into his face. "What does your uncle have to do with the prisoners escaping?"

"It is a long story, *mi amor*." He traced the line of her lip with one finger. "And I have other things to occupy me at the moment."

She kissed his finger. "We have all night, Alejandro."

His hand slid over her hip. "I have other plans for this night."

"Tell me," she insisted, pushing his hand away.

He sighed and turned onto his side, propped his head on his hand, and looked down at her. "My uncle would like nothing better than to see some of the prisoners escape. Because any escape would be my fault, it would give him the perfect chance to…well, to make sure I paid fully for it."

"But why? What is there between the two of you that makes him seem to hate you?"

"He doesn't just seem to hate me. His hatred of me is very real. For many years my parents had no children. Ignatio, in the meantime, had several. He was sure that when my father, his older brother, died, the title and the family land would be his or his son's. Then I was born. I am an only child, Maria. If something were to happen to me…"

"But that is not reason enough to want you dead, Alejandro. I mean, it is a strong reason, but there must be more to it than that."

"You are too perceptive. My uncle has always resented me, but when I was small, he was sometimes actually kind. It was he who gave me my first lessons on the lute. But as I grew older, I…I do not look very much like my father, Maria."

"So he not only blames you for being born, but for taking what he feels should rightly be his because he thinks you are a bas–"

"Yes."

"And you think he would actually go so far as to use an escape to–"

"Yes." He shrugged. "Think about it, Maria. There are no more incompetent soldiers in the militia than the three he assigned to me. He ordered me to take the prisoners out to Ft. Mose which is the most northern of all our defenses. I am not even sure there are soldiers to man that fort again even if it is repaired. So far, Ignatio has done nothing overt, but I am sure he is hoping for an incident."

She put her arms about him and laid her head on his chest. "But even if the worst would happen, what could he do to you? You are a noble of Spain."

The arm he had around her tightened and his hand gripped

her arm. "He could have me shot."

Her head jerked up and she looked into his face with widened eyes. Her breath seemed lost somewhere. "Surely not!"

He gave a laugh. "Do not worry about it, *querida*. It has not happened yet, there is but one more day, and I will be vigilant."

His laugh and reassurances did not persuade her. She sat up and looked into his eyes, fear for him drenching her heart. "How could he have you shot? That is an extreme punishment for such a failure. He would not get away with it."

"Certainly there would be repercussions, Maria. Certainly there would be censure. But I would still be dead and my uncle, or his son, would still inherit."

Mariette shuddered and clutched him to her, burying her head against his shoulder. She could not stand the thought of Alejandro being stood up against a wall and shot. And to know it would be her fault, that she could bring that on him, she could have his death on her head…it was more than she could bear. She could not help the wracking sobs that began.

"Here, here, *chiquita*, there is no cause for this. Nothing is going to happen. There is but one more day and then the prisoners will be gone. There is nothing to worry about." His reassurances only made her cry harder. There was only one more day and something would happen. And if it did, Alejandro would die. And if it did not, her brother would die. If not from a dark prison cell, then when someone discovered who he was and used him to exact revenge for their father's successful raids against the Spanish in this horrible war. How could she choose?

Alejandro held her tightly, soothing her with soft words mumbled into her hair, one hand patting and caressing her back. Comforting the very one who could bring about his downfall and death. Who must bring death upon him or let it fall upon her twin. They had apparently been lax in finding out just who their prisoners were here in St. Augustine, but she could not count on that happening in a Spanish prison. Matt must know that, too, or he would not have capitulated so easily to her plan to rescue him. But once he knew he would be sent to a prison in Spain...

She knew her twin. He was like a plant that needed sun to live. She had seen the difference in him in the last week. Many of the prisoners had complained about being forced to work. A few of them, like Douglass, had even declined from the labor. But Matt had thrived—strengthened—in the fresh air and sunlight. If she did not go through with the plan to rescue him tomorrow, she might as well be signing his death warrant. But if she did...

She lay awake long after Alejandro had fallen asleep, pondering what she should do. What she had to do. What other course she had. But there was no other course. It was not until deep into the night that she had an idea. It might work. The more she thought about it, the more convinced she was that it was the only thing that would work. Once Matt and Douglass were safely aboard the *Fortune*—or *La Fortuna*, as she and Nate had repainted the name— she would turn herself in to the Spanish authorities.

She cringed when she thought of what that would mean for her. Certainly death, perhaps even by burning at the stake. Perhaps Ignatio would even... But she could not let herself think of that. She would endure what she must. Surely Alejandro would be spared if there was an English spy to blame instead, a spy who was also the daughter of the infamous Sean Fortune. Yes, she had lived in his house, but she had also been warmly welcomed into Ignatio's home. Yes, it was the only way. She knew her brothers would not let her do it. But they would not be able to stop her. She would tell them only that she wanted to stay with Soledad. Then, once the *Fortune* had sailed, she would march herself into the fort and confess. Alejandro would be spared. And Matt would live.

The next morning dawned sunny and bright and Mariette thought how little the day reflected her mood. She was glad that it would be the last day her brother and Douglass would suffer imprisonment, but it was also her own last day of freedom. She could not be glad of that.

Alejandro had awakened in the early morning hours to make love to her and she had relished every touch, every caress, every murmured endearment, knowing it would be the last he would give her. By nightfall, he would know her for the spy and enemy she was. How would he feel about her then? Would he hate and despise her? Or simply be angry at being duped and used?

When Alejandro began to stir, Mariette clung to him as she had done all night. His arm went around her pulling her closer. He seemed as reluctant for the day to begin as she. As long as she was here in his arms she could pretend that all was well. But at last he roused, kissing her before he even opened his eyes. He looked at her then, giving her a smile that she could not return. She could only hold him tighter. He held her quietly for a time then stretched and got up.

Propped on one elbow she watched him dress, looking her fill at the magnificence of his naked form one last time. She followed him out to the patio—he to shave, she to start a fire to heat his morning chocolate. When he was finished, she handed him a steaming cup and he sat at the little table sipping it.

She glanced at the position of the sun. He had never dawdled so long. Usually he was up and gone in minutes.

"Are you going to take the prisoners out today?" Almost she hoped he would not. It would excuse her for failure to rescue Matt. She would not have to die to save the two men she loved.

"I was hoping to persuade you to leave earlier and I would wait for you this morning," he said.

Wait for her? She had things to do before she went to the fort for the escape. She had to find Irish so she could go with them and take Paddy to Nate to put aboard the *Fortune*. She could not do those things with him here. There would be no way to explain them.

"There is no need," she said, waving a hand. "I will come later as I usually do."

He leaned close, caught the hand she waved at him and kissed it. "There is a need. My need to look at you every waking moment."

And what woman would not want to be looked at the way he was looking at her now? As if she were the most precious thing in his life. As if he could devour her. As if his very soul was in his eyes. She wondered how he would look at her this evening when she walked into the fort and told his uncle what she had done, how she had planned from the beginning to deceive and use him.

"I have never seen you look at me that way," he said to her.

She looked away. Was her soul also in her eyes, she wondered? She knew there was hunger there for him. And love. She loved him and yet she had to continue to deceive him and use him. At least until Matt was safe.

She turned back to him. "You asked me a question the other night, Alejandro. A question I was too preoccupied to answer then."

A smile curled his lip and he kissed her hand again. "I was a bit preoccupied myself, *querida*, I have forgotten the question."

"You said, 'Why tonight?'"

"Mmm." He tasted her fingers one by one. "And now you have an answer for me?"

"Yes." She squeezed his hand so tightly her knuckles whitened. "I love you, Alejandro."

He looked like someone had just given him the desire of his heart. But just as quickly dismay seemed to cloud his features. He opened his mouth to say something but she placed her free hand across his lips.

"You do not have to say anything, Alejandro. I know you are leaving soon. I know I cannot go with you. I expect nothing from you but one thing."

His brows knotted with his unspoken question.

"Remember that I love you. Believe and remember that no matter what happens. Never doubt it." She looked into his eyes as if she would brand him with her love. Tonight, he may no longer believe her, but for now, she would see her love reflected in his eyes.

"I will carry that with me forever."

She closed her eyes. That was all she could ask. He might hate her for a while, but surely he would come to understand, would know that she had not had to come back to save him but that she did it because she loved him.

He kissed her then on the mouth, softly, tenderly, as if she were cherished.

Alejandro insisted on waiting for her and walked her as far as the fort. He invited her to come in, to ride in the cart to Ft. Mose with them, but she looked up at those tall, gray walls and shook her head. She would be imprisoned within them soon enough.

"I will go ahead to my village and see you at noon with your lunch."

He stood uncertainly for a moment with his hands on her shoulders, looking down the road that led to Ft. Mose and her village. Finally, he nodded, gave her a quick kiss and let her go, watching her until she was nearly out of sight.

When she reached the village, Nate started toward her in alarm. "What happened? Why didn't you wait for me to come get you as usual?"

She smiled and patted his arm reassuringly. "I just thought I would come early today, to check to make sure everything is ready."

Frowning, Nate placed his hands on his hips. "We were ready yesterday!"

"Alejandro couldn't take the prisoners out because of the rain. I thought you would know that."

Nate's brows shot up. "Alejandro? You're calling him Alejandro now?"

Mariette could feel herself blushing, but she refused to let Nate annoy her. Not today. Not the last day she would ever see him. She never realized how hard this was going to be. There he was scowling at her as she had seen him do so many times when she tried to talk him into something he didn't want to do. She couldn't help throwing her arms around him and hugging him close.

"Mari?" he asked gently, using his childhood name for her, "is everything all right?" He put his arms around her and patted her back.

She nodded, then pulled away. "I guess I'm just a little nervous. This is the day we've worked toward and I just want everything to go smoothly. Most of all, I don't want anything to happen to you."

He straightened like the typical young male who seemed to think he was invincible. "Nothing is going to happen to me."

She took his arm. "You be sure it doesn't. If anything goes wrong— anything—you promise me that you will get out and go home, even if you have to leave me here. Even if you have to leave Matt and Douglass."

"We won't have to leave anybody."

She gripped his arm tighter and looked into his eyes as fiercely as she ever had when she was trying to get her way. "Promise me, Nate."

"All right, but–"

"No but's. You get out. Matt and Douglass are already prisoners. I'll be all right here. You're the one at real risk."

He gave a grudging nod. She wasn't sure she believed him, but it would have to do.

She let go of his arm. "Okay, tell me how things stand. Did you and Cato mark the path so we can find it from Ft. Mose?"

"We tied a yellow rag on a bush. It's low, about this high." He marked the height with his hand. "It's just above the height of the weeds and easy to spot but I doubt anybody would pay any mind to it unless they knew what it was."

"I'll tell Matt and Douglass what to look for. As soon as they get to that spot I'll cause a distraction so they can slip away. They might need help, so you be waiting for them, but don't come too close. If there's trouble, I want you out of it."

"The rain helped in one way, Mariette. The creeks are higher. Cato and I checked this morning. I'll be able to get the *Fortune* right up to the end of the path. We won't need the skiff at all. As soon as Matt and Douglass and you are aboard, I can sail her to another hiding place I have picked out until the tide turns and we can sail home."

"I might not be able to get to the ship. I'll be causing the distraction, remember? If I'm not with Matt and Douglass, you go ahead without me and I'll meet you back here later on." He opened his mouth to protest but she held up a hand. "I know, make sure I get here in time to catch the tide."

He grinned and nodded. "We're going to do it, Mariette. We're going to get them out and we're going home. Today."

She smiled, but she knew it was not true. One of them was not going home. Her.

Chapter Eighteen

MARIETTE ARRIVED EARLY AT WITH ALEJANDRO'S LUNCH just in case the prisoners reached the path sooner than she and Nate expected. Nate had left the village when she had, both of them hugging Soledad in tearful farewell and with many thanks. Mariette had pressed a coin-filled pouch into Soledad's hand and Soledad had given her a last batch of her sweet potato muffins along with her blessing.

Cato would help Nate with the *Fortune* then return to the village. Nate should be aboard his little ship by now, sailing up the rain swollen creek. By the time Matt and Douglass made their way down the cut path, Nate and Cato would have the *Fortune* turned about and Nate would be waiting for them somewhere along the path.

The prisoners were spread out in the field around the fort cutting weeds. Matt and Douglass worked side by side. Matt used his sickle smoothly, working with a steady rhythm that Douglass could not seem to match. But he managed to stay close to Matt and they were both positioned closest to the woods. When they reached the path, it would not take much of a distraction for them to slip into the woods and out of sight.

Mariette shaded her eyes, looking for Nate's yellow signal

cloth, and it took her a few minutes to spot it. It blended with the colors of the high, sun-ripened grass making it inconspicuous, but plain for someone looking for it.

And then she saw Alejandro. He turned in the saddle and caught sight of her at the same time, then craned his head upwards, checking the position of the sun. She was earlier than usual but he called a halt to the work. Sending the prisoners to an early lunch, he cantered toward her, sliding down from his horse and directly into her arms in one smooth motion.

Hidden for the moment behind his horse, he took the opportunity to kiss her thoroughly. And she took the opportunity to thoroughly enjoy it. It would probably be her last. She clung to him, feeling the hard length of him and remembering the look of those same muscles naked in the candlelight.

"You didn't have to stop yet. I am early," she murmured against his chest.

He chuckled. "I was hungry."

She looked up at him. "So soon? Breakfast was late and I am early."

"Not for food." He bent to kiss her once more, nibbling along her lip. "For you."

Alejandro was going to kiss her again but his horse gave a big snort and sidestepped, exposing them fully to the prisoners. Mariette moved away from him, looking sideways at the prisoners to see if any of them had noticed.

Of course, Matt just had to be looking her way just then. There could be no doubt that he knew exactly what she had been up to behind that horse, not with the scowl he was giving her. But that scowl was nothing compared to the look he gave Alejandro. As if this was all Alejandro's fault. She could only be thankful that Alejandro would never find himself at the mercy of her twin. Or that Matt did not know that she would sacrifice her life for

Alejandro later this very day.

When they settled down to eat, she could not manage a bite. She handed Alejandro his food and watched him, savoring his every movement, every smile he gave her.

"You do not eat, *querida*."

She shrugged. "I am not hungry. I will have something later."

When he finished, he leaned back against the wall of the ruined hut where they had taken so many lunches together, and closed his eyes.

She could not eat, but she did sit there enjoying the feel of the breeze on her face, the smell of the horses, the fresh cut grass. The colors seemed more vivid and she felt more alive than she ever had. Was this how it felt to know you would soon die? Is this the way soldiers felt before a battle, knowing they may not survive it?

Mariette looked at Matt. He and Douglass were both leaning against a wall, but they were not sleeping like the other prisoners. How could they, knowing freedom was not far away?

Alejandro was sleeping soundly and she knew why. Neither of them had had much sleep the night before. Two of the guards were beginning to nod off, as well. Only Raúl seemed vigilant, pacing impatiently back and forth, slapping his thigh with his whip. He glanced their way a few times, looked up at the position of the sun, then paced some more. Finally he approached, and, keeping a watchful eye on the prisoners, cleared his throat loudly to awaken his captain. Alejandro opened one eye and looked up at Raúl.

"*Capitán* it is past time to rouse the prisoners and put them back to work."

Alejandro stretched and got up. "It is their last day, Raúl. There is no need to stick to schedules now. We will work them only another hour or so then take them back to the fort so they can have time to bathe one last time before their journey."

Raúl's tightened lips gave notice of his disapproval with this concession to English prisoners of war, but he clicked his heels and began nudging guards and prisoners alike to get them moving.

Mariette stood and looked at the field as the prisoners marched back to their work. Could Matt and Douglass reach the path before work was halted for this last and final day? They would have to. Even if they got within a few yards of it, they should be able to slip away if the distraction she had planned went as she hoped.

She did not wait long before she began taking water to the prisoners. They had long ago accepted her presence among them and many of them smiled and said pleasant things to her. Things she had to pretend not to understand. Others still made occasional suggestive comments. And she had to let those pass as well as if she did not understand. It was only the one they called Jackson who had done more than make comments. Today, she would make him pay for all the foul words she had had to ignore, for all those little touches that he had made seem so accidental and then leered at her. Today he would pay, and that payment would buy the freedom of her twin and Douglass.

As she worked her way down the line of men she purposely skipped Jackson and ignored his calls to her to come back to him. When she reached Matt and Douglass, Matt watched as Douglass drank and said, "We're running out of time, Mariette."

She nodded and refilled the cup for Douglass. "You're almost to the path Nate cut."

"Where the yellow rag is tied?" he asked without breaking his rhythm.

She started, worried that the rag was more obvious than she thought. But then she realized that Matt would have noticed. He noticed everything, especially in the wild. He had been half-raised by native Indians and would have no trouble finding his way down that path to the *Fortune*.

She nodded.

He stood to take a cup of water from her. "What were you and the captain doing behind his horse?" He looked into her eyes and she squirmed inwardly.

She lifted her chin defiantly. "Does it matter?"

Matt tossed out the remnants of his water and handed the cup back to her. "I don't know. Does it?"

She ignored the question. "Watch for my distraction then get into the woods. I'll be right behind you if I can. If not, don't wait for me. I'll meet Nate later at Soledad's."

He nodded and bent to his work.

The prisoners worked steadily and the oppressive heat of the afternoon began to dull wits. Mariette noticed Alejandro looking up at the position of the sun and knew that he was thinking of calling a halt to the work. Matt and Douglass were still a few yards from the path, but close enough if her distraction could give them a few extra moments. She would have to chance it. They might not have another opportunity.

There were only two more prisoners to give water to before she came to Jackson. She had skipped him twice now. He should be ready to snap. It would just take a little nudge to provide the distraction she needed, especially if she had judged his character correctly. She sauntered up to him and, giving him the nastiest smirk she could, she drank from the cup slowly, deliberately letting some of the water dribble onto the ground.

"You stupid slut," he snarled. "If you were smart enough to understand English I'd let you know exactly what I think of you. Always teasin' a man, swingin' them hips but thinkin' yer too good fer the likes of me. I bet yer givin' it to that heathen captain."

Mariette slowly poured another cup of water and acted as if she would pass him by again.

He wiped his mouth with the back of one grimy hand. "You better not skip me again." He held out his hand for the cup of water she held.

Shrugging, she stepped closer to him. Closer than she had ever dared before, and held out the water to him. But as he reached for it, she deliberately bumped his hand, dropping the cup and spilling the water.

Jackson's face reddened. His eyes bulged. "Stupid bitch!" Then he backhanded her across the face.

Mariette staggered and would have fallen if another prisoner had not been watching the exchange and caught her. The blow surprised her, but she managed to cry out as loudly as she could, dropping the water jug, putting her hand to her cheek and continuing to wail. The other prisoners came running. So did all three of the guards and Alejandro. One of the prisoners socked Jackson in the jaw sending him to his knees and another kicked him in the side, knocking him to the ground.

Alejandro waded into the throng and grabbed her by the shoulders. "What happened?" he asked over the sound of several prisoners trying to tell him in English.

Mariette pretended to sob louder. "He struck me! I was just giving him water and he hit me!"

Mariette had seen her brothers get angry. She had seen expressions on their faces that could have congealed blood if she hadn't known they would never hurt her. But she had never seen a look like the one on Alejandro's face. She almost pitied Jackson.

"Go home," he said. "I will be there shortly."

She nodded in humble acquiescence while her heart soared in triumph. She pushed her way through the prisoners and headed for the path. Already there was no sign of Matt and Douglass. Her distraction had worked. She heard a whacking sound and knew from the many fights her brothers had engaged in exactly what was happening to Jackson. Then, just as she made it to the woods she heard Alejandro calling for the guards to line the prisoners up and get them back to the fort.

Mariette was surprised to see the yellow rag still tied onto the bush. Matt was usually not so careless in hiding his trail. He must have left it for her. She pulled it free and tucked it into the waist of her skirt, accidentally breaking the branch as she did so.

As soon as she stepped into the woods she saw the blood. Was it Matt's? Or Douglass's? How had they gotten injured? Brows knotted with concern, she followed the path.

Alejandro rubbed the knuckles of his right hand. He had never in his life struck a helpless man. But he had never been this angry at one either. At least he had been able to control himself enough not to hit the man more than twice.

He glared at the prisoner as Raúl hauled him to his feet. Raúl didn't actually grin, but Alejandro could see the delight in his eyes. "Shall I have him flogged, *capitán*? I will do it myself for the insult he has given to the little *señorita*."

Alejandro turned his glare on the soldier. Raúl and Jackson were cut from the same cloth. Raúl didn't care about Maria. He was only looking for an opportunity to swagger and whip a prisoner.

Alejandro shook his head. "He's going to a prison in Spain in the morning. That's punishment enough. Let's take these men back to the fort and get them cleaned up."

Sickles were collected and a ragged line of prisoners was soon formed.

"*Capitán*," Francisco gave him a rather wilted salute and then pulled his uniform back down over his ample belly. "I have counted twice, *Capitán*, but there are two prisoners missing."

Alejandro blanched. He counted them himself. Eighteen. Not now! Not the last day! He scanned the field for two prisoners who were simply slow, or perhaps had taken the opportunity provided by the fight to sit down and rest. He could see no one. Two of them had taken advantage of the distraction, all right, but to try to escape. They could not have gotten far. And where could they go? He ran to his horse and mounted to have a higher vantage point. There was still no sight of the two men. And then his heart lurched. There was also no sight of Maria.

Her water jug lay where she had dropped it and the basket that had held their lunch still sat beside the hut. The road back toward St. Augustine was clear. The escapees had taken a hostage.

His hand tightened on the reins and he took out his pistol. He would kill them. He put his pistol back and drew his saber. He would kill them slowly. There was only one way they could have disappeared so quickly. They had taken to the woods.

Francisco stood looking up at him, his fleshy face crinkled with worry.

"Paco! Raúl! Get these men back to the fort and give them a chance to bathe. I'm going after the two who are missing."

Raúl's eyes gleamed. "You will need help. I will go with you, sir!"

"There are only two of them, Raúl. They are chained and un-armed. I will find them and bring them back." The horse would be no use in the woods, not with undergrowth so thick. He dismount-ed and handed the reins to Paco. "It should not take me long."

Alejandro walked along the edge of the woods looking for signs where the men might have entered. He was certain it would have been close to where they had finished cutting weeds. There! Grass and weeds were trampled ahead and what was that on the ground? He bent and touched a finger to the red stain. Blood. He gripped his saber. If they had harmed Maria, they would die a thousand deaths.

There was a broken branch on a bush. Alejandro pushed by it to enter the woods. More blood showed him he was close on their trail. The undergrowth was not so bad here as he had expected and he took a few steps, then stopped. One of the plants known as Spanish bayonet had been hacked down, its razor sharp leaves cast aside. He looked farther ahead. Another bush had been cut, and recently. Those men had known somehow that this path was here. They had known. Someone was helping them with their escape. Someone who might be just ahead and armed. He pulled out his pistol. Holding it in one hand, and his saber in the other, he followed the path.

It did not take Mariette long to catch up to Matt and Douglass. It was Matt who was limping along leaning on Douglass. Blood ran down his leg. They heard her and turned.

"What happened?" she asked, lifting her skirt to rip off a strip of petticoat.

"I did it," Douglass said, reddening.

"You?" Mariette bent to staunch the flow, putting pressure on the wound and quickly wrapping the makeshift bandage around Matt's leg.

"When you started that brawl it startled me, and I accidentally sliced Matt's leg with my sickle."

"It's a bad wound, Matt," Mariette said. "It will need stitches."

"You can do whatever you want to me once we're safely aboard the *Fortune*," Matt said, his voice strained with the pain of his wound, "but for now we'd better get moving."

They had not gone far when they heard something ahead of them. They stopped. First they saw the pistol. Then they saw Nate appear.

"Nate!" Matt reached out to take his little brother's hand but Nate was looking beyond them, raising that pistol.

Mariette turned to see what had drawn Nate's attention.

Alejandro was just coming into view around a curve in the path. He stopped when he saw them, then he raised his own pistol.

Mariette heard the cock of Nate's pistol only a moment before she lunged for her brother's hand to keep him from shooting Alejandro. There wasn't a better shot among them, and if Nate were aiming to kill, that's exactly what he would do. The gun went off as she shoved Nate's hand, causing his shot to go wild. But not wild enough. She turned just in time to watch Alejandro crumple to the ground.

"Alejandro!" Mariette ran to where he lay. His weapons had fallen from his hands and were quickly snatched up by her brothers as she fell to her knees beside him.

There was blood. Too much blood. Tears started to blur her sight but she quickly dashed them away. Her grandmother had taught her that her first duty was to tend the wounded. Crying over them didn't help. If she had to cry, she could do it later.

"Come on, Mariette, we have to go!" Nate said, nudging her shoulder.

She shot him a quelling glance then turned back to Alejandro. The wound was on his head but she knew he was alive because blood continued to flow. She put pressure on the wound with one hand and lifted her skirt with the other, reaching for her already abused petticoat.

Matt's hand came over hers, freeing her to tear a strip of material. She gave him a quick smile of gratitude.

"I guess that business behind his horse was important, after all, wasn't it?"

She didn't answer but bent to her task, wadding some of the petticoat against the wound and wrapping the rest about it to keep the pressure and staunch the flow of blood. Head wounds always looked worse than they were because they bled so much. When she was finished Matt took her arm and pulled her to her feet.

"You've done what you could. Let's go while we can."

She dug in her heels.

"What now?" Douglass asked.

"There might be wild animals. We can't just leave him." And that was when one of the wildest ideas she had ever had came to her. It would not be easy to convince her brothers, but it was a way to save Alejandro from his uncle as well as save herself.

She looked at her brothers and Douglass waiting anxiously for her to follow. They weren't going to like what she was going to say. But she had decided and she would not back down. She squared her shoulders and dared them to argue with her as she said, "We're going to take him with us."

Three male voices bellowed, "What?" at the same time, but she stood firm.

"I don't have time to explain right now, but believe me, this is the best thing to do. Doug, take his feet. Nate, get his shoulders. Let's get him aboard the *Fortune*."

The two of them looked at her as if she had suddenly gone stark raving mad. Only Matt seemed to consider her order, albeit with narrowed eyes. She looked back, pleading with him. He glanced once between her and Alejandro, then nodded. "If you're sure, Sis."

Mariette bit her lip to hold back the tears. Matt understood. He had seen her daily with Alejandro. He had seen them together today. He knew there was more to her demand than wanting to save one Spanish enemy from wild animals. He couldn't know the whole story, but he was her twin and more than any of her brothers, he understood and trusted her.

"I'm sure," she answered him.

He nodded. "Pick him up and let's go."

Doug and Nate stared at him open-mouthed as if he had caught whatever had afflicted her.

"Do it!" he said in that way he had of commanding obedience, then he turned and limped down the path.

Nate and Douglass exchanged a perplexed shrug then bent to pick up Alejandro.

Alejandro's head was throbbing, but that was all right because he could hear someone speaking English and knew he must be safe in England. Why was his head throbbing? Had he fallen out of that old apple tree again? Memories swam through his consciousness. Memories from a long time ago. Playing with Lord Randall's children, daring each other higher up the tree, Quinten shaking the branch, falling. But that had been a long time ago.

He struggled up through the blackness, remembering today, the English prisoners escaping. A shot. Had Ignatio put him in front of a firing squad? Alejandro came out of the blackness and into pain. Not bad pain, but enough to make him wince.

"I think he's coming around, Mariette."

"I'm glad I got him stitched up while he was still unconscious." That was Maria's voice. Maria? Mariette? The two names chased themselves around in his head.

"I'm sorry I don't have anything to give you for the pain, Matt." Maria's voice again. Matt?

"Don't look like he needs it." Some male voice.

He heard Maria chuckle. "He needs it, Douglass. He just refuses to show it. He spent too much time with his Indian friends growing up. You could cut his heart out and you'd never know you'd hurt him at all."

Alejandro frowned trying to make sense of what he was hearing, where he was. He wasn't in England. He was in Spanish Florida, but that whole conversation had been in English. The English prisoners. And another man. One of them had shot him. But how could Maria be speaking English?

He opened his eyes. He was lying on some kind of bunk bed and from the movement he felt, he was on a ship. Mateo was sitting on the bunk across from him and Maria was sewing up a gash in his leg. The second English prisoner was looking on, holding a pan of water for her and in the doorway stood the one who had shot him.

That young man was watching him intently with a pistol trained on his heart. "Lie still Spaniard or I'll shoot you again."

Maria snipped a last thread and turned to Alejandro with a smile. She's smiling? How could she be smiling? They were both prisoners of these Englishmen. And then it all came together. He looked from one face to another. All of them had been speaking English. Including Maria. And she did not have the slightest trace of an accent. She was English. She was the one who had helped the two prisoners escape. Even knowing what it would cost him, she had helped the prisoners escape. She had betrayed him.

Chapter Nineteen

ARIA. HIS MARIA. SHE HAD USED HIM AND BETRAYED him and now she was smiling. A pain in his heart grew to match the pain in his head. But he could squelch the pain in his heart. Squeeze it until it became a hard knot of anger. The pain in his head just kept going. There was something wrapped around his head, but when he tried to lift his hand to touch it, he felt a weight and heard a rattle of chain. He looked at the manacle around his wrist, the short length of chain fastened to the wall, then he looked at Maria.

"Nate, put that pistol away," she said. "He knows he's not going anyplace."

The one called Nate stuck the pistol into the waist of his breeches then leaned in the doorway with arms crossed. Alejandro looked from him to Mateo. They had the same bright blue eyes, the same hair, the same features. Brothers, he would guess.

He tried to sit up but Maria moved to sit beside him, pushing him back down. She looked intently into his eyes one at a time, then held up one finger. "Watch my finger," she ordered in Spanish and moved her finger up and down and sideways watching the movement of his eyes.

"There is no concussion. You will be all right. Your wound was not as bad as it looked at first. It only took six stitches."

"You're English," he said. It was not a statement. It was an accusation.

She didn't try to deny it. "Yes. From Charles Town. These," she pointed to Mateo and Nate, "are my brothers, Matt and Nate. Douglass," she nodded toward the sunburned man with pale eyes and hair, "is…a friend."

And I? he wanted to ask. What am I to you? Instead he looked around and asked, "Where are we? What ship is this?"

Nate straightened in the doorway. "It is my ship, the *Fortune.*" Nate seemed hardly more than a boy, but he could see the pride in his eyes, the set of his chin. He might be young, but he was already a man. He would not give him less than his due. Besides, Nate had already shot him once—and had threatened to do so again.

Alejandro nodded but then turned back to Maria. In spite of this being Nate's ship, she seemed to be the leader of this little pack. "What do you plan to do with me? Keep me as a hostage until you reach safety, then dump me overboard?"

Mateo chuckled. "Not a bad idea, Captain de Silva. But I doubt that Mariette would let us. For some reason, she seems to want to keep you."

Maria, or rather, Mariette, glared daggers at her brother and blushed.

"You used me. You betrayed me."

Her chin came up at his accusation but again, she did not deny it. Nor did she seem the least bit ashamed by her deception. "Yes," she admitted.

She looked steadily into his eyes and only her hands, tightly clasped in her lap, gave indication that what she had to say was difficult. He imagined that she would face a firing squad with the same equanimity.

"I could not let Matt and Douglass languish, perhaps die, in some Spanish prison. I had to do what I could to free them. I talked Nate into bringing me down here." She turned to give her younger brother a brief grin. "Not a difficult thing to do." Nate grinned back and she continued. "I had to have information, come up with a plan. Who better to provide it than a Spanish officer? It was pure luck that you happened to be in charge of the very prisoners I had come to free."

"Not so lucky for me, though, is it?" He held up his manacled wrist.

"But do you not see? It has all worked out for the best. We will take you with us. Your uncle cannot wreak his vengeance on you if you have been taken hostage by the escaping English prisoners. And when the war is over, you can go back to Spain or wherever you want to go."

So she had thought of him. His indignation eased a bit. "And what if I had not followed you? What of me then?"

Her chin jutted out determinedly. "I was going to come back for you."

"Come back for me? Just like that?" He snapped his fingers. "Why would you think a Spanish officer would come with you and not arrest you and turn you in?"

She bit her lip and glanced sideways at her brothers before she took a deep breath and said, "I was not planning to come back to take you with me. I was going to turn myself in and take the blame for the escape so your uncle could not blame you."

He could see that she clasped her hands tighter to still their trembling and he could not help but place his free hand over them, squeezing gently.

"Did you not know that you would have been shot—or worse?"

She nodded. "I knew." She looked at him with anguish in her eyes.

"But how could I choose between my brother and…and you? I could not. It was the only way I could think of to save you both. But when you followed us, when you were wounded, that is when I thought that if we took you with us, I could save us all." She leaned close to him, pleading with him. "Do not hate me, Alejandro. I did what I had to do."

He reached up to caress her cheek. "You would have sacrificed yourself to save me?" He was touched beyond words at what she had planned. But when she nodded and a tear touched his fingers he was nearly unmanned.

"It would not have worked, you know," he told her softly. "My uncle would probably have shot us both."

She shook her head. "Not when I told him who I am."

He lifted a questioning brow.

"My last name is Fortune. Do you not think your uncle would have been pleased to have the daughter of Sean Fortune in his grasp?"

"You're…" Alejandro looked from Maria to her brothers. They nodded.

"You can see why I had to free Matt."

"Yet you were willing to take his place. For me?"

"What else could I have done, loving you both as I do."

There was a harsh sound from the prisoner named Douglass and Maria's, or Mariette's, eyes widened with alarm. "Oh, Douglass! I'm so sorry. I… I didn't know you could speak Spanish–"

Douglass stopped her with a hand to her shoulder. "Oh, I've picked up the odd word here and there. But it's all right, Mariette. I think I've known for a long time, maybe from the very beginning that what you felt for me was not…was not what I felt for you. I don't think I ever really believed my good…" he chuckled mirthlessly, "my good fortune in having you accept my proposal."

She reached up to clasp his hand. "Douglass, I really do love you. It's just…"

He pulled his hand free and patted her shoulder. "I know. Like a brother."

She nodded.

"Then I will leave it to you and Captain de Silva, who is now our prisoner, to work out what is to become of him."

Alejandro wanted to sweep her into his arms, but a manacled wrist—and the presence of the others—prevented him. "It does seem that what you have done has truly worked out for the best, Maria, er, Mariette. I will go with you to Charles Town, and quite willingly."

"You have no choice, Captain de Silva," Mateo growled, his brows furrowed as he glared at his sister. "You are our prisoner now, chained where you lie, and Nate still has his pistol quite handy."

Alejandro could see the surprise on their faces when he began to laugh. It was time to reveal his secret. "I said I would go with you willingly." He looked at each of them then switched to English… and watched surprise light their faces. "You see, I am half-English myself. I came to St. Augustine to try and find some way to get to an English colony. Charles Town will suit me just fine. It was only bad luck in my case that my friend Governor Montiano had been replaced temporarily by my uncle, who, as Mariette knows, is look- ing for any chance he can to see me dead."

Three pairs of male eyes turned to Mariette for confirmation. She nodded. "He told me last night that his uncle wanted to see him dead because he suspected that Alejandro was not the true son and heir of his father." She turned to Alejandro. "But he did not tell me his real father was English."

Alejandro shrugged. "It is not a thing one bandies about. What does it say for one's mother, after all? I didn't know myself until a year ago when my mother was dying." He sat up further in the bunk and leaned against the wall. "My mother and the man I always thought of as my father did not have children for several years. Then, one year my father accompanied the Spanish ambassador to England. There they became quite friendly with a certain lord from Devonshire. My mother, apparently, became very friendly with him. Over the years, as I grew up, I spent summers in England with this lord, played with his children as if they were my siblings. Which, I later learned, they were.

"When my mother was dying, she told me all this. My father happened to overhear our conversation. He had suspected all along, but was too proud to let himself believe that it was true. After he heard us, he could no longer lie to himself. He threw me out of the house.

"It was not long after that I began to have little accidents, accidents that could have killed me had I not been lucky. Then I was attacked twice on the streets. I realized that although my father was too proud to denounce me publicly, he had no qualms about ridding the family of me by more permanent means. The bloodline was very important to him, I was not of his blood, yet I would inherit—unless I was dead.

"I decided to find my way to an English colony and take up life as an Englishman. But when I arrived in St. Augustine, my uncle was waiting to take up where my 'father' had failed. If I go back to St. Augustine, my life will be forfeited."

Mariette turned to her brothers. "Which is why I insisted we bring him with us."

"There is only one flaw in your story, Captain de Silva," Douglass stood with furrowed brow and his hands clasped behind his back. Everyone turned to him. "You have no proof."

Nate nodded. "You're right, Douglass." He looked at Alejandro. "Why should we believe you?"

Mateo crossed his arms and looked at Alejandro with a lifted brow. "Douglass has a good point, Captain. But I suppose it doesn't matter since you're going to Charles Town, willing or no."

"I assure you, I am quite willing." Alejandro lifted his chained wrist. "I am even willing to go as a chained prisoner. But I do hope that once we are in Charles Town, you will release me?"

Mateo looked at Douglass. "What do you think, Douglass? You're the lawyer here. Can we legally loose a Spanish prisoner of war on Charles Town once we get home?"

Douglass shook his head. "Since we are currently at war with Spain, I'm afraid the Captain will have to be turned over to the authorities." He looked at Alejandro and shrugged. "I'm sorry. Without proof–"

"I do have proof." Alejandro gave a mirthless laugh and leaned his head back against the wall. "But it is in my house in St. Augustine."

"What kind of proof?" Douglass asked, the lawyer in him keenly focused.

"When my mother told me about my real father, she gave me some papers from him that she had kept hidden, letters claiming me as his son and letters of credit if I ever found my way to an English colony."

Douglass nodded. "That would probably be sufficient. If we could get them. Since we can't, perhaps you could send a letter to him for more."

Mariette jumped to her feet, hands on her hips, facing the three men. "And what is he to do in the meantime? Languish in a jail cell? Getting duplicate papers could take months."

Alejandro reached out and took her by the arm, pulling her down beside him again. "A few months in prison versus being shot? I think I can tolerate that." He caressed her arm. "And in the meantime, perhaps my incarceration could be lightened by a visit or two from an English lass who speaks impeccable Castiliano?"

"I'll do better than that." She lifted her chin in a defiant gesture that Alejandro was coming to know—and be leery of—as well as her brothers. "I'll go into St. Augustine and get your papers."

It was not just her brothers who shouted, "No!" It was all four of the men.

Alejandro gripped her arm. "Mateo. Matt." He sat up and leaned forward. It made his head hurt, but he shrugged off the pain. "Do not let your sister do this. Even if you have to chain her, as well. It is too dangerous."

"I agree," Matt said firmly, receiving agreeing nods of approval from Nate and Douglass. "This time, little sister, I'm putting my foot down."

Mariette glared at Matt. "Little sister? You might be my older brother, but only by about two minutes, you heathen. And that's not enough to give you the right to order me around."

"I agree with Matt and Captain de Silva," Nate said, crossing his arms.

"And as captain of this vessel, I have the right to clap you in irons if you disobey."

Matt grinned up at his brother.

"You don't understand," Mariette said, leaning forward with palms open and pleading.

Nate and Matt exchanged a wary look. "We never do," Matt said, "until you totally confound us with convoluted explanations that convince us to go along with your hare-brained schemes." He shot a menacing glare at Nate. "Such as talking your little brother into sailing you into enemy territory during a war."

Mariette gave a perky toss of her head. "And aren't you glad I did?"

Matt leaned over to confront her nose to nose. "We aren't out of this yet, Twin, and to let you go traipsing back into St. Augustine for something that can be obtained another way would be pushing our luck just too far."

"I agree, Maria." Alejandro caressed her arm but stopped when he saw Matt scowl at his proprietary gesture. "It is too dangerous."

She crossed her arms. "It would be safer for me than for any of the rest of you. And besides, there is another reason I have to go back."

Matt and Nate matched her crossed arms with equally determined crossed arms of their own.

"I have to get Irish."

That statement took the starch out of her brothers' stance and she pounced on that weakness.

"I've told you how she's been beaten." She turned to Alejandro for support. "You can tell them how that witch of a mistress treats her."

Against his better judgement, Alejandro nodded. "It is true that the Irish woman has been badly treated, but I would not see you risk your own life to save her, Maria."

"Mariette," three male voices corrected him.

He shrugged.

Maria, or rather, Mariette, looked at each of them in turn. "I have to go. If she had not helped me when I needed her..." She turned to Alejandro. "I have a confession to make. I can't cook. Irish cooked several of your meals and taught me enough to keep you fed. She and a friend who lives here did most of that cooking. And now Irish has become a friend. I can't abandon her."

She turned to Matt and Douglass. "You both know what it's like to be a prisoner of the Spanish. At least you had hope of being released when this war is over. Irish has none. She's a slave, and will live and die a slave unless we help her escape."

"Even if we wanted to help her," Nate said, "we don't have the time. The tide turns in less than an hour. We have to catch it at it's height or be stuck up this creek another day. And that would be too dangerous. The Spanish probably already have patrols out looking for us."

"They will be looking for two bedraggled, chained, escaped slaves on foot," Mariette answered. "Not a ship." She leaned forward earnestly. "But don't you see? This is perfect! We can sail on the tide to the docks and I can go to Alejandro's house to get Irish and his documents and be back in a quarter hour. We'll be gone again before they even realize we're there."

Nate's fists went to his hips and he nearly growled at her. "You want me to sail the *Fortune*"—he jabbed a thumb at his chest—"my ship right under the guns of *El Castillo*?"

Mariette grinned smugly. "*La Fortuna.*"

She stood and took one of Nate's hands. "Irish is my age. She has already been beaten, half starved, she still wears the clothes she was captured in six months ago. Can you sail away without at least trying to save her?"

Alejandro looked at the wavering expressions on the brothers' faces. Surely they wouldn't endanger Maria—Mariette—and allow her to talk them into this scheme? "I vote no," he stated emphatically.

The three siblings turned to him and said almost as one, "You don't get a vote."

"Then let me add my plea." He glanced at the two brothers. "A voice of reason, if you will." He ignored Mariette's glare. "I sympathize with Irish. Perhaps when this war is over you can do something to help her. But to let Mariette go back into town is too dangerous for her." He looked at Mariette. "You forget about my uncle." Turning back to the others he continued. "A vicious, evil tyrant if there ever was one. If he corners Mariette—"

"Your uncle will not be looking for me," she argued. "He'll be too busy looking for two escaped prisoners and his nephew." She turned back to her brothers and batted her lashes a time or two, making her eyes look bigger and more soulfully pleading. Her lips formed a pretty little moue. The two brothers bit their lips and looked at each other.

Alejandro rolled his eyes. "You're not going to let this act of hers convince you to let her have her way, are you?"

Matt gave him a speculative look through narrowed eyes but Mariette gave him a quelling glare before she turned her pleading back on her already half-whipped brothers. "A quarter of an hour. That's all I need. A quarter of an hour to save not only Alejandro from months of languishing in a jail cell–"

"Which I am perfectly prepared to do rather than have you take foolish risks with your own neck," he interrupted with a quelling glare of his own.

"–as well as saving an innocent woman from years of torment as a slave at the hands of those evil Spanish."

"I also happen to be Spanish and you didn't seem to think I was so evil a moment ago!"

"Half-Spanish," four voices chorused in unison.

Alejandro threw up his hands.

Nate and Matt looked at each other and shrugged.

"One quarter hour," Matt said, again nose to nose with her. "Any longer and I'm coming after you."

"One quarter hour," Nate said, punctuating his words with a jabbing finger. "Any longer and I'm taking my ship out of danger and leaving you there."

"I really wish you'd reconsider, Mariette," Douglass said with a worried frown on his face.

"You're all insane," Alejandro said crossing his arms in a huff.

Mariette gave him her prettiest smile yet and patted his arm. "Aren't you glad? Otherwise we wouldn't have met, and you wouldn't have a free ride to an English colony!"

Alejandro lifted one brow and held up his shackled wrist. "And that is supposed to make me feel better about all this?"

Mariette hurried through the streets toward Alejandro's little house. She carried a small hamper from the ship. She thought it would look more normal to carry it since she usually brought Alejandro's dinner home from Soledad's every day. When she and Irish left, she could use it to carry Alejandro's papers as well as a few clothes for him. He hadn't asked her to bring anything, including his papers. He had only wanted her to get Irish and get back to the ship. But since she was going to be there anyway, it wouldn't hurt for him to have some of his things.

She hadn't mentioned it to her brothers but there were a couple of more things she wanted to bring—the dress she had worn to the dance, and of course, Paddy.

As soon as she arrived at the house she set the hamper in the bedroom and went out to the patio, where Paddy was. He began wagging his tail and licking her everyplace he could reach. She gave him a quick pat, but for once he would just have to wait for his dinner and play time.

Irish was usually washing dishes out on her patio at this time of the evening and Mariette prayed she would be there. All four of those males who thought they were in charge had given her strict orders to come right back to the ship if she didn't find her friend immediately, and for once she not only said she agreed, she really did agree. It would be too dangerous for the *Fortune* to stay at the docks any longer than necessary. If Irish wasn't to be found, and quickly, she would have to be left behind. For now.

When Mariette peeked into the next door patio, she breathed a deep sigh of relief. Irish was just hanging up her dishpan. A few moments longer and she might have already been inside and inaccessible.

Making sure her friend was alone, Mariette pushed open the gate. Irish turned and Mariette motioned for her to come with her. As soon as they were inside Alejandro's patio, Mariette shut the gate and took Irish's arm in a tight grip. She had thought a long time about how she would approach Irish about going with them, and had decided that she must make sure she really did want to escape before divulging that she was English. Sometimes, in spite of what her brothers thought, she could be very cautious.

Speaking low and in simple Spanish, Mariette looked intently into Irish's eyes. "You said once that you would do anything to escape to an English colony. Do you still feel that way?"

Irish's brows knotted, "Why do you ask?"

"Just tell me."

Irish's eyes narrowed suspiciously, but she nodded. "Yes, I would escape if I could. Why?"

"I can help you get away. Now."

Her friend's eyes widened and Mariette could see hope filling them. "How?"

Mariette straightened and switched to English. "I am English, with more than a bit of Irish in me as well, and I am on my way back home to Charles Town. You can come with me, but we have to go now."

Mariette could see the questions, the demands for explanations springing up in Irish's expression. She shushed her. "There is no time for questions now. If you want to go, you must simply trust me for now and do what I tell you."

It did not take Irish long to give a quick nod of acceptance. "What do I do?"

"Do you have anything you need to take?"

Irish shook her head. "I have nothing but the clothes I stand in. I'm ready."

"Good. You get Paddy, his dish, and a little food for him while

I gather a few things from the house. Then we'll go."

Irish bent to call Paddy from the far corner of the patio where he was sniffing at something. "Where will we go?"

"My brother's ship, the *Fortune*, is waiting at the docks. I'll just be a moment." She headed inside to get Alejandro's documents.

"Maria."

Mariette turned. Paddy was waddling toward them and Irish grinned up at Mariette. "It's good to speak English again."

Mariette nodded. "But when we get to the street, we must speak only Spanish until we are safely aboard my brother's ship."

Irish nodded and clapped her hands softly for Paddy to hurry to her.

Mariette stuffed her dress and a few of Alejandro's clothes into the hamper and then began looking for his documents. At first he had refused to tell her where they were, saying that he did not want her to risk the extra time to get them. But when she said it would just take her even more time to find them on her own, he had relented.

She looked down at the floor. This room was covered in tiles and she counted seven tiles from the door and bent to pry up the tile that Alejandro had assured her was loose. It came up easily and she pulled out a leather pouch. It was heavy with coin but when she opened it, she found the papers also folded inside.

It was just as Alejandro had said. Letters of credit and a document claiming him as the natural son of Lord Randall. She didn't take the time to read the rest. That could be done later. She was in the process of stuffing the documents back into the pouch when the door of the bedroom slammed open.

With a start Mariette turned. Ignatio stood blocking the doorway, a lecherous grin on his face. "Well, my dear, I have had men watching for you and was wondering when you would return."

Chapter Twenty

MARIETTE HID THE POUCH BEHIND HER. FEAR CLOTTED HER brain. Sweat began to dampen her palms. Alejandro had been right. She did not know his uncle. She had never expected Ignatio to come after her when he thought he might soon have Alejandro's head.

She forced herself to smile. "Alejandro will be home soon. I will tell him you stopped by."

Ignatio advanced a step into the room. "Alejandro will never be home again, Maria."

"I don't understand."

"You are very beautiful, Maria, but like most women, you are sadly lacking in wit. Alejandro will not be home because the militia has orders to shoot him on sight."

Mariette's heart began to race and her eyes widened. "But why?"

Ignatio gave her a smile that she thought would have looked right at home on a snake. "For helping two English prisoners to escape."

"But he didn't help them."

"Oh, I am sure I can convince a carefully picked tribunal that he did."

"And what if he brings them back?" She tried not to sound smug.

Ignatio shrugged. "As I said, he is to be shot on sight." He rubbed his thumb and fingers together as if fingering a coin. "I am sure that any poor soldier will swear that he was fleeing with them rather than bringing them in."

The blood seemed to drain from her head, yet knowing that Alejandro was already safe aboard the *Fortune* gave her the strength to remain standing. But she had to get away. If she didn't return to the ship, she was sure Nate would not sail away without her. One of her brothers would come looking for her and then her whole plan could come tumbling down about them. They could all be caught and shot, right along with Alejandro. She lunged for the storage room door. Ignatio caught her easily. Far easier than she would have expected, given his bulk. She screamed and he backhanded her, knocking her to the floor. She tried to get to her feet but he scooped her up and tossed her onto the bed. She kicked out at him but he fell across her and grasped her by the wrists.

"Get off of me! Let me go!" she cried.

Ignatio put both her wrists together to hold in one hand. That was when he spotted Alejandro's pouch.

"What is this?" Still lying across her and holding both her wrists in one hand, he snatched up the pouch.

Her eyes widened in fear. Ignatio held in his hand all the proof he needed to stand Alejandro in front of a firing squad. If he caught them, if he took the *Fortune*, the fact that Alejandro was chained to the bulkhead would not make any difference to Ignatio—or to any 'handpicked court' he put together.

"Something of importance, is it?" he asked, gripping her wrists so tightly she winced in pain.

She fought him harder then, kicking and screaming, but he only laughed. "Scream all you want, my lovely little bitch. No one is coming to aid you. The two guards outside the house know my tastes well. They will expect to hear you scream. And it will only sharpen their anticipation for when I give them their turn with you."

He tossed the pouch onto the bed beside her and pulled off his neck cloth. With practiced ease he tied one end of it around her wrists and looped the other end about one bedpost.

Taking out a knife he held it up in front of her, moving it to catch the light. She could not take her eyes off that knife, she could not breathe. She tried to shrink away from its edge, but there was nowhere to go. This is what he wants, she told herself. To see your fear, to taste it. Determined not to give him anything he wanted, she tore her gaze from that glinting blade and glared at him, clamping her mouth shut, not giving him the satisfaction of asking what he was going to do with it.

He chuckled. "You are very brave, Maria. This is going to be so much more fun than I had anticipated." With a vicious grin he turned and used the knife to cut the hem from her skirt, cutting the strip into three pieces.

Using his body to keep her legs still, he tied a piece around each ankle and tied her ankles to the bottom bed posts. Then he freed one of her hands long enough to tie the third piece around that wrist and bind her spread-eagled to the four bedposts.

Gleefully he surveyed his work. "How lovely you look with your arms spread wide waiting for my embrace and your legs spread like a whore's waiting anxiously, I am sure, for what you are certainly going to get." He chuckled again. But we are not going to be too hasty, my lovely Maria. There is too much fun to be had before that final"—he chuckled again— "climax."

He picked up the pouch. "First, let us see what you were in the process of pilfering from your 'employer', shall we?"

Maria jerked her hands hard against her bonds, but her struggles only seemed to tighten the knots that held her.

Ignatio hefted the pouch, listening to the clink of the coins it held. "A thief caught in the very act. Tsk, tsk, Maria. I shall have to punish you for that. And one of us is going to enjoy that very much." He pursed his mouth in mock sympathy. "What a shame it won't be you."

She would not give him the satisfaction of denying his claim that she was a thief. She knew it would do her no good anyway.

He also heard the crinkle of the papers inside. "But what else have we here?" He opened the pouch and pulled out Alejandro's documents, quickly scanning them. "Ha!" he crowed with delight. "My dear, you have delivered my enemy into my hands. I might never have found this on my own. I must find a way to thank you properly." He ran a hand up one of her legs. "Aah, but I have already found a way, haven't I?"

Irish watched Mariette go into the house then scooped Paddy up and squeezed him tightly and happily to her. She held him up and looked into his little face. "We're getting out of here, Paddy." He tried to lick her nose and she chuckled. "I don't know where we're going or to what, but it's got to be better than this, as long as no one ever finds out who I really am."

Tucking him under her arm she went to the stove and found a few scraps of meat Maria had laid aside for him. She gave him one piece and wrapped the rest in a cloth.

She couldn't help humming happily to herself and swaying to the rhythm of her own melody. Once again, there was hope. Real hope. Not the many false hopes she had encouraged herself with over the last six months.

Her head came up and her tune stopped. Her money! She wasn't going to leave without her money. It was all she had in the world and she wasn't going to leave it here. Besides, she might need it wherever she was going. Thank goodness she had left it here, in the captain's back room.

She went into the storage room from the patio and was just tucking her few coins into her bodice when she heard Maria scream. Momentarily paralyzed, Irish could only listen to the sounds of struggle coming from the bedroom. Surely it was not the captain in there with her friend. Irish crept to the door that led to the bedroom and edged it open a crack. It was the commandant of the fort. She had been in the crowd that had greeted him when he had arrived three weeks ago and marched through the marketplace. She shut the door and put her hand over her mouth, biting her lip. He had a knife and was threatening Maria with it. She could not fight a man with a knife. She had to get help for Maria. But where? Captain Alejandro could be anywhere, the fort, out with the prisoners he was guarding...

Think! She leaned her head against the wall and she could feel tears threatening. Not only was Maria in danger, but that small hope of her own freedom was beginning to dim. If something happened to Maria, she could remain a slave here for the rest of her life.

She lifted her head. Maria's brother! Maria had said he was waiting for her at the docks. They were only a few blocks away. Irish slipped back out of the storage room, scooped up Paddy and went out the back gate to the alley. She hurried toward the docks as fast as she could without attracting undue attention.

When Irish arrived at the docks, she was struck with dismay. There were so many ships! How was she going to find Maria's brother? The name of his ship. Maria had told her the name. Of course, the *Fortune*. She had thought at the time that it was her good fortune that she would be taken to freedom in a ship named the *Fortune*. She looked up and down the docks but could not see a ship called the *Fortune*. Then she spotted it. It had the look of an English ship, but it was named *La Fortuna*. Could that be the one? It had to be.

"¡*Holá! ¡Alli en La Fortuna!*" she hailed them in her still wretched Spanish. She did not dare use English in case she was wrong, or some of the people nearby heard her.

A face with incredible blue eyes appeared over the railing of the ship and looked at her, then up and down the docks. "¿*Sí?*"

"Are you Maria's brother?" she asked in Spanish.

The man's eyes narrowed. "Who are you?"

"My name is Irish."

Those blue eyes widened in alarm. "Where is Maria?"

"She's…are you Maria's brother?"

"Si. Where is she?"

Irish looked around. Their conversation was beginning to attract notice. "Can I come aboard?"

The face disappeared, a gangplank was lowered to her, and Irish hurried aboard. The man waiting for her seemed not much more than a boy at first glance, but one look into the depths of those eyes told her that beneath that boyish slimness was a man. He pulled in the gangplank before facing her, hands on hips. "Where is my sister?"

Irish switched to English. "She's in trouble."

"I knew it!" Grabbing her arm he dragged her down into a small cabin where three men sat on bunks. Irish recognized one of them. "*Capitán* de Silva!"

The captain smiled and nodded to her but when he saw that she was alone, he sat up in alarm. She was not given time to ask why he was there.

The man who had brought her to the cabin said, "Mariette's in trouble."

"Damn!" cursed a man with eyes as blue as the first one.

The captain stood up and took her arm, urging her to sit beside him. Her eyes widened at the sight of his chained wrist.

"Tell us what happened, Irish," the captain said calmly.

She blinked, momentarily surprised that he spoke perfect English. "She came to me and said she would help me escape." She looked around at the men and was relieved to see them nod their heads as if they already knew that. "She went into the house to get something and told me to get Paddy." She held up the puppy who was now squirming to get loose. "I remembered that I had hidden some money in your storage room, Captain, so I went to get it. That's when I heard her scream." The captain's grip on her arm tightened so much she winced. "I peeked through the door. The commandant of the fort had her…" She bit her lip remembering, but made herself continue. "He had her tied to the bed and had a knife. She had told me that her brother was waiting for us on his ship. I decided to come for help."

The blue-eyed man on the bunk stood up, gasped with pain from a wound on his leg and held out his hand to the other blue-eyed man. "Give me your pistol, Nate. I'm going after her."

A tall, blond man pushed him back down. "You can barely walk, Matthew. I'll go."

"A blond, sun-burned man in ragged clothes? Really, Douglass, you're who the patrols will be looking for," the first man, the one called Nate, said. "I'll go."

"You little whelp," Matthew said, "you're not going anyplace. If something happens to you, who's going to sail this ship?"

The captain stood up, jerking at the chain that bound him. "None of you is going anyplace. I'm the only one who can."

"Do you really believe we'd let you loose?" Douglass asked.

"Who else can go? You've said it yourselves. He"—he pointed at Nate—"is needed to sail the ship. He"—he pointed at Matt—"can barely walk, let alone face my uncle. And you"—he pointed at

Douglass—"stand out like a sore thumb and can barely understand Spanish, let alone speak it."

Alejandro looked at the three of them. "Besides, none of you knows where my house is, nor how to get in the back way without attracting attention."

The three men glared at him a moment, then looked at each other.

"We're wasting time! Who knows what he's done to Maria by now!" He held out his wrist imperiously.

Matthew, standing with his weight on his good leg, gave him a long considering look, his hands on his hips, then said to Nate, "Let him go."

"Are you crazy?" Nate cried. "What if everything he's said is a lie and he turns us and her in? How do we know we can trust him?"

"I think we can trust him, Nate." He looked directly into the captain's eyes. "I've seen how he looks at Mariette. He's the one who didn't want to let her go into town in the first place. He's not going to turn her in. And he's right. We have no choice. He's the only one of us with any chance of getting to her and getting her back here. Let him go."

Douglass pursed his lips then nodded in agreement. Nate glared at Alejandro, but pulled a key from his pocket and unlocked the manacle.

Alejandro put his hat on, adjusting it to cover the bandage then grabbed Nate's gun and knife, tucking the pistol into his own waist and the knife inside his waistcoat. As he started out of the cabin Matt gripped his arm. "You'd better bring her back, Captain. She's my twin."

"And she's the woman I love," said Alejandro and he went flying up the steps to the deck.

"Make it fast or we'll lose the tide!" Nate called to his retreating back.

The woman I love? Where had that come from? Alejandro asked himself as he hurried down the dock and into town. From my heart, was the answer. It had been her beauty that had first attracted him. Then her innocence had held him at bay and made him look at her anew. She had surprised him with her intelligence, her medical skills, her compassion for the suffering of others. She had even taken in Paddy.

He gripped the butt of the pistol. He had to clear his thoughts. He would need all his wits about him if he was going to save Maria. Mariette. He could not help but smile. She had deceived him, but he understood the reason why. He would have done the same thing if he had had a brother in trouble. And thinking about it now, he had to admire her cleverness in planning and carrying out her scheme. And her daring. Most women he knew would faint at the thought of going into an enemy stronghold in disguise in hopes of rescuing someone they loved.

Mariette had not only been willing to put her life in danger for her brother, but would have sacrificed herself for him if things had not worked out as they had. How could he not love her?

Alejandro slowed when he spotted a soldier standing at the next corner, his musket at the ready. Alert. Had Ignatio stationed him there to watch for the two English prisoners who had escaped?

He cut down a side street to avoid the man. He did not have time to answer questions about the prisoners or why he sported a head wound. He had to get to Mariette. There were only two more blocks to his house, but knowing his uncle, there would be guards posted outside the front door. He would turn down the alley at the end of the next block, go through the patio to the storage room and surprise his uncle.

He had just entered the alley when someone called his name.

Alejandro turned, reaching for his pistol, but his hand froze just as his fingers touched it. Raúl, the militiaman who had served under him guarding the prisoners, stood at the end of the alley with a pistol aimed straight at his heart.

Mariette thought Ignatio took an extraordinarily long time folding his coat to lay it over the back of a chair. Not that she was looking forward to what was coming next, but the commandant carefully laid the coat over the chair then turned toward her, rubbing his hands together, eyeing her with a lascivious grin, then turned back to adjust the arms of the coat just so. Again he turned to her, then back to smooth a wrinkle from the coat, adjusting it neatly, then back to her once more.

She was beginning to grit her teeth and just wish he would get on with it when she realized that he was dallying for the sole purpose of tormenting her, making her tense in anxiety, relax in reprieve, until she was ready to scream. He was enjoying using this little tactic to torment her, to draw out his own anticipation. Whatever he had planned for her could very well take all night. He seemed determined to draw every last sip of pleasure he could from her defilement, and all at her expense. Tiring of his little coat folding game, he finally stood beside the bed rubbing his hands together and looking at her from head to toe, as if gleefully trying to decide where to begin.

Mariette was sure he knew exactly where he would start, what he would do. He just wanted to keep her in suspense and terrorized. And he was succeeding. He reached out to touch one of her breasts and she could not help but give him the satisfaction of flinching.

"Oh, dear, dear," Ignatio said, a pained expression on his face. "This will never do." And then he grinned maliciously. "There is much too much play in your bonds, my dear. I would not want you to have too much freedom." He sighed heavily as if the fact that she could move her arms and legs a bit was entirely her fault. "I suppose I must tighten them."

He untied the strip that held her right arm outstretched then quickly pulled it tighter and re-tied it. He ran his fingers lightly down her arm, muttering, "Better, better." She tried not to flinch from him, but still, he shook his head and said, "But not good enough. Perhaps the other arm, as well."

Slowly he walked around to the other side of the bed, pausing to flick imaginary specks from his shirt sleeve. Mariette tensed, ready to jerk her arm away and hopefully gain her freedom when he released her. But he was prepared for her attempt, perhaps even hoping for it, for as soon as he loosened the knot and she tried to yank her arm free, he caught her wrist in a paralyzing grip and laughed delightedly.

She felt sickened when he tightened her bonds then ran his fingers down her arm, smiling to himself and again muttering, "Better, better."

Then he loosened one foot and tightened that bond, then the other, each time running a hand up her leg, smiling broader and broader the higher up her leg his touch went...and the more she tensed. Grinning, watching her closely, Ignatio touched the tip of one breast. She could not help herself. She writhed away from that evil touch. He clucked his tongue, shaking his head sadly from side to side. Then he began the tightening process all over again, going from one limb to another, tightening her bonds, stretching her tightly. He was an expert at this and soon had her nearly immobilized. She was tied with strips of cloth but still her wrists and ankles ached with the strain.

She would not cry, she told herself, nor beg. It would only give him satisfaction and she was sure he wouldn't release her no matter how much she pleaded with him. When he had her bound as tightly as he was able, he stood at the foot of the bed and looked at her. "Ah, Maria," he said, and his hand went down to stroke himself, growing the bulge in his breeches, "how lovely you look. You are almost ready for me, are you not?"

She did not deign to answer, only glared at him. Her look did not bother him in the least. He merely chuckled. Then he cocked his head and tapped one thick finger against his lips as if in deep thought. "Hmm. I do think we could do better."

Mariette almost cried out then. How could he possibly tighten her bonds any more? Already she ached with the pull. But it was not her bonds he had in mind this time. It was her clothing.

"I love to see a woman's leg," Ignatio told her, as if discussing a particular flower in his garden. "What a shame that they are kept hidden." He pushed her skirt up to her knees and stroked her legs. His hand lingered at her ankle where the strips cut from her skirt bound them. "And how wonderful to see such a lovely limb stretched out and bound just for me."

He moved to the side of the bed and pushed her sleeves up to her shoulders, stroking along the length of her arms. "Lovely, but women often bare their arms," he said shrugging. Then his gaze went to her breasts and she sucked in her breath.

No! she thought. But he pulled on her chemise, tugging it down over her breasts, baring both. Slowly, slowly he traced around one breast with his finger, circling closer and closer toward the tip. Then he pinched that tip enough to make her wince and gasp. He chuckled and again stroked himself, his eyes half-closed with pleasure.

Mariette bit her lip to keep from crying out in humiliation. She had always imagined a rape to be quick and violent, not this deliberately unhurried degradation.

"Perhaps a little more leg," he said, and pushed her skirt and petticoat and chemise up past her knees.

A sharp rap sounded at the door and Ignatio jumped, his eyes round and frightened like a little boy who has just been caught doing something naughty. But that glimpse into the commandant's mind lasted only a split second before his expression became violently angry. He cursed and spun around to face the door. "I told you I was not to be disturbed," he growled, his hands clenching and unclenching.

"Commandant, we have *Capitán* de Silva!"

Ignatio's expression changed from angry to triumphant as he spun back to her. "Well! It seems you were right, my dear! My nephew has returned after all. Now it seems I will have the pleasure of personally taking care of the both of you."

He chewed a lip thoughtfully for a moment, looking from her to the door as if unsure which of his pleasures to take first. At last he stepped back to her side, yanked her skirt down and her chemise up. "No need to let those louts enjoy the sight of you before I am done, is there?" Then he went to the door and jerked it open. Mariette could not help the whimper that escaped her lips when she saw Alejandro…with two pistols at his back.

Chapter Twenty-one

RAUL'S PISTOL SAVAGELY JABBED IN THE BACK. ALEJANDRO stepped into the room, and didn't know which sight he hated worse—the triumphant grin on his uncle's face, or Mariette bound to the bed, her wrists and ankles already red from the tightness of her bonds.

He glared into Ignatio's eyes. "What are you doing with my housekeeper? Let her go."

"Tsk, tsk," Ignatio said, holding up one fat finger in warning. His grin broadened and he bounced on the balls of his feet. "I will ask the questions here. And I will make the demands." He took his coat from the back of the chair and nodded to Paco, who held the second pistol. "Tie him there."

Raúl shoved Alejandro down into the chair and stepped back to keep the pistol on him. Paco looked around for something to tie him with.

"Imbeciles!" Ignatio pulled out a knife and with a gallant nod of his head to Mariette, cut away a strip from the bottom of her skirt and tossed it to Paco. It was the same material that bound her, Alejandro noted.

Paco pulled Alejandro's arms behind him and began to tie his wrists. Alejandro clenched his fists and strained his muscles to make his wrists larger. Along with Paco's typical overeager inefficiency, it might just be enough to enable him to get loose.

"I found him in the street, Commandant." Raúl boasted. "I know you said we could shoot him on sight, but I thought you would prefer a trial and a firing squad for this traitor."

"Yes," Ignatio drawled, "just so." He nodded toward the door. "Now get out."

"But Commandant–"

"Get out, I said! And don't interrupt me again. No matter what you hear." He looked at Mariette. "As I said before, you might hear a bit of screaming." Then he nodded toward Alejandro. "And you might hear a little something from him, as well." He smiled at the two guards brightly. "But don't worry. I'm sure there will be plenty left for the two of you to enjoy when I am through."

Raúl ogled Mariette. "Thought you were too good for me, didn't you, you slut? I'll teach you to service me and beg me for more." Looking down his nose at Alejandro he shoved Paco out the door ahead of him and left the room.

Alejandro worked at the strips that bound his hands. "Why did you order me shot on sight, Uncle? I have done nothing."

"You have allowed two of the prisoners to escape, 'Nephew'. And now I will have you shot."

"That is not reason enough to shoot me."

Ignatio smiled, picked up something from the bedside table and held it up in front of Alejandro…his leather pouch. "It is when I can prove that you are an English spy sent here to help the prisoners escape."

"Shoot me if you will, Ignatio, but let her go."

Ignatio backhanded him across the face, splitting his lip and knocking his hat to the floor. "I give the orders now, my 'noble nephew'!" To prove his point he swaggered to the bed to run his hand over Mariette's breast. "I will indeed stand you up in front of a firing squad, but only after you have watched me have my way with your little 'housekeeper'. I'm so glad you replaced the one I had hired for you. It will be so much more fun having sweet little Maria than that old whore."

Alejandro swore under his breath as he watched Mariette bite her lip and flinch from Ignatio's touch. For that alone, he should kill the man.

"Never again will I have to give way to a bastard usurper simply because my older brother was too pigheaded to believe that his mealy-mouthed wife had cuckolded him. Thank God he came to his senses. He told me in a letter that he'd finally learned the truth about you, Alejandro, and that you were coming to St. Augustine. How fortunate that I was able to volunteer to help out dear Governor Montiano and greet you at your arrival."

Alejandro tried to remain unperturbed. He had to keep his uncle talking, boasting—anything to keep his attention off of Mariette. Anything to give him time to work himself loose.

"You will not get away with shooting me, Uncle. Even if I am a bastard, I am still the son of a noble house."

Ignatio backhanded him again. "Uncle! I have never been your uncle. I have put up with the title because I have had to, but no more! Never call me uncle again."

Alejandro nodded as if graciously acquiescing to a humble plea from an underling. "It will be my pleasure to disavow any familial connection with you."

"Bastard!" Ignatio sneered.

Alejandro shrugged nonchalantly. "I believe we have already established that status as it pertains to me. Now as to you—you are working your way to claiming that same title for yourself with every breath you take, and without any help at all from your mother."

Enraged, Ignatio leaped at Alejandro, reaching for his throat and knocking the chair backward to the floor. But Alejandro's efforts to free himself, combined with the ineptitude of Paco, had met with success. Alejandro shook off the strip of Mariette's skirt even as he fell and he was able to grab Ignatio's shirt front, taking the commandant to the floor with him.

Ignatio's fingers were fat and thick but surprisingly strong, cutting off Alejandro's air. Alejandro brought his hands up between Ignatio's, and, using his arms, managed to break Ignatio's hold and throw the commandant off him. Ignatio landed hard, and Alejandro heard his head bang against the stone tiles. The commandant groaned and tried to sit up, but fell back.

Alejandro scrambled to his feet, pulling Nate's dagger from inside his waistcoat. Standing astride Ignatio, he reached down and grabbed a handful of the commandant's shirt, and jerked him upright. Alejandro realized Ignatio must have hit his head even harder than it had sounded for his eyes were unfocused, his brows knitted in an effort to concentrate. Shoving the man ahead of him, Alejandro went to the bed and cut through the fabric that bound one of Mariette's wrists. Then he handed her the knife to finish freeing herself.

Mariette lost no time cutting through the strips of cloth. "When I saw you come in with Raúl's pistol at your back, I thought all was lost."

Alejandro was glad to note that, in spite of what she had been through, Mariette's voice held only a slight quaver.

"We are not out of this yet," he said. He tightened his grip on Ignatio, whose eyes were no longer so unfocused as they were.

Mariette looked at her erstwhile captor and nodded, sliding off the bed. As soon as she was off, Alejandro shoved Ignatio down onto the mattress and began tying him with the same material he had used to bind Mariette.

Some of the pieces were too short now that they had been cut, so Mariette sacrificed a few more strips of her sadly shortened skirt and helped tie Ignatio. He began to struggle as they finished and Alejandro used a last piece to form a gag.

Ignatio was glaring at them, hatred burning in his eyes. He tried to call for the guards, but his cries were muffled by the gag.

"You might as well relax, 'Uncle'. Your guards will not disturb your fun. At least not for a good long while."

Ignatio raged at him, jerking on his bonds so hard he shook the massive bed.

Alejandro tucked the pouch containing his documents and money into his waistcoat. Mariette already stood by the door to the storage room, a hamper slung over her shoulder, the knife tucked inside her waistband. She looked fierce enough, and ragged enough, to be a member of one of the bandit bands that plagued Spain.

"Unless there is something particular you want to take, I have already packed some clothes for you," she said.

"There is." He reached into the corner and picked up his lute. He paused to look down at Ignatio. "I should kill you for what you have done to Maria, Ignatio. But at times you were like a true uncle to me. Perhaps the only reason you taught me to play the lute was because my father disdained it so much, but you did teach me. At least I can thank you for the gift of music you gave me."

Ignatio's only answer was a fierce growl and an angry scowl.

Alejandro scooped up his hat from where it had fallen on the floor, put it on, gave Ignatio one last salute of farewell and followed Mariette out the door. He hurriedly grabbed a few more of his belongings from his trunks as he passed through the storage room, tucking them into a bag.

On the patio, Mariette was looking around frantically when Alejandro took her arm and pulled her into the alley.

"Where is Irish?" Mariette demanded. "We can't leave without her."

Alejandro pulled her along. "She's already aboard the *Fortune*. How do you think we knew you were in trouble?"

"Thank goodness she is safe! But I cannot believe my brothers let you come for me."

Alejandro shoved her behind him as they came to the end of the alley. He peered around the corner of a high coquina wall, then, seeing no soldiers, took her arm to continue on their way.

"They had no choice. They didn't know where my house was and could not very well show their faces in town with every militia-man looking for escaped English prisoners."

As they hurried toward the docks a few people looked at them strangely. Alejandro was sure they would remember a Spanish captain and a bedraggled Mestiza with half her skirt shredded when Ignatio got loose and began asking questions. He could only pray that Nate's little ship was fast enough to get them all well on their way before Paco and Raúl dared to open that bedroom door and set Ignatio free.

As soon as they were within sight of the *Fortune*, a gangplank was shoved out onto the dock. They hurried up it onto the deck. Matt hugged Mariette briefly and nodded wordless thanks to Alejandro, their gazes meeting and holding for a long moment of mutual approval.

Irish took her turn to hug Mariette with a wiggling, licking Paddy between them.

Nate did no more than nod to them before he was loosening sails and directing Douglass at the tiller. Alejandro was soon pressed into service, hauling at a sheet and tying it around a belaying pin in response to Nate's crisp orders. Within moments they were underway, the sails of the little ship filling with the breeze as if it were as eager as its passengers to get home.

Once the sails were set and the *Fortune* was moving steadily out of the harbor, Alejandro went to stand at the rail, looking back at the walls of *El Castillo*, watching as the last of his life as a Spaniard slid away. He gripped the railing hard, knowing that, for him, there could be no going back. He felt a touch on his arm and turned to see Mariette standing beside him.

"You can never return to Spain, can you?"

He shook his head. "No."

"I'm sorry." She leaned against him and he put his arm around her, holding on to her as if she were a lifeline in a stormy sea.

"There is nothing to go back to. My mother is dead. My father…" He straightened, lifting his chin. "My father is in England."

Nate joined them at the rail with a big grin on his face. "We did it! We snatched Matt and Douglass right out from under the noses of the Spanish!" He made a swooshing motion through the air with the flat of his hand. "We sailed right in and right out. An English ship, sailing right past the walls of *El Castillo* and not one shot fired. Don't know why Oglethorpe had so much trouble."

Alejandro had to laugh at Nate's youthful enthusiasm. "Don't get too cocky, Nate. If Ignatio hadn't stripped the garrison to send them out looking for me up by Ft. Mose, you just might not have made it. Governor Montiano would not have been so foolish. Fortunately for us, Ignatio was more concerned with revenge than the well being of the colony."

There was a good deal of congratulations, back slapping, and thanks as they all watched *El Castillo* disappear behind them and the open sea stretch out before them. Dusk turned to night and everyone settled down to sleep, Mariette and Irish in the little cabin below, the men wrapped in blankets on the deck, Nate standing the first watch at the tiller.

It was shortly after Nate roused Matt to take his place that Alejandro heard Mariette come on deck. He watched her standing at the railing very close to where he lay.

"Can't sleep?" he asked as he stood up to join her.

"Still too wound up, I suppose," she answered.

He put his arm around her. "You've had quite an adventure."

"It was worth it to save Matt and Douglass, but I might think twice before starting another one."

"I'm glad you started this one."

She turned back to face the sea. "What will you do now? Will you go to England?"

He looked at her in surprise. "I thought I would stay in Charles Town. How could I leave you?"

He saw her fingers grip the rail. "You were going to leave me in St. Augustine. You told me so."

He nodded. "Yes, when I thought you were Maria, a simple woman of mixed blood."

"But not now that you know I am a wealthy Englishwoman? Is that what makes the difference, Alejandro?"

"No!" He gripped her shoulders, forcing her to face him. "It is true I would have left you behind when I thought you were Maria. I had no idea how I would get to an English colony myself, what dangers I might have to face. Maria had a home, brothers, parents. How could I ask her to leave with me, go to another colony, another culture where no one spoke her language, perhaps never see her family again? It was tearing me apart, loving you but knowing it would be best for you to leave you behind."

Mariette's jaw dropped. "You love me?"

"How could I not? I wanted you from the first moment I saw you in the marketplace. But then I realized what a good person you were, how special, how knowledgeable. You were always surprising me. I fell in love with that woman. With you. Now that I know who you really are, how can I love you any less? You are still that sweet, compassionate woman I came to love, but you are so much more it is hard for me to take it all in. Daring, brave, loyal–"

"I can't cook."

"What?"

"I can't cook. If you are going to ask me to marry you, I thought you should know that first. I would make a terrible wife. I'm a disaster in the kitchen. My friend made those sweet potato muffins."

"We'll hire a cook," he said, trying hard not to laugh. He pulled her close and put his arms around her. "So, will you?"

She cocked her head, a teasing twinkle in her eyes. "Will I what?"

"Will you marry me?"

"I thought you'd never ask."

He did laugh then, full and heartily, throwing back his head. "How could I not?" Then he kissed her, tasting her anew.

"If you are going to kiss my sister like that, Captain de Silva, I hope you are willing to marry her."

Alejandro and Mariette jumped apart. They had forgotten all about Matt at the tiller just a few feet away.

"I will," Alejandro answered. "I mean I am. I just asked her and…" he turned to Mariette, "I think that kiss was a yes."

"It was," Mariette took his hand. "And now that I have a witness, you're stuck with me even if I can't cook. I did warn you after all."

"I'll have to warn him about a few other things if he thinks he's brave enough to take you on." Matt grinned at Alejandro. "But somehow, I think he'll be able to handle you. And without boring you to death, either."

Matt stood up and stretched. "If you two are going to stay up half the night talking, why don't you take the tiller? I could use the rest."

"I'm afraid I don't know much about sailing," Alejandro said.

"I do." Mariette slid into Matt's place. "There isn't a Fortune born who doesn't know how to sail. Of course, some of us, like Nate, are a lot better at it than others."

"You can sail a ship but you can't cook?"

"I'm a Fortune, and if you're going to be part of this family, it's time you started to learn to sail."

Alejandro sat down beside her. "So what do I do first?"

It was nearly noon on their second day of sailing when Nate suddenly stuck his spyglass into his belt, kicked off his shoes and scurried to the top of the mast. Mariette watched her brother steadying himself with one arm around the mast while he set the spyglass to his eye, studying the sea astern.

"What is it, Nate?" Matt called, standing on tiptoe and peering in the same direction.

Nate didn't answer for several moments but when he did, his voice was grim. "It's the *Eagle*."

By the time Nate slid back to the deck, everyone was looking at the white speck of sail on the horizon. Alejandro set his arm across her shoulders and Mariette leaned into him for comfort. But he was all hard ridges and tense muscles.

"Are you sure?" Matt asked.

Nate handed him the glass. By now there was no need to scramble to a higher vantage point. The ship behind them was closer.

"The *Eagle*?" Irish looked from one to the other in puzzlement.

"A Spanish ship of the line." Nate's fists went to his hips and he leaned back to study the set of the sails. "A warship."

Irish clutched Mariette's hand. "Do you think they'll intercept us?"

Matt snapped the spyglass shut. "You can count on it."

"But maybe they won't. Maybe they'll veer off."

Alejandro began shedding his coat and rolling up his sleeves. "They won't veer off, Irish. They're pursuing us. The *Eagle* was in the harbor when we left St. Augustine."

Nate peered up at the sun. "They must have left soon after we did. Probably on the very next tide."

"Is there any way we can get any more speed?" Alejandro asked.

"A little, but they're bigger and with a lot more sail. They've spotted us by now. There's no way we can outrun them."

"What weapons do you have aboard?" Douglass asked. "I've no mind to be a prisoner of the Spanish again."

"Nor I." Irish's eyes were blazing with determination.

Nate looked around at the expectant faces waiting for his answer. He sighed. "There are a couple of sabers, one pistol, one musket, and one three pounder stern chaser. Not much up against forty cannon."

"How far are we from Charles Town?" Mariette asked.

"Several more hours," Nate answered. "The *Eagle* will overtake us long before we reach safety."

"What about Savannah?" Douglass asked.

Nate shook his head. "We passed Savannah about an hour ago."

"Then we run and then we fight." Alejandro looked at Nate. "If our captain here will handle the sailing, I have some experience with cannon. With your permission, Captain Fortune?"

Nate grinned, but it was a grim, humorless grin. "You are now in charge of artillery."

Douglass bit his lip. "Just how much damage do you think you can do to a ship that size with one three pounder, de Silva?"

"Not much. Even if I'm lucky enough to knock a hole at her

waterline I doubt it will slow her down very much." He looked at Mariette and reached out to caress her jaw. "But what else can we do?"

Turning, he went to the stern and began uncovering the small cannon.

Douglass brought out the two sabers and gave one to Matt and one to Alejandro. Nate already had the pistol tucked into his belt. Douglass set himself to helping Alejandro bring up a keg of powder and load the cannon. Nate trimmed the sails to capture every scrap of breeze while Matt held the tiller.

Mariette could feel a slight increase in their speed, but the Eagle continued to loom larger. It wouldn't be long before they were within range of her guns.

"Mariette, you and Irish get below and set up a sick bay," Matt ordered.

Mariette nodded her agreement but had no intention of obeying. Matt just wanted her somewhere safer but she wanted to know what was going on.

And it wasn't long before something was indeed going on. A puff of smoke from the Eagle's bow announced the arrival of a sighting shot that landed with a splash just a few feet from their stern. Now that the Eagle's gunners had their range, their next shot would find them.

Mariette pulled Irish down beside her behind the mast where they would be somewhat protected but could still see.

"If I had a pistol I'd take one or two of those Spaniards down before I let them get their filthy hands on me again," Irish growled.

Mariette grinned her approval and patted the knife stuck into her waistband. "I'll not let them take us without a fight."

A second shot from the Eagle roared overhead tearing a huge hole in the mainsail.

"Damn!" Nate shook his fist at the enemy vessel. "That was a brand new sail!"

"If we get out of this, Little Brother," Matt called from the tiller, "I'll buy you a new one."

Nate tightened the sail hoping to keep as much wind in it as possible. "I'll hold you to that!"

Irish yelped with surprise when Alejandro set off the *Fortune's* cannon.

Mariette felt the ship shudder from the recoil. She stood up to see if Alejandro's shot had had any effect. It had hit the other ship, but glanced off. The *Eagle's* bow did not present a very good target.

Another shot tore through the rigging, ripping holes in the sails.

"At least they won't sink us if they keep aiming so high," Irish muttered, ducking falling debris.

"They're not trying to sink us," Mariette said. "They're trying to stop us by damaging our sails. They want to capture us, not sink us."

"Saints preserve us!"

"Amen to that."

The little stern chaser had cooled enough for Alejandro to load another shot. With the *Eagle* this close, surely even a three pounder would do some damage if he hit them.

"He's going to fire the cannon again," Mariette warned Irish, putting her hands over her ears. There was a roar and Mariette felt the recoil, then Matt and Douglass were pounding Alejandro's back in congratulations.

"You did it," Douglass cried. "Right at her waterline!"

"Aye," Matt agreed. "She's shipping water."

Alejandro nodded. "But not enough to slow her."

"Alejandro! Surrender! You know you don't have a chance!" came a call from the Spanish ship.

"Ignatio!" Alejandro spat out.

"Go to hell!" Nate answered through cupped hands.

They were close enough now that the Spanish were firing muskets at them.

"Surrender, Alejandro!" Ignatio called. "I'll spare Maria."

Mariette leaned forward to call to Alejandro. "Spare me for what? I'd rather die than surrender to what he has to offer me! How soon can you fire that cannon again?"

Alejandro turned to grin at her. "It's almost cool enough now, *Bandita!*"

Another shot raked through the Fortune's rigging, bringing curses from Nate and raining down splinters and pieces of sail.

Mariette felt the little ship falter to a halt with no means left to catch the breeze. Alejandro had time to get off one more shot before the *Eagle* was upon them. It went into their rigging, bringing down a few large splinters but not doing any real damage.

Grappling hooks were thrown from the *Eagle* and the *Fortune* was drawn tight against her side. Six muskets were trained on the *Fortune*'s crew from the higher deck of the Spanish ship. There was nothing left to do but drop weapons and raise hands in surrender.

Three Spanish sailors dropped down onto the deck of the Fortune, pistols at the ready. Two went below and one began prodding their English prisoners to climb the rope ladder up to the deck of the *Eagle*. Alejandro was the first to climb that ladder, followed by Matt and Douglass. Irish went next, glaring at the Spanish sailor who shoved her forward.

Mariette saw Nate take a last, long look around the deck of his ship, one hand fondly caressing the railing and a knot grew in her throat. This was her fault. Nate was going to lose his ship, his freedom, and maybe even his life, all because of her.

Then a musket poked her in the ribs and she turned to climb up to the deck of the *Eagle* with Nate close behind. As soon as Nate was aboard, Matt leaned close to him. "Not very many men for a ship this size, are there?" he asked his brother.

Nate scanned the ship with a sailor's judgmental squint. "They were in too much of a hurry to leave port to round up all the sailors. It's my guess they barely have enough to man her."

"I've counted a dozen, including the commandant," Matt said.

"Maybe there's more below?" Irish suggested.

Nate shook his head. "Only one cannon was firing. If they had more men, they would have used more cannon against us."

"Two of their men were wounded by that last shot from our cannon," Matt added.

A glint appeared in Nate's eyes. "Then they'll need help getting her back to port."

"I know what you two are thinking," Mariette whispered. "But even if we can take this ship, we don't have enough people to sail her."

"We'll deal with that problem when the time comes," Matt said. "Right now, just keep watch for any opportunity."

Douglass and Alejandro nodded their agreement and Irish's red head jerked once in a defiant nod.

"Well, well!" Ignatio came toward them rubbing his hands together gleefully. "It seems we have caught the two escaping English prisoners and the two traitors who helped them." He arched one brow at Alejandro and ran a lascivious look down Mariette making her feel soiled just from his gaze.

Alejandro stepped in front of Mariette. "Leave her out of this, Ignatio."

Ignatio's nostrils flared. "As soon as you turned traitor, Alejandro, you lost any right your position as heir gave you to tell me what to do."

Mariette could see Alejandro's jaw clench.

"Leave Maria out of this," Alejandro repeated, his tone more humble. "It's me you want, Ignatio."

Ignatio chuckled. "And it is you I have. Along with your co-horts." He looked them over, seeming to notice Irish for the first time. "Who is this lovely *roja*?"

"No one. A slave we forced to come along," Alejandro answered.

"Or one who is also trying to escape, I think." He leered at Irish.

"Perhaps we can work something out, *Roja*, and I will see that your master does not punish you too cruelly for your attempted escape."

Irish's head came up and she glared at Ignatio.

"Or perhaps I can suggest a few ideas for your master to use to punish you. Perhaps he will even allow me to take care of the matter for him."

Mariette noticed that Irish paled, but still she continued to face him with defiance.

Ignatio merely shrugged off her glare and went to stand in front of Nate. "And this last member of your treasonous group, Alejandro—who is he?"

"No one. Just a sailor we hired to take us away."

"Hmm. A lot of no one's here. Perhaps the log book from your little ship will give us more information. I believe our captain is looking through it now." He turned to call over his shoulder. "Captain Agrait, what have you found out from the log book?"

The Spanish captain came forward, a look of astonishment on his thin face as he thumbed through Nate's carefully kept log. "Commandant, do you know who we have here?"

Ignatio frowned impatiently. "That is what I asked you, Esteban."

Captain Agrait held out the logbook to Ignatio but Ignatio

batted it away. "You know I do not speak that heretic tongue. Tell me what it says."

Agrait looked at Nate. "That ship belongs to Nathanial Fortune who purchased it from Sean Fortune."

Ignatio grabbed the book. "Sean Fortune?" He scanned the page until he found that name then he looked up at Nate, a grin of complete triumph on his face. "And you are this Nathanial Fortune?"

Alejandro spoke before Nate could. "I told you he is no one, Ignatio."

Ignatio backhanded Alejandro so hard he reopened his split lip. The two Spanish sailors who were guarding them gripped their pistols tighter, anticipating having to use them. But Alejandro merely wiped the blood away with the back of his wrist and said nothing.

"Nathanial Fortune!" Ignatio rocked back and forth from the balls to the heels of his feet. "Sean Fortune's son, perhaps?"

Nate clamped his mouth shut and refused to answer.

"Just how did you get involved in helping English prisoners to escape?"

Captain Agrait reached to turn a page of the logbook. "There, Commandant," he said. "He wrote that he brings his sister, Mariette, to St. Augustine to rescue their brother, Matthew, and her fiancé, Douglass, from the Spanish."

Mariette's hopes sank. Dear, sweet Nate and his meticulous logbook had doomed them.

Ignatio's eyes widened as he swept his gaze over her. Mariette stood still as Ignatio walked slowly around her, looking her over anew from head to toe, his brows raised. "Maria, Mariette. So, *puta*, whore, you have done what few women have ever done. You have surprised me."

His gaze went to Douglass then to Matt. "You must be the

brother they came to rescue." He nodded toward Nate. "The resemblance is obvious." He stepped back shaking his head. "To think I had the son of Sean Fortune in my hand all along and did not know." He shrugged and a smirk grew on his lips. "But perhaps it was for the best because now I have three of you." He looked from one Fortune sibling to the other and then to Alejandro. "As well as this traitor who will not live to see the sun rise again." Ignatio leaned forward, going onto tiptoe to sneer directly into Alejandro's face. "A traitor caught in the very act does not deserve a trial. You will hang from a yardarm within the hour."

Mariette looked at Alejandro standing there unfalteringly, glaring at Ignatio without fear. He might die. Today. And it was all her fault. Her impulsiveness had brought him to this. If not for her, Matt and Douglass would not have escaped and Alejandro would not be in this mess. Nor would her brothers or Douglass. She swallowed hard. Or Irish.

She looked away. She could not look at any of the people she had led into disaster. That was when she saw the wounded Spanish sailor and what was about to happen to him. "Stop!" She had to shove Ignatio aside to get past him, but she didn't give that a second thought as she rushed to the wounded man's side, all her medicinal instincts taking precedence. "Stop!" she repeated in Spanish to the second sailor who was about to remove a huge splinter from the man's thigh.

The man stopped in bewilderment, looking to his captain for guidance. Mariette also turned to the captain. "Don't let him remove the splinter without applying a tourniquet first. Otherwise, he just might bleed to death before the wound can be stitched."

Ignatio gripped her arm and tried to pull her away but the captain stopped him. "How do you know this?" he asked Mariette.

Mariette calmed herself and tried to look as competent as she could. The Spanish were even worse than the English in thinking a woman couldn't possibly know how to stitch a wound. "I am a trained doctor. I can help him."

Ignatio started to protest but the captain held up a hand. "He is Spanish and your enemy. Why would you help him?"

"Right now he is merely a man in need of medical attention. And I have promised to care for any I could." True, she had never formally taken the Hippocratic oath, but she had promised her Grandmother Fortune to use her skills to help any who needed them. She took that promise seriously.

The captain hesitated and then Alejandro spoke. "She is skilled, *Capitán* Agrait."

Ignatio again started to protest but the captain froze him with a glare.

"That man is my nephew, Commandant. Unlike you, I care for my nephew."

He nodded and Mariette bent to examine the wound.

A sailor hastened to bring her the things she needed, a basin of salt water, a medical kit with needles and thread. All else faded away as she concentrated on her task, applying the tourniquet, then working quickly because the tourniquet could not be left in place for very long without damaging his leg.

She pulled out every splinter she could find, washing the wound with the salt water several times, thankful that her patient had fainted. The splinter had just missed the large artery, so he had a good chance of recovery. She set several stitches in the deeper muscles of the leg then closed the wound and wrapped it. Then she turned her attention to the second wounded man, a matter of a few minor cuts that were quickly sewn.

Mariette washed her hands and looked up. Everyone had been watching her in amazement. The captain bowed gravely to her. "Thank you, my lady, for what you have done to save my nephew."

"There is still a danger of infection, Captain," she warned him.

He nodded. "But now he has a chance." He held out a hand to help her up but she shook her head. "I should stay here with him for a while."

The captain smiled and nodded agreement, and moved away.

Mariette watched as everyone's attention went back to their other prisoners. Anyone could have sat by the side of these men while they slept, worn out from their wounds and the stitching. But she had spotted a pistol behind the second wounded man and once everyone was busy, she might be able to get it.

Ignatio was continuing to gloat, boasting of everything he planned to do to each of his prisoners. Pretending to shift the sailor to a more comfortable position, she reached behind him and slid the pistol under her skirt. When she sat back, she could feel it against her knee. With her back to the others she lifted her skirt and checked the weapon. It was loaded and primed. It felt good to slide her fingers around the pistol. She might be a doctor, but she would not hesitate to shoot someone to save her brothers and the others.

"I think it is time to return," Captain Agrait said to Ignatio. "You can carry out your macabre threats once we reach the safety of St. Augustine."

Ignatio sneered. "You prate like a woman, Esteban. This is a Spanish warship."

"And seriously undermanned." The captain gestured toward the *Fortune*, still lashed alongside. "That piece of garbage was no challenge, but I do not think we could face a bigger and better armed English ship."

Mariette saw Nate's fists clench to hear his pride and joy referred to as a piece of garbage.

"Then rig up a tow line and let's go," Ignatio said impatiently.

The captain looked disdainfully over the side at the *Fortune*. "She's not worth towing and she would just slow us down."

"Then what do you suggest we do with her?"

Captain Agrait shrugged. He gestured to two sailors who leaped down onto the deck of the Fortune as soon as he said, "Sink her."

A roar of outrage bellowed from Nate and he launched himself at the captain, tackling him and bringing him down. The captain's head hit the railing with a heavy thud and the man went limp. At the distraction, Alejandro and Matt each took on the guard nearest them. Alejandro struggled with his guard for his weapon, his hand gripping the sailor's wrist. Matt used an Indian wrestling trick to quickly bring down his opponent and disarm him. A whack on the head with the pistol butt left the sailor lying limp on the deck.

Irish had leaped onto the back of another sailor and had her arms around his neck trying to choke him into submission. Douglass had found a saber and was fighting another sailor. Although he had only indifferent skill, desperation spurred him on.

Matt used his stolen pistol to shoot a sailor advancing on him with an upraised saber and caught the saber from the dying man's hand as he fell.

The captain had landed on top of his weapons when he fell and Nate was trying to free them to use when Mariette saw Ignatio aim for her little brother. He was aiming at Nate's back, a broad, impossible-to-miss target at that range. Nevertheless, he was taking his time, taking careful aim, cocking the weapon with a malicious snarl on his face.

Her protective instincts coming to the fore, Mariette lifted her pistol and fired without thinking, without pause, and watched Ignatio fall, a fountain of red blossoming across his chest.

"You little bitch!"

Mariette looked up into the face of Raúl. He stood over her, his face contorted with anger. On her knees between the two wounded men and with an empty pistol, she was helpless. She watched as he drew his saber back, raising it high to bring it down in a slashing arc that would eviscerate her. She scuttled backward as far as she could, coming up against the ship's rail, but it was not far enough to escape from that blade. But when the blade came down, it was with a soft groan from Raúl and the saber fell from his fingers to land unused on the deck. Then she saw the line of red and the saber tip that stuck out of him just below his rib cage. He fell to reveal Nate standing behind him, his face white with the shock of having just killed a man, even if it was to save his sister.

Alejandro had subdued the guard and with a blow of the pistol butt knocked out the sailor Irish was struggling with. The man Douglass was fighting lunged at him but overreached himself. Douglass was able to sidestep the thrust, knock the sailor's saber out of his hand and bring his foe to submission.

Matt grabbed the captain's pistol from Nate's shaking fingers and pointed it over the side at the two remaining sailors, telling them to throw down their weapons.

The Spanish sailors and their captain, now sporting a rather large goose egg on the back of his head, were soon imprisoned belowdecks. The dead, Raúl, Ignatio, and the sailor Matt shot, were laid out on deck and covered with sailcloth.

Mariette stood beside Alejandro as he looked down at his uncle. He had not said anything when the battle was over and he had realized that Ignatio was dead, and by her hand. Now he turned to gaze at her and she wasn't sure what to expect from him.

"I'm sorry," she said, and even to her, it sounded inadequate. But he reached for her and pulled her close.

"If you hadn't shot Ignatio to save your brother," Alejandro said, "Nate would not have been alive to save you when Raúl tried to kill you. Of the two of you, I would far rather it be Ignatio lying under that sail than you."

She put her arm about his waist. "For that matter," Alejandro continued, "I'm glad it isn't Nate under there, either."

The six of them sat down near the bow to decide what to do.

"I don't think the six of us can sail a ship this big, can we, Nate?" Matt asked.

Nate looked up at the rigging, considering, then shook his head. "No, it would take at least three or four more good men to do the job."

"I don't think we should risk letting any of the sailors help us," Douglass said and everyone nodded agreement.

"Then how will we get to Charles Town?" Irish asked. "I'm not much of a sailor, but I don't think we can go in the *Fortune*."

"You're right," Nate agreed. He glanced at his brother. "She'll need a lot more than a new sail before she's fit again. But the *Eagle* has a longboat. We can leave her crew locked belowdecks with plenty of food and water, set sea anchors, and take the longboat. We should be able to reach Savannah within a few hours."

"And send a ship back to bring in our prize," Matt said.

"A prize?" Irish asked.

"Aye," Nate answered. "We took it. A Spanish warship. So now it's ours. Except," he added glumly, "we'll have to share it with whoever helps us bring it in."

Suddenly there was a loud roar and they all jumped to their feet as a cannon ball shot across their bow, the seaman's warning to surrender or fight.

"Where did that come from?" Mariette wondered aloud looking around for the source of the cannon fire.

But it was Nate who called out, "It's the *Jessica*!"

"The *Jessica*?" Irish asked.

"Papa!" Mariette said happily grabbing Irish by the hand.

"How many ships does your family own?" Irish's eyes were

wide with incredulity as she saw the huge ship bearing down on them.

Mariette laughed. "Several of them, but the *Jessica* is the biggest and best armed of them all."

Nate turned to grin at her. "It looks like we'll not have to share our prize with anyone except family after all."

Mariette grinned back. "You are now completely forgiven for leaving that letter behind for Mama and Papa to find."

"Ahoy, aboard the *Eagle*!"

Mariette turned and began to wave happily with her whole arm at a tall, dark-haired man aboard the *Jessica*. "Papa!"

"So it is your father who has come to our aid?" Alejandro asked.

"Yes!" Mariette was leaning on the rail, still waving when another figure appeared at the railing. "Mama!"

"Egad! Your mother, too? Have I fallen in with a family of warriors?"

Mariette laughed. "Mama did try to raise us as good little English ladies and gentlemen but I'm afraid she failed miserably." She shrugged. "Except for Ty, of course, my oldest brother."

Mariette's mother was crying happily at the sight of her children and Douglass.

Grappling hooks were thrown to draw the two vessels together. As soon as they were secured, everyone climbed aboard the Jessica for a happy reunion and introductions.

The story of Matt's and Douglass's and Irish's rescue was briefly told and Alejandro was introduced.

"He had to escape St. Augustine, too," Mariette said, "when his uncle found out that Alejandro's father is really an English lord. And," she paused for effect, "he has asked me to marry him."

"With your permission, sir," Alejandro said holding out a hand to Mariette's father.

A grin tweaked Mr. Fortune's mouth as he took Alejandro's hand. "I suppose I must say yes. You look like a man who would not take no for an answer."

Alejandro did not answer but he did draw Mariette possessively closer to his side.

"Well, children," Mariette's father said sternly, arms crossed, "especially you, Mariette, and you, Nathanial—you have a lot to account for, going off into enemy territory like that and getting yourselves captured." He glared at each of them in turn, but could not hide the twinkle in his eyes. "So what do you have to say for yourselves?"

Mariette shrugged. "You and Mama have told us often about your adventures with pirates and how you met. Aren't you glad your daughter now has her own tale to entertain her children and grandchildren?" She looked up at Alejandro who leaned down to kiss her there in front of everyone, a promise that those children would soon be on their way.

Historical Note

Ft. Mose is located just north of St. Augustine. It was originally manned by African-Americans who had fled slavery in the English colonies. It was these people who guarded Spain's northern frontier and who met and defeated James Oglethorpe's land forces in 1740.

The African-Americans who lived near the fort came back after the siege and rebuilt their lives. But when the English took the colony from Spain in 1763, they left their homes to continue living in freedom in another Spanish colony.

Ft. Mose was rebuilt but on a different site and has now been excavated. The original Ft. Mose, the one in my story, still lies somewhere nearby under several feet of water.

**Keep reading for an excerpt from
Fortune's Pride, sequel to Fortune's Foe**

About *Fortune's Pride*

As long as no one knows who Irish really is, she will be safe. But Tyrus Fortune seems determined to uncover all her secrets. Can she fully love him without revealing her true self to him? But if she does, will it also put him and his family in danger?

Tyrus Fortune returns home after two years determined to unmask the woman who has found her way into the hearts of his family. He is sure she is a fraud--until he begins to fall in love with her. Now he only wishes she will trust him with her secrets and her love so they can face the future together.

Excerpt from Fortune's Pride

Chapter One

As soon as Tyrus Winthrop Fortune saw the Irishwoman, he was sure there was something not quite right. He had spotted that red hair while still on board his brother's little ship, the *Fortune*, coming up the river. He had seen the easy way she laughed with his other brother, Matt, while they waited for Nate to dock his ship. He had seen the way she helped his heavily pregnant sister, Mariette, make her way down the dock of his family's plantation.

As he kissed his mother on the cheek and accepted an enthusiastic but unwieldy hug from his sister, he had seen how easily his family accepted this interloper as if she were one of them. As his brother, Matt, wrung his hand, gave him a hearty backslap and huge grin, Ty noticed how the Irishwoman pushed an undisciplined strand of curly red hair out of her eyes and looked at him with one cocked eyebrow, as if assessing him and finding something slightly amusing.

There was nothing amusing about him. He was quite properly dressed in the latest London fashion. She, however, looked like a hoyden.

His mother pulled her forward. "And this is Irish."

Oh, he knew who she was. His family had mentioned her in several glowing accounts in the letters they had written him while he was in London.

Irish presented her hand to him with a challenging tilt to her head, as if she half expected him to dismiss her out of hand. But the gentlemanly manners his mother had tried to inculcate in all her children had taken strong root in him. He would not be so dastardly as to ignore the hand of a woman his mother was presenting to him in good faith. Not even if he had a niggling suspicion that faith was misplaced.

He took her hand and made a very courtly bow over it, even though he could not help noticing that "Irish" had neglected to wear a fichu tucked into her bodice. Yes, it was quite a hot summer day, but it was shameful to display such a heathenish amount of skin. Creamy white skin that looked as soft as satin and the enticing curve of two perfect breasts that should have been decently covered.

Her hand was not soft. It was firm and competent and the palm slightly calloused. But when he touched his lips to the back of that hand he found the skin there as soft as the upper curves of her breasts looked. The feel of it against his mouth took him quite by surprise so that he gasped and jerked erect, then wished he had an excuse to kiss that hand again. He couldn't, of course. That wouldn't be proper. But he couldn't help running his thumb over the back of her hand...before he remembered himself and hastily let it go.

"Irish...?" He left the question hanging, waiting for a proper name. A surname. Something he had asked his family a time or two in his letters over the last two years. Something his family had failed to mention with irritating consistency. Now he waited with his own cocked and questioning brow for the answer.

She gave him a smile that was almost coquettish. But he had been flirted with by the most accomplished women in London. He was not going to accept a mere smile for his answer. Not after waiting for one for two years.

She shrugged, causing those breasts to momentarily lift, and entice. He forced his gaze upward to her face.

"Just Irish," she said, clipping the words off with finality, locking and barring the door.

Her voice was as strong as her hand and he could hear her Irish brogue even in those two words, the lilt, the extra attention to the "r". Just Irish, indeed. But what else?

He started to ask again, to demand more information of her, but his mother was taking his arm to introduce him to his sister's husband. He turned away from the little baggage, but not without a scowl that promised he would not forget to return to the topic later.

Ty approved of Mariette's choice of a husband immediately. He shook hands firmly as they took each other's measure. The man was half-Spanish. England was presently at war with that country but Alejandro's father was English, and Ty had made it a point to meet him while he was in London. Alejandro came from good stock, and it did not matter so much in the colonies if a man were a bastard.

"Welcome home, Tyrus," Alejandro said, one arm lovingly about Mariette.

"I'm glad to be back," Ty answered, noting with approval that Alejandro spoke without a trace of a Spanish accent, and didn't cut his name short the way the rest of his family did.

"Shall we go into the house?" his mother suggested. "Dinner should be ready."

"I'll just pop into the kitchen, then, and see how that stew is coming along." Irish picked up her skirts and turned to skip up the steps to the house, and Ty caught a quick glimpse of trim ankles and outlandish green dancing slippers. Dancing slippers?

He nodded in approval at the retreating backside of the Irishwoman about whom he knew as little now as he had in London. At least she seemed to know that she wasn't part of this family. She knew her place was in the kitchen. It only made him wonder why she had been down on the dock with the family to welcome him home.

"Irish has been such a comfort since she came to stay with us," Ty's mother said as she took his proffered arm to walk at a more sedate pace up the steps.

At the top they paused to wait for Mariette who, with the help of her husband, was taking the steps one at a time, breathing heavily. Matt and Mariette were twins, and looking at the size of his sister, Ty wondered if she could be having twins, as well. It seemed impossible that his impetuous, sometimes wild and irresponsible sister, was now settled down with a husband and about to be a mother.

Ty's gaze swept to the docks where Nate was directing the unloading of his ship, piling Ty's luggage up to be taken into the house. The river looked the same as it always had. He turned back to look at the house he had been born and raised in. There was the addition on the side his mother had written about, a sun room with large windows. Otherwise, it was also just as he remembered it—grand and sprawling, two storied, and now, with the addition of the sunroom, the two wings of the house were nicely balanced.

"It was Irish's idea to add the sunroom," his mother said, making him grind his teeth. "Do you like it?"

"Hmm," he answered noncommittally. "Do you always take the suggestions of servants on such monumental matters?"

His mother shrugged. "If it is a good idea, does it matter where it comes from?"

He hated to admit that whoever had had the idea, it had been a good one. He was spared the necessity of answering, however, because Mariette had finally made it to the top of the steps and his mother urged him on into the house.

Ty took a few minutes to freshen up then joined his family in the dining room. The table was set with his mother's wedding dishes and he was surprised to see that a place had been set at his father's place. He wondered if his mother did that every night while his father was off chasing Spaniards in this horrible war.

Alejandro helped Mariette into a chair and Ty held his mother's chair for her. Nate and Matt sat down and Ty reached for the chair at his traditional place at the table next to his mother, but her hand on his stopped him.

"Sit there, Ty," she said.

He stopped, incredulous. "Father's place?"

"Your father isn't here and you are the oldest. It's proper."

He nodded his acquiescence and took his place at the head of the table, wondering why an extra place had been set. It didn't take long for him to find out.

Irish came in bearing a huge bowl of stew. He tried not to appear condescending as he smiled pleasantly at her, as if giving her permission to serve. She, however, was not cowed into proper humility at all. She gave him a saucy grin and a wink as she set the stew in front of him, and he could not help himself from taking advantage of the view he had of some very deep cleavage. He could feel himself growing warm and tore his gaze away. Insolent wench!

It was then that the Irishwoman managed to totally surprise him. She moved around the table and sat down, cool as you please, right in his traditional place next to his mother. He would have thought she was doing it just to flummox him except no one else seemed to note anything unusual at all. Had she managed to worm her way into the very family circle?

"Tyrus, will you say grace?" his mother asked.

Ty managed to unclench his teeth long enough to say the prayer.

The same two servants, Ruby and Dee-dee, who had been there all his life, began to ladle out the stew and serve the meal. They grinned at him and welcomed him home, placed bread at his side and a bowl of stew in front of him.

"Tell us about London," his brother, Matt, asked.

"Yes," agreed his mother. "Are we terribly out of style here in the colonies?"

"You could never be out of style, Mother," he answered chivalrously but truthfully. "But I've brought fashion dolls for you and Mariette so you will be able to see for yourselves just what the ladies are wearing in London."

"No matter how up to date your dolls are, Ty," said his sister, rubbing her distended abdomen, "I'll still be hopelessly out of style by the time I can fit into a normal gown again."

"Has parliament considered passing a law against impressing our sailors into the navy?" Nate asked.

Ty looked at his youngest brother, now nineteen and already a man with his own two ships plying the coastal trade. "You seem to do all right, Nate. I didn't notice a lack of men to help sail the *Fortune*."

"That's because I'm willing to pay better than anyone else. I want the best on my ships."

Ty could hear the pride in Nate's voice. His brother was doing well. He listened as his family began talking of trade, and sank into that familiar atmosphere he had missed so much the last two years. He looked around the table. Anyone could tell that they were a family. Nate and Matt looked much alike with their black hair and remarkable blue eyes. Ty's eyes were blue, too, like their father's, but of a grayer shade. Mariette had black eyes like their mother and all of them, including their newest family member, Alejandro, had black hair. They all fit. All of them except that bold splash of red at the end next to his mother.

Irish didn't have blue eyes or black hair. Her hair was red and unruly and her eyes were green. She was obviously not part of this family. She didn't belong at this table. So why was she here?

Yes, he knew the story. Mother and Mariette had both written to him telling him how the woman had helped Matt and Mariette escape from the Spanish. But that didn't explain why she now seemed to be included in the family. It wasn't right. But he would talk to his mother about it tomorrow. Today was a day to catch up and just be glad to be home.

Ty took a taste of his stew, then another. It was delicious. He picked up a roll and pulled it apart to butter it. A yeasty fragrance wafted toward him. Bread was his favorite food, and as he bit into the roll he thought it had to be the best one he had ever eaten.

"Do you like the rolls?" his mother asked.

"Mmm," was all he could answer, his eyes half-closed as he savored the rich flavor.

"Irish made them," Mariette said.

Ty's eyes sprang open and he nearly choked. Irish again! He put the roll down before he crushed it in his fist. "I'm glad you found someone to replace Mary," he managed to grit out, "but I'm surprised that our new cook is eating with the family."

There was dead silence for a moment. Then Mariette burst out laughing. She laid one hand on his arm with the other at her breast, as if trying to catch her breath from laughing so hard. "Oh, Ty, we've missed your dry sense of humor."

The rest of the family took up the laughter.

Had they all gone insane? What spell had this red-haired witch put on them?

But that red-haired witch was not laughing. She was looking down at her stew, pushing the rich chunks of meat and vegetables around aimlessly, her spoon clutched tightly in her hand. She was the only one who seemed to know that he had meant every word he had said, that she was not fooling him in the least. She did not belong at this table and they were the only two who seemed to know it.

Then her head came up and she looked right at him with a

challenge in her eyes. She scooped up a spoonful of stew, stuck it triumphantly into her mouth and began to chew. She might know that she didn't belong at this table but she was letting him know that she was staying, whether she belonged or not.

The battle lines were drawn.

For the rest of the meal he tried to ignore Irish's presence at the other end of the table. He answered his family's questions about England, heard about Matt's most recent visits with his Indian friends, Mariette's description of hers and Alejandro's home, and his mother's concerns for his father's safety.

Near the end of their dinner a gangly dog came padding into the room as if he belonged. Ty started to get up to shoo him out but no one else seemed to pay much attention, and the dog lay down beside Irish. He noticed that she reached down to pet him and slipped him a piece of meat from her stew. Now was not the time to say anything, but that would have to stop.

Dessert was his favorite—apple turnovers. He didn't ask who made them. He just enjoyed them, eating three and savoring every bite.

Mariette's condition made her tire easily so the women left the table soon after, and Ty spent the next hours talking to his brothers and getting to know his new brother-in-law. He drank a little more than he usually did but not enough to keep him from walking fairly steadily up the stairs to his room, loosening his stock and undoing the buttons of his shirt on the way.

Irish lay back stiffly onto the soft pillows of her bed and stared wide eyed around her room trying to unclench her jaw, her hands. She had thought she was safe. She had thought she had a place with people who cared for her. Now all that seemed threatened. She should have known there would never be any safety for her.

When she had arrived in Charles Town with Mariette, the Fortune family had welcomed her warmly. They had assumed that she was a well-to- do woman beset by tragedy, and that tragedy had made her reluctant to talk about herself. She had not disillusioned them. When they had asked questions, it had been easy to change the subject or pretend a sadness too great to reveal.

As the days and weeks passed, they seemed to forget that they knew very little about their guest...and certainly none of the truth. They offered her the best they had in return for the little part she had played in helping Matt escape from the Spanish. They treated her as if she really were one of the family.

Only she knew what a fraud she was, what a lie she was living. Every day she walked a tightrope of fear. Fear of discovery, fear that the Fortunes would suddenly decide to question her in earnest, fear that they would ask her to leave.

They had been more than generous with her, even letting her have part of the money from the Spanish ship they had brought into Charles Town as a prize. Now that bit of money had grown thanks to Nate allowing her to invest in his shipping business. But she didn't have enough, yet. Certainly not enough to keep her safe. Maybe she would never have enough. As if she even knew how much that would be.

She had made herself as useful as she could to the family, hoping they would come to think of her as indispensable. And she was glad to do what she could for them. They had given her so much. When their old cook Mary died, she'd taken over supervision of the kitchen, teaching some of the servants how to make various dishes. When Mariette and Alejandro moved into their own home, Irish had taken over supervising the servants in their household chores. Whatever needed doing, she did with a willing hand and a glad heart. She had thought she was safe.

Mariette and her brothers had spoken often of this eldest

brother who was away in London. They spoke of his stiff pride and his perfect manners, the way he never seemed to get disheveled or dirty no matter what he was doing, how he insisted that they all behave with propriety, and how they had worked together to thwart him with their antics. They spoke of his priggishness and they spoke of his compassion, but always they spoke of him with love. And they looked up to him almost in awe. Their perfect brother who could do no wrong. When they had learned he was coming home, they had been joyous.

But Irish had been apprehensive. Tyrus Fortune had seemed different from the rest of the family. They had told her how easily he saw through them and usually caught them when they tried some outlandish prank. Would he see through her as well?

Now that she had finally met the great Tyrus Fortune, she was sure he had looked into her very soul and found her sadly wanting. But she had also seen into his soul. He acted stern. He scowled at her. He looked so prim and starched she was afraid he might crack. But underneath it all, he seemed to be the one who most feared that he might crack—that if he unbent just a little, there would be no stopping the unbending.

For some absurd reason she wanted to be the one who taught him to let go. She wanted to see his stock loosened, the ends dangling beside the open throat of his shirt. She wanted to see if his chest was as hard and perfectly molded as it seemed beneath his coat and waistcoat and shirt. She wanted to see him relaxed with one leg thrown over the arm of a chair, to see the bunch and release of those strong thigh muscles as his leg swung casually back and forth. She wanted to see him...smile.

She was sure it could happen. She knew he was capable of melting. When he had kissed her hand, when his lips had touched her, it was as if something hot had run up her arm. Something hot and melting. And he had felt that melting heat, as well. She was sure of it. It was why he had jerked away so quickly, why he had looked so surprised, why he had forced his mouth back into the hard, firm line it had momentarily lost. The heat of that simple kiss had started to melt something inside him and he had been as afraid of her as she was of him. Afraid and attracted.

She knew he was afraid because he had jerked away, and attracted because he had allowed himself that brief caress of her hand with his thumb before he let her go. A caress that had sent another surge of warmth through her.

But if he was afraid and attracted, so was she. It would not be easy walking a tightrope of fear and attraction. She had to be careful. She could not let her attraction for Tyrus Fortune overcome her caution. If she gave away too much, if he found out who she was, how long would it be before he asked her to leave?

Or would it be worse than that? Would he root out her every secret, find out who she was and turn her over to the law?

She squeezed her eyes shut and tried not to cry. Life had been so good. For two years she had lived as she had never hoped to live. She ran her hand over the clean, smooth sheet, rolled her head on the down pillow, felt the light silk nightgown she wore. In a moment it could all be taken away.

She still had her money. Even if they turned her out, she had enough to live on for a while. Or would they take that away, too, if they found her out? Or worse, would she find herself in jail?

She had thought she was safe until Tyrus Fortune came into her life. She had worked hard today to make sure the house was in good order and the dinner a special one for the returning eldest Fortune son. Her mouth twisted wryly. He had seemed to be enjoying it until Mariette told him who made it. She had seen the way he had looked at her at the table. He wanted her gone. She was as much a threat to him as he was to her. She was a mystery he did not understand and it bothered him not to understand everything around him. And he didn't understand his attraction to her.

Why was he so suspicious? Would she be able to allay his suspicions as she had the rest of the family's? Perhaps she could use his attraction to her to keep him off balance long enough for him to accept her presence in his family. She would flirt and flatter but keep him at a distance. That was the key—to keep him at a distance.

Attraction was a double-edged sword, it could end up unbalancing her, make her lose her caution. She must not let that happen. What she must, must, must do, was keep this place she had made for herself. This place she had been safe in for two years. This place she wanted to remain sealed in forever. It was too good a place to lose. She would hang on in every way she could.

Paddy gave a whine and she reached down to pet him where he lay on the floor beside her bed.

"Don't worry, Paddy. We've come this far. We'll be all right. We'll show Tyrus Fortune he can't get the best of Kathleen Moira O'Conner." She spoke softly, especially those words that she must never say out loud to anyone. Her name.

Tyrus Fortune had laid down a challenge and she would meet it, just as she had met his glare at the table with an impertinent bite of stew. No matter what she had to do, she would keep her place. She would be safe.

With that determination to comfort her, she fell asleep.

Ty made his way down the long upstairs hallway, putting a hand out once or twice to steady himself against the wall. Surely he had hadn't drunk that much. It must be the darkness of a moonless night. He found the door of his room and fumbled with the knob until it finally swung open. A growl greeted him.

"What the hell?" he muttered.

The growling stopped and a soft thumping began. There was

the click of nails and the soft pad of paws crossing the wooden floor, then his hand was being licked. Absently he patted the dog, assuming it was the same one that had made itself at home in the dining room earlier. "What are you doing in here, fella?" He felt a wagging tail whip against his legs as he turned to open the door again.

"Go on, get out," he said softly.

The dog just whined and sat down.

"Oh, hell, stay then. Just don't expect me to feed you from the table."

Ty pulled off his shirt and kicked off his shoes. He shook his head wondering where his coat and waistcoat were. It wasn't like him to shuck them off and leave them lying like Matt usually did. Oh, yes, he had given them to a servant to take to his room. He unbuttoned his pantaloons and stepped out of them, folding them neatly over the back of a chair with his shirt. He lined his shoes up neatly under the chair. It was too dark to put them into the wardrobe tonight and he didn't feel like lighting a candle.

Wearing only his drawers he padded to the window to open it, but it was already open, a soft breeze moving the curtains. For a few moments he listened to the sounds of insects filling the night. He had missed those sounds. He took a deep breath. He had missed the smell of the land and the rice paddies. He had missed this house and his family. He was glad to be home at last.

He went to the bed, pulled back the sheet, and sat down on the edge. That's when he realized that the dog wasn't the only invader in his bedroom.

Chapter Two

IRISH WOKE UP WHEN SHE FELT THE SHEET LIFT AND THE BED dip. "Paddy?" she murmured and reached to pat the dog. But it was not Paddy's soft, floppy ears or wet tongue her hand encountered. It was firm, warm flesh. Puzzled, she splayed her hand over that flesh. The skin was smooth, the muscles hard and the body leapt off the bed.

"What the hell?" a deep masculine voice yelped.

She sat up, pushing hair out of her face. Her eyes widened as she recognized her intruder. "Tyrus Fortune! What are you doing here?" she demanded.

"What am...?" He seemed genuinely confused, but that changed quickly to belligerence. "What are you doing here?"

"Sleeping."

She was wide awake now and could see him dimly against the window.

He was certainly one fine figure of a man, with or without clothes. She saw him plant angry fists on his hips and lean forward.

"Did my brothers put you up to this?" He threw up his hands. "I thought they had grown up a little. I'm going to have their hides for this."

"What are you talking about?" she asked.

"You—being here."

"Why should your brothers have anything to do with it?"

His fists went back to his hips and he stalked closer to the bed, blocking out what little light there was with his broad shoulders. "So this is all your idea?"

She rubbed her eyes. Maybe she wasn't quite awake. But this was too bizarre even for a dream. Of course it was her own idea to be asleep in bed in the middle of the night. "Yes," she said.

He reached over and jerked the sheet away, uncovering her, then, taking her by the arm he began pulling her from the bed.

"What are you doing? Let go of me!" She struggled, but her strength was no match for his. Panic began welling inside her. This couldn't happen again. She wouldn't allow it! This wasn't St. Augustine and this family was good and upright. But maybe one of them had learned a few things while he was in London. By this time she was on her feet beside him. She opened her mouth and began to scream. He stopped her with a hand clamped over her mouth.

"Do you want to wake the whole house, you little tart?" he snarled.

Yes, that's exactly what she wanted to do. They would believe her. They had to. She had been safe here for two years. She tried to free herself but he held her tighter.

"Be still," he commanded. "I'm trying not to hurt you, but if you keep this up you'll only hurt yourself."

Oh, no, he wasn't going to hurt her. A man never seemed to think that a little unwanted 'poking' hurt a woman. It was what they were made for, wasn't it? She struggled harder. She was not about to be used by any man, ever again. Suddenly she was swept off her feet and tossed onto the bed, the full weight of Tyrus Fortune on top of her, pinning her down, his hand still clamped over her mouth.

She could feel his hard length, but his elbows were propped on the bed on each side of her, keeping most of his weight from crushing her. She went limp. Maybe if he thought she had given up he would let down his guard and she could escape.

"I'm going to take my hand off your mouth," he said. "Just keep quiet."

Like hell, she thought. As soon as his fingers moved away she took a deep breath, but before she could scream he clamped his hand back across her mouth.

"So that's your game, is it? It won't work, you know. No one is going to force me to marry you just because they find us in bed together. Especially since you obviously came to my bed. I certainly didn't force my attentions on you in yours."

Her eyes widened. Was he insane? Then her brain began to work and she realized what was happening. She could smell the wine on his breath. He had mistakenly come to the wrong room, and the wrong conclusion. She struggled to free herself but he held her closer. Too close.

"Will you stop struggling!" It was a command, not a question.

Feeling him rise hard and long between her legs, she stilled instantly.

He took several deep breaths. "Now will you keep quiet if I let you go?" She managed to nod and he slowly took his hand away. When she didn't scream, he rolled off of her to lie face up beside her, taking slow, deep breaths and scrubbing his hand over his face.

"All right, now get out," he said, "and we'll pretend this never happened."

"You insufferable cad!" She kicked him in the side and began pushing him toward the edge of the bed with her feet. He was so surprised by her attack that he toppled over the edge and landed on the floor in an undignified heap.

He sat up, rubbing one shoulder. "You're insane!"

"You're the one in the wrong room," she countered.

He looked around. "It might be dark in here but I think I can recognize the room that—except for the last two years—I've slept in my whole life."

Now she understood what had happened! She started to laugh. She drew up her knees and hugged them, laughing harder.

"You really are insane," he grumbled, getting to his feet.

"Your room is next to this one," she explained.

Those fists were back on his hips. "I told you, this is my room. I'll thank you to get out of it."

"Out of your room, out of your house, and out of your life. That's what you'd like, isn't it, Mr. Tyrus Fortune?" She lifted her chin. "But I'll do none of them. Your mother gave me this room when I first came here. 'Tis mine now and I'll be keeping it, thank you. You'll find your things in the guest room next to this one. I prepared it for you myself. Now, if you don't mind, I'd like to get a wink or two before the sun comes up. I've a fine lot of work to be doing in the morning." With that she plopped back onto the pillows, pulled the sheet up and turned her back to him.

"Get back to sleep? I got the impression you were expecting someone, Miss Irish," he snarled at her.

She turned back toward him. "No, Mr. Fortune, I was not expecting anyone. What gave you the idea that I would welcome any man to my bed, seeing as how I'm not married?"

"Then who is this Paddy you were reaching for so eagerly?" he asked triumphantly.

The click of dog nails interrupted, they both looked down and saw Paddy outlined beside him wagging his tail.

"Oh," he said. "Oh, the dog."

She could imagine his face turning a bright red. It was surprising that it didn't light up the room. At least she had the good sense not to laugh out loud as she heard him stomp across the room, grab his clothes, and leave.

www.michelestegman.com

About the Author

Michele Stegman has loved history all her life. She lives in an 1840's log cabin with her husband, Ron, and enjoys spinning wool into yarn then using it for her weaving or knitting projects. She has learned to make her own soap and bakes her own bread.

From the time she was a child and realized that books were written by people, she wanted to be one of those people. In graduate school one professor told her she put too much romance into her history papers. Instead of taking it out, she put more in and began writing historical romance novels.

Fortune's Pride, a sequel to ***Fortune's Foe***, is available at all major online book retailers.

Visit Michele's website for information on her other books and to read excerpts: www.michelestegman.com. Or connect with her on Twitter at twitter.com/michelestegman, or on Facebook at facebook.com/MicheleStegmanAuthor.

www.ingramcontent.com/pod-product-compliance
Lightning Source LLC
Chambersburg PA
CBHW020332180626
46812CB00001B/172